I0818413

BY MILA KANE

MAFIA

Vicious Vengeance Duet

WICKED HEIR

SAVAGE THRONE

Made of Mayhem Duet

MALEVOLENT KING

RUNAWAY QUEEN

Devil's Own Series

KING OF THE CAGE

Original Sin Series

UNHOLY VOWS

BRUTAL LEGACY

SACRED RUIN

BULLY

Hellions of Hade Harbor

BAD INTENTIONS

DARK DELIGHTS

TWISTED DEEDS

WICKED ENDS

VICIOUS OBSESSION

BRUTAL LEGACY

MILA KANE

DELL • NEW YORK

BRUTAL LEGACY

A NOVEL

Dell
An imprint of Random House
A division of Penguin Random House LLC
1745 Broadway, New York, NY 10019
randomhousebooks.com
penguinrandomhouse.com

2026 Dell Trade Paperback Edition

This work was originally self-published by the author in 2025.

ISBN 9798217299683

Printed in the United States of America on acid-free paper

1st Printing

Cover design: Angela Haddon
Cover photograph: Wander Aguiar

BOOK TEAM: Production editor: Dennis Ambrose • Managing editor: Saige Francis • Production manager: Linnea Knollmueller • Copy editor: Lawrence Krauser • Proofreaders: Michael Burke, Kathleen Fridella, Caryl Weintraub

The authorized representative in the EU for product safety and compliance is Penguin Random House Ireland, Morrison Chambers, 32 Nassau Street, Dublin D02 YH68, Ireland.
https://eu-contact.penguin.ie

Welcome to Mila Kane's New York. It's not the city you know, and here the kings and queens of the underworld reign supreme.

Along with life and death, love, darkness, and mayhem rule this corner of the book world. This book contains some darker themes, including graphic violence, kidnapping, and captivity, arranged Mafia marriage, suicidal ideation, and PTSD. Descriptions of panic attacks, microchipping, and surveillance will also be found here.

If that's your thing, read on. If not—please skip this one!

BRUTAL LEGACY

Prologue

GEORGIA

The shots rang out in the restaurant, sending panicked cries and screams up from the patrons. People hit the floor, and I was no different. Broken glass littered the tile, cutting into my knees.

I crawled under the table. Someone was crying, and someone else shushed them. Whimpers of fear filled my ears. A room full of people desperate to live.

A hard crunch sounded.

Footsteps over shattered glass.

Crunch.

Which way were they going?

Crunch.

Were they getting louder?

Crunch.

Dark dress shoes appeared in front of my hiding place. Shiny leather brogues. They looked expensive. Handmade for sure. My terrified brain fastened onto the mundane to keep me from screaming. I clamped my hand over my mouth to muffle any sound from escaping.

The shooter shifted, taking a step to the left, and I nearly fainted with relief as they walked around my table to the side.

He'd gone. Moved away to terrorize another table.

The relief had barely hit when the table above me scraped hard over the floor. One second, I was cocooned in reassuring darkness, the next, I was crouching in a pitiful, cowering ball while the table shielding me flipped over and crashed on the floor.

Light stung my eyes. I was totally exposed. I could feel the gunman standing over me. His presence sent goose bumps over my skin . . . like Death himself had come to collect me.

This is it, Georgia, the end of the line.

Maybe I should have gone to church once in a while in the last fourteen years, or believed in something . . . Maybe then, kneeling before my end wouldn't feel so desolate.

What did I have to show for my thirty-three years on the planet? A shitty apartment with half a dozen unfinished designs? A broken heart that had never healed right, and a grudge the size of the moon? So big that fourteen years of carrying it had destroyed the possibility of anything else good in my life.

Silence had fallen and stretched out endlessly. Was this when your life flashed in front of your eyes? Was this like in the movies when everything moved in slow motion? Or was the man with the gun really just standing over me, staring down?

Did he want me to glance up at him before he killed me? Just in case that was true, I kept my chin tilted mulishly down. I was nothing if not stubborn as fuck.

"Get up," a deep voice commanded.

I tensed even more. Everything screamed at me to refuse.

"Get up, now, or I'll shoot a person in this room every ten seconds until you do," the deep voice continued, unbothered. Like he wasn't just threatening to kill people.

"Ten, nine, eight . . ." he started.

I pushed myself to my feet, fighting a gasp as my hands ground into the jagged glass on the floor.

"I'm up. Don't hurt anyone else." My voice was surprisingly stronger than I'd thought it would be.

"I won't as long as you do what I say, but every second we waste here, their lives are in danger."

His odd wording sent my eyes up to his face, finally.

He was tall, well over six feet, and dressed like he'd been in a stock portfolio meeting and decided to step out and shoot up a restaurant. A custom-made black suit, crisp white shirt. He had that aura of power that only emanated from the truly wealthy.

But he wasn't your average rich guy . . . there was something very different about him. Maybe it was the tattoos liberally decorating the backs of his hands and neck; clearly the guy had some serious bodywork going on beneath the three-piece suit. Or maybe it was how his face was spattered with someone else's blood.

But on closer inspection, no, it wasn't just the tats or the flecks of red against his cheek, though they certainly added to the aura of his presence.

It was just him. The way he stood, cocksure but ready. Lethal and confident. A man who had done terrible things and would again. A man who could take any danger.

A man who *was* the danger.

He wrapped a hand around my arm and tugged me to him. My feet had forgotten how to work, and I fell clumsily into his chest. He didn't even sway at the impact.

"Where are you taking me?" I asked, searching the little I could see of his face.

He had sunglasses on, fitting for the California sun falling through the long windows of the restaurant. His jaw was square and tanned, shadowed with just a hint of dark stubble. He had strong cheekbones and an aquiline nose. Dark winged eyebrows and shorn black hair. There was something vaguely military-esque about the strictness of that cut.

He was criminally good-looking. Shouldn't there be a rule that the most dangerous guys couldn't also be the hottest ones?

"Wherever I want," he said simply.

"What? You can't!" I squeaked out in a panic.

"And who is going to stop me?" he asked.

"You can't just steal a person," I murmured, knowing I was wrong. This madman could. He was.

"I can do whatever the fuck I want." He turned from the carnage of the restaurant and pulled me beside him, pushing me out an exit.

A hard object poked into my side. *The gun?* I couldn't see it, but clearly he had it pressed into my rib cage. I had to fight. I had to do something. I tried to step on his foot, but he barely flinched.

"Let's be clear. If I say jump, you say how high. I say kneel . . . you hit the fucking deck, got it?" he growled at me, perfectly certain that I would comply. His hand was around my neck, his strong fingers biting into my skin.

"Or?" I shot out, anger at his unshakable confidence pushing my fear from my mind for a second, before it came back, tenfold.

He spoke with that same perfect confidence. "Or—you'll die."

1

ELIO

La Seta was packed to the seams with Napoli's most beautiful. Skin carefully revealed in titillating patches, perfumes meant to seduce, hair swinging and enticing, smiles tempting . . .

But not to me.

I moved through the swaying mass of desperate, clawing people like a dark arrow through a cloud of cotton candy. I wasn't here for fun. I was here for one purpose.

To do my job.

Ahead, my target was laughing at the bar, downing shot after shot, lowering his guard even more. Some people really made this easy.

I leaned against a nearby pillar and watched him in the mirror across the way. My biggest problem somewhere like this was blending in. I didn't sway. I didn't smile. It kind of made me stick out in a place where everyone else was riding a chemical high of some kind, be it drugs, alcohol, or pure endorphins.

"*Ciao, bello,*" a female voice purred beside me. A hand snaked down my chest. "I haven't seen you here before."

I had her wrist in a tight grip before she saw me move. Her hazy, half-closed eyes widened in alarm.

"And you haven't seen me this time," I advised her quietly.

Her smile returned; she assumed I was flirting back. She leaned into me, and the manufactured scent of her perfume was harsh on my nose. Femininity in a bottle. I wished I could unsmell it.

"Sure, I haven't. Why don't we get out of here and not see each other a little more?" she suggested.

I let go of her wrist. "I'm afraid that's not in the cards. I'm not what you're looking for."

"You're a man, aren't you?"

Debatable.

"Maybe so, but I don't have the parts you want."

She pouted for a moment and then leaned in. A last-ditch attempt to seduce me. Her hand landed on my crotch, and she squeezed me through my dress pants.

"You feel like you have everything I need."

This time, I didn't bother moving her hand. I simply dropped my mildly pleasant mask and let her see the man beneath. She stilled as my eyes drilled into hers, and she saw it all. The madness, the anger, the simmering violence only just contained. The monster without his man disguise.

She dropped her hand and stepped back.

"That isn't the part I'm missing, *signorina*."

"What is it then?" she asked, muted now. "What are you missing?"

I caught sight of my target leaving the bar ahead of me and stepped forward. My missing parts were far more vital than some appendage. My missing parts made me incapable of mercy, or gentleness . . . It had been that way for as long as I could remember.

Since *her*.

"A heart," I told her curtly and stepped past her, intent on my target.

He was a De Sanctis made man. I'd also been a De Sanctis for the greater part of my life. Service to my capo and the *famiglia* had been my sole reason for living for the last decade. The family was rooted in Naples, though that grip was weakening gradually with the decline of Salvatore De Sanctis's health. I lived in the second De Sanctis stronghold, New Jersey. My capo, Renato, Salvatore's nephew, was visiting Italy with his new wife, and where they went, I went. I was his shadow, his right hand, and his personal executioner.

Since I owed him my and my sister's lives, it was only fitting. One of the most satisfying parts of my job was rooting out corruption in the heart of the family. Death before disloyalty was a motto I lived by. I wasn't a merciful man, but I conducted the bloody and violent business of being *sottocapo* to a brutal Mafia as professionally as possible . . . But a traitor in the *famiglia*? They got special attention.

I enjoyed delivering them the consequences of their actions, and I was so very good at it. I was a natural-born killer and could never be anything else. I'd lived in hell and brought the demons back with me. I might as well use them in service of my family.

I followed my target toward the back of the club. I had no worries about repercussions from the police. The Italian police were some of the most corrupt I'd ever met. I'd learned that lesson young. Let them chase their tails.

My mark had entered the men's room. I stood outside and kept my face carefully angled away. I had a black baseball hat on and tinted glasses, as strange as it was to wear them in a dark club. Thankfully, enough Italians were fashion-conscious for me to get away with it as a normal outfit.

There wouldn't be any cameras in the restrooms; it was against the law. There was a handy CLEANING IN PROGRESS sign just around the corner from the bathroom. I waited a few moments before entering the room. I wanted my target to be midstream and not easily distracted. There was only one other man in there, and he took one look at me and left quickly. No, not everyone was a drunken idiot. He stepped around the cleaning sign, which I'd placed in the doorway, and took off.

My target was using a urinal. I waited until he finished and started to zip up, then slipped a garrote from my pocket. With a flash of explosive power, I had the wire around his neck before he could even realize there was someone else in the room.

The man struggled, his hands clawing at my face, but he was too drunk, and I was too strong for him. I pulled him against my body, bending backward so his entire weight hung from the wire around his neck. The crack was satisfying and clean. I dropped him to the floor and removed the garrote, washing it carefully in the sink. The whole thing had taken seconds, and there was always time to clean up your instruments. That was only one of the habits ingrained in me by my long years in the military. Precision. Clarity. Focus. I glanced in the mirror and wiped a streak of blood from my cheek. Emotionless. In that whirling storm inside, I lived in the silent eye.

Untouchable.

I left the club, careful to keep my head down. As I strode away, turning this way and that down the warren-like streets, I found myself in Scampia, a neighborhood nestled in the heart of Napoli. I could have walked the whole way with my eyes closed. I grew up in that very neighborhood. A few streets down on the right was the house where my mother died. A little farther was the place where my sister was taken by the state and my father was arrested in the street, facedown like a dog on a rainy day.

If I were a man who could feel, then this walk down memory lane might be depressing.

Luckily, I wasn't.

I didn't feel much of anything at all.

Just the way I liked it.

Spring storms rattled the thin old windows of my hotel room, howling up the skinny cobbled streets of Naples.

It didn't interrupt my routine. It didn't matter where I was. At home in New Jersey, or doing work abroad for my capo, my routine was unchanged.

Even here, in the city of my birth, dark dreams chased me from sleep in the small hours. Especially here.

A clock in the hallway beyond my room chimed the hour. Four A.M. I didn't need the clock to tell me the time. I was well acquainted with the particular kind of darkness that descended right before dawn broke. The deepest, most desolate kind.

I was awake, like I usually was, sitting at the table in my room, cleaning my guns. It was my nightly ritual. I had started it in the military, where the hours of night felt like days and your conscience was a boulder crushing your lungs.

I learned the measure of a man's soul in that darkness. In the quiet between spaces where normal life should be. Every night, at four A.M., I was back there, sand beneath my feet, sweat running down my back, and the knowledge that in the morning, I'd lose a little more of my soul.

I wasn't sure how much was left to give.

The gun in my hand shone in the low light from the dying fire in the corner, painstakingly cleaned and oiled. I enjoyed the weight of it. It was comforting. Other men turned to drink and substances to numb the terrible pain of being alive, but those did nothing for me. There was only one thing that calmed the storm inside, and that was my nightly ritual.

I laid out my collection and cleaned each piece carefully, my mind blissfully blank.

After, when there was nowhere to go but back to my bed and the nightmares that waited for me there, I loaded a single bullet, spun the chamber, and played my Russian friends' favorite game.

Click.

Another stay of execution. Another miss.

The shutters on the window were open, so I could watch the lightning lingering over the city's silhouette. The air was thick and damp, heavy with the coming rain. Ozone and petrichor flooded my senses. Below, a car drew up and stopped outside, blocking the narrow lane.

Men in dark suits got out, and then a stooped, shuffling figure emerged. It was late for guests, but the man outside was no guest in this city. I left my gun on the table and went to meet the Godfather of Naples himself.

They were in the parlor by the time I got downstairs. Renato, my best friend and capo, was well put together in a silk dressing gown, like he was on his way to the world's most lethal pajama party.

Salvatore De Sanctis, his uncle, was in a three-piece suit, like he usually was. The only concession to his age was the jeweled walking stick he gripped in his gnarled hand. Time had passed here in the city of my birth. Sometimes it felt like it hadn't. Time had stopped for me decades ago, on hot, foreign soil, baking under the sun, unsure whether there was a tomorrow. Somehow, life had paused, and it had never restarted.

But looking at Zio Sal, it was undeniable. Time was ticking, bringing me every day closer to death. It shouldn't have been comforting, but it was.

"Elio, boy. Why does it seem like you were already up? I take it you already cleaned up Franco, the idiot who thought he could undersell me?" Zio Sal rasped at me, shooting me a warm glance when I entered the room.

My errand tonight had been for Zio Sal.

I nodded and took in his guard detail. As I scanned them up and down, Zio Sal chuckled.

"Be careful, boys. You'll be getting a performance evaluation in a minute, so stand up straight."

Renato inclined his head toward me. "Since we're here, Zio, if you want Elio to do some training, I'm sure we can twist his arm."

Zio Sal shook his head. "I lost too many men last time. I can't afford another of Elio's trainings."

"Fair enough. To what do we owe this early call? I thought we were having lunch?"

Zio Sal shrugged irritably. "This is lunch. I can't sleep for shit anymore. If it's not the aches and pains, it's visiting the fucking toilet. Don't laugh, it's not funny. It'll happen to you, too, one day, if you're lucky to live as long as me."

Renato smoothed his face into a sympathetic expression. "Of course. Forgive me, I don't want to wake Charlie so early. She needs her sleep."

Zio Sal waved a hand dismissively. "Don't gloat about your new wife and all the fun you're no doubt getting up to. We will meet again later. I want to see the woman who has tamed the great Renato De Sanctis."

I held back a smirk at his statement.

"Very funny," Renato said, irritated.

Zio Sal pointed at me. "He got it. Anyway, this isn't a social call. I wanted to see you boys." He turned his head to the guards standing around the room.

They swiftly headed for the door. I moved closer, knowing I

wasn't included in the silent command to get the hell out. If there was important De Sanctis business, then I was there. After Naples, and the shit show that had unfolded, my sister and I had become De Sanctis inner circle, and they were more family to us than our own had ever been. I sat on the couch opposite Sal. There were three of us left in the room, and the door had been closed a good few minutes before Sal felt safe enough to talk.

"We have a minor problem." Zio Sal pulled a cigar out of his pocket and lit up. "An old friend of mine, you might remember him from when you were younger. He's finally gotten in trouble for taking bribes and who knows what else . . . He's going down, and word on the street is that he could sing to cut a deal, lessen the sentence." He gestured with the cigar, the lit end dancing circles in the air.

Tension hit my system. One thing I'd developed while scraping by and surviving in my twenties was great gut instincts. I could just tell before something devastating happened. Before the bomb went off, before the mission went to shit, before the bullet rang out. I could just tell.

Like a bullet flying through the air from a hidden sniper, Zio Sal's next words zipped straight through my hollow chest.

He sighed heavily. "It's Prosecutor Bellisario."

I could practically feel the impact of the name I hadn't heard in more than a decade thud through my body. My cool, indifferent mask shuddered under the sound.

Ren glanced my way and then looked at his uncle. "Does he have anything on us?"

"On me, everything. That old *volpe* turned the other way for every big thing I needed done for twenty years. He could sink us with the information."

"So, we take him out before he gets to say a word to anyone."

"Just hold on a second . . . it's complicated. Alfredo, the *furbo* old fox that he is, figured that would be your solution. He says he's passed on the information . . . it'll be released in the event of his untimely death."

Renato snorted. "He's bluffing."

"Maybe, but you don't know him like I do. He's smarter than he appears. Just to complicate things, we weren't the only people he was doing favors for. Word is that the Ravelli family also has a lot at stake if he sings. They want him eliminated . . . and so, he wants our protection."

Ravelli? The name was familiar, but I couldn't quite remember why.

Renato raised an incredulous eyebrow. "You're shitting me. He's threatening us into protecting him?"

"I told you, he's smarter than he appears. Moreover, he wants protection for his daughter."

The words washed against the bastion around my heart.

"His daughter?" Renato snorted. "Let them kill them both and we'll deal with whatever evidence comes out. Actually, I'll bet he sent the information to her. Two birds with one stone."

"*Basta,* Renato. I don't want that. It's undignified. I'm old, and soon, I'll no longer be of this earth. I don't want to be dragged into interview rooms, or worse, a cell, before I die. Allow me to die with dignity . . . at my country estate."

Renato hid a smile of affection for his cantankerous old uncle. He'd been a hell-raiser in the past, but you'd never know it from his stooped posture and fragility now.

"If killing her is off the table, then the most obvious course of action is to marry the daughter off, of course, to a De Sanctis man," he said. "She's our collateral against him spilling his guts and Salvatore's history to the law in order to reduce his sentence. He clearly cares about her welfare . . . So she becomes a De Sanctis, and as long as he plays nice, she lives."

"You've forgotten that she's already married," I reminded Renato before he could get too carried away with his ridiculous idea. Sal gave me a strange look, as if a husband should be no impediment to making her one of the De Sanctis family.

"And what about the threat from the Ravelli family?" I pressed on, trying to force him to see reason.

"Protecting the father in prison is no big deal, half the guards are ours, and half the inmates. Protecting the daughter can fall to her new husband . . . the tax on getting a wife like Georgia Bellisario. Once Alfredo dies, he can do what he wants with her."

Georgia Bellisario.

The name stuck like a claw in a furrow scored across my heart.

A remnant of a time when the organ I housed in my chest used to beat.

I used to be a living, breathing man.

I used to have hopes and dreams and hot blood running through my veins.

Georgia Bellisario had been the end of all of that.

The day I met her, I started my descent into hell. Now, I lived there.

"Of course, it's Georgia Conti now, isn't it?" Renato mused. "Now she's the Conti widow."

Widow. She's the Conti widow. A widow. The word threatened to send me into a spiral.

"She's what?" I managed.

"A widow. Her husband passed not too long ago. Some illness. Everyone is dying," Zio Sal said, dramatic as ever. "You didn't know?"

I shook my head tightly. No. I didn't know. I didn't let myself check on her. I didn't let myself wonder. My life only worked if I continued to be a cold, emotionless machine, performing tasks and following orders without question. Looking up the woman who had ripped my heart from my chest and left me to bleed out didn't fit. It wasn't *allowed*.

"Ah, yes, she married the Conti boy, didn't she," Zio Sal muttered, nodding. "Those two were always inseparable."

Right. Inseparable. The reminder that Georgia had married her childhood boyfriend after all, when my life had burned to ashes, was just the reminder I needed to reinforce my indifference to her situation now.

"Who do you suggest for the husband?" Renato asked.

I glanced at him and met my capo's eyes. There was a question in them. Something that saw beneath the steel cage enclosing my mind.

I looked away.

"That's not my decision. It's none of my business. But I pity the poor bastard."

Renato chuckled softly. "I'd bet my fortune that Georgia is still a handful. I've only ever heard of one man handling her."

"Renato," I interrupted him. I had no desire to walk down memory lane. I'd decided long ago that the woman in question was dead to me. She'd died on a warm, late summer day, lying under the shadows of an olive tree. She'd died. She was gone forever. I didn't care about what was left over.

Sal watched us and then waved his hand. "The details are for you to work out. I don't know. I'm old and I want to get back to bed. Make this go away."

"*Ho capito*. Rest up, and I'll let you know when it's done."

Leaving the hotel, we stood on the steps and watched Zio Sal disappear into his town car.

"What do you really think I should do with Alfredo Bellisario and his daughter?" Ren asked, staring up at the slice of early morning sky visible between the old buildings surrounding us.

She's a widow. *A widow.* I silenced that small voice inside.

I shrugged. Mask in place. "Whatever you want. It's not my business."

"Oh really? I'd have thought there was no one more your business than her," Ren mused.

I held my tongue and avoided his probing gaze.

Renato blew out a breath, sensing my determination not to get dragged into the situation. He thought, nodding decisively. "Jimmy. Jimmy will marry her."

"Jimmy . . . Jimmy who I think is skimming off the casino Jimmy?" I asked, surprised.

Jimmy De Luca was a low-level made man, one who I was pretty sure was a traitor and deserving of the same punishment I'd dispensed last night.

Renato nodded. "He's the right age and single. Maybe it'll make him less annoying . . . or Georgia will kill him. Either way, it's a win-win. You got a problem with that?"

He cut his eyes to me.

I studiously avoided his gaze and shook my head. "No. No problem. It's not my business."

"Right." Renato sighed as though I was the most trying person he'd ever met. "One part is your business, however. Georgia lives in L.A. Her fiancé lives in Atlantic City. Someone needs to go and get her . . . and that someone is you."

"Me?" I repeated.

Ren nodded. "You. Once all this business with Bellisario gets out, you don't think the Ravelli family will have the exact same idea as us? Right now, it's about who can act fastest to help old Alfredo make the right choice about who to rat out. I don't trust anyone else to bring the daughter back in one piece but you. Cheer up. You'll only have to put up with her for a few days, then Jimmy will do his duty and take over."

"I can send a trusted man," I stated flatly. Everything inside me resisted the very thought of seeing Georgia again, never mind talking to her, being around her . . . I wasn't sure either of us would make it to the wedding in one piece.

"Don't overthink it, Colonel. Just follow orders." Renato gave me a grin.

He knew exactly how ingrained the habit of following orders was for me. When you'd dedicated your entire life to serving your country, questioning orders—or worse, refusing them—felt like an unforgivable betrayal.

"Still, I didn't intend to see her again," I pointed out, knowing the battle was lost. My capo's mind was made up.

Renato's hand landed on my shoulder. It reminded me of that day, a lifetime ago, when we'd first met, and I'd tried to steal his wallet, only to get caught immediately and hauled in front of the prosecutor.

"It seems like fate has other plans for you."

2

ELIO

THEN

I made it to the third day in Castel Amaro, when I knew I had to find a way to eat. The village was tiny, a speck on a map. I had caught a ride that far with a farmer. Hitching on the back of someone's truck was easy enough. He'd caught me at a rest stop on the outskirts of the village and run me off with a shotgun.

So much for the countryside being friendlier than the city.

I was heading south. I needed to get the hell out of Napoli and the legacy my father had left me . . . son of a rat.

I wandered during the day, keeping out of sight of the locals, and slept in someone's barn at night. There was a hole in the roof, and through it, I watched the stars.

I missed my home. Napoli. They called it the city of the seven castles, but I'd always think of it as the city of thieves. It stole your heart, while its inhabitants stole everything else. Well, at least they had in my neighborhood.

My father had worked for a local Mafia and done a shit job of it. When he went down, he'd rolled over and sung like a birdie for the local police and made it impossible to stay in the city. Then the family he'd ratted on got to him and he'd joined my mother in the dirt. There was only me and my little sister, Giada, left. The state sent her to stay with some distant relatives they'd dug up from somewhere, whereas me? I was on my own. I was old enough to take care of myself and answer for my old man's crimes . . . I couldn't have stayed in the city. That life, and everyone I'd ever known, was over for me.

It was better that Giada was with family right now. They could at least feed her. She could sort out the rest herself. She might be small, but she was mighty. Once I was settled somewhere, had a job and a way to support her, I'd steal her out of her bedroom one night. The Santori siblings belonged together.

The aroma of roasted lamb threaded through the air, making my stomach cramp painfully. Fuck, I was hungry. I'd been hungry before. Since our patriarch was arrested and then died in prison for being a rat, there had been more than enough nights when I'd gone to sleep starving. Somehow, caring for my sis had pushed the mundane needs of the body out of my head. Now I had nothing to distract me from the certain knowledge that if I didn't get something to eat today, then tomorrow, walking, stealing, or just standing upright would be a challenge.

The church bells rang overhead. It was Sunday, and the locals of Castel Amaro were out in full force for church and lunch, and the *passeggiata*. It was the time to see and be seen, and I had my eye on someone in particular.

There was a family in town that was miles above the others in terms of wealth. An older, distinguished-looking man, and a younger man who could be his son, or even grandson.

Lifting one of their wallets would ensure a full belly for more than a few nights.

I waited until the men retired to the bar inside the restaurant where they'd just eaten a lavish lunch, and when one went to the bathroom, I made my move.

It was a tiny *taverna*, and the bathroom hall was cramped. I peeked into the bathroom through a crack in the door. My mark smoked a cigarette at the window, leaning on the sill and talking on the phone in a rapid stream of English.

His cigarettes and lighter were perched on top of his wallet behind him, beside the sink.

My first stroke of luck in years. Maybe ever.

Pushing the old door open only as far as I needed to snake my arm in, I reached for the wallet.

I moved slowly. Rushing caused mistakes. Holding my nerve for the endless amount of time it took to reach out and grab the soft leather felt impossible, but somehow, I managed it. It wasn't like pickpocketing clueless tourists in Piazza Garibaldi. It was quiet here, and there was nowhere to run if the man turned around.

I gripped the wallet, tilting it so the cigarette pack and lighter slid off quietly. There was a small clatter, but the man was talking so loudly he didn't hear. I retracted my arm, my whole body sweating. Gently, I pulled my arm through the gap in the door and let it fall shut.

I'd done it.

Somehow, I'd done it.

"What are you doing?" The voice just beside me sent my hands flying up defensively.

"Hey!" the person exclaimed as my knuckles met soft skin.

A young woman stood in front of me, her hands on her slim hips, glaring up at me.

Her cheek was red where I'd hit her to shove her back.

Crap. I'd smacked a girl?

"You hit me!" she cried.

Before I knew what I was doing, I clamped a hand over her mouth and maneuvered her into the ladies' room.

She fought me, scratching my wrists and biting my fingers, like a wildcat in a sack.

"Shh, stop! I didn't mean to hit you, it was an accident," I whispered in her ear.

She continued to fight, so I held her firmer and gave her a shake. She was breathing hard, and her high, firm breasts were pressing into my forearm. It was distracting.

"Listen. It was an accident, okay? I thought you were about to hit me, so I hit you first . . . I'm sorry," I hissed.

I had her pressed against the door, her body bucking into mine. Her face was trapped by my hand, and her huge dark eyes were glaring up at me, pure fury in their depths. At my words, some of the fight went out of that fiery glare. She sighed.

After a moment, she relaxed and mouthed a question behind my fingers. Gingerly, I freed her lips.

"An accident?" she repeated. Her voice was husky, like she'd injured her throat through screaming against my hand. Her lips were full and dark red. My touch had slightly smudged her lipstick.

"An accident. I'd never hit a woman on purpose," I told her firmly.

She narrowed her eyes at me. "If it was an accident, then you'll let me hit you back to even the score."

I blinked at her. *What the hell?*

"I don't have time for your little game," I snapped at her and tried to step past.

"Leave and I'll scream that you stole Ren's wallet," she countered.

I stilled and frowned at her, grinding my teeth.

She smirked and tilted her head back, resting it on the door. "Didn't you know that's who you were stealing from? You got a death wish, or are you just clueless?"

"I was actually trying not to die, but thanks for the information," I said roughly. *Fuck.* Who the hell had I messed with? Maybe I could still put the wallet back.

"Why were you going to die?" the girl asked.

She was pretty. Now that I took a second to notice, she was uncommonly beautiful. If we were caught alone, the fact that I was only trying to get away from her would be hard to believe. With her lush body, tousled hair, and smudged lipstick, who would believe I'd been able to keep my hands off such a temptation? She could cause me more than a headache.

I took a deep breath and blurted out the truth. "Not eating for nearly a week tends to have that effect," I muttered and looked toward the window in the ladies' room. That should be my escape route.

"You've not eaten in a week?" she exclaimed and then peered at me closer, a thorough up-and-down inspection. "Are you homeless?"

I let out a bitter laugh. "Why? Is that a crime too, here in your perfect town?"

She wrinkled her nose. "That's not an answer. You smell like you're homeless."

"That was the cattle truck," I fired back.

She opened her pretty pink mouth to say something else, no doubt something that would piss me off, just as the ladies' room door slammed open and a hand reached inside and grabbed me.

"Here's the thief, right here. Georgia, did he hurt you?"

The guy she'd called Ren was studying her carefully. She narrowed her eyes at me. I waited for her to tell the man that I'd hit her. Her cheek was still red.

She shook her head. "No, he didn't. He didn't touch me."

I stared open-mouthed at the girl as the man pulled me out of the bathroom and clapped a heavy hand on my shoulder.

"Come on, kid, you're coming with me."

I sat on the soft leather seat of a town car, staring hard out the window and wondering how the fuck I was going to get out of this one. A man sat beside me. One of the men from the restaurant. Not the rich one and his son. His driver had addressed him as *Signore Procuratore*. Mr. Prosecutor.

My mama, God rest her tired soul, had always said I was born under an unlucky star. Every single day, the fucking universe proved her right.

The car pulled to a smooth stop outside a squat building painted a faded light blue, jerking me from my moody silence.

Carabinieri.

The local police office. I'd managed to escape Napoli and the people who wanted to hurt me and spit on my traitor father's grave, just to be arrested in the fucking countryside. There wasn't a soul in the world with the ability or means to come bail me out. I'd rot in there.

I clenched my hands tightly into fists on my thighs as I considered fighting my way out of the car and making a run for it. My stomach growled, a sense of nervous anticipation running through my thoughts.

"Hungry?" a gruff voice said from beside me.

The prosecutor was watching me carefully.

I shrugged and turned away, putting a hand on the door. I didn't need this fucker gloating. I tried the handle. It was locked.

I looked back at the man.

He was staring at my tattered jeans and sneakers, one of which was held together with string.

"Did you run away from home?"

I snorted softly. "Run away? How old do you think I am?"

He mirrored my shrug from before. "It's hard to tell. You're tall but skinny . . . underfed. You've got swagger and confidence . . . but the eyes, they tell a different story. You're hard to place, and you're old enough to get arrested, I suppose. You fucked around with the wrong person. The De Sanctis family aren't people to cross."

My face drained of color, and sudden nausea hit me like a punch. I'd just tried to rob a De Sanctis? The De Sanctis family was infamous in Italy. I'd never seen any of them in person . . . not until today.

"You're lucky that they've let me deal with your sentencing."

I glanced meaningfully at the police station. "Yeah, really lucky."

The man watched me for a long moment. "Do you know who I am?"

"A prosecutor, I guess."

The man nodded. "I'm not just the prosecutor, but the moral compass of Castel Amaro. Mercy is a good look for a man like me . . . I'm thinking of running for office in a few years."

"Weren't you having lunch with the De Sanctis men?" I pointed out.

The prosecutor smirked and nodded. "Indeed. I love the law, but it doesn't pay like it ought to. A man can't be blamed for supplementing. I have staff to pay and a daughter to support."

I shrugged again, unsure where this man was going with his confession.

"You don't care that the prosecutor was having lunch with a mob boss?" he wondered idly.

I shook my head. "That's your business, not mine. I just need to eat something."

The prosecutor chuckled and slapped me on the shoulder.

"I like you, kid. You're a survivor. Scrappy . . . I like that. I'll tell you what. I'm going to give you a chance to pay off your transgression. Here is your sentence: Don't go to jail, work for me. I need a new stable boy. You can sleep in the barn. It's still warm enough. You can eat from my kitchen, except dinners, that's for me and Georgia."

I turned to face the man who held my future in his hands, trying not to show my pathetic hope.

"Just shovel horse shit, that's it? What's the catch?"

The prosecutor shook his head. "No catch. Work for me, do what I say without question—within working hours—and you get room and board. We got a deal, kid?"

Do what I say without question? That remark alone had my hackles rising, but I couldn't afford to refuse. I could run away easier from some bougie house than a jail cell.

"Deal."

The man smiled with satisfaction. He nodded to the driver and the car started again, carrying us away from the police station.

"I'm Alfredo. Alfredo Bellisario. I run this town, unless Salvatore De Sanctis is visiting his country house." He chuckled.

"You're friends?" I ventured. I wanted to find out a little about this mercurial man who'd spared me an uncomfortable night on a bench in a cell.

"Old, old friends. Sal grew up around here, before he started the family business. He scratches my back, and I scratch his. Don't worry about the wallet. I'll tell them we've come to an agreement."

The car stopped, pulling in behind an apple-red Mini. The door was opening, and someone was emerging.

The driver exited to let Alfredo out. I opened my own door; I didn't think the new stable boy merited the chauffeur opening his door for him. My feet sank into the gravel of the driveway, and I peered across the impressive forecourt at a pale terra-cotta villa surrounded by fig trees. Shit. This place was nice. Well, clearly it was nice if they had stables, but still, I'd never set foot in a house this nice.

The sun beat down on the back of my neck. God, it was hot. I hadn't washed in days. I felt disgusting in that moment. Starved and reckless, dirty and desperate.

That was when I saw her.

The girl from the restaurant.

The prosecutor's daughter. Of course it was her.

She shut the door of the red Mini and stared at me, raising an elegant eyebrow before sliding on huge sunglasses, shielding her eyes from me. She glanced over at her father, who was deep in conversation with a man who, from his uniform, seemed to be the gardener.

She walked across the gravel. She had red heels on and a white dress with printed cherries scattered across it.

"I thought you'd been arrested," she said. Even her voice was beautiful. Deep and smoky, older than her years.

I shoved a hand through my unruly dark waves and hoped I didn't look as dirty as I felt.

"Yeah, well, your dad realized he needed a hand around here, and I was more than happy to oblige."

She wrinkled her nose. "You're going to be working here?"

"I'm sure stranger things have happened," I said.

She tossed her hair back over a shiny brown shoulder. "They haven't. Nothing ever happens around here. You'll see. I give it a week and you'll be wishing you were arrested because you're dying of boredom."

"I don't know, I like boredom. I think it's underappreciated, and besides . . ." I let my gaze drop down to her slender ankles, up her bare legs, and over her body, meeting her gaze again, wishing I could see her eyes. "I think living here will be plenty interesting."

"Is that right?" Her red-tinted lips tilted at the corner. "What's your name?"

"Elio. Elio Santori. And yours is Georgia."

A slow smile spread over her beautiful mouth. "And you know that how?"

"I heard it at the restaurant."

"Interested, were you?" she teased.

I chuckled and shrugged. "Just curious about the girl who lied for me. The prosecutor's daughter. I don't know if your daddy would approve."

She sighed, and I had the feeling she'd just rolled her eyes.

She crossed her arms over her chest, and I stepped closer. Her father was still occupied, and I'd be damned if I didn't want to smell the lemon and lavender clean scent of this girl again. It was surprisingly addictive.

She watched me come closer and wet her lips. Was she nervous? Her little pink tongue darting out and swiping over her full red lips sent my blood pumping downward.

"So, 'Elio'—for the sun god? What are you named for?" she asked, a hint of nerves in her voice. Ms. Confident could be flustered too, then. That was interesting.

I tutted and shook my head. I had reached her. I leaned a hand on the back of her car, the metal hot under my palm, and shoved the other into my jeans pocket. A denim handcuff to keep me from touching something that would get me fired before I'd even worked a day.

The prosecutor's daughter.

"No, my mother didn't hold with the Greeks. She was a superstitious woman, and her gut instincts were never wrong. She named me Elio for the Latin . . . *alius*."

Georgia considered that, tilting her regal head an inch as she mulled over the word.

"*Alius*? Other. Different . . . right?" she finally asked.

I nodded. "Clever girl," I murmured, genuinely impressed.

Few bothered studying the classics anymore; fuck knew I certainly hadn't. But Georgia was a Renaissance woman. The whole package. Beauty, brains, and moxie.

I was a fucking goner.

Then a heavy hand landed on my shoulder.

"Georgia, darling, time to go and study. I'll show Elio around the place. You two needn't interact much. In fact, you'll hardly know he's here."

Georgia nodded, her cheeks flushed a delicate pink I couldn't tear my eyes from.

I watched her walk into the house, and her father watched me watch her.

"Lay so much as a fingertip on her, and I'll make you wish I'd dropped you off at the police station."

I glanced at him.

His jovial face was serious.

"My daughter is forbidden. Touching her means a fate worse than death for a punk like you . . . Got it?"

I swallowed the knot of anger and resentment in my throat and forced myself to nod.

"I hear you. She's off-limits. That's the rule," I muttered.

Alfredo nodded, patting my back consolingly.

He didn't know I'd never been very good at following rules.

3

GEORGIA

NOW

"Hold still, or I swear, you'll know what pierced nipples feel like," I warned past a mouthful of pins.

"Ha! More fool you, I've always wanted pierced nipples—oh, and a Venus piercing, too . . . if you happen to get near my clit." Erica, my friend, muse, and pain in my ass giggled at me.

"Pass. Something has gone seriously wrong with this design if I stick a pin anywhere near your pussy." I sighed, pulling the last pin from my mouth and tucking in the sweetheart neckline of the gown. I stepped back and eyed the design critically.

Erica turned around and looked at the floor-length mirror behind her, and gasped dramatically.

"Oh my God, I'm a goddess," she murmured reverently.

"That's undeniable, but there's something not quite right about the waist."

I reached for my measuring tape, and she stuck a hand up in front of me.

"Halt! It's nearly midnight, and you promised me drinks tonight. We are going out. I've been your mannequin for three hours. I've earned my fifteen-dollar cocktail."

I raised an eyebrow at her. "Fifteen dollars? If you want to drink branded spirits, then we are going to the Weaver."

Erica huffed. "Great, so you can buy me a free drink? There's never anyone cute there."

"Then statistically, it's due for a visit from a hottie." I grinned at her and tidied up. My tiny apartment was hardly big enough for dressmaking. The only spot was between the refrigerator and the sitting room sofa. It made cleanup easy.

I stabbed my last pin back into the pincushion on my wrist and tugged it off. My apartment was groaning under the weight of the extra work I'd brought home from the dressmaking shop I worked at, so I had to keep everything tidy and in its place, or I'd disappear under bolts of fabrics and jeans needing to be hemmed. I should have been trying to catch up on my work—there was always an endless amount of tailoring needing done—but it was the weekend, and I'd wanted to work on my passion project for one evening. I'd have to make up for it tomorrow.

I reached for my measuring tape. "Come on, let's go, or if you've changed your mind, we could redo the entire hem—" I started.

"I'm going!" Erica blurted and tried to take the dress off, letting out a short scream.

"Watch the pins!"

Ten minutes later, we were both dressed and in the hall outside my apartment, my design on a hanger, dangling on a clothes rack, and I was wrestling with my front door lock. The damn thing always jammed.

"You need a new door." Erica watched me critically.

"I've got it, it just needs to be jiggled the right way," I said, trying my damnedest to make the damn thing turn. *Come on, don't embarrass me now.*

"You need a new apartment. You can't stay here for long. It's a miracle you haven't been mugged or robbed yet." Erica peered down the stairs like the building was the ninth circle of hell. Clearly, she didn't know about the damn loan shark who came sniffing around looking for repayment of my late husband's debts every month, and it was going to stay that way. The only person more broke than me was Erica, and knowing her, she'd try and help, putting herself last.

"To be fair, I have nothing to steal, so more fool them. Anyway, my lock might be a difficult little bitch sometimes, but she's mine and she doesn't let just anyone in."

Erica narrowed her eyes at me. "Are you talking about yourself or the lock?"

"Fuck off." I grinned at her and turned the key triumphantly. "See? Easy!" I forced the pant from my voice.

"Whatever," Erica said and headed down the stairs.

I followed, taking a step and pulling my vibrating phone out of my jacket. It was a text message. In Italian.

I dragged my thoughts away from the doom spiral before it began. Step one to recovery was to recognize the thought patterns that marked the beginning of an emotional deep dive. Then, try to stop yourself from plummeting. I was better at that when I had someone else to focus on.

I paused on the stairs and read. I was embarrassed to admit my mother tongue was rusty. I'd been living in America for fourteen years.

A deep chill spread through my limbs, and the hand holding my cell went numb. I didn't need to refresh my Italian to understand the message.

Mrs. Conti, I am a lawyer representing your father. I need to speak with you urgently. Please contact me at your earliest convenience. I am awaiting your call.

The first rule of continuing to live when your heart has been broken into a million pieces is not to think of the past. Draw a line through it. Stay away from thinking about things associated with it. Push it all away. That was the reason why I hadn't seen or spoken to my father in more than ten years. He reminded me too much of the worst day of my life. In the beginning, I'd sent him updates on my life, entirely false, pretty, rosy images . . . to keep him and his concern away. Over time, even that had stopped. It hurt too much.

To my father, my life was a carefully curated feed of happy photos and cheerful memes. A lot of people scorned social media for setting unrealistic expectations for others, but sometimes, that was what I valued the most about it.

Why should I have to bare my soul, and every excruciating disappointment and stress in my worthless existence, to curious outsiders? I didn't. I could hide behind the perfect shot and a holiday card written in a cheerful tone. Sometimes, the fact that no one else knew how low I'd fallen was the only thing that kept me going. Even after all this time, I still had my pride. I didn't have much else to my name, so I figured I should be grateful.

Why was a lawyer contacting me about my father? Had he died?

"What's up anyway? Since we left your place, you've moped like your cat died. Cheer the fuck up!" Erica demanded.

I blinked at her. My mind was far, far away from the dive bar we were sitting in.

In my mind, I was thousands of miles away, in a small town, overlooking a different sea, young and naive . . . and about to be irreparably shattered.

"Sorry, I'm not feeling good. I should go. I'm cramping your style." I nodded toward a hipster-type dude at the bar giving Erica the eye.

"You don't have to go," she pouted, sending a smile in the hottie's direction.

"Yes, I do . . . Have fun." I summoned a smile for her from somewhere and grabbed my jacket and left. It wasn't cold. L.A. seldom got cold enough to wear anything heavier than a light jacket.

I wandered home along quiet streets, lost in the halls of memory.

I couldn't get the text out of my head. It was too early in Italy to call, with the time difference. I had to wait. It was sure to be a sleepless night until I spoke to someone.

I got home and fiddled with the lock. It refused to open.

"Just open, *fanculo*!" I rasped, tears pressing on my eyelids.

I rattled the door, twisting the key this way and that, until the damn thing bent. I sank down against the wall and leaned my head on my knees, tears pushing up and out, uncontrollably.

Why could nothing ever be easy?

My work paid well enough, but living alone in the city was expensive. Being a widow in her thirties, I didn't want to share a space with roommates, so here I was, in a place where the door didn't even lock and I was too scared to call the landlord about it.

I couldn't go home to Italy; I'd rather die in my little apartment alone than relive all that I'd experienced there. Not to mention the paralyzing fear of flying I'd discovered when I left. So, I was stuck. Life had stopped, and there was no restarting it.

By the time the knees of my jeans were soaked through and my cheeks burning with salt, a soft sigh sounded. I looked up just in time to see Old Albert standing at his door across the hall from me.

"The lock again?" His voice was the result of a pack-a-day habit over the last seventy years. He sounded like the Crypt Keeper and yet was the healthiest ninety-year-old I'd ever met.

I nodded.

He shuffled out of his apartment, screwdriver in hand.

"Nothing to cry that much over," he remarked lightly, jiggling the lock.

I watched him work. His gnarled old hands were like knots of wood. A rush of gratitude threatened to overwhelm me.

"I'm not crying about the door . . . I'm just wishing you could be my dad," I muttered.

Old Albert chuckled. "Dad? More like granddad."

"Whatever. Family, I guess." I glanced down at my hands. "I'd trade my own family in a heartbeat."

"Family is as family does. You can choose your own, I reckon, if you want," Old Albert said kindly and swung the door open. "There you go. Right as rain."

I stood and impulsively hugged him.

He patted my back.

"Go on in and get to bed. Everything will feel better in the morning; take it from someone who's been around the sun a few times more than you."

I nodded and gave him a smile. He went back to his apartment, and I waited until the door closed safely behind him then slipped into my own. My tiny, piece-of-shit, hole-in-the-wall with a door that barely worked, no AC, and a landlord who liked to come over in person for the rent and remind me that I could pay a reduced rate if I let him watch me shower once a week. Not free rent, just reduced. How flattering.

I caught sight of myself in the hallway mirror as I set down my keys.

My dark eyes stared back at me. Erica was right. I seemed off. I was haunted—but that made sense, in a way.

I'd always been haunted by the past. The year I'd turned nineteen, a bomb had imploded my world, and the aftershocks were still rocking me.

I'd never get over them.

My necklace glinted in the darkness, and I pulled it out from under my hair and held the beautiful silver locket between my fingers, rubbing my thumb over the smooth metal. Inside the locket was a perfectly preserved sprig of heliotrope.

It was my altar to the past. My tribute to all I'd lost.

A hard bang at the door startled me. I jumped and dropped my necklace. I turned. Dark shadows cut through the light at the bottom of the door.

"Georgia? You home? Let me in!"

Bang, bang, bang.

Oh my God. Not again. Was it the end of the month already?

I backed away from the door, my sadness and worry for my father disappearing. A very real fear of the present worked through me. Jackson Howel was a local lowlife and loan shark. Tom, my dearly beloved late husband, had gone into a lot of medical debt at the end, and now that the dust had settled, I was finding out that he'd borrowed to pay that debt in less-than-ideal ways.

There was a sharp sound of metal clicking against metal, and then the door swung open. I spun, making a dash through the apartment, then a hand landed in my hair and tugged me back ruthlessly.

Howel was a small guy but strong and mean. His gold teeth caught the light from the window as he leaned over me. He'd dragged me to the floor, and my scalp was on fire. He'd ripped a good chunk out, I could just tell.

"Well, look who was home after all. You don't inspire confidence in our payment plan, you dumb bitch, when you don't answer my calls."

"I'm sorry. I've been busy working, trying to get the payments together," I told him as emotionlessly as I could. Fuck, I had to fight every instinct I had to kowtow to a man like this, but I had no choice. I had no power, no influence, and I was broke as hell.

"And you need to tell me that, loud and clear . . . so we can think up alternatives," Jackson snarled and twisted my hair back so hard that blood dripped down my forehead.

"I've got your payment," I panted, tapping his hand, trying to convince him to let me up.

"You do?" He studied me and then smiled.

It was so greasy and cunning I shuddered.

"You should have said. I don't like hurting paying clients."

He held my hair for a second longer, making it clear who the boss was, and then released me. I fell to the side, panting.

"Get it then, now," Jackson said.

He drew out a chair at the kitchen table and sat, watching me scramble around. Tears of pure frustration and anger threatened to push through, but I drove them back.

Fuck this guy. I wasn't going to let him see me cry.

I went to my dressmaking dummy and reached inside the hollow interior for the envelope I'd been carefully stuffing all month. I brought it out and handed it to him.

He took it and started to count.

I crossed my arms over my chest, leaned against the kitchen counter, and watched, counting with him in my head.

"Well, look at that. It's all here." Jackson smiled and eyed me up and down. "I can't say I'm not a little disappointed about that."

"So, that's all you need. You can leave. I'll see you next month, right?" I strove to be strong, at least in my tone. He didn't get to see how much he'd scared me.

Jackson studied me. "You can pay it off faster, you know, if you pay more. The way you're going . . . you're only paying off the interest."

I swallowed. "It's all I can afford right now."

Jackson smiled. "Then I guess I'll be seeing you next month and the month after . . . as long as we both shall live, *bella*."

I stiffened at the word. Jackson was connected to some low-level Mafia thugs in the area. I didn't know much of anything about them, except that since Tommaso had died, they'd made my life a living nightmare.

After Jackson left, with much swagger, lewd glances, and promises to be back next month, I locked the useless door and sank down on the floor.

Fuck. What was I going to do? Jackson was no financial genius, but it didn't take one to know I wasn't paying off Tom's debt fast enough. I'd been to the cops, and they couldn't do anything about it. I either had to pay up or run. Leaving everything I'd worked for in L.A. made me feel like my life up to now had been a waste of time. Sure, it wasn't much, but the small life I'd pieced together for myself from the tattered remains of my dreams mattered to me. It was all I had to live for.

Well, that and my memories. I gripped my necklace tight between my fingers and closed my eyes. I was the memory keeper, and if I didn't house those precious moments, they'd be lost forever.

Alone, in the dark, I let the tears come.

4

GEORGIA

THEN

"Make me something," Tommaso pleaded, holding up a pink-sequined bolt of fabric in front of the mirror.

I shook my head and tapped the ash off the end of my illicit cigarette.

"Your father would shoot you if he saw you in that," I pointed out.

Tommaso pouted. "I would hardly show him. It would just be for me . . . and whatever in-the-closet rando I invited into my boudoir."

"And yet, you'd still get shot at the end of the day. Babe, wait until you move to America, and I'll make you whatever you want for Pride." I held my pinkie up. "I promise."

Tommaso sat, and set aside the fabric. "I suppose you're right. God, I can't wait. Promise you'll join me next year. You'll get into design school, and I'll be a hotshot businessman of some kind, and we'll live together in a fabulous loft, drink margaritas for breakfast, and just be ourselves for once."

I took Tommaso's hand. Sure, it was the twenty-first century, but being the only son of a local businessman and pillar of the church, Tommaso had as much chance of being accepted as a gay man in our backward, uber-religious little town as a devil worshipper had. "Sure. I can't wait." I gave him a wan smile. Would I really get into Parsons one day? I had no idea. Would my father let me leave Castel Amaro? Again, I had no idea, but I doubted it. Since my mother died, he liked to keep me close.

Just the idea of being left alone in the suffocating town I'd been born in was enough to make me scream. I couldn't stand any of it. The gossiping *nonnas* watching from their doorsteps, or the nuns from the convent on the hill. The local school system, whose books were as antiquated as the community, or the fact that anything that wasn't church, cooking, or farming was frowned upon. If it wasn't for the internet, people like me and Tommaso would have perished of boredom long ago.

I lay back on my bed and blew a smoke ring at the ceiling. Okay, it was supposed to be a smoke ring, but in reality it was a puff of smoke that brought on a cough.

"I don't know why you're bothering learning to smoke. It's gross."

"Because my dad wouldn't like it. I just need to push through . . . It has to get good at some point—otherwise, why would everyone be so obsessed with it?"

Tommaso peered out the window and down to the garden. At the far end, there were stables where a procession of stable hands came and went each day, to his delight.

"You should ask the new boy to show you how to do it." Tom turned a wicked smile my way. "He seems like he knows all about the kinds of things that would make your daddy angry."

I sat up and followed his gaze.

Striding out of the barn, a pitchfork balanced on his shoulder, was the new boy. Elio Santori. The *cittaiolo*. City boy. He approached a pile of hay like it was trying to start a fight with him, stabbing it violently with the pitchfork.

"What do you mean?" I wondered idly.

He'd taken his shirt off and only had low-slung, ripped jeans on. His body was something else. He was nice to look at, I'd give him that. He even had some ink. I'd never seen a real tattoo before. In Castel Amaro, tattoos were akin to the Devil's mark.

"I mean, that kid's been through some shit, you can just tell. He's trouble . . . a bad boy." Tommaso wriggled his eyebrows suggestively. "I bet he's a wild ride."

"If you think so, go and try your luck."

"I'm not the one he stares at like a juicy steak. He eye-fucks you every single time you walk past him."

Heat flushed through me. "He does not."

"He does. I bet my right hand you in your skimpy shorts, or that yellow bikini you wear to swim in out back, are what he pictures when he's sleeping in the stables . . . jerking it hard and imagining it was you."

I threw a pillow in Tommaso's direction. "Shut the fuck up."

"Why? Does it turn you on to think about it?" Tom grinned.

Yes.

"I'm sure I'm just a spoiled little daddy's girl to a guy like him. A guy with real problems." I watched Elio Santori work in the late afternoon sun. It was my latest hobby.

Elio had set his pitchfork down and was heading toward the house.

I stood and smoothed my romper. It had polka dots on it, and I'd made it myself. I was happiest behind my sewing machine.

"Do you want another soda? I'm going to get one," I murmured.

Tom laughed. "You do that, you thirsty bitch. Say hi to the *cittaiolo* for me."

I gave him the finger and left the room, skipping downstairs to find Elio's boots already off at the door. I wandered through the house, wondering if he'd gone to the bathroom, and arrived at the kitchen.

The fridge door was ajar, and Elio Santori, in all his sweaty, bare-chested glory, was standing in the gap. He straightened up when I approached, a glass bottle of lemonade in hand.

He put the bottle to his lips and tilted his head back, taking long gulps of the juice. I watched, transfixed. I was so lost in the vision of him drinking, I jumped when he spoke.

"Can I help you? Don't tell me you're here to get me in trouble for touching something in the fridge?"

I wandered farther into the kitchen, pasting nonchalance across my face.

"I'm not the boss of the refrigerator. Do what you want," I murmured.

He watched me impassively and then took another drink.

I let my gaze slide down his torso. He was twenty, only a few months older than me, but he felt so much older. It was his worldliness. I had none, and he had it all. He'd lived a thousand lives in the city, dangerous, difficult lives, while I'd been here, playing with dresses and dolls and being spoiled by my dad.

"How's your face?" Elio suddenly asked. He shut the refrigerator and set the lemonade bottle on the counter. He turned, and the movement brought him close to me.

"Fine. You barely brushed me." For some reason, being seen as weak in front of this man felt unbearable. Also, it had been more than a week since he'd accidentally hit me. What kind of damage did he think he'd done?

He brought a hand up and gently cupped my cheek. Heat ripped through me like nothing I'd ever felt before.

"You lied for me," he said, his tone suspicious. "Why would you do that?"

I swallowed the hard knot in my throat. "Why not? It didn't cost me anything, and like I said, you barely brushed me."

He tilted his head. "So, it wasn't pity? You didn't feel sorry for the broke pickpocket who hadn't eaten in a week?"

I scoffed. "Feel sorry for you? Why should I? Boo-hoo, the bad-boy gangster was hungry . . . cry me a river."

"Gangster?" he repeated, dropping his hand from my cheek.

"I heard your dad was Mafia."

Elio snorted. "He wished. He was a bottom-feeding wannabe. If Renato De Sanctis is a white whale, my father was krill. I don't aspire to that kind of life."

"You don't? Then what do you aspire to?" I asked.

He was still standing so damn close.

Elio leaned in. Was he going to kiss me? He was so near.

"I don't have a fucking clue, but I know it won't be here in this shithole town. I'm getting out of here, as soon as I can. If you're as smart as I think you are, *topolina*, you'll do the same."

"*Topolina?*" I parroted the word, unsure whether to be offended or not. *Topolina*. Little mouse.

"Haven't you heard the story? *Il topo di città e il topo di campagna*. I'm the city mouse, you're the country mouse."

I raised an eyebrow at him. "Wasn't the city mouse rich?"

Elio regarded me and then chuckled. His wide, full lips drew back in a heart-stopping grin. It was the first smile of his I'd ever seen.

"*Vero*. Still, the nickname suits you."

He pulled back, the bottle in his hand. He'd been reaching for the bottle, not getting close enough to kiss me.

Heat washed into my cheeks.

He drank steadily, looking me in the eye the entire time. His strong throat bobbed, glistening with sweat from his outdoor work. I tore my eyes away with great effort.

"So, what's your plan for getting out of here, then? Share with the class," I challenged him.

He just shook his head. "It's not time yet." He set the empty bottle on the counter and stepped around me. "Ask me again later." When he was level with my side, he touched my ear, making me jump. "I saw this in the garden." It was all he said.

"How will I know when it's time?" I called to him, gingerly touching my hair. He'd tucked a little flower behind my ear.

He paused in the doorway. "You'll know, because I'll be gone. See you around, *topolina*," he said, winking at me and sauntering away. I went into the hall after him, and caught sight of myself in the mirror on the wall. A dark purple flower with neat little petals sat behind my ear. A heliotrope. I turned to thank him for the pretty little present, but he'd already gone.

ELIO

I'd never been religious, but since moving to Castel Amaro, I never missed church.

The reason for that was far from good and pure. I didn't give a shit about the sermon, or the blessings. I wasn't going there to save my stained soul . . . I was there for one reason, and one reason alone.

Her.

As soon as I'd moved into the stables of the terra-cotta villa at the edge of the town square, I'd realized that Alfredo Bellisario had been more cunning than I'd imagined in keeping his daughter out of my way. Unless Georgia sought me out, I was powerless to see her.

She was either at school, being tutored, or with her boyfriend. Tommaso Conti. I'd never hated another man as much as I did that fucker. He spent endless hours with Georgia up in her bedroom—with the door closed, I was furious to note. Once, I'd snuck up there to check, only to hear the soft murmur of their voices through the wood.

The fact that Alfredo Bellisario let Conti, the rich, stuck-up cunt, be in Georgia's bedroom, alone with his precious daughter, while he went out of his way to make sure her path never crossed mine, pissed me off.

Sure, I knew I was nothing more than a homeless gutter rat to the Bellisarios, but I wasn't dangerous. I'd never hurt Georgia. I just wanted to see her.

And so, I'd started coming to church.

She always stood at the front with her father. The place was always packed on Sundays.

There wasn't much going on in a town like Castel Amaro. Good, honest farmers did their work out in the fields, mothers stayed at home with their children, the local priest held his Sunday services, and Georgia's father, the upstanding citizen, waged a one-man war against the local Mafia. Except he didn't; he bent over for Salvatore De Sanctis and took all the bribes he liked. Of course, what went on behind closed doors wasn't anybody's business but their own. Castel Amaro liked to pretend to be squeaky-clean and godly on the outside, but it had its secrets, just like anywhere else.

Castel Amaro was the kind of place where people liked to think that they knew where their children were, even if that wasn't quite true. Boys should be strong and silent; girls should be quiet and obedient. The younger generations should respect the old, never raise their voices, wash their hands before dinner, and keep their thoughts and opinions to themselves.

But not Georgia Bellisario. She was an exotic bird, fluttering around that old villa. She laughed loudly, and no one shushed her. She spoke her mind, and the staff just nodded along. Her father indulgently listened to her opinions on topics and kissed her on the head afterward. Georgia wasn't like any other girl in the village.

She was magic.

They say there are turning points in life you can only see when you look back.

For me, there was the day my sister was born, mine to protect and look after for all time. There was the day my father was arrested, the last day I'd ever seen him. There was the day I'd stolen the wallet from Renato De Sanctis.

Then, there was the day I'd caught Georgia staring at me across the aisle in church, dust motes floating in the strands of sunlight between us. Another turning point.

A life-changing event.

An awakening.

She met my bored gaze, her big brown eyes full of amusement and teasing, unlike any I'd seen before, especially in church. Of course, I'd peeked before. A man could hardly avoid staring at such beauty. She wandered around her house in all types of skimpy clothing and half-sewn designs. I stole glances and guarded those illicit memories carefully. But a woman like that didn't need anything from a thug like me. We both knew what I was. We both knew our value in this world was wildly different. I was a hustler, a wannabe gangster's son. Someone going nowhere fast. She was a different breed altogether. She was going somewhere. The world was at her feet. And she deserved all of it.

But that afternoon in church, something had changed. A turning point I'd never forget.

She'd held my gaze while the priest intoned his sacraments.

The rest of the church lowered their heads obediently to pray and left us alone. We were the only two people in the world for that stolen moment.

Then she stuck out her pointy pink tongue, rolled her eyes back like she was dying along to the words of the Lord's Prayer, and pulled a rusty laugh from my lonely chest.

And just like that, I'd fallen.

5

ELIO

NOW

I left Naples a few hours after Renato's orders. Since keeping a low profile was important, considering that we didn't know what force the Ravelli family had sent to capture the prosecutor's daughter, I flew commercial.

Without exception, being in a crowded airport and stuffed into too small a space with other people meant I was tense. I also had to leave my favorite guns on Renato's jet to make the return flight to New Jersey.

My hands itched without my means to defend myself.

In the stifling Naples airport, I set up my laptop at a coffee shop and downloaded the file my sister had sent me only minutes before.

I drank three espressos while waiting for the damn airport Wi-Fi to download the large file.

Georgia Conti.

And there it was, suddenly sitting on my desktop.

There had once been another with the same name, long since deleted. I'd asked my sister for it when I'd left the Col Moschin,

Italy's very own Special Forces unit. Finally a civilian once more, my debts all paid and left behind, I'd been prepared to find her. I'd find her and she'd answer for the past. It was all I'd thought about for years while in active service. The thought of being face-to-face once more had kept me warm many a night, sleeping outside in the rain and cold. It had lulled me to sleep while in active conflict zones and soothed my brow when I'd lain in medical for weeks at a time, my body injured once again.

Then, the day I'd walked free, I'd sat in a coffee shop, just like the one I was in now, and opened the file for an excruciating couple of seconds before closing it and deleting the entire thing.

The first image that had popped up was Georgia, holding her husband's hand, beaming at the camera.

In the military, I'd learned how to control myself. I hadn't thought anything could crack that calm, until I saw that photograph.

In seconds, my blood pressure rose, and anger like nothing I'd ever felt flooded me. It tasted like blood and ashes on my tongue. I slammed the laptop closed and then picked the entire thing up and smacked it against the table.

When that didn't work, I bent the entire fucking thing in half.

As the stunned coffee shop had gone silent and everyone stared at me, I'd sat there feeling like a land mine. Lethal, unpredictable. Unacceptable.

"Dude, if you've got a virus, just restarting usually works."

I could still hear the exact perplexed timbre of the guy working at the table next to me. Normal people didn't carry rage like that inside them. Normal people didn't feel like they could light the sky up just by looking at a photograph.

If you've got a virus. It was a very fitting way of thinking about the woman who'd destroyed me so completely. Wiped me clean.

The military had been a clean slate. A total reboot. I couldn't afford to be re-infected with Georgia's poison.

I'd finally wiped the virus from my OS. I couldn't go back.

That was when I'd realized it was too dangerous for me to search for Georgia. I had my freedom from the Col Moschin, and Renato De Sanctis waiting for me to take up the role of *sottocapo* in his Cosa Nostra. I'd learned how to live emotionlessly, in the eye of the storm, where nothing hurt.

I wasn't giving that up for anyone.

Especially not her.

Now fate, and my capo, had brought her back into my life, and I had no choice but to see her or defy orders.

I opened the folder, and there she was.

This time, the picture wasn't anything glamorous. Black-and-white CCTV footage of her arriving at a dressmaking studio. Giada, my sister, was a tech genius. If there was a camera within a viable radius of her target, she'd find them.

She had Georgia walking to the supermarket and returning home with heavy bags. Georgia checking the prices of every single item she bought. Georgia taking the bus. Georgia waiting for the bus. Georgia in a coffee shop, sketching on a pad, lost in her own thoughts. Georgia and her friend leaving a bar late at night.

I forgot my coffee and the crowd as I stared at her. The footage wasn't perfect, but it was clear enough to make out the strong line of her jaw and the same sharp little chin I remembered so well. It had fit in my grip just right.

With a discipline honed over nearly two decades, I closed the photos and scanned the information.

Widowed, employed at a dressmaking atelier, her address. No hobbies listed. She didn't seem to leave her apartment much except for going to work. No mention of any family other than her recently deceased husband.

Good.

It would be just me and Georgia, alone . . . Just like old times.

When I arrived in L.A., I went straight to her apartment. Breaking in was child's play. She was out, as I'd expected her to be at that time in the morning. A momentary fiddling with the door admitted me to her private space.

The apartment wasn't what I was expecting, not at all.

When I'd known Georgia, she'd been the overindulged, spoiled little princess of one of the most well-known men in town. Her boyfriend, Tommaso Conti, who she went on to marry, had been the son of a local millionaire.

Fourteen years later, and his widow was living in a tiny apartment with peeling paint, no air-conditioning for the L.A. heat, and the sound of a loud argument from the upstairs neighbors. How the mighty had fallen.

I glanced around her kitchen, finding only instant noodles and one cucumber to eat, and then moved through the tiny space. I didn't touch anything. Georgia was my virus, after all, and even curiosity about her situation was unacceptable.

Instead of poking around, I set up small cameras, one in the corner of each room. I needed eyes on her, and anyone who might be looking for her, like the Ravellis. I was also pretty sure that her father had sent his collateral to his only daughter. He had no one else he could trust. When you'd fucked over as many people as Prosecutor Bellisario had, allies were few and far between.

He'd sent the collateral to Georgia, or instructions on how to access it. I was sure.

If I could find that . . . this whole ordeal and the arranged marriage would be unnecessary. We could just have the good prosecutor killed in prison, before he sang on Salvatore. Easy, mess-free.

If she had the evidence, there would be some sign of it, and considering how often she stayed in, I was betting the cameras in her house would be very illuminating.

She'd lead me to my collateral sooner or later, and I'd be waiting . . .

And watching.

6

GEORGIA

"Hey, did you finish those alterations over the weekend?" Eddie was my manager at the dressmaking shop I worked at, and a sweetheart.

I nodded and pointed to the pile at the end of my desk.

He blew out a long breath. "Thank God. There's some actress insisting that we got her dates wrong, and she needs it today."

"It's done. I hope she doesn't need anything further, though, and that I got it right," I worried.

Eddie patted my shoulder. "You always nail it, don't worry."

He answered his furiously ringing cell and wandered away. I sat back and stretched this way and that, feeling my spine decompress. God, I felt old lately. I knew I wasn't old, not really, but I felt it.

I reached for the moisturizer I kept on my desk. My hands were sore, my knuckles swollen from hours and hours of careful needlework. I'd have arthritis in them before I hit thirty-five, I was sure of it. Maybe I already had it. I wouldn't know. Me and health insurance had parted ways many years ago.

I looked up at the small slit of a window that ran along the top of one side of the dressmaking studio. Upstairs was a luxurious showroom, offering high-end tailoring of the most expensive designer clothes money could buy. That's where we did the fittings. The work part, grueling hours spent hunched over a desk, was down in the basement. Don't get me wrong, it was clean and safe, and brightly lit. There were far worse places to work, and I was well aware of that . . . but it would be nice to see the sun now and again.

"Georgia!" Eddie called, hurrying back over to me. "Update on the dress for the actress. We need to take it to her. You want to go? I could call a courier or . . ."

I couldn't have shot up faster. "Or I could go for a walk and get some fresh air on the clock?"

Eddie smiled. "Enjoy it. Take your lunch while you're over there. She's at some hotel charity benefit, and there's always free food up for grabs. Just make sure to get the dress taken up to her suite for her later. I'll send her assistant's number to you in case you have trouble."

Impulsively, I leaned toward Eddie and hugged him. "Thanks."

He chuckled and waved me off. "Have fun."

I left the building and spilled out into the early afternoon daylight with relief. The air was as fresh as L.A. ever got, and best of all, I had a little time to myself while I ran my errand. There was something I had to do.

As soon as I was away from the building, I pulled out the calling card I'd bought that morning and painstakingly typed in the information, before calling Italy. The phone rang briefly, and then someone answered. I spoke haltingly, aware that this was my first time speaking proper Italian out loud in a while. Since Tommaso died . . .

She put me on hold, and before I knew it, a deep male voice greeted me.

"Mrs. Conti, thank you for returning my call."

"No problem. You had information about my father?" I perched on the edge of a stone fountain outside the office building.

"Yes, I'm not sure if you know, but he has been arrested."

"What?" The shock radiated through me. "What for?"

"The charges are pending, but the initial warrant cited bribery and corruption. The new director in charge at the Direzione Investigativa Antimafia is very insistent in rooting out the criminal infrastructure that has allowed the Mafia to run unchecked in Southern Italy."

The lawyer's tone didn't make it clear whether he approved of the DIA's actions or not.

"My father doesn't work for the Mafia," I said.

The lawyer was silent for a while. "The investigation will reveal more information."

"He doesn't! Salvatore De Sanctis was his childhood friend, that's all . . . The police are just confusing—"

"Mrs. Conti. I am not a jury; you don't need to convince me of anything. Your father wanted you to be informed, and I am doing so. I also believe you should know that your father might choose to cooperate with the law in the prosecution of some of the people he allegedly worked with. That could pose a significant threat to your family."

"My family? I'm the only other Bellisario . . ."

"Exactly. I suggest you think on that and take the necessary precautions. I will call you again to update you with any progress in his case."

"Wait, what am I supposed to—"

The call cut off, and an electronic voice informed me that I had used all my credits.

After the call ended, I sat as long as I could afford to, trying to get my head around my new reality. My dad had been arrested.

The self-proclaimed moral compass of Castel Amaro, arrested for bribes and corruption. I felt sick. Sure, I knew my father had his faults, but I'd never thought of him in the same category as the De Sanctis family.

Had I been wrong?

When I couldn't afford to linger any longer, I got up and made my way onto the bus, slinging the dress over my shoulder. I rode downtown with the masses, pressed tight in the midday rush. I loved to people-watch on the bus. I loved to look at the ladies who wore beautiful heels and bright dresses. Gorgeous colors and patterns, innovative and fresh fashion. It was still my passion, but unfortunately, not my reality. I couldn't help catching my reflection in the glass doors and reminding myself how far I was from a chic existence. I wore comfy mom jeans and sneakers, layers of old T-shirts, and a light sweater on top to adjust to whatever temperature the sewing room would be on any given day. My hair was always braided or kept in a ponytail. Sensible and practical. I had no jewelry, and my hands were callused, dry, and painful.

The time in my life to think about pretty fabrics and luxury garments for myself was long behind me.

There was a crawling sensation on my neck that had me glancing around. Paranoia crept over me. I was the last Bellisario . . . and my father had crossed the wrong people. Would I really be a target?

I got off the bus hurriedly, still feeling those silent eyes on me. Was I being followed? I kept twisting around to look, but everyone was minding their own business, talking to friends or keeping their eyes glued to their phones.

After endless minutes of walking, I arrived at the hotel where I was to drop the dress off. My stomach growled as I made my way into the foyer and over to the wall of elevators. The assistant had already given me the room number. I had to leave the gown with the actress's glam team, and then I could go and see if there was any food left over from the function.

I made the handoff on the penthouse floor, enjoying the luxury of the hotel.

It had been a very long time since there had been any kind of luxury in my life. On the way out, I grabbed a few soggy sandwiches and stepped back out onto the busy sidewalk.

My phone vibrated in my pocket and I was surprised to see the lawyer's number flash across the screen.

"Hello?" I answered around a mouthful of chicken salad.

"Mrs. Conti, further to our previous conversation, I'm afraid I forgot to pass on an important piece of information. Your father has sent something to you. Have you received it?"

"What? No! Where did he send it?" I immediately worried.

The lawyer read out my old address. I hadn't lived there in years. I'd stopped being able to afford it long ago.

Shit.

"Did you get it?"

"No, not yet. I'll see if I can get it," I said.

The lawyer was quiet a beat, then spoke. "It's a very important package. I'd recommend retrieving it as soon as possible."

"Right, I know," I muttered, distracted as I put my phone on speaker and started trying to look up post offices around my old zip code.

"No, I don't think you do. It is very important, Mrs. Conti. It could be the difference between life or death for a man like your father."

I paused, something about the lawyer's careful wording catching my attention.

"A man like my father?" I repeated.

"A man with many enemies," the lawyer clarified. "Please call me when you have it. I need to pass on that it is safe."

He hung up, and I looked up a bus that would take me to my old neighborhood. Great, my father had sent me something so important, I needed to waste my lunch hour tracking it down. I guessed it wasn't his fault that I had moved and not given him my new address, but still, it was annoying.

I worked steadily through the afternoon and into the early evening. I always took on a lot of commissions and extra jobs. It helped pay off Howel and his never-ending payment plan. I supposed I should be glad he didn't just kill me, but then again, what good would that do? You couldn't get money from a corpse, and there was no one to go to after me. The real danger was that he'd hurt me to teach me a lesson and scare me into paying faster.

It's only a matter of time.

The thought should have scared me more than it did. But the truth was that I was pretty numb. I moved through my days in a haze, shell-shocked in the aftermath of my life. What should have been the happiest time had turned out to be the most painful.

What was there to look forward to?

I wasn't sure what the answer to that was, but it wasn't in my nature to give up.

I was a stubborn bitch until the bitter end. I wasn't built to tap out.

I'd go down swinging, every time.

I commuted home in a dream, and only realized I'd been on autopilot for nearly the entire journey when I found myself walking down my street. It wasn't too late in the evening, and traffic was still moving sluggishly down the main road. People were out and about, going to dinner or meeting friends. A family with a baby in a carrier were just getting out of a car. I watched them as they walked up to a much nicer building than mine. Good. I wouldn't wish my building on anyone, especially not a new family with a little baby to take care of.

I was looking for my keys when I was struck again by the strange sensation that someone was watching me. An itch between my shoulder blades. I glanced along the street. Shadows were gathering in the corners.

I couldn't see anyone, but the feeling persisted.

I headed upstairs and fought with the door for a few seconds prior to entering my apartment.

I let my heavy bags down with a sigh of relief and glugged some water from the bottle in the fridge. Damn, I was low on groceries.

I only had noodles. Tommaso had abhorred them and scoffed at the thought that such a freeze-dried concoction could be related in any way to real pasta. I'd eaten them more in the year since he'd passed than in all the years that had come before.

Just the thought of my late husband sent my mind spiraling back to Castel Amaro, and I remembered the package that I'd tried to pick up from the post office. Apparently, since no one had been at my old address to receive the package my father sent, it had been taken to a sorting center. The hours were insanely inconvenient, so I hadn't managed to pick it up today. I'd have to go again.

I turned to the sink and ran water to boil for noodles. God bless the person who'd invented instant ramen. As an Italian, it was a very specific kind of betrayal to my heritage to live on dehydrated noodles, but there was nothing I could do about that right now. Maybe one day.

"Beneath the frozen river, currents still run."

Even in my memory, his deep voice had me shivering when I remembered how it had stroked across the words.

Absentmindedly, I grabbed the pot handle, forgetting it was hot, and gasped. I dropped it. Scalding water spilled out and hit me in droplets of fire.

I jumped back, letting out a yelp. I stared at the mess of the kitchen, pot sideways on the floor, water everywhere, and started to laugh.

Maybe I was an eternal optimist, and really did believe deep down that one day, things would change . . .

Or maybe I was just losing my mind.

7

GEORGIA

Another day, and another chance to personally deliver a dress on my lunch break. Seeing as the actress needed on-the-spot adjustments, I was out again. This hotel wasn't as far from my office as the one yesterday, so I took my time to walk through a park and take a quick break on a bench, then jumped on the bus. It was a hot day, the L.A. sun baking down on me. My clothes were better suited for working in an overly air-conditioned office, not walking around on the street. I was sweating already.

At a leisurely pace, I headed to the hotel where I'd do my out-of-office adjustments. I had the dress, plus a heavy backpack with everything I could possibly need to fix the item of clothing.

A little later, I was knocking on the door of a suite, at the very top of a very fancy hotel.

The actress's assistant let me in. I'd met Alexandra a handful of times before. She worked hard as hell and she never failed to impress me. Today, she took my heavy backpack from me right away.

"I hope you brought an abundance of patience, you're going to need it," she warned me.

"What? Why? Did Elise gain?" The one thing that I didn't have in my bag was the ability to make the dress I had designed bigger.

"No, nothing like that. Her boyfriend is here . . . or the guy she wishes was her boyfriend."

Well, that was a relief. I could ignore any canoodling, that was no big deal, but the dress needed to be ready tonight.

I followed Alexandra into the sitting room and paused as I took in the scene. Elise was a French actress who everyone was talking about. The kind all the boys wanted to be with, and all the girls wanted to be. Right now, she was putting on a show for a man dressed in black, slouched arrogantly in an armchair. The worst part was how he was staring at his phone instead of the bombshell gyrating in front of him.

His eyes flickered over to us.

"Excuse me, Elise, the dressmaker is here to do alterations."

Elise straightened up and looked at us with a hazy expression. Her pupils were small. Was she on something? I'd seen it all in my years working for the Hollywood elite, but Elise had never been high or drunk or unprepared for our meetings before.

She stood and swayed.

"Okay, fine. Give me it."

I approached. "I'll help you put it on."

"Whatever." She sighed and pulled off her dressing gown. She was completely naked underneath.

I grabbed it off the floor and held it in front of her.

"Maybe some privacy," I said pointedly to the man sitting in the chair.

Now that I was up close to him, he didn't seem like Elise's type at all. He seemed too disreputable to be an exec and too tattooed to be another actor. I'd have recognized him if I'd seen him in anything, so he'd have to be a newbie. But there was no way this man was new to anything. His confidence oozed off him.

"Are you talking to me?" he asked, arrogance striking through in his tone.

Something about it was so fucking annoying. I felt like I'd spent my entire life being ordered around by arrogant men, and after last night with Howel, I'd had enough.

"Yes, I am," I blurted, before Alexandra could step in to smooth things over.

"What we mean to say is—" Alexandra waded in.

"I think she knows exactly what she means to say and has, in fact, said it." He stood, adjusting his suit. He had a slight accent. Something Eastern European.

"Don't worry, there is nothing here I haven't seen before," he said and stopped in front of me. The man was tall. "Except for a woman who isn't trying to impress anyone."

"Is that supposed to be a compliment?" I heard myself ask before I could stop myself.

"Georgia," Alexandra murmured to me in warning.

The man chuckled softly and reached into his pocket. "My name is Roman. Roman Sokolov. If you ever find yourself in Philadelphia, give me a call." He held out a matte-black business card.

"I won't." I made no move to take it.

After a long, tense moment, Roman tucked it into my jeans pocket and nodded to Elise.

"*Do svidanya,* Elise. Be good."

And with that, the menacing man left. I took a deep breath as soon as he'd disappeared.

"Well, that was intense," Alexandra muttered when Elise stepped into the other room to put on her dress.

I'd make whatever adjustments were needed once I saw it on. "Was it? What was that guy's deal anyway?"

Alexandra just shrugged. "Some guy Elise started to pursue

after meeting him when she was shooting on location. He was here for business, and she basically begged him to stop by."

I winced. "Well, he seems awful."

"He does, doesn't he, and dangerous."

I knew danger from men like that. I'd grown up in Castel Amaro, home to the De Sanctis summer estate.

"Well, at least Philly is far away from here. She'll be fine," Alexandra said and clapped when Elise came out, the designer gown frothing around her. She had an awards ceremony that night, and she was going to rock the red carpet.

"You look amazing," Alexandra enthused.

Elise nodded, distractedly. Her hair was untidy and her eyes glassy. A deep twinge of empathy moved through me. I knew better than most how the wrong man could wreck you.

"Let's get you all cleaned up and finish fitting this dress. You're going to be the belle of the ball tonight."

She gazed at me, a hint of fragility dancing across her delicate features.

"Really?"

"I promise."

Once I'd fixed Elise's dress, she passed out in her room. Alexandra grabbed her purse and nodded toward the door.

"Have you had lunch yet?"

I shook my head.

"Me neither. My treat. Let's go."

We sat in the dining room of the hotel. I'd never have eaten there if Alexandra wasn't paying. I ordered the cheapest thing on the menu and sipped at my water while she talked about the Hollywood scene.

It all sounded utterly exhausting.

"And how about you? How's it going? Dating anyone new?" she asked.

I laughed. "Nothing can compare to your fun and games . . . I'm boring."

She raised an eyebrow at me. "That's a no, then?"

I nodded. "It's a no. I don't have the time or inclination."

"I get that, but what about sex? Battery-operated devices just don't compare to the weight and smell of a real-life man."

"Smell? Pass." It didn't seem like a good time to explain that it had been so long since I'd had sex, I was worried cobwebs had formed down there.

We ate while making easy small talk. These were the kinds of things I lived for nowadays. Interactions, lunch and pleasant conversation, a walk in the sun. Simple pleasures. Simple but priceless.

While we waited for the bill, Alexandra left to visit the ladies', and I relaxed back in my seat. I glanced around the room, watching the other diners.

That feeling of being watched was still niggling at me, but there was no one in sight. Literally no one was looking at me. My father's news had made me paranoid, clearly. Like anyone was going to bother traveling from Italy to the U.S. just to threaten me . . . I hadn't even seen my father in fourteen years. *Right. So, everything is fine.* I didn't quite believe it.

I drank a little more and tried to shrug off my worries. I was probably giving myself far too much importance.

The sad truth was, outside my father and maybe Erica, no one in the world really cared what happened to me.

That stark fact was my final thought before the first shots rang out.

8

ELIO

I followed my sister's intel on finding Georgia's workplace and grabbed a coffee at a place across the street. I watched the building. With a newspaper as a cover, albeit an old-fashioned one, I watched the entrance, while also looking for anyone else who was doing the same.

It didn't take long to see the other man watching the building.

He wasn't nearly as casual as he thought he was, lingering outside the office on a motorcycle, a messenger bag slung over his shoulder as his disguise. Amateur hour and confirmation that the Ravelli family had indeed decided to get to Georgia. It made sense. With the threat of Bellisario in custody and out of reach, and Georgia being his only living relative, there was no other way to send a message.

I had to get her back to Jersey and married quickly so I could move her into Casa Nera, the sprawling De Sanctis compound that Renato called home. I had to make sure Alfredo Bellisario understood that his precious daughter was our hostage.

I was distracted from my thoughts by the sight of a dark-haired woman leaving the atelier. Everything in the street seemed to stop around me. Noise died away; cars stopped moving on the road. The world held its breath as I got my first glimpse of the girl who had shaped my world.

No, not a girl anymore . . . a woman.

And she was beautiful.

The promise of her youth had blossomed beyond expectation. For a second, I couldn't look away. For a second, my pulse sped up, my heart remembering that once, a long, long time ago, it had known how to beat. It only lasted a second before the familiar coldness I'd spent more than a decade perfecting surged through me, providing comfort and distance. Georgia Bellisario—no, Conti—wasn't someone I knew. I'd known a wild and shining girl, a burning flame, captured in a moment of reckless youth, a moment that had cost me everything. The woman before me now? I didn't know her, and I wouldn't. I didn't care enough to. I didn't care much about anything. That was the legacy of my childhood love.

The waitress dropped a tray behind me, and the world crashed back into life.

Georgia walked across the courtyard in front of the building. I didn't need to check if it was her. It was obvious. She crossed the street and headed toward a park.

The guy on the motorcycle shifted around, speaking to someone on the phone. Reporting in.

I paid for my coffee and went out to the street, taking a cigarette I had no intention of smoking from a pack in my suit jacket and holding it between my lips. The guy on the motorcycle hadn't glanced at his surroundings even once. No situational awareness whatsoever.

Georgia went into the park and found a bench just inside, still in sight of the road. I put the cigarette in my mouth and watched her. She made no move to call anyone or browse her phone. She just stared into space for a while then stood. As soon as she was on the go, I was behind her.

I had to take out the guy on the motorcycle sooner or later, but I wouldn't do that until I had to. Keeping a low profile would be the best strategy here.

Georgia wandered up a busy sidewalk, and the motorcycle guy followed. Seconds later, I followed as well. Weaving in and out of the crowd, I kept the back of her head in my sights, as well as the guy carrying a motorcycle helmet.

She jumped on a bus just before it eased away from a stop. I hailed a cab to follow.

Before too long, she left the bus, and I paid my cab and followed her on the sidewalk again. Her head was swiveling back and forth. Once or twice, her eyes nearly met mine. Could she feel me watching?

She went into a hotel, and I settled at a coffee shop across the street to watch her. I pulled up the hotel on my phone and checked for other exits, then messaged my sister, the De Sanctis eyes in the sky, to monitor the back doors.

The biker had parked right outside the hotel and was talking on the phone. I wasn't close enough to hear, but I imagined he was shooting a rapid stream of Italian down the line, asking for instructions.

When Georgia failed to emerge after half an hour, the biker got impatient and went inside. I followed slowly. Inside the hotel was a bank of elevators on one wall and a banquet hall and restaurant on the other. The biker was still on the phone, pretending to be a courier of some kind.

I settled into a seat that faced the street, but had a handy mirror angled just right to keep an eye on the elevators. Then she appeared. Walking with another woman, she went into the restaurant.

The biker waited, so I waited until his back turned then made my way into the restaurant. I asked for a seat near the door and sat out of Georgia's eyeline. I could see her, though. I could see her . . . and I couldn't look away.

She ate as if she hadn't seen food in a week. She talked and laughed, her beautiful face creasing into easy smiles.

She licked her lips, and my body turned to stone. I could still remember the taste of her . . . the only woman I'd ever wanted. The only one I'd ever touched. The fact that she still affected me just as much as she had then, despite the fourteen cold years between us, pissed me off.

Her friend got up and went toward the bathroom. In her absence, a movement from the biker grabbed my attention. He'd finished his furious conversation on the phone.

The Ravelli rival was lingering near a flower arrangement, sticking out like a sore thumb. He was going to do something. I stood, ready for whatever he was about to do.

Then, he turned and saw me.

I didn't have anything particularly identifiable about me, but still, the reaction was immediate. He flinched and reached into his jacket.

The fool was about to shoot up a room full of people, for no reason other than the pure fear he felt at seeing me. It should have stroked my ego, but it was too much of an inconvenience.

He drew a gun, and his first shot went wide. Screams filled the air, and people dove for cover. I couldn't spare a look for where the first shot went. I was running toward the shooter before he could line up the next shot. I caught him around the waist and bore him to the floor. He landed hard, his hand flying upward. Unfortunately, he didn't drop the gun. I reared back and punched him, two hard shots to the jaw, and reached for the gun. As I took it from his hand, he managed to turn it toward me. I fell to the side as two shots rang out, hitting the ceiling above us. A millisecond faster and they would have gone directly into my chest.

Shit. Had Zio Sal gotten the information late? The Ravelli family was already here and already armed. I'd flown commercial and had yet to pick up a gun. All I had was my training and whatever weapon I could grab. Just now, that looked likely to be a salad knife. It would just have to do.

I punched the biker one more time and reached out and grabbed his fallen helmet. Bringing it around in a hard arc, I clocked him with the heavy object just under his chin. The knockout sweet spot, and he was down.

I couldn't afford to forget where I was. Sure, I could get away with garroting someone in a dark and dingy corner of a Neapolitan nightclub with just a baseball cap and shades as a disguise, but this was different. I had the shades on, but otherwise I was perfectly visible, in front of about a hundred witnesses and cameras, in broad fucking daylight. Not only that, but killing a random, errand-running Ravelli made man wasn't my mission today.

My mission was hiding somewhere. I got to my feet. It was deathly silent apart from the tinkle of glass still falling from a shattered chandelier.

I walked around, inspecting the various heads of the people huddling and hiding. Finally, I made out the toe of the sneaker I had noticed Georgia wearing. She was under a table. Clever girl.

I stopped just in front of her for a moment. Fate had brought us full circle. I could just leave her here and tell Renato that I'd been too late. I'd be forgiven. We were late to this party, clearly. The Ravellis were already in place. If not for gross incompetence, they'd have her right now. I could just walk away and abandon this woman to her fate, as she'd abandoned me to mine, a lifetime ago.

I reached for the table and flipped it back easily. A wave of murmurs rose. Everyone was too shit-scared to look up and see what was really happening. They had no idea if it was the gunman walking around or someone else. I could use that to my advantage. Georgia was staring stubbornly at the floor, her arms over her head like that could protect her from anything. Like that could protect her from me.

I snagged a spoon from a nearby table and pressed it into my palm.

"Get up," I commanded.

She tensed, unwilling to move. I didn't want to haul her up. I didn't want to touch her more than I had to. I knew from experience how poisonous her touch was.

"Get up, now, or I'll shoot a person in this room every ten seconds until you do," I warned her. Sure, I didn't have a gun, but she didn't know that.

Still, she failed to move. Even as a grown woman, a widow, no less, she was stubborn as fuck.

"Ten, nine, eight," I started.

She lurched to her feet, gasping as her palms pressed against the broken glass on the floor.

"I'm up. Don't hurt anyone else." Her voice was yet another thread to the past. It was still her, just deeper. Richer, somehow. She sounded genuine, but I knew better.

Georgia Bellisario had never cared about anyone but herself.

"I won't as long as you do what I say, but every second we waste here, their lives are in danger." My impatience to get out of the room before the cops showed up was making me rough. She flinched and then looked up and met my eyes.

Her look felt like a slap. My reaction was hidden behind my shades. I had to get it the fuck together. I couldn't afford to show weakness, especially in front of this woman.

I reluctantly wrapped a hand around her arm and tugged her

to me. Clearly, she wasn't going to move without some encouragement. She stumbled and fell against my chest. I ruthlessly shoved her away to put some distance between us.

"Where are you taking me?" she asked, her eyes searching for mine behind my dark shades.

"Wherever I want," I said simply. Here wasn't the place or time to explain to her how fucked she was.

"What? You can't!" she exclaimed in a squeaky voice.

"And who is going to stop me?" I asked, with an edge of arrogance to my tone that I knew would piss her off. To cement my control, I pressed the end of the spoon into her side, hidden from view.

She stiffened, clearly believing that I had a gun pressed against her. I fucking wish I did. Everything would go more smoothly once I had a proper weapon in my hand.

"You can't just steal a person," she stuttered as I put her in front of me and started forward.

"I can do whatever the fuck I want," I murmured to her.

She gasped and squirmed as I pushed her through the side door and into a short hallway, heading for the emergency exit at the end. Alarms had gone off, and there was no one in sight.

Then Georgia stopped and stomped her foot on top of mine, as hard as she could. It would be laughable if I were the kind of man partial to a good laugh. Instead, her bravery and stubbornness only pissed me off. I whirled her against the wall, pressing the hilt of the spoon harder into her side. I put my other hand at the base of her neck and squeezed slightly.

"Let's be clear. If I say jump, you say how high. I say kneel . . . you hit the fucking deck, got it?"

"Or?" she panted, her dark eyes wild with fear, her pulse thundering under my fingers.

"Or—you'll die," I told her with perfect confidence. Sure, I wouldn't be the one to kill her, but I was pretty sure the Ravellis would.

She blinked at me, and a tear dashed down one cheek. It nearly transfixed me for a second. While our past had hardened me into an empty, frozen shell of a man, she still burned as brightly as ever. Her emotions were so potent, I wanted to pull back before she infected me with all that feeling.

Messy and uncontrollable. Chaos bottled in one volatile package.

"Got it?" I pulled myself back to the very real threat of the cops busting in at any second.

I pressed her pulse point a little harder when she failed to respond.

"Got it," she spat at me. Defiance, even now?

My *topolina* hadn't changed. Not at all.

"Good, because I won't repeat myself. Now, move."

9

GEORGIA

The madman holding me tightly against him led me down the alleyway behind the hotel and out to the street. We were around the corner from the entrance. People passed us on the street, looking curiously at the building, with its shrieking alarms and large crowd of upset patrons standing outside on the sidewalk. They'd evacuated, it seemed, every room but the restaurant.

Cop cars screamed toward us, and hope fluttered in my chest. I stumbled for a second, seriously considering ripping myself out of my captor's hold and making a run for the road. I could throw myself in front of one of the cop cars and point out the gunman.

"Don't even think about it." His deep, low voice was a growl in my ear.

He prodded me with the gun and herded me toward the wall of a nearby building.

"I wasn't thinking anything," I muttered hopelessly as he pressed me against the building, into the pose of a couple wrapped up in each other and oblivious to the commotion down the street.

"Sure you weren't."

His tone was so overly confident, something in me snapped, and I spoke without thinking.

"Don't pretend like you know me. You don't know anything about me."

He stared down. I wished I could see his eyes. What kind of eyes went with a man like this? A man who would shoot up a room and take a woman hostage?

A muscle worked in his tight jaw.

"You'd be surprised," he ground out and glanced over his shoulder. "If you want this to be as painless as possible, consider keeping your mouth shut from now on."

He pulled me to him, and we were walking again. This time to the road. Cabs were lined up along the street, with some of the drivers out and watching the action.

"You'd be surprised."

His voice worked through my mind, playing on repeat. It was so familiar, somehow, and yet different. He had no accent. His tone was clipped. And yet . . . I could have sworn I'd heard it before.

We got to a cab, and my captor rapped hard on the hood to get the driver's attention.

"You working?"

The cabbie nodded and ducked back into the taxi. We got into the back, the damn gun digging into my side the entire time. I caught the driver's eye in the rearview mirror and tried to tell him with my eyes that I needed help.

"Where to?" the driver asked as we turned away from the hotel and police. Turned away from any sign of help.

"Boyle Heights," the man answered confidently, then rattled off my address.

My address.

What was the point of trying to get away, when this man

clearly knew where I lived? He probably knew where I worked, too.

I blinked at the taxi driver in the mirror, my eyes crying out for help.

"Nice photo on the dash. You got kids?" my captor asked the driver.

He nodded. "Four of them, if you can believe it!"

"Wow, four kids . . . a lot of mouths to feed." My mystery man in black glanced at me.

The subtext of his look was clear. He'd hurt the driver if I said anything to him. I got it. I wasn't getting anyone killed.

We drove in silence. I watched the city pass by outside the window, envying the people walking freely to and fro. Just an hour ago, I'd been one of them. I hadn't appreciated that simple action until now. In an hour, my life had been upended, and I couldn't get my brain to accept it. The change was too dramatic.

A new, starkly terrifying thought hit me.

What would happen when we were alone? What did this man want? Was he here to hurt me? Was it because of my father? Was he going to kill me?

Panic threatened to close my throat, my lungs seeming to seize up. I could barely drag enough air into my chest. Spots danced in front of my eyes, and a wave of dizziness hit me. I was having a panic attack. I was no stranger to them. I'd been having them since I was nineteen years old and my world fell apart.

I closed my eyes and focused on three things. Three things I could smell. Asphalt from the slightly open window. Air freshener. My shampoo. Then three things I could feel. My jeans. The leather of the seat. A gun in my side. *Nope.* Not helpful. Finally, I let my eyes open and focused on three things I could see. The back of the driver's head. The sunlight falling in the window and landing in a square on my leg. The dark glasses of the man who was holding me at gunpoint. He seemed to be watching me, but it was hard to tell. He could have been asleep for how impassive his face was.

"Have you received any international mail recently? Something from your father?" my mercenary asked.

Shit. The package that I hadn't collected yet.

"No. Why? Should I have?" The lie left me before I could stop it. Why was I lying? The only reason I had was that this man was dangerous, and if he wanted whatever my father had sent me, it might be important. I needed a bargaining chip to protect myself. I couldn't let him have it.

The cab pulled to a stop, and fear slammed back into me. Before I could think about trying to call out to the driver, we were back out on the street.

I lunged away when my captor turned to close the door, and he yanked me back, hard.

"What did I say about repeating myself?" he murmured ominously. "Now, be a good girl and invite your guest upstairs."

"You're not my guest," I muttered.

"Fine, how about the man who decides your fate?" he replied, just as quietly.

I glanced at him but found his face still as impassive as ever.

We started up the stairs to the top floor. He was right behind me the entire way, breathing down my neck.

"What's going to happen when we get inside?" I asked, risking a glance over my shoulder.

"I wouldn't like to spoil anything . . . You'll just have to wait and see."

His uncaring tone nearly brought tears to my eyes. I forced them back. *Get a grip! Don't let this asshole see you cry.* He had to lower his guard at some point, and then, I'd be ready.

We got to the top of the stairs, and I fumbled for my key, taking way longer than I needed to, putting off the moment when we'd be alone.

"Don't drag it out, Georgia." His tone was lethal.

I grabbed my key and put it in the lock. The damn thing jammed, because of course it did.

I wriggled it around as my captor watched me in stony silence.

"What did I just tell you?" he growled when I'd failed to open the door for several moments.

"I'm not dragging it out, it's broken." I jiggled the key in the lock.

He sighed and brushed past me, taking the key from me and trying himself.

The door swung open.

"I made it easier for you," I said, about to brush past him and go inside.

He took a step back, and the position put him near the top of the stairs.

I didn't even think about it. My survival instincts were pumping. I just acted.

I twisted and shoved him as hard as I could, both hands to the solar plexus. He swayed back. The stairwell below him was steep and long. A fall would injure him, maybe even render him unconscious.

At the last moment, his hand snaked around my wrist and pulled me with him. I don't know how he managed it. The speed of his reflexes had to be otherworldly, because he didn't fall. Instead, he grabbed me and used the momentum to spin us both around on the top step. My back slammed into the wall, and then he was there, pressing me against the tile without mercy. Somehow, his hand had ended up behind my head, thank God, as it cushioned the blow of the wall.

Now he used that grip to tilt my head back, exposing my throat to him.

"I told you not to fuck with me, Georgia. You're out of your league. Accept it now, or the future is going to be difficult for you."

"Like you care about my future," I snorted.

I needed him to back up and get away from me. His rigid body leaning into mine was a display of power I didn't need. I already knew how outmatched I was. And his scent . . . this close, there was something disturbing about it. It was almost too nice to inhale. It was too pleasant . . . It made me forget what he was. I needed space from it.

"Don't try and play games with me . . . you won't like the games I play back, *topolina*."

The nickname froze me to the spot. A bucket of ice water over the head.

The voice clicked into place in my head. It all went together. The way he carried himself . . . it was different, and yet, the same. There was a new predatory grace and trained precision to his movements that he hadn't yet developed in his reckless youth. His face, once just bearing the promise of the man he would become, had embodied every drop of it. His scent. The way it called me closer . . . even after all these years.

The smell of home.

His sunglasses hadn't budged an inch, even in our tussle. I reached for them, and he knocked my hand away. If I could see his eyes, then I'd know for sure. No one had eyes like Elio Santori.

"Elio?" I whispered.

It was hardly audible, yet as loud as a gunshot.

He stilled. An eerie kind of absence of motion. He didn't breathe. It seemed like his heart didn't even beat.

Then he tilted his head to the side.

"Who?" His tone was cold, disinterested.

"Elio, is it you?" I murmured. My heart was hammering, threatening to break through my ribs. Did I ever think about the man who had broken my heart into pieces? Only every single day, but hey, I'd improved on the first few years of my twenties, when I'd thought about him every few minutes.

He sighed, the lower part of his face still not giving a single thing away.

"Again, who? I don't know who you're talking about."

"Liar. You're him." I was convinced. I could hear him murmur *topolina* again and again in my head. It had tripped off his tongue so naturally, there was no mistaking it.

He shrugged. "Think what you want, Signora Conti. It doesn't matter to me, and it won't change anything for you."

It felt like the world slowed to a crawl as he reached up and pulled at the arm of his sunglasses. They came off slowly, and every second lasted a lifetime while I waited to see if my ghost, the man who'd haunted me every day since he'd left, had come back into my life.

The glasses fell away, and he looked right at me.

And his eyes were brown.

Dark brown.

Emotions I couldn't name swirled inside me. Relief, disappointment, fucking confusion.

"Are we done here?" the man murmured.

I nodded mutely.

"Good. Now get the fuck inside, and stop testing me."

10

GEORGIA

THEN

When you lived in the countryside, you had to get creative when you got old enough to want to party on the weekend. The local hot spot for parties in Castel Amaro was just a little too far out of town to comfortably walk to. Down by a hollow near the river, where we'd played as kids on a tire swing, now, as teens, we lit a fire and drank.

I didn't get to go out much. I went to school, of course, but my father made sure to fill up all my free time with tutors. English, mathematics, economics . . . all sorts of subjects I had no interest in. My passion was design and dressmaking, but my father thought that was beneath the Bellisario name. I had no idea who he wanted me to be when I was older, but I was certain it wasn't the real me.

He had no idea who that was.

Only my English tutor got my full attention. I needed to be able to speak English to go to Parsons, after all. Also, my mother had been an American. She had passed when I was too young to have a single memory of her. All I had was my American-inspired name, for the state she'd been from. For her, I wanted to speak English, and one day, live in her country.

I brought my beer bottle to my lips and sipped, then winced. Tepid beer wasn't a great taste, but it was all that was left around the bonfire. My classmates had gotten increasingly wasted and disappeared in pairs off into the bushes.

Even Tommaso had abandoned me.

I swigged my beer and wished Elio Santori was there.

Right, and why would he be interested in what a bunch of little country mice were up to? I frowned at the dark, moving water of the river just beyond the hollow.

It had been a month of the Neapolitan bad boy sleeping in the barn, just outside my bedroom, and absolutely nothing had happened.

Clearly, he didn't want to know.

Despite my knowing that, a monstrous crush had developed on my part. I was obsessed. I watched him out the window whenever I had a moment. I contrived meetings whenever I could, but it was tough to catch him. I'd even started to enjoy church, since I usually saw him there. He had to know, right? He had to.

I rested my back against a wide tree trunk and scrubbed a hand over my face, wrinkling my nose at the feeling of my heavy mascara. The fact that was becoming impossible to deny was that he knew, but he wasn't interested.

A rustling in the bushes sent me sitting up straight. Tommaso crashed through the undergrowth and fell to his butt beside me.

"What's going on? Where have you been?" I scanned the bushes behind me for a sign of who he had been getting busy with.

He raised a swaying finger to his mouth and drew an imaginary zipper along his lips.

"That's for me to know, and you to never find out."

He grinned at me, and his smile was so infectious, I found myself smiling back. It was rare to see my best friend so happy and uninhibited.

"Well, that's exciting." I elbowed him in the side. "I'm glad one of us is having fun."

Tommaso clapped his hands together and cackled. "Oh, honey, I'm not going to be the only one having fun! You're welcome. I'm going to leave with my secret paramour."

"Hey! You're my ride," I reminded him quickly.

He patted me on the shoulder. "Not anymore. You're welcome."

With that, he stood and staggered back toward the bushes.

"Toma? Come on," I called, pushing myself to my feet. *Damn it.* I glanced around to see if there was anyone else left at the party who might be heading back to town. I didn't fancy walking alone. Walking the long, winding road to town alone in the dark didn't sound enticing.

Damn Tommaso. I swore at him furiously in my head when I leaned down to grab my bag, and the world swayed. Whoa. I'd drunk more than I'd thought.

No, you're just a lightweight.

Yeah, that was right. With my dad around, there weren't many opportunities for drinking at home.

I draped the strap of my bag over my shoulder, slinging it across my body. I could do this. I wasn't some damsel in distress.

I walked gingerly out of the dark hollow, tripping and swearing. The ground was littered with bottles and fallen branches. We'd need to come back tomorrow to clean up.

I climbed out of the thin copse of woods that lined the riverbank and made it to the road, only to stumble immediately. Out of all the places to put my foot, I'd managed to aim right for a sizable pothole. My knees buckled, and I was going down, until a strong hand wrapped around my shoulders and jerked me firmly upward.

All the air forcibly left me as I was hauled against a warm, hard body. A familiar smell wove its way into my lungs. Straw and spice, leather and musk.

I looked up into Elio Santori's eyes and felt like my heart might break through the fragile cage of my ribs, and right out of my chest.

"What are you doing here?" I blurted and stared at him.

"Coming to get you home, what else? Since your boyfriend couldn't be bothered not to drink and drive. He messaged one of the other stable hands, who then told me. The fucker wasn't even going to check you got home." A dark frown passed over Elio's face.

His scowl was formidable, but I was too drunk and relieved to see him to be scared.

"My boyfriend?" I repeated. "What boyfriend?"

"Conti—Tommaso, the one who is always holed up in your room with you, who else?" Elio muttered, a muscle clenching in his square jaw.

"You think Toma is my boyfriend?" I asked and then burst into laughter. He thought I had a boyfriend? All this time, while I'd been pining after him, nursing a killer crush . . . he'd thought I had a boyfriend?

"How much have you had to drink?" Elio demanded.

I swayed in his hold, unable to stop laughing.

"Enough," I finally gasped out, swallowing my laughter down. "I've had just enough . . ."

"Just enough for what?" he asked.

I put my hands on his chest, and he stilled completely. A sudden absence of movement that felt nearly unnatural. I slid my hands upward. He only had a T-shirt on, even though the nights were getting cooler lately. I placed a hand over his heart, all my mirth chased away. I felt reckless and free.

He didn't move. I pressed my hand on that sacred place and counted his heartbeats.

"Just enough—to do this," I murmured and pushed myself up on my tiptoes, and before I lost my courage, fused my lips to his.

He jerked with surprise. I ran my tongue along the seam of his sealed lips. I had no kissing experience. That was probably pretty obvious. But in movies, they just kissed, and it all seemed to work out.

This was not that.

He didn't open his lips or move them at all to match mine. He was as still as the grave.

Nerves crowded in, my panic clearing my brain fog and all remnants of the beers I'd had earlier.

I tore my mouth from his and staggered back. He caught me, and I shoved his hands away.

"If you don't want to kiss me, just tell me so, you don't need to embarrass me." My voice was full of hurt and rejection. I wished the ground would open up and swallow me.

"I don't recall being asked, *topolina*. If you had, I'd have told you I don't kiss drunk girls."

I turned to him. He had his fingers on his lips. Wiping away my touch?

"I'm not drunk," I protested.

He shrugged. "You look drunk to me."

"I'm not!" I barely resisted stamping my foot like a toddler.

He chuckled, the bastard, and reached out to take my arm. "If you wake up without a headache tomorrow, then you come and tell me I was wrong," he said firmly and tugged me toward the road with him.

"Oh, right, and you'll do what?" I grumbled.

We were at the edge of the road, and Elio pulled me to a stop. He stared down at me and brought a hand to my mouth. I paused, my heart suddenly lurching into a frantic beat. He rubbed his thumb along my bottom lip and then slid his hand into the hair behind my ear, gripping it in a way that tilted my head right back, making my face his tribute.

"I'll kiss you like you're meant to be kissed. I'll kiss you like I've wanted to since the moment we first met."

I stared into his pale eyes. No one had eyes like his. Pale green in the daylight, and at night, they caught the light of the moon and glowed.

I wet my lips, my mouth suddenly drier than a desert. The tug from my scalp where he held my head was delicious. I wanted more.

I lost track of how long we stood like that, lost in each other's gazes. The only thing that yanked me from that magic was a loud, inelegant snort I was sure hadn't come from either of us.

I blinked, the spell broken, and twisted my head to the side. Right there, tied to a low branch, was a horse.

I laughed. "You're right. I must be drunk. I see a horse."

Elio eased back and stepped toward the animal. "You're not imagining it. It's a horse. It's your ride home."

"What?" I demanded.

"I couldn't find any car keys to steal . . . so a horse it was."

I stared at him. "You came to pick me up . . . with a horse?"

He grinned at me. "Just call me your knight in shining armor. Now, get up here. You're in charge. I can't ride for shit."

ELIO

The village gathered to celebrate every single saint's day, and in Southern Italy, that was a whole lot of gatherings. Huge pots of pasta sat on the doorsteps, waiting for the kids to carry them to the picnic tables in the village square. Wine was unearthed from basement stores and decanted into glasses, sparking lively debate about grapes and vintages. Meats were roasted and salads tossed. The smell of spicy extra virgin olive oil and garlic frying filled the air as children ran amok and the church bells rang.

That year, I didn't see any of it. I'd left the feast preparation to sit in the olive grove above town. I had my notebook and pencil. Even though I was destined to live a life of petty crime or manual labor, I had dreams of being a writer. No, not just a writer. A poet.

These were silly imaginings and destined never to come true, but it didn't stop me from jotting down lines here and there. In Castel Amaro, there was often nothing to do but dream. I had to find a proper job so I could afford to go see my sister, but that project was on the back burner until I paid off my debt to the prosecutor's satisfaction.

It was the day after the party at the river, and Georgia's drunken kiss. I needed to tell someone about it, even if it was just the pages of my tattered notebook.

I'd just sharpened my pencil with my pocketknife when I heard her voice.

"What are you writing?"

Anticipation drove a fist into my gut. I'd spent half the night remembering her touch, stroking my cock and picturing her hand on it. I'd tortured myself with all the things I would have done to her if only I didn't inherit my mother's morals. *She was drunk. She probably regrets it. Maybe she doesn't even remember.* It was always my father's voice in my head when the darkest, most hateful thoughts slithered through my mind.

I sat up, straddling the branch, and peered down.

Georgia stood on the hill below, arms crossed as she gazed up at me. Her white dress had lemons on it. It showed her smooth, nut-brown arms and legs. Her long brown hair brushed her waist as she tilted her head back to watch me.

I gripped the branch above me and slowly lowered myself down to the ground, dropping the last few inches. I'd gotten taller in the last year, passing six feet, and although Georgia wasn't short, she had to look right up to meet my eyes.

"Nothing. Aren't you going to the feast?" I hoped she'd say no and stay here with me. Getting the prosecutor's daughter alone was a rare thing.

"Aren't you?" she shot back, a grin playing around her red lips. "Someone told me to come and find them when I wasn't drunk... though for the record, I was perfectly coherent last night."

A bumblebee flew near Georgia's face, and she recoiled. I reached out, my hand as quick as a whip, and closed my fist loosely around the bee.

Georgia gasped. "You'll get stung!"

I twisted away from her and gently opened my fist. The bee had landed on my palm, and had indeed stung me. We both watched its fuzzy black-and-yellow body fly off lazily.

"It didn't die, so it didn't sting you," she said and picked my hand up. "Right?"

"That's just honeybees that die," I told her. "Bumblebees don't. So, aren't you going to the feast?"

"Not if you're not. Did you get stung? Your hand is red," Georgia said, holding my palm open and frowning at it.

"It's fine."

"Why'd you touch it?"

"You were scared," I pointed out.

She narrowed her eyes at me. What was she thinking behind those doe-like brown eyes?

"You didn't kill it," she observed.

"Why would I? It's just doing what it needs to survive. I can't blame it for that. It's what we all do," I said quietly. I wished my heart would stop racing. I made to tug my hand from her grip. Maybe that would help my body calm down. The blood was rushing everywhere but my head right now.

She held my hand firmly and refused to let go.

I raised an eyebrow at her questioningly.

"Thank you. You're not like the other boys in the village," she said slowly and raised my hand toward her face.

I watched her with rapt attention. She held my open palm to her mouth and pressed a sweet kiss to the bee sting.

That simple gesture lost me the battle to stay in control of my body. I stepped forward and slid a hand around the back of her head, sinking it into her hair and gripping tightly.

"What are you doing?" I asked, my voice low and urgent.

"Thanking you," she said softly. Alarm had lit her features, but now they melted into excitement. "For the bee, and last night."

A pulse jumped in her throat, beating madly. I brought my other hand to linger there, against that thrumming place. Savoring the evidence that she was just as affected as I was in this moment.

"If you want to thank me, shouldn't you ask what I want?" My voice was a low scratch in my throat.

She tilted her head closer, leaning into my chest. "What do you want, Elio?" she asked, her tone unbearably throaty.

"You know exactly what I want," I whispered and stepped back, taking her with me.

The olive tree met her back, and then I was pressing her against it. Her soft breasts pushed into my chest.

"Since that moment in the bathroom . . . since our first touch, you've known, and don't pretend that you haven't. There's no space for pretending between you and me, *topolina*," I murmured.

Her pulse leapt again, and she swallowed, the movement brushing my palm.

"Well . . . then take it, *cittaiolo*," she teased. "If you dare—"

I captured her lips in a searing kiss and cut off her words. Her lips were as soft as they'd always looked, and her mouth tasted like vanilla. Her tongue slid out and stroked my lips boldly, and I jerked back, surprised. It felt wrong, somehow, that a girl as perfect and protected as Georgia would be so forward. Was she after something? Was she trying to steal something, or was she going to accuse me of kissing her and then get me fired? Surely she couldn't be kissing me like that because she wanted me? Surely not. Things like that didn't happen to men like me.

She appeared rumpled and debauched, her breath coming in quick pants. Her lipstick was smeared. I couldn't stop staring at her mouth.

"What's wrong? Don't you want me?" she asked in a whisper. Her teasing was long gone. Something real lived in the depth of her hot, vulnerable gaze.

"Why?" I tried to calm my racing thoughts and the desire to pull her up into my arms and push up her short dress. I wanted to tumble her to the soft earth of the grove and settle between her thighs and claim her as my own before God and nature. I wanted to plant my seed deep inside her and ensure she'd be mine forevermore. My wife. My lover. The mother of my children. It was hard to think straight around that overwhelming need.

"Why what? Why do I want to kiss you?" She wet her lips, leaving them shiny. "I'm nearly twenty. I think I'm due a first kiss. I don't believe that sinners will go to hell or any of that other bullshit my father and his friends talk about . . . and I don't think they believe it either. God, the Devil . . . they're just monsters under the bed to scare kids into being good."

I blinked at her. No one spoke like Georgia Bellisario did. She was irreverent and opinionated and fucking fearless.

The first man to touch her was me. I wanted to be her first

everything. I wanted to leave my fucking fingerprints on her soul so no one could doubt that she was mine.

"Why me?" I clarified and waited for the answer that would change my life or break my hopeful heart.

She sighed and let her head fall back on the trunk of the tree.

"Why? You don't want to kiss me?" she asked, but there was evasion in her tone.

I brought my hands up to the tree trunk and caged her in.

Excitement leapt back to her dark gaze.

"I said . . . Why me? You could have anyone . . . Why. Me?"

Her gaze glided over my face. I wondered what she saw there.

"Because, *cittaiolo*, you're not like the rest of them in this godforsaken place. You'll get out of here one day . . . and I want you to take me with you."

Her attention fell to my lips and bounced back up. Her tanned cheeks warmed with pink roses. Georgia didn't blush often. She wasn't the type. She was too confident for that. But not now. Now, with everything else stripped away, she let me see her.

All of her.

"I guess I want you to save me, Santori. I want you—" She took a halting breath. "I just want you."

"That feeling, Miss Bellisario, is entirely mutual," I murmured.

Her hot breath hit my lips when I leaned back in and kissed her hard. Her arms twined around my neck, and she pressed her body to mine.

And nothing would ever be the same.

11

GEORGIA

NOW

Inside the apartment, the man closed the door and locked it. I flipped the lights on and rounded the table to stare at him.

He glanced around the room, and I saw it through his eyes. Every secondhand, scarred piece of furniture; all the shabby, pitiful evidence of my pathetic life.

"What now?" I asked, keeping the shake out of my tone.

"Now"—he looked me up and down—"you show me to your bedroom."

He stepped closer to me, and I flinched back. My pulse was racing, and I felt like I might faint. I'd never been so scared.

"Why?" I demanded softly, a plea in my voice.

He tilted his head to the side. His beautiful face, so like the one love of my life, was stony, giving nothing away.

"Because I told you to," he said flatly and jerked his head toward the small hallway beyond the kitchen.

I turned around and fought a sob. How had my life come to this? I'd been poor, but getting by, sad but surviving, and then, overnight, my life was full of danger and threats.

"Is this about my father?" I offered and walked in the slowest steps possible toward my room.

"What about your father?"

"I know he's been arrested, but that's all I know . . . I don't know anything else about his business. I'm sure he hasn't done the things they are accusing him of. He's sure to be out soon." I stopped, sucking in a breath as we drew closer to my cramped bedroom.

I was lying, but telling the truth right now didn't seem like a good idea. The chances were very slim that I could persuade this lunatic to believe me. No, he didn't have the air of a lunatic. He was tightly controlled, perfectly disciplined. He was more like a mercenary.

"Oh, Signora Conti, if you really believe that, you're more naive than I'd have ever imagined. Still, maybe it's a case of willful ignorance."

"What?" I asked, my indignation giving way.

We reached the bedroom, and I stopped in the doorway.

He nudged me from behind.

"Hurry up."

"What do you want me to do?" I blurted and stepped into my room.

He followed. The air instantly felt claustrophobic. He was too big for the small space. Too raw, too masculine for the soft, feminine room. Net curtains and soft throws and embroidered pillows, remnants of a life when I'd had money, didn't go with his bloodstained face and lethal grace.

"Lose the clothes," he said.

My stomach dropped. This was it. It was really happening. I stared at his face, so achingly familiar. If he had been Elio Santori, would I have expected mercy? Yes. As stupid as it was to believe in the boy who'd abandoned me, I'd have felt safer.

Instead, I was here with this stone-cold stranger, who wore Elio's face like a mask and had no heartstrings in reach to tug on. A man without mercy or compassion. A monster, or worse, since technically monsters could feel. Frankenstein's monster felt loneliness and sorrow. This man didn't seem capable even of that. He wasn't a monster. He was a machine. Cold metal inside his chest and processors that didn't allow for feelings. How could someone be so incredibly impassive?

I shook my head, a tear dripping down my cheek.

"Don't hurt me. Please. I swear I don't have anything to do with my father anymore. I haven't spoken to him in years."

"Not my problem. Strip, or I'll do it for you."

He'd slipped his hand into his pocket, gripping a hard object.

The gun. I'd forgotten about that in the confusion and panic. Like this man needed a gun to hurt me.

I brought my hands to my jacket and shrugged it off, then tugged my T-shirt up, gasping as glass cut into my hands once more. I looked closer at my clothes. The splinters of glass from earlier were embedded in the soft material, probably from when I'd lain on the floor to hide.

Carefully, I pulled my jeans down, trying not to cut myself.

I rose, only in my underwear.

The man was watching me with an unreadable expression. I tossed my glass-littered clothes in the corner and folded my arms over my chest, trying not to blush from the tips of my toes to the roots of my hair.

It's underwear, Georgia. Just like a bikini. You're okay.

"Why did you call me *topolina*?" I asked in Italian.

The man stared for so long, I started to think he wasn't going to answer. But then he did.

"You live in a filthy attic, you're malnourished and scrawny . . . like a little mouse, scurrying this way and that, desperate to survive. It's a fitting name for you." He spoke in English, with only the slightest trace of Italian to his voice.

The subtext was clear. He didn't want to communicate with me in anything other than English. I shouldn't look to build any camaraderie in both of us being Italian.

A jagged laugh left me at his cruel description.

"I guess I am," I mused. "But I'm just doing what I need to, to survive. You can't blame me for that . . . Someone important to me once told me that."

The man was quiet again. Not even a hint of a reaction showed on his perfect face.

"I think you're misunderstanding something, Signora Conti. I don't care what you do, or don't do. Before today, I wouldn't have cared if you'd starved in this shithole. I don't care about you beyond taking you where I need to take you."

"And where is that?" I immediately pounced, relief hitting me so hard I nearly had to sit down.

He had to take me somewhere. He wasn't going to kill me here and now, tonight.

"You'll find out soon enough." He eyed me up and down. "Put some clothes on and go to sleep."

"It's five in the evening."

"I don't care. Sleep, or don't, just don't leave this room. I've had enough of you today," he tossed over his shoulder as he headed toward the door.

"Elio—wait," I called, unable to stop myself. *Elio.* Why had I called him Elio again? He clearly wasn't, no matter how sure I was.

"I'm not your Elio . . . whoever he was."

I scoffed softly. "He was never mine . . . but yeah, I won't call you that again. I just don't know what else to call you."

"You don't have to call me anything."

"No, I do." Try to humanize yourself to your attacker, wasn't that the advice? "I'll call you 'the mercenary' then, if you don't suggest something."

"Call me De Sanctis, if you must call me anything."

"You're a De Sanctis? You work for Renato?"

"Enough questions for tonight. Sleep, read, tear your hair out . . . just don't bother me."

He shifted, and in the light from the hall, I made out an odd shape in his hand.

A spoon?

Suddenly, it clicked. He'd used the spoon to pretend he had a gun. He didn't have a weapon. He didn't have a fucking weapon.

I didn't think, I just went for his eyes.

I wasn't the type to go easy. I couldn't help it. Dumb or not, resistance was in my DNA.

The only advantage I had was the element of surprise. My mercenary was clearly not expecting to be attacked by a half-naked madwoman intent on tearing those dark brown eyes from his face.

They were wrong. All wrong.

I neared, and he opened his arms instead of sidestepping, and I fell into his embrace. My knee came up immediately, and I nearly got him, but he twisted at the last moment, protecting his balls from my vicious attack with a hard hip-check. I fell backward and he was on top of me, pushing the breath from my lungs when I dropped onto the bed.

I gasped for breath for a split second, then I fought against him. This was it. My only chance to get away. I pushed at his face and tried to get up and away from him, but his body was too heavy, and he covered me too thoroughly.

"Enough!" he roared after I brought my head up sharply and hit my lip hard against his chin.

His hands fastened around my wrists like steel manacles.

"I said enough. You can't get away from me. There is no escape from me, or what's coming, or the sins of your father. I'd advise you to stop testing me. I am not a merciful man. Test me one more goddamn time and I'll put you across my knee and turn your ass so red, you won't be able to sit for a week. Test me twice, and you'll be hog-tied and gagged and in a luggage trunk for our flight. A third time? You really don't want to know what'll happen a third time. So, be good. Got it?" he asked.

His voice was careful and controlled. He didn't seem like a man who lost his cool easily. Even when he'd threatened to spank my ass, he'd behaved as though the act was a perfectly rational response to someone annoying you . . . like there was nothing at all kinky about it.

Kinky? Why was I even thinking about kink right now? I'd gone too long without sex. It was official. This man who felt all man, and sounded all man, and pissed me off just like a man . . . was pressing his hard, heavy body into mine, and I had nowhere near enough clothes on for my body not to get confused.

"Answer me when I speak to you!" he demanded.

"Yes, sir," I snarled out, pissed off that I'd missed my chance to escape, and also that he could just toss me around like I weighed nothing. I was powerless. Utterly powerless, and it was terrifying. My go-to response to terror was anger, so that tracked.

I was furious.

"Good. And watch your tongue. I've had enough rebellion and enough questions. Understood?" His tone made it clear that he was expecting to be obeyed. The man was a total control freak.

I just nodded, clenching my jaw to keep myself from arguing.

He nodded. "Good girl," he said and patted my goddamn head like I was an errant puppy.

"Now, don't bother me again tonight, or I'll handcuff you to the shower, gagged, and turn it on. How much hot water do you get here? Half an hour, max?"

I looked away. My little rebellion was clearly over, because I couldn't risk being in a cold shower all night.

Slowly, he raised himself off me. Everything about him was solid. Even his cock. He'd been pressed between my legs, and if I hadn't been furiously fighting for my freedom, I'd have noticed it a lot more.

He stood, and I could make out the bulge when he turned sideways. He made no effort to hide it. I was glad it was dark, because I was pretty sure my face was scarlet. It felt like it was burning. The fact that this monster was hard, had me half-naked on the bed, and yet didn't cross any lines was vaguely reassuring.

Yes, because threatening to spank you, tie you up, and gag you isn't threatening at all.

He moved toward the door. He was going to lock me in this room. The window was a useless escape route. I couldn't even open it, it was painted shut so well. The only window in the whole place that opened was the living room one. Maybe I could get him to let me sit in the living room, and then if he went to the bathroom . . .

He'd already reached the door while I deliberated my next move.

"Wait!" I called, but he just closed the door behind him.

I sat there, forgetting I was nearly naked until a shiver worked across my bare flesh.

Think, Georgia. Just think. He'd given some information away. I had to figure out what this meant.

He worked for Renato De Sanctis, which meant that was where he was taking me. My father and Salvatore De Sanctis had been close friends, once . . . I pulled on a T-shirt and shorts and lay down, staring at the ceiling. I didn't have my cell phone; my mystery man had taken it. I couldn't tell work that I wouldn't be back. I couldn't call the cops, or the lawyer, or Erica . . . or anyone.

The bedspread felt silky against my bare legs, and a rush of goosebumps moved up my body. I felt aware of myself for the first time in fourteen years. Being married to a gay man had switched off the part of my brain that felt anything sensual. And in the end, when Tommaso had been so ill, slowly fading away, nothing else had mattered but keeping him comfortable. I had cut the cord to my own sexual feelings. I was barely aware of it. But stripping off in front of my captor had forced me to be aware of my body. It had forced me to think about my underwear and near nakedness. Now, I was waking up. Tingling in all kinds of unwelcome places.

Relax, Georgia, it's just the Stockholm syndrome talking, since he made you change out of your ruined clothes instead of forcing himself on you.

I wasn't going to be the woman who fell for a kidnapper because he showed the slightest sliver of kindness. I might have only had sex with one man in my life, and basically forgotten about my body from the waist down, but I wasn't that desperate.

I had to keep a clear head and remember that I was completely alone with a man who was more machine than flesh and blood. He was taking me somewhere, and I needed to be ready to run, whatever chance I got. If only I could figure out why this was happening.

I had to focus on what I knew . . . there were threads here, I just needed to weave them together. I lay on my bed and watched the evening sun move across the ceiling, my mind working furiously over the past.

I had nothing else to do, after all.

12

ELIO

Not a single sound came from Georgia's bedroom, if you could call it that. It was smaller than the walk-in closet at my penthouse in Atlantic City.

I paced the living room–cum–kitchen, which took me about five strides. A fucking rustle from somewhere near the fridge had my senses snapping to attention. I pulled a knife from my pocket, and when something moved, I threw it with deadly precision. It hit the rat squarely in the side, and the clueless thing wriggled against the wall for a few seconds before dying. *Shit.* It bothered me that the kitchen was rat-infested. It bothered me that the fucking door wasn't great, and I could hear the neighbors talking upstairs. It all bothered me.

Most of all, it bothered me that this place smelled like her.

I needed air.

I needed to find out what the situation was with the Ravellis. That guy had recognized me on sight alone. Usually my eyes were my most distinctive feature, and I was used to wearing brown contacts to conceal them when it suited me, but that hadn't helped today.

Georgia had fucking recognized me. *Because you called her "little mouse."* Right, I'd fucked up first. Being around her, I was slipping up like I hadn't in years. For the past decade I'd formed a hard shell of ice to stay behind, but an hour in Georgia Bellisario's company and there were visible cracks.

The contacts had thrown her. She was doubting herself. Three months together followed by fourteen years of separation. Her logical mind was telling her that it was impossible. I didn't look like the lanky twenty-year-old who had been all knobby knees, easy smiles, and clean-shaven cheeks. If I hadn't slipped with the nickname, she'd never have voiced her suspicions. I had to be more careful.

If I were smart, I would get her to New Jersey and married to Jimmy as quickly as possible. That was what had to happen. Those were Renato's orders, and the capo's orders were to be followed. That was my forte.

I pulled out my cell and called across the country.

"What's up? Kidnapped any snitches' daughters yet?"

"Hello to you too, Giada."

"Hello. How's it going? Did you find her?" Giada was the little sister who'd been taken away by the state when I'd been too young and poor to do anything about it. It had taken me years to get Renato to step in and get her moved to the De Sanctis estate.

"Hmm, I found her. Now, I need to find a way to get her home without getting us both killed. The Ravellis are already here. I need you to check if it's just the one or more."

"On it. So, how is she? The traitor's daughter?" The sound of keys clacking in the background floated to me.

"She's—what you'd expect." It was a lie. She wasn't what I'd expected. Humbled, living in poverty, defiant even in the face of death.

"So, she ran kicking and screaming from coming with you?" Giada teased.

"She tried."

"Let me guess, she didn't get far."

"They never do," I muttered, though this was my first time kidnapping a woman, and I planned for it to be my last. My usual remit was protecting my capo with my life, working on strategy, and keeping the made men in line.

Giada hummed while she worked. "Shit. You feel like driving cross-country?"

"Pass. Too many opportunities for her to run away."

"Hmm, and you're sure there's no other way to make sure Prosecutor Bellisario keeps his mouth shut about us and blabs about the Ravellis instead? I'm not a fan of the ol' kidnapped bride scenario, especially not when it involves Jimmy De Luca. The man's breath can clear a room in less than five seconds," Giada complained.

"It's not our problem." I sighed. The very thought of Jimmy De Luca and his thieving fingers touching Georgia pissed me off.

"Maybe it should be . . . You do remember that you are also single. You could do worse than a nice Italian woman—"

"I'd rather die than be the one to marry Georgia."

"But if memory serves, isn't this the woman you once asked me to look up, years ago, and nothing came of it?"

"*Basta*." Enough.

Giada was quiet, silenced by my fatal tone, and then whistled. "Okay, calm down. Don't get your panties in a twist, brother dearest. You just go on being the most reclusive monk in all the land and die alone one day."

"I'm not the marrying kind, *sorellina*. But don't worry about me. I don't intend on living that long."

"Hey! Stop it. You're being a major downer, and I'm telling Bran. Now, back to the business at hand. As we both know, the Ravellis are cockroaches, and where there's one, there's a hundred more, just out of sight. I can see an infestation all around L.A., including the airport."

"They know I'm here."

"I'm sure they do! Renato De Sanctis's right hand . . . bagging and toe-tagging you would be quite the score for them."

"Unfortunately for them, I'm not so easy to kill. Charter me something private, leaving as soon as possible."

"On it. I'll send you the details." Giada hesitated a second before hanging up. "Try not to get killed, okay?"

"Got it."

I headed out after midnight. I needed a gun to protect myself and Georgia and had a few contacts who could get me one. If not, the plan was simple. Go to a bad part of town, wait for someone who was carrying, and make them an offer they couldn't refuse.

An hour later, I was on my way back, this time suitably armed.

I hadn't even had to go far from Georgia's neighborhood to find trouble. She lived in a truly shitty part of the city. It was dangerous as hell for a woman living alone here. What the fuck was Tommaso Conti thinking, to leave his widow in this desperate situation? If he hadn't been dead and buried already, I'd kill him myself.

He'd died of some disease, as far as I knew, but that didn't excuse not planning for Georgia's future. She lived in a rat box; her fucking door didn't even work. Anger lashed at the walls of my composure as I made my way into her building. It smelled like a urinal on the ground floor, and that only made me more furious. Why was she living here? How had her life become this? This was what she had chosen, over me. It would be ironic if it weren't so fucking infuriating.

I headed up the stairs and felt the change in energy as soon as

I neared the top floor. Something was wrong. I'd barely been gone, and I'd made sure my sister had removed all traces of Georgia's address from any online system. Nothing tied her to this place. I'd made sure of it.

I raced up the last few stairs and found her shitty door standing open, mocking me.

Holy hell. I'd made nothing but mistakes since I'd gotten here. Being around Georgia was already fucking with my head and making me sloppy and undisciplined.

I drew my gun and stilled just outside. I had to be ready for whatever was inside. I needed to get control back, or both of us could end up dead.

She could die.

I fought the panic that threatened to devour my focus and stepped into the apartment. There was the low droning sound of a man talking up the hall, near the bedroom. I walked silently along the hallway.

"You were just here—you said you'd see me next month." Georgia's voice was hard, but there was a hitch in it that betrayed her. She was scared.

Something dark writhed in the pit of my belly.

"Well, you know, I gave it some thought and realized that I could help you out with getting ahead. Like I said, you need to get the interest down on your loans . . . or you'll never be free of your late husband's debts."

Her husband's debts? So, this had nothing to do with the Ravellis.

"I don't need your help with a payment plan, thanks. Just leave," Georgia's voice rang out, courageous as always.

A chuckle floated to me in the hall.

"No, I don't think I will. I think you'll have to make me."

Then Georgia gasped, and the sound of a struggle filled the air. I took the safety off my gun and stepped into the room, taking in the scene on the bed.

Georgia was fighting back with all she had, while the guy attacking her was trying to pin her down. I crossed to the bed in two long strides and pressed the gun to his temple.

"How about *I* make you, motherfucker," I growled.

The struggle stopped, and Georgia's huge, dark eyes stared up at me.

"Move. Now." My tone held no room for refusal.

Georgia jerked into action, wriggling out from underneath the man.

"Listen, buddy, we can talk about this . . . we can make a deal," the man was saying, his rank sweat stinking up the room.

"Pass." I pulled the trigger.

The sound was loud in the small, close room. Georgia screamed as the side of her attacker's head blew outward, his brains spattering against the wall beside the bed.

She fell to the floor and crab-walked backward until she hit the wall. Her eyes were fixed on the bed.

A red haze had descended over my eyes, a veil, and it was taking its sweet time to clear. What the fuck had I just done? There were a hundred ways to kill a man silently, and I'd acted like a hothead and shot him. A countdown started in my head for how long it would probably take the LAPD to show up. I had time. I needed to get a fucking grip.

"What did you do?" she panted, looking faintly horrified.

"Took care of your problem. You're welcome." I wiped the muzzle of my gun on the bedsheets.

"'You're welcome'? You want me to thank you for shooting someone in the head right in front of me?"

"You can thank me for getting you to move. If not, you'd be bathed in the dead man's blood right now."

"Right . . . I didn't get dirty, so I guess I'm fine," she murmured faintly.

I shoved the gun in my waistband and grabbed a bag off the floor.

"Pack your things. We're leaving. You have three minutes."

"Three minutes. When are we coming back?"

"Never. Take anything you absolutely need, leave everything else. And it has to fit in the bag."

"Wait! I can't just leave." She reached out and grabbed me as I went to leave the room.

"You can and you are. You now have two minutes."

"Shit!" She scrambled to her feet, bursting into action.

"Georgia, let's go." I banged into her room two minutes later.

She spun around, in the process of trying to shove a box into her bag. I grabbed it and tossed it on the bed.

"Leave it, it doesn't fit."

"No! I have to take it," she insisted and grabbed the box.

"I said leave it," I growled at her, aware of time ticking away.

"No! No, I won't leave it!" Her suddenly agonized shout grabbed my attention.

I focused on her properly. She was about a second away from a panic attack, it looked like. That would slow us down more than anything.

I slowly lifted my hand and pointed the gun at her.

"Leave. It. We're going right now."

I leveled the gun at her head, hoping the shock of it would bring her back to her senses.

She shook her head and shocked me by stepping forward and

pressing her forehead against the barrel of the gun. The sight of it on her skin was unsettling. I wanted to move it. It was wrong on a bone-deep level. I wasn't here to kill her, after all, but she didn't seem about to back down and do what she was fucking told.

"If that box doesn't come with me, I'm not going anywhere either. You can shoot me in the head, too, and just get it over with." Her teary eyes met mine. They shone like glassy jewels in the moonlight flooding through the window.

"Don't tempt me," I ground out, stepping forward and dropping the gun. Instead, I took her chin in a hard pinch. "I told you not to play games with me."

She trembled in my grip. "I'm not. I'm serious. I'll die before I leave without that box."

"What the fuck is in it?"

"None of your business."

An incredulous laugh left me at her prim tone. The sound shocked me. I rarely laughed, and starting when I was on the run from the police, surrounded by evidence that I'd just killed a man and had a woman to kidnap, seemed like a bad time to start. I glanced at the box. What could be so important to her to push like this? Mementos of her dearly departed husband? A wedding photo album?

"Are you the bravest person I've ever met or the dumbest?"

She pulled out of my hold and raised her chin at me, like a queen. Regal just like she'd been as a teenager in Castel Amaro, when the world had been at her feet. *Ah, there she is.* My Georgia, still as imperious as ever.

"I don't care what you think about me. I'm not leaving without it."

I could see the resolution in her gaze. Of course, I could just drag her kicking and screaming without it. I could knock her out, but then I'd have to carry her, and that would slow me down.

Why was she so attached to it? Could it be the collateral I was sure her father had sent her?

I backed up and reached for the box. I took her open bag and shoved the bulky shape inside, forcing the zipper shut.

"Now, if there isn't anything else, we're leaving."

I turned and grabbed her arm, slinging her bag onto my back, and pushed her toward the hallway.

"Thank you."

The words were so quiet, I might have imagined them.

Then a loud banging at the door echoed through the apartment, and I froze.

"LAPD—open up!"

Shit. Their reaction times were better than the NYPD's, I'd give them that. Or, more likely, they had a strong presence in this shitty neighborhood.

I turned toward the window running along the living room and checked where it would come out. It opened up to a fire escape in a dark part of the alley. Best of all, there was a point halfway down where it passed close enough to the neighboring building's fire escape to move across it.

I surveyed Georgia's sneaker-and-jeans outfit and nodded, my mind made up.

I shoved open the window and turned for Georgia, only to see her standing across the room. She had moved quickly and quietly while I was still assessing the situation.

My eyes met hers, and I knew what she was going to do.

"Don't . . . They can't save you from me, and you'll only piss me off," I warned her in a low tone.

Her hand reached out for the lock on the door. I considered my options in a flash. I could try and get to her before she opened the door. The apartment was small, but not that small. I'd fail. The only other option was to withdraw and bide my time.

"Don't say I didn't warn you . . . I'll see you again, soon." With that, I stepped out of the window onto the fire escape and ran down as fast as I could, jumping stairs wherever I had the chance. Upstairs, the sounds of the LAPD entering the apartment filtered down. I heard them shout at Georgia to put her hands behind her back. I jumped to the fire escape on the building beside hers and climbed again, keeping to the shadows. There were two cop cars in the street outside her apartment. I climbed to the top and onto the roof just in time to see Georgia being led from the building in handcuffs and put in the back of a squad car.

They wouldn't hold her for too long. She had a good story, and besides, there was no weapon there or anything to tie her to the shooting. I didn't trust cops as far as I could throw them, but Georgia wasn't the kind of person they were looking to go hard on.

They'd release her soon enough . . . and I'd be waiting.

13

GEORGIA

THEN

The stables smelled like hay and leather, with subtle undertones of horse shit and sweat, nearly completely drowned out by the sweet fragrance of the lavender bushes just outside and the night-blooming jasmine that lined the walkway to the stone building.

I followed the path, tonight, more than other nights, eager to reach my destination.

I smoothed my hands down my dress. Creamy white satin. It was ankle-length, and there wasn't a hint of cleavage at the top, but it clung to my body like a second skin. I didn't think my father had thought about that scandalous possibility in the cut and material when he'd let me design my own dress for tonight. *Cena dei cento giorni.* The last dinner for my high school class. Americans called it prom and went all out, or so the movies made it seem, while in Italy dinner was the focal point. We'd eat together and later go and dance somewhere. School had finished a few months ago, but punctuality had never been my friends' strong suit.

I'd been Tommaso's date tonight, since he couldn't take the guy he'd really wanted to go with.

Now, finally finished, I wanted someone else to see me in my dress.

I crept into the stables. My heels sank into the packed dirt. They were silver with sharp stilettos, and they might even bring me up to Elio's sternum, if he was barefoot.

I'd been signaling with the little flashlight I kept in my bedroom at the window for a while but had gotten no response. It was our little code. *Come to me* in Morse code, and expressed with flickers of light. Since there'd been no reply from the stables tonight, I was taking matters into my own hands.

"*Cittaiolo?*" I whispered into the night stillness. I was here to see my city boy, after all; why else had I bothered with the new dress? The design was mine, but my father had picked the color. Pure as snow, virginal white. It didn't take a rocket scientist to figure out what my father wanted to convey to the village with this dress.

She's off-limits. No one touches my daughter. Don't get close.

Unluckily for him, the *cittaiolo* didn't care about his rules.

Elio Santori was a rule-breaker by nature. His very existence seemed to bend the fabric of the world itself. No one should be so damn charming and troublemaking all at the same time. No one should make me feel like he did with one slow smirk.

I tried to hide how much he affected me. Playing hard to get was all the rage. Yet, when he cornered me after church or caught me in the kitchen when no one else was around, it was like I was melting. Everything in my life ceased to matter except his touch, his smile, the way his fingers played with my hair.

I was a goner.

"Elio?" I whispered again when the stables remained silent to my call.

I advanced, checking out each stable. Sometimes he bedded down in the hay with a sick horse and stayed the night. He was a natural with the animals; it was a shock to find out that he'd never so much as seen one outside the racetrack until he'd come to town.

I reached the end of the aisle that ran between the berths and peeked in the last one.

There he was.

Sun-darkened olive skin glowed in the low lights. His arms, lined with slim muscle, were stretched over his head. His T-shirt had crept up his flat belly, and there was a trail of hair that circled his belly button and ran downward, disappearing into his jeans. I longed to trace it and see where it went. I wanted to see every single part of this boy who had turned my boring life upside down and painted it with brilliant colors.

His face was soft in repose. He was usually scowling at someone, or something, or laughing. His face was lively, expressive as hell. He couldn't hide his thoughts; they were painted across his brow. Now, his face was slack with sleep, and I got to simply stare, just like I always longed to.

He was classically beautiful. He had the kind of face that would have inspired a marble bust back in the day. My art history teacher would sigh over him if she ever caught a glimpse. A strong jaw and aquiline nose, slightly bumped on the bend, just enough to be intriguing. He was no angel, that was certainly true. He caused too much mischief and mayhem for that comparison to be drawn.

I hovered over him, reaching out a fingertip to lightly trace down his cheek.

I didn't see the knife coming.

One second, I was bent over, trying to balance in my heels and tight dress. The next, there was a flash of silver and a blade at my neck, and Elio's hot, hard body pressed against me.

"*Cittaiolo,* it's me. Wake up," I murmured, my heart racing.

He made a noise. Something between agreement and complaint. The knife remained where it was even as Elio tipped my chin up with his other hand, and his eyes hit mine. Those eyes. If I forgot everything else about this man, surely, I'd never forget that pale-jade stare. Thick dark lashes surrounded those eerily beautiful eyes, and dark winged brows framed them. The man was distractingly good-looking.

"Thank fuck I was only dreaming . . . For a second there, I thought I was a goner and had arrived at the pearly gates. It's the dress . . ." he murmured, leaning back to gaze approvingly at me.

"You thought I was an angel, and you still pulled a knife?" I wondered.

He grinned. "Yeah, well, maybe I could threaten my way into heaven. It's worth a shot, right?"

"You're ridiculous." Heat crept into my cheeks at the way he was staring at me. He'd drawn back for a better view and now, he continued to stare.

"Hmm, yeah, when it comes to you, I am . . . and you are—" He broke off and brought his eyes back to mine.

I tipped my chin back and enjoyed his reaction. This was the moment I'd sweated over at my sewing machine for more than a week, wasn't it? I wanted to be seen by him, and every single time, he delivered. That didn't make it any less thrilling.

"And I'm?" I prompted.

He leaned closer and shook his head slowly, tutting under his breath. "You know what you are . . . you don't need me to say it."

I mirrored his slow head shake. "No, I really don't."

He couldn't know how true that was. Brought up by my father alone since I could remember, always at home, cloistered and spoiled and hidden from the world, I really didn't know.

He let out a long exhale and ran his finger down my cheek.

"Beneath this skin, a world waits to be discovered.
Beneath this mundane existence, galaxies stir in wonder.
Beneath the frozen river, currents still run.
Beneath stone and concrete, seeds push through—
And those seeds can lift whole buildings."

Elio's deep voice spoke his words like cool water running down a deep ravine. I drank them all up. They ran into my lonely, parched soul, and sated it.

"And?" I urged.

Every single poem in progress that he'd shared with me, he'd ended the same way. It was my favorite ending of every single ending that ever existed.

"And I was hers, and she was mine . . . and no one could take her from me . . . and no one ever would."

I smiled contentedly at him. He slid the finger he had on my cheek down my neck and past my collarbones, weakening my knees. Lately, kissing hadn't been enough to satisfy either of us. I wanted more, and I knew Elio did, too. Every kissing session we indulged in brought us closer and closer to crossing the line between us.

One thing that Elio didn't know was how badly I wanted to cross that line. I wanted to erase it.

"It was my *cena dei cento giorni* tonight," I told him, shivering under his touch but not wanting him to stop.

"Oh, I know." His eyes were decidedly hot and bothered by my dress.

"You did?"

He nodded lazily. "Why do you think I'm not in bed?"

"A sick horse?"

"I'm waiting around to see what time that motherfucker you hang around with brings you home at."

I laughed. "What motherfucker? Tommaso?"

Elio nodded. "Mm-hmm, the one your father likes. The good boy. The suitable choice."

I rolled my eyes at him. "Please, the jealousy is so childish. We're best friends. He's like a brother to me."

"No, he's not, and I can guarantee that he doesn't think like that," Elio said shortly and pushed a hand through his flopping waves.

I couldn't out Tommaso's secret to Elio, no matter how much I'd love to reassure him that he had nothing to worry about from my best friend.

"I don't care what my father thinks . . . don't you know that by now?" I changed the subject. I stroked his face and stared into his eyes. "Sage green. One day, I want to paint our bedroom sage green," I murmured. "Just like your eyes."

"Why?" Elio murmured.

"It makes me feel safe. It makes me feel . . . everything," I admitted with a sigh. I was starting to feel that if I didn't touch him, I'd die.

I tugged at the hem of my dress, pulling it up so I could swing a leg over Elio's lap and straddle him.

His eyes went darker than the blackest coal as I settled my weight on him.

"What are you up to, *topolina?*" His warm murmur was more than half growl.

"What does it feel like?" I asked, mock innocence painted across my face. I knew exactly what I wanted, and it was this man. I wanted all of him. I wanted to end my youth right here, tonight, on the floor of the stables, with the man who would take me from this hopeless backwater. The man I'd face the world beside. We were meant to be, I knew it in my bones.

"It feels like you're playing with fire." Elio flexed his hips beneath me.

He was hard. The long, probing length of him was pressing against me through his rough jeans. My whole body shuddered.

I simply nodded, biting my lip. I wriggled my hips on his lap, rubbing my needy pussy on his bulge. I could probably come just like that, humping his jean-clad hard-on like it was a pillow in my bed. I had one that was just the right shape, but it was nothing compared to the real deal.

"Georgia," Elio warned. He grabbed my chin in a firm grip and stopped my lazy gyrations.

I blinked back into focus and took in his dark, possessive gaze.

"*Topolina*, you're not the kind of woman a man fucks casually." His eyes searched mine.

"You don't want me?" I asked.

"I was born to want you. I will always want you. I will live every day wanting you and I will die that way, too. Wanting you is in my blood. It is my legacy to want you . . . but I want more than tonight. I want forever."

The hand holding my chin slid up my cheek and sank into the hair behind my ear, his grip holding my face in place, so near his.

"I want you to marry me, Georgia. Be my wife, and I will give you everything you want. I will save you every day. I will dedicate my life to your happiness. Marry me."

"Marry you? Everyone will say we're too young," I protested, my mind reeling.

"I don't care."

"You don't have to say that . . . for me to want to . . . you know," I muttered, heat warming my cheeks.

Elio chuckled, so low and gruff that goose bumps swept up my arms and over my chest. I was so cripplingly aware of him: his touch, his scent, his voice.

"On the contrary, you *do* have to agree for anything to happen," he said. "I told you that you're not a woman to fuck casually, you're a woman to wait for, and to marry . . . We'll fuck as a couple about to get married or not at all."

"Why?" I wondered at his dogged insistence. Most young guys I knew wanted to hook up and definitely not get a fiancée out of it.

"Because, I can't take having you just for one night. If I have you, I need to know it's forever. Anything else would break me."

His quiet confession felt sacred somehow. An admission of weakness from the strongest guy I knew.

"I've fallen in love with you, Georgia, and I'm not a man who intends to love like this more than once. I need to marry you like I need air to breathe. I don't have much of anything right now, but I swear, I'll give you a good life. I'll find a way to give you what you deserve."

I didn't know what to say. My heart swelled; my skin flushed with fire. I couldn't breathe. Thoughts were racing through my head, and yet above the din, there was one word that emerged above all else.

Yes.

I leaned in and kissed him, sliding my tongue over his, and let my hand trail down his flat, packed abs, then to his belt. I tugged at it, showing him my intention.

He gripped my hair and tilted my face back. "Tell me you'll marry me. Give me your answer," he demanded.

"Isn't it obvious?" I asked.

He shook his head slowly, his gaze running over my face. "Not to an unworthy soul like me. I need to hear it."

I took a deep breath and leapt. "I'll marry you. I'll be your wife."

A smile crept over his face, a blinding sunrise.

"My wife," he whispered, repeating my words. "I like the sound of that. You will be my wife."

I nodded, his smile so infectious, I was grinning madly back. "I will be your wife, so why don't you do your husbandly duties?"

I gave him a wicked smile and pulled his belt free, undoing the top button of his jeans. His breath hitched, his eyes turning even more molten, a feat that shouldn't have been possible.

"Let's seal this deal the old-fashioned way." I delved my hand fearlessly into his unbuttoned jeans.

"What, a handshake?" Elio raised his hips slightly.

I ruthlessly tugged down his boxers and jeans just enough for his cock to spring free. I'd seen one before; I lived in the age of the internet. And yet, the feel of Elio's, warm and pulsing in my hand, was fascinating. I scooched back, straddling his knees now so I could peer more closely at his dick. He was big, of course; I'd suspected that, given the bulge he showcased in his jeans even when not hard. Big but beautifully formed. I ran my hand up and down the shaft, and his breath caught.

Oh, I liked that. I felt powerful like I never had when I held this man who I loved's cock in my hand and explored it. Worldly, confident Elio Santori, the *cittaiolo,* all-knowing city bad boy, didn't seem so bold, suddenly. He was hungry . . . hungry for me.

"Sure, we can shake on it." I ran my thumb over the slit at the top of his cock and smeared the clear liquid there. "Don't forget to spit first," I added and brought my hand to my lips, spitting into my palm, then returning to my indulgent exploration.

He tensed, letting out a tight hiss. He jerked, his cock leaking against my palm. It was so alien and strange-looking, and yet, I couldn't turn away.

"*Topolina,* keep touching me like that, and this isn't going to last very long." He caught my wrist.

"I brought protection," I blurted awkwardly when he maneuvered me to the hay. He'd spread a large blanket under us. The lights were burning low, and it felt like we were the only people in the world.

He moved my dress up my thighs and stopped when my pussy came into sight.

"Tell me you didn't go to dinner without panties on?"

I giggled. I could feel his hot breath on my skin.

"I only don't wear panties when I know you're going to be there."

He smirked at me. "That's my girl. Now, let me see that pretty pussy."

I squirmed beneath his gaze. He was staring right at me, pushing my knees apart so I was spread wide open, with nothing to hide behind.

"Don't be shy, Georgia. You're perfect. Everything about you is perfect to me." He leaned in. "I want to taste you."

"Taste!" I nearly squeaked.

"You tasted me. It's only fair," he murmured.

Yes, that was right. I had tasted him. The salty musk still lived on my tongue.

Then his tongue touched me, and I couldn't think about anything else.

"You're so good at this," I panted, a worrisome thought taking form. Had he had a lot of other lovers?

"I must be a natural since I've never done it before," he said against my skin, seeming to read my mind.

"You haven't?" I asked breathlessly.

He pulled back, wiping his mouth on the back of his hand. He tore the condom wrapper open with his teeth and spoke around it.

"Mm-hmm, I haven't. I haven't done any of it . . . I haven't really had time to think about it much." He lowered his hand to his hard-on and rolled the condom down his pulsing shaft. "Besides, I've never met anyone I wanted to do this with . . . until you."

"Well, likewise." I smiled up at him.

"Your boyfriend, Tommaso, is going to be disappointed." Elio positioned himself over me and put the tip of his cock at my entrance.

I laughed. "For the hundredth time . . . he's not my boyfriend."

"Damn right he isn't . . . I am . . . I'm more than that," Elio grunted, pushing just inside me.

I was so turned on I couldn't bear it. I lifted my hips, trying to pull him deeper.

"I'm going to be your husband," he said and sank deeper inside me.

I cried out at the twin sensations of pain and pleasure meeting. He was so big, it was an invasion I wasn't nearly prepared for, but somehow the stretch was delicious. It felt primal, like accepting this man who I loved into my body was changing us both. When we were remade, we'd never be the same.

He rested his forehead on mine and pushed in as deep as he could.

"Shit, *topolina*, being inside you is a holier feeling than being in church." He kissed me softly. Withdrawing a little, he glanced down and swore.

I followed his gaze. Blood was smeared over the condom.

"Does it hurt? I don't want to hurt you," he began.

I grabbed his face, cupping his strong jaw, and shook my head. "It doesn't hurt. It feels right. Keep going."

He let out a shuddering sigh as he moved again, sinking back inside me, a jolt of pleasure chasing the tail end of pain away. Slowly, he developed a languid pace, his lithe hips gyrating against mine, his cock rubbing places I'd never known existed inside me.

He scattered kisses across my face. A kiss for my cheeks, another for my eyebrows, most for my jaw.

His hand sank into my hair and tightened, and his pace

increased. I moved with him, raising my hips to meet his thrusts. I wanted everything from this man. Every single experience . . . I wanted it with him.

He stroked my face. "This is my sacrament. The only body I will consume and the only blood I will spill."

A surge of pleasure shot through me, foreign and unexpected. I gasped, chasing after the elusive feeling. He changed the angle of his hips, hitting me the same way again, his pelvic bone grinding down on my clit.

I cried out, sinking my nails into his arms.

"Are you going to come?" He sounded almost as surprised as I felt.

"I—I don't know," I panted, squirming beneath him. "I feel like I'm going to wet myself," I admitted.

"Go ahead, *cara*, we're already in the barn," he said.

I laughed and slapped his shoulder as he chuckled.

"Hey, this is serious," I moaned; he somehow managed to catch my clit with every thrust.

"Oh, it is . . . really fucking serious. I have a new addiction, and it's being inside you . . . my soon-to-be wife." He groaned and fucked me harder.

"Are you going to come?" I asked him back, feeling a difference in his movements.

He nodded. "I can't stop it . . . you destroy me, Georgia," he said, his voice strained.

I couldn't answer, because pleasure was streaking through me. That odd feeling of pressure returning, I was rising. Rising. And then I fell.

Pleasure I'd never before felt burst inside me like an overripe peach, juices spilling, flesh soft and liquid-feeling. Wetness hit my thighs, but it didn't feel gross. It felt right.

Elio growled in my ear, his hand pulling my head back, baring my throat to his teeth and lips.

"Fuck, you just squeezed me like you were trying to fucking kill me."

He panted and then shuddered, his whole body going rigid. His hips slammed deep and stayed there. He pulsed inside me. It was hot and wet. *Should that happen with a condom?* I didn't care. I wanted to be marked by him forever. Joined in a way that could never be reversed.

That moment there, in the stables, lying on a makeshift bed, the moon shining down outside, full of him, our hearts beating against each other's, I felt fate press down on us both. He pulled out of me, and I felt him hot and wet across my thighs.

"The condom broke." He reached down to take it off. "Fuck."

"I don't care. I didn't like it anyway," I confessed. "I want to feel you . . . all of you. I'll go on the pill."

He stared at me and ran a hand through my hair, then cupped my cheek.

"You do kill me, *topolina*, you know that? I can't live without you," he said, his green eyes staring into my soul.

"Likewise." I met his unflinching stare.

He nodded and placed a single kiss on my forehead. A sign of worship. Devotion.

He pulled me close, then guided my head to his shoulder and spoke softly. *"And I was hers, and she was mine . . . and no one could take her from me . . . and no one ever would."*

14

GEORGIA

NOW

"Girl, I swear, you don't do things by halves. Your life was totally boring, and instead of joining a book club or something, you go and get kidnapped by some criminal and held at gunpoint."

I didn't bother correcting her. *Spoonpoint* didn't have quite the same ring to it.

"Yes, it was all my choice," I sighed, downing a large gulp of coffee.

Erica perched on the barstool next to me. "What was the police station like? Did they bring out a hard-boiled detective to interrogate you?"

I shrugged. "I don't know . . . just some tired guy and his partner asking all about Jackson and the loan. I guess they're used to dealing with this kind of thing. I mean, gangs fighting among each other and loan sharks threatening people."

Erica watched me. "Are you sure your mystery man was really Mafia?"

"I'm sure. Believe me . . . I know Mafia. The man he works for is a big deal on the East Coast. If they can find him." *If they do that, I'll be safe.* I didn't bother saying the last part, because the stark truth was that until they did, I wasn't safe. I wasn't safe at all.

"Are you sure you're okay to go to work today?"

I nodded. I needed to go. I wouldn't make rent if I didn't. I'd been given two days off for my trauma, and it was all I could afford to miss.

"I'll be fine."

"What about going back to your place? Can you really sleep there after what happened?"

I forced a smile. "It's fine. I'm tougher than I look, and I'm going to find a new place anyway, like you said, in a better neighborhood."

Erica brightened. "Maybe near me?"

"Maybe."

There was no way I could afford to live near Erica. She had a good deal on a studio because the owner was friends with her aunt. But the studio was truly tiny, and I couldn't impose on her any longer. I knew it was hard for her to have someone stay, even if she'd never say so directly.

I left Erica's. I had no idea if my De Sanctis stalker was sticking around to find me. The LAPD had said they'd put a security detail on me. I didn't see a single sign of them, so I wasn't sure if that meant they were just very good at their job or that they hadn't really bothered.

Could they truly stop a man like my mercenary?

On the way, I stopped by the post office and finally got the package my father had sent me. I sat in the little lobby and stared at the envelope with trepidation. Did he have what my mercenary was looking for? Would it save me or damn me?

I reached inside and withdrew a flash drive. It was small, tiny enough to tuck into my bra. I went to the bathroom and did just that, throwing the envelope in the trash on the way out, and then stopped. The flash drive felt like a neon sign over my head.

INCRIMINATING EVIDENCE HERE!

I couldn't leave it there. It felt too obvious and easy to lose. I opened my bag and rummaged through it. The other week my cheap lipstick had fallen out of my purse and smacked onto a tile floor. The entire inner tube had slid out, separating from the larger case. I'd forced it back in at the time. Now, I dropped the shiny black case on the floor and broke it again. Tossing the inner tube of lipstick in the trash, I slipped the tiny flash drive into the empty lipstick container and snapped the lid on. It wasn't a bad little disguise. Not at all.

I tucked the lipstick into my bag and headed to work.

I needed to see what was on the drive. *And then what?* Then I'd lose plausible deniability. Like my mercenary cared about that. He'd already deemed me guilty by association with my father, and sentenced me to whatever it was he was taking me to.

A headache pressed at my temples, but I got to work and got settled, while Eddie made a pile of the work I'd missed out on.

My eyes glazed over as I looked at it. I'd be here a week at least, trying to catch up.

So, in addition to getting on the LAPD's radar, sitting through an interrogation, and having nightmares of seeing a man get shot in the head, I had another thing to thank the black-clad asshole who'd dragged me around all day for.

I worked steadily through the day, grateful for a distraction from my worries.

While it was comforting that the LAPD was searching for my captor, I didn't have high hopes of them finding him. He seemed like a man with skills, and he'd been confident that he'd get to me again.

It was all because of my father. Clearly, there was a lot I didn't know about how he'd lived his life, and it had been far from the squeaky-clean image he'd projected. He'd been best friends with Salvatore De Sanctis, of course, I'd always known that, but I'd been naive.

Willful ignorance. The man in black's voice echoed through my mind. His disdainful tone had made it clear how little he believed my protests of innocence.

Before I knew it, it was time to go home, and my coworkers were on their way out. It was the weekend, and they had places to go. I had nowhere to go and nothing to do that was more important than catching up on my missed work.

I chewed on my lip and thought of my half-sewn designs. I'd been dumb enough to stuff them into that hastily packed go bag, along with my most precious possession. The box of my mementos.

Now they were at the mercy of that man. He'd probably tossed them in the trash the first chance he got, ridding himself of the deadweight and any vestiges of mercy for me. I focused on sewing to drown out the hopelessness I felt when I thought about my belongings abandoned somewhere in L.A.

When I lifted my head up again, it was dark outside, and my lamp was the only pool of light in the workshop.

I checked my watch and was shocked at the time. *Eleven P.M.? How?*

Something had jolted me out of my work-focused delirium. I listened for it—the soft sound of rain falling. It had started raining? That was pretty unusual for this time of year in L.A. I didn't normally hear it in the workshop, underground as we were.

I listened to it, enjoying the sound before it stopped.

Wait, it stopped? I stood and stretched, walking to the sliver of window that ran along the top of the wall, and glanced up. Raindrops streaked down the glass. So, why had the sound stopped?

It was like a window had been open and someone had closed it.

Or . . . a door.

Fear blew through me in a sudden rush, setting my nerves on high alert. I strained my ears, trying to hear something, anything, from whoever else was still in the building.

Maybe it was just a coworker upstairs in the showroom. That seemed doubtful, though; it was late. Really late.

I hurried back to my desk and clicked my lamp off, plunging the room into semidarkness. After a few moments, my eyes started to adjust to the gloom, and the meager amount of streetlight falling through the small window.

Outside on the street, several pairs of legs passed by the window, walking quickly. There was only one thing in the direction that they were going, and it was the emergency exit to the showroom.

Panic hit me hard. There were men creeping in here . . . for me.

I had to get out of here. If the men were coming in through the back, then I had to make a break for the front.

I crept along the row of desks and sewing machines, past the heavy-duty iron we used to press the designs, and the cutting table. My legs cramped at the position I was rolled into, but I pushed the discomfort out of my mind. This was serious, and there was a good chance I wasn't going to be leaving here under my own control.

I nearly made it to the stairs. I was so close. Whether I'd have really gotten out, typed in the security code, and pushed the metal grate up in time, I'd never know.

I never got the chance to find out.

Hard arms wrapped around me from behind, and a hand clamped over my mouth, sealing in my sound of surprise.

I wriggled and fought, but the grip was too damn strong.

"You might want to cut it out, unless you want to die here tonight," a deep, familiar voice murmured in my ear.

My mercenary. He pulled me against him, holding us flush against a wall near the coffee maker, about five feet from the stairs.

"Who are they?" I whispered when he finally removed his hand from my mouth.

"Friends of your father, or I should say former friends. They might be under the impression that he sent you the information that would sink their boss, should your father meet an untimely end in prison."

"What? They think my father made me his insurance?" I could have laughed. "I told you, we don't really talk."

"Still, who else does Alfredo Bellisario have in this world, other than his precious only daughter? Are you trying to lie to me that he hasn't sent you anything? I see you, Georgia . . . I'm always watching."

The man was just as tall and broad as I remembered. Being pressed against his chest, the promise of his protection, shouldn't have been a comfort. But it was. It felt like gaining an unexpected ally. Get *real*. I had given the police this man's description and tried to get him arrested for murder. There weren't any warm and fuzzy feelings from his side.

"That's why Renato wants me too, isn't it? My father could expose everything Salvatore has been up to in Napoli for decades . . . He could cut a deal and fuck the De Sanctis family in return." I knew in my bones I was right. My father had never really cared much about anyone but himself. Of course he would cut a deal and hang me out to dry.

"What if I told you that your father wants Renato to protect you?"

I scoffed softly. "Protect me? So they sent you? The Terminator? You just want to use me to scare him, right?"

The man was staring down at me, and for a second, I thought

he might answer. It was an obvious one. I knew I was right. It was just the way things worked in our world.

"Would you rather I handed you over to the other guys? I can do it right now. The gang's all here . . . I could hand you over and be back in New Jersey tomorrow and forget you ever existed."

"Then you'd fail your little mission, and I have a feeling that's important to men like you," I said, raking my gaze over him. He had to be former military; there was no mistaking his upright carriage and the precision of his movements.

"Men like me?"

"Rule-followers. Mercenaries. I've met toasters with more empathy," I blurted out before I could stop myself.

He studied me and then grinned. There was more warmth in an ice storm.

"In that case, why don't you decide who you want to go with. Them, or me. Decide now. I'm happy to break the rules and give you up, if that's what you choose."

My throat tightened, swallowing the rush of words I wanted to spit at him. But in reality, what could I say?

"Come on, Signora Conti, choose. Them, or me." His arms tightened around me.

"Don't call me that," I muttered, distracted by my impending doom. I had no idea what the other men wanted, but this one was taking me to Renato De Sanctis. At least that would buy me time . . . and I knew Renato. He'd never been a true monster.

"Fine, I choose you. Take me to Renato and let me plead my case. I know him. He won't kill me." I raised my chin and tried to feel as confident as I sounded.

My mystery man tilted his head to the side. "If you think that's the worst he could do, you're going to be sorely disappointed. Now, where do you keep the knives in this place?"

"Knives? Don't you have a gun?" I was distracted from his ominous warning by his question. There were dangerous men sneaking into the building as we spoke, and he didn't have his gun?

"Yeah, because I'm going to wander around L.A. while the cops are looking for me, carrying a murder weapon. Great idea. No, I don't have a gun, but I don't need one for these fuckers. Kindly direct me to something with a sharp edge."

"There has to be at least ten of them," I said.

"Your point being?" He raised an arrogant eyebrow at me.

Wow. Someone was confident in their killer moves. I just had to hope he had the skills to back it up.

We didn't have actual knives in the workshop. Why would we? But there *was* something we had plenty of. I reached around the corner we were hiding behind and grabbed two shiny objects glinting on the cutting table.

I handed both pairs of fabric shears to him. He stared at them for a second, nodding.

"Now, get down and don't make a sound." His hand landed on my shoulder, and he pushed me toward the floor.

I hit it unceremoniously and shot a scowl at him, crawling under the nearest desk. My mystery man took a pair of fabric shears in each hand, melting into the darkness.

Silence fell, punctuated by the thump of the metal door at the top of the workshop stairs. They had entered our level.

Low male voices speaking in Italian filled the space. They moved down the stairs, their footsteps echoing around the dark room.

Sweat rolled down my neck. I felt sick. There were other men who wanted to get to me to threaten my father? I felt like there had been a huge, glowing bull's-eye on my back since I'd gotten that call from the lawyer. I was fucked. How was I going to get out of this mess?

As I thought furiously about how I could possibly get rid of the target on me, murky shapes moved at the other end of the workshop. My eyes had adjusted to the dark enough that I could make out the other guys. I knew they weren't my very own personal robot/killing machine, because they weren't nearly as big as him, nor as graceful.

They moved in a line, talking quietly among themselves. One from the back of the line disappeared and didn't reappear.

One down.

The men continued on, while my mercenary picked them off one by one. The only sign he'd been there was a glint of metal every now and again.

Eventually, the men realized what was happening, and all hell broke loose. They started to shoot blindly behind them, hitting each other at times. My man in black glided through the middle, an avenging angel, sidestepping shots as if he were bulletproof. He swayed and ducked with perfect elegance. He made killing look like a dance. When someone landed a kick to his chest, he caught his leg and sliced his Achilles tendon with one hard snip. His shears flashed as he stabbed them into his opponents' chests. Rapid cuts that sent them to their knees. He whirled and finished one off by slashing the side of his neck, releasing a great spray of arterial blood right across a roll of raw white silk.

I shuddered at the sight. Fuck, after this, I could never come back here.

Ever.

He worked his way through the group of men, and faster than I could believe, silence fell again. My mercenary dropped the shears into his pocket and surveyed the mess, shoving a hand through his hair. The motion triggered a flood of recollection. He was like someone ripped right from my memories at that moment. But he wasn't him . . . the bloody carnage on the floor of the workshop was more proof of that than even those dark brown eyes. Elio Santori had never wanted to become a man like his father . . . a gangster.

I stared, and he brought his bloodthirsty gaze to meet mine.

I held that blistering stare for a good while, then he glanced away.

"We're leaving. Try to run away this time and I'll leave you to the next wave of these guys. Don't be fooled that this is over. It's just begun."

With that, he turned on his heel and made for the door. I pushed myself from my paralysis and grabbed my bag, running after him.

15

GEORGIA

We didn't get far from the building before my mercenary dragged me into a dark alley. His hand took mine, and he tugged me along the back entrances to a row of stores. At the very last one, he picked the lock on the back door and shoved me inside, closing the door behind us.

It was pitch-black, and he was close; so close I forgot how to breathe. He hustled us through the lobby and into a room beyond.

He moved around, confident somehow, despite the darkness. A lamp clicked on over an exam table. *Wait, an exam table?* The sound of barking floated over to us.

This was a vet's office.

"Come here," he said briskly and patted the table.

"I'm fine. I'm not hurt," I protested.

He looked at me. "I said come here."

Knowing that arguing with him was like debating with a wall, I sighed and went to sit on the table.

He took off his jacket, revealing a black T-shirt beneath and sleeve tattoos. He rummaged around in a cabinet and then reached into his pocket for something.

"Are you hurt? I'm fine," I pointed out.

"So I see . . . for now," he said curtly.

That was ominous, to say the least.

Then he added to the menacing feeling by turning around and snapping on latex gloves. I stared as he smoothed them over his thick wrists. There was something about seeing his tattooed arms straining his T-shirt, the blood flecked across his face, and those gloves . . .

He reached for a silver tray, and all other thoughts left my head when I spied the hypodermic syringe on the tray.

"What the hell is that for?" I panicked, trying to stand up.

He tutted, circling behind me.

One hand snaked around my neck from behind, and then suddenly a sharp pain pierced my neck. *That fucker.* The tray had been a distraction. He had been up to something else the whole time.

"I wouldn't move if I were you," he said calmly, injecting God knew what under my skin, while holding my neck hard enough to make breathing a little challenging.

"What are you putting inside me?"

"Nothing you'll notice."

"What the hell is it?"

The needle withdrew, and I flinched when it left my skin. I twisted around to glare at him.

"Tell me! Did you poison me?"

His lips twitched. The action was alarmingly close to a smile. It was disarming. I hadn't seen him display much emotion at all until this point. Well, except for the moment when he'd shot the loan shark in the head, and when I'd opened the door to the police. He'd been more human in those moments than all the others combined.

"Funny that you think others are the poison and not yourself," he said.

What the hell did that mean?

"No poison . . . Nothing too nefarious. You know those little trackers they put in naughty pets that keep running off?" He moved around my front, taking off the gloves and throwing them toward the trash can with perfect aim.

"You microchipped me like a cat?" I asked, the words sounding hollow.

"Seeing as I don't imagine anyone would take you to a vet's office to have the chip scanned, not quite. I chipped you with something far superior. Don't be thrown by the location. It's the only place we passed with sterile equipment."

"So . . . it's a chip?"

He nodded. "It's a chip, but nothing that exists on the market. This one is special. A GPS that tracks you in real time. The tech isn't used outside the Special Forces at the moment."

"So, how did you get it?"

He shrugged. "Everything has a price."

I shook my head, staring him down. "Not everything. Not people." I didn't know why it felt important to say that right then, but it did. This was a man who followed orders for a paycheck, no matter how dark and vile they were, like kidnapping an innocent woman.

"The fact that you think that confirms how naive you are," he said darkly and jerked his jacket on. "Get up. We're leaving."

"I don't suppose you'll tell me where we're going?"

He started toward the door. To my surprise, he stopped and waited for me and actually answered the question.

"To Casa Nera. It's time for you to meet the King of Atlantic City."

"Renato? He doesn't scare me, just so you know." I followed him out onto the dark street. My neck throbbed a little where he'd injected me. "I knew him when he was younger. He doesn't scare me," I repeated, maybe more for my own reassurance than anything else.

My mercenary just shrugged, his eyes alert and checking every corner.

"Maybe he's not the one you should be worried about."

16

ELIO

I was glad I was wearing black when we walked through the cheap motel I'd been hiding out in near the private airstrip. It concealed the blood just enough not to freak out the bored clerk on duty in the small hours of the night.

Georgia was silent for once. So, that's all it took to shake her confidence. Slaughtering ten men in front of her. Good to know.

We got into the double room, and I locked the door behind us. I'd been keeping a low profile and hiding from the cops for days since Georgia had given them a detailed description of me. Luckily, they seemed to lose interest in both of us when they worked out who the dead body was in Georgia's apartment.

It was no big surprise they'd pulled her building's security detail, as crappy as it was. The LAPD didn't care about the murder of a man like the loan shark who'd broken into Georgia's apartment in the night. They were glad he was dead. One less lowlife to manage on the streets.

Still, I needed to get us out of there. The Ravellis were stepping up their efforts, no doubt seeing how Georgia, their leverage, was about to slip through their fingers.

I moved farther into the room and started to strip down.

"What happens now?" Georgia asked. Her voice was faint. She'd seen a whole lot of nightmarish shit in the last few days, probably more than in her entire life put together.

That wasn't my problem.

"Now we wait while our flight gets rearranged." I pulled my soiled shirt over my head and flung it toward the bathroom.

Georgia was staring at me in alarm. "What are you doing?"

"Taking a shower, what does it look like? What, you need one too?" I turned to her.

Her gaze hit my torso and slid down and around. Thank fuck that I'd only had a couple of tats back in my youth, and now, combined into sleeves like they were, they were pretty indistinguishable.

"Don't tell me you're an environmentalist? You want to save water and shower together?" I stepped closer to her. "Isn't that what all the kids are up to?"

I wasn't quite feeling like myself. I was exhausted, adrenaline dumping out of my system. In the week since I'd been back in contact with this woman, I was feeling more things than I'd allowed myself to feel for over a decade. It was untenable. I felt like a kettle, overfilled and destined to boil over.

Georgia wet her lips, and I couldn't fucking look away.

"We're not kids anymore," she said quietly, her gaze darting around my face.

I knew what she was looking for. She still suspected me of being Elio. Of course she did. She wasn't stupid. Despite the changes in us over the years, her gut told her the truth. But something was throwing her off, maybe even more than the contacts. She'd never imagined that the Elio she'd known could become a man capable of the bloody acts I'd committed tonight. That, more than anything else, told her that her instincts were wrong.

"Hmm, guess not." I turned away and grabbed a fresh towel, heading to the bathroom.

As soon as I was inside, I turned the lock and leaned against the door. I glanced down. I was fucking hard as hell. It wasn't anything unusual to be hard after a tough fight. A celebration of life. Your body urgently demanding you go and pass on your genes immediately, in case next time you don't walk away.

But that wasn't why I was hard right now. There was no point in lying to myself.

I was hard right now because of the woman in the next room and the way she smelled. The way her body fit against mine. The way her lips had shone after she'd licked them.

Fuck.

I turned the shower as cold as it would go and stepped in. My breath left me as the freezing water rained down on me, shocking my system, and I let the sudden drop in temperature cut through my heated thoughts.

I was more than flesh and biology. The dark hell that I'd lived had broken fundamental parts of me, and it had all been because of her.

I placed my hands on the tile and let the water run along the ridges of my cock. My sister wasn't wrong; I did live like a monk. My body was a line I didn't let another human cross. It was the only thing I had left of my own. I had no silence inside my own head, no peace, no place to hide from the memories of war. But my body? That was mine and mine alone.

After Georgia, there had been no one else. I didn't trust another woman to come too close. Lust was a stranger to me, and if it did come, in the night, alone with my memories, I just thought of the terrible things I'd seen, in far-off places. Atrocities. Soul-killing evil.

I'd been in the Esercito Italiano long enough to forget how to want, and then in the Col Moschin long enough to forget I'd ever known desire in the first place.

I hadn't been lying in the club when that woman attempted to hit on me. I wasn't a whole person. I was missing some parts. Pretty important ones.

For the first time in over fourteen years, I felt those parts inside me wake up.

It was unacceptable.

Un-fucking-acceptable.

I lost track of how long I stood under that burning cold, but it wasn't enough to cool the heat slumbering in my soul. The fire that one woman, and one woman alone, had ever managed to rouse.

I had a bad feeling, deep down in my gut, where all my best instincts came from . . .

I was already fucked.

After the shower, I froze out Georgia and her attempts at conversation. I bunked down on the floor near the door, and she lay in the double bed. After a while, despite the stress of the day, I managed to drift off. It was a skill learned in the military. You had to sleep when you had the chance.

In my dreams, I was lost in memories. Sitting in a truck, a second before the convoy is attacked. In a medical tent when the guy you sleep next to is brought in, legs blown away. Watching a target approach a school, ninety-nine percent sure that he's got an explosive on him, waiting for permission to take him out.

I woke with a start, bolting upright in my makeshift bed on the floor, a knife gripped in my hand. My breath was rasping in and out, my body drenched in sweat. So much for the shower. Little by little, the room came into focus. I remembered where I was and who I was with.

Stiffly, I stood and looked over at Georgia, just a shape under the blankets with a dark rope of hair spread against the white pillowcase.

The dreams hadn't been so bad in a long time. Feeling much of anything at all, thanks to this woman, was going to make everything worse. The silent storm inside me, always twisting and turning, threatening to drag me under, might actually get me this time if I couldn't find a way to stop my walls from crumbling. They were there for a reason. To protect my mind. I needed them, and this woman threatened them. I needed to get away from her as quickly as possible.

I sat at the table. I had no gun to clean, so instead I laid out the knife collection I'd managed to accrue since Georgia had run to the cops. Since getting caught with weapons while wanted by the police wasn't the smartest idea, I'd left them at the hotel. Collecting weapons was simply a habit at this point.

I took a soft piece of cloth and started to clean the blades, slowly and methodically. I could be doing anything, as long as it was slow and steady and gave me something else to focus on, but cleaning weapons had become my way of coping with the endless nights.

"What are you doing?" Georgia's voice was rough with sleep.

I tensed. The last thing I wanted was to speak to her right now.

"I said, what are you doing?" she repeated, as if there was any chance I hadn't heard her in the silent room.

She got out of bed and approached the table. A single spotlight shone over it, and she stepped into the light. She had on an oversized T-shirt and nothing else. Her dark hair was pulled into a long braid that snaked over her shoulder. Her face was bare and effortlessly beautiful.

Just like that, I was rock-hard again, putting all that time under cold water to waste.

"I heard you. Go back to bed." My tone was not welcoming.

Despite that, Georgia perched on a chair and reached out to touch one of the knives. I caught her wrist tightly, stopping her motion.

I looked at her for so long, she shifted impatiently and raised an eyebrow.

"Ever killed anybody with a knife?" she asked, her hand twisting in my grip.

"Yes."

She swallowed hard, her slender throat bobbing. A sure sign that she wasn't as composed as she pretended. Her pulse jumped beneath my fingers.

"Were you in the military?" she asked.

I didn't answer. I had no intention of taking this stroll down memory lane. Not when the entire way was littered with mines that could end me.

"I mean, clearly you have been trained professionally. What do you do for Renato? Are you a hit man . . . or maybe a bodyguard?" she continued. "Hello? I'm talking to you."

"Oh, are you? I thought you just loved to hear yourself speak."

Her mouth hung open; she was outraged. "Well, it's polite to make small talk, you know. It's an asshole move to make others fill the silence all the time."

"I'm not making you fill the silence. And if you think calling me an asshole will hurt my feelings, I can assure you, I've been called much worse."

She snorted softly. "I'll bet."

I shook my head, and the movement seemed to catch her attention.

"What is it?" she asked.

"Just . . . you seem awfully curious about a man like me. I can only warn you, that is a very bad idea. Curiosity killed the little mouse, didn't you hear?"

She sighed. "I told you not to call me that, and I can't help it if I'm curious." She was studying the side of my face intently.

"I'm not him," I told her, once again, and dropped her arm.

She nodded. "I'm starting to see that. He'd never be a man like you."

I set down the knife I was working on and looked at her, wiping my hands on the rag.

"Considering your terrible taste in men, I think it's for the best," I told her.

Her hands balled into fists. "My what? I don't have terrible taste in men."

"Of course you do. You didn't know what was really going on with your dad. You married a man who started out rich but was so piss-poor at managing himself and his money that he left his widow at the mercy of a loan shark, living one step above a cardboard box on the street. You have poor taste in men."

Her eyes grew glassy, like my words had actually upset her. The look bothered me.

"Yeah, well, you think that, and you don't even know about my first boyfriend . . . the one who asked me to marry him and told me he loved me, just to run away. The one who broke my heart. If you knew about him, then you'd really know how shitty my taste in men was," she murmured.

Venom laced her tone, but her words, her words made me see red.

I tightened my hand on the knife I was holding, the dull edge biting into my palm as I squeezed it. She was trying to get a rise out of me. She wanted me to give myself away. I wouldn't give her the satisfaction.

"He sounds like a real monster," I ground out.

She stared at me for a long time. She seemed vaguely disappointed.

"He wasn't anything as grand as that. He was just a man . . . a thief. A grifter. And none of that would have mattered . . . except that he never loved me like I loved him. That's the truth."

Like fuck it is.

The words to disagree with every falsehood she'd just uttered consumed me. I burned with the need to remind her who had been the one lacking love, but that was dangerous. Lifting the lid on the past wasn't something I'd ever allowed myself to do. I wasn't changing that now.

I stood suddenly, the chair scraping back, and her eyes widened. I was hard as hell, my cock straining up my belly, and the whole fucking room smelled like her skin. I couldn't stand it. She needed to get back to fucking bed, and there was only one way I could think of to convince her of that fact.

"If you're cold and lonely in bed, just ask me to join you, Signora Conti. Don't go about making meaningless small talk in the middle of the night. You wouldn't be the first desperate housewife to want to fuck a monster."

Her eyebrows flew up, and red tinged her cheeks. Her mouth fell open, incredulous and outraged. I enjoyed her anger.

"You think I want you?" she managed to get out. "I don't!"

I glanced down at her hard nipples meaningfully. "Tell your tits that."

My hand was reaching toward her chest before I could stop myself. Her soft breast filled my palm and sent a jolt of electricity through me. I burned.

When she didn't stop me, I thumbed her nipple, the hard bud begging for more.

"Should we check how wet you are—"

Her slap took me off guard. Just another reminder of how far I'd fallen in only a week. I didn't touch unwilling women. I didn't touch women at all. I hadn't felt compelled to in so long . . . I'd thought that part of my life was over. And then in walked Georgia, just as fucking infuriating as always, and set my blood on fire.

Anger at myself, and her, and this whole fucking situation burst through me. I yanked her close, holding her in place with one hand on the back of her head, fist in her hair, and the other on the small of her back.

Her hot breath hit my neck as I tilted her head back so I could look her in her eyes. Those mesmerizing eyes that I'd once lost myself in.

I wasn't sure, right then, if I'd ever found myself again. Maybe she'd kept the best parts of me all along.

"Do you have a death wish, Signora Conti? Or just really poor survival instincts? I'm surprised you've made it this long."

"You don't know me or what I've survived," she spit at me, anger making her resemble a warrior goddess.

She was pressed against me, her soft belly surrounding my hard-on. She swayed, and the pressure nearly undid me.

"I've survived worse than you. I've lost everything before . . . so you don't scare me," she breathed. Her gaze ran over my face and dipped to my lips.

I've lost everything before. What the fuck was she talking about? She had to mean her late husband. She'd lost everything when that thieving *bastardo* Conti had died.

"Yet," I said and smoothed her hair back gently.

The unexpected softness of the touch seemed to shake her more than anything. I rubbed my thumb lightly across her parted lips, and her breath hitched.

"You don't fear me—yet . . . We've got time for that, Georgia, all the time in the world."

I slid my hand down her chest and found her hard nipple again. A murmur of pleasure left her as my finger brushed the hard point. *Interesting.* Then I pinched it hard, and her eyes snapped back into focus.

"Until then . . . be a good girl and you might survive this."

"Fuck you," she rasped at me, pulling her head from my grip.

"Again, just say the word, Signora Conti . . . I'll fuck your husband's memory right out of you."

She gasped at me and then turned on her heel and stormed back to bed. I'd finally shocked her into leaving me the hell alone.

I sat heavily, my cock throbbing with blood, and I did my best to ignore it. I picked up my cloth and continued to clean, though my thoughts were consumed by her. As insidious as a poisoned kiss, the weakness she created was ebbing into my system, infecting me with every breath.

I had to stay away from her. It was the only way. The sooner she was married off, the better. I held the knife too hard. So hard, the blade split my skin. Ideally, I'd love to punch something. Maybe a wall, or a mirror, but that would give away too much.

I couldn't let her see the wreckage inside me. I just couldn't. I just had to make it until the wedding. If I could make it until the wedding, she'd be someone else's problem.

Right. I couldn't even convince myself of that.

17

ELIO

THEN

There are moments so massive, they set the entire direction of your life. I'd arrived in Castel Amaro a drifter. Untethered from connections or meaning. I had no parents, my sister was being looked after by family more capable than me, and I . . . I was starving, barely able to take care of myself.

Then, I'd met her.

Mia ragione.

My reason for being.

My country mouse.

With her beside me, I was stronger than I'd ever been. I was more certain of my path. I had purpose. My life had meaning.

It was time to give Alfredo Bellisario the chance to give his blessing.

I knocked on the door to his office and waited. He took his time to call for me to enter.

I went in and shut the door behind me. The late afternoon sun blazed behind thick shutters shrouding the room in darkness.

"Santori? What is it?" he asked, irritably glancing up from his desk.

"I have to speak to you about something important, sir."

I unclenched my hands and took a deep breath.

"What is it? I don't have all day. You want to be released from your debt?" Alfredo eyed me up and down, measuring my worth.

I shook my head. "No, sir. It's nothing to do with work. I need to speak to you about Georgia."

He sat back now, giving me his full attention.

"What about Georgia?" he demanded.

"There is no way to sugarcoat what I have to say, so I'll say it directly. I'm in love with her, and she's in love with me. I want to marry her. I've asked her, and she's said yes."

Silence surged in after my words died, so thick I could have choked on it.

"Is this a joke?" Alfredo said.

"No, sir. It's no joke. I'm in love with your daughter, and we're going to spend the rest of our lives together."

Alfredo was silent. He slowly got to his feet and rounded his desk.

He studied me. "I can't tell if you're really being serious or if you think this is funny."

"I'm deadly serious. She has agreed to marry me."

Alfredo flinched, his face paling.

"I understand this shock. I know I'm not the man you pictured for your daughter, but I'm the man she chose for herself. I know I don't have much . . . now, but I vow I will find a way to give her the life she deserves."

Alfredo looked away from me, his hands working to hold on to the edge of his desk.

"She loves you?" he said finally, his voice rough.

"She does," I confirmed.

He was staring at a picture on the wall of him and Georgia eating ice cream. She was a few years younger than she was now.

"Georgia has always done whatever she wanted to. She's always rebelled against my rules and plans for her . . . I see that, even now, she knows her own mind and isn't afraid to make her demands." He turned back to me. "Well, what are you going to do to be worthy of her?"

I blinked. This wasn't going like I'd thought it would. I'd thought he'd beat me, at the very least.

"Whatever I have to," I said, my response immediate.

"*Whatever I have to,*" he repeated. "I seem to remember a promise just like that when I gave you a job instead of letting you go to jail."

"I'll apologize for going behind your back, sir, but not for loving your daughter. I can't apologize for that," I said quietly.

He tilted his head to the side. "So, you have a code of some sort, then? I could be forgiven for thinking that you didn't. The boy who tried to steal, got caught, and was given a lenient sentence . . . only to seduce the daughter of the man who saved him."

"I didn't set out to seduce her. We fell in love."

Alfredo gave a heavy sigh. "I suppose I should just be thankful that you want to marry her. Too many men don't like to take responsibility these days . . . they don't want a wife at your age."

It seemed like a low bar to pass under, but I wasn't going to say anything to discourage him from accepting the idea.

"What really bothers me, however, is the disrespect. If you love a woman, you should respect her father."

"I do respect you, Procuratore."

"Why don't you show me just how much? I don't want a son-in-law who isn't going to work in the best interests of my family . . . I need to trust you."

"I'll do anything," I said, another immediate response.

"I've heard that before." Bellisario stood. "I'll think about what you can do for me to prove yourself. Georgia wouldn't like it if we were at odds, so let's try to get along." Alfredo looked at me. "I've never had a son. I've always hoped that the man who Georgia picked could feel like that to me . . ."

"I'd like that, too, Procuratore."

He nodded slowly. "Let me think about all of this. Go back to work, and I'll be in touch when I think of a way we can become closer . . . build trust."

I headed for the door. My palms were sweating, and I needed to drink about a gallon of water, but I'd done it, and I was leaving intact. It was more than I'd ever hoped for.

"Oh, and Santori?" Alfredo called.

I stopped on the threshold of the doorway.

"Georgia's fabric delivery came in, and someone collected it in error. She needs to pick it up, so let her know. I'm afraid our little meeting has set my schedule back today."

"I'll go and get it, Procuratore," I said, closing the door and walking down the hall, feeling like I'd just survived a firing squad.

I decided to go and get Georgia's delivery before I went back to work. I needed to make Alfredo like me. It wasn't for me. I couldn't have cared less what the man thought of me, but Georgia cared, so that meant I cared. I'd told her I would take care of everything, and I meant to.

I cut through town, a whistle on my lips and a spring in my step. Swinging by the post office, I found out that the delivery had gone to the De Sanctis house by accident. The walk to the De Sanctis summer estate was a good five miles. I didn't see a single car going in my direction, so I was stuck walking. The day was warm, and my mood was light. I was marrying Georgia. The very idea thrilled me every time I thought of it. I was marrying the love of my life.

For a gutter rat from Napoli, it was a good ending, after all. Who'd have thought?

I made it to the estate and went in the side entrance. I was used to using it to run messages between the houses. I'd been working for Alfredo Bellisario nearly half a year, and I'd gotten to know more about the family who summered in Castel Amaro. Salvatore De Sanctis was Mafia royalty. Renato, the heir, lived in America some of the time and occasionally came here to work under his uncle.

I headed through the gardens, toward the kitchens.

There was security everywhere, from the black-suited guards who patrolled the gardens to the CCTV cameras sitting on top of every wall.

I was a familiar face to the security detail at this point and was allowed in. When I stepped into the kitchen, I found it deserted, a rare occurrence.

"Ah, Ms. Bellisario's things are by the fridge," a harried staff member called to me as he bustled through the room. "And take the bag, too, it's from Mr. De Sanctis for Procuratore Bellisario. You'll save me a trip later."

I found the bag and package easily enough. I'd moved quite a few packages between the two houses. I never peeked to see what was in them. De Sanctis business wasn't something I wanted to get caught up in. I was just a messenger.

I grabbed the box and the leather duffel and made for the door.

I headed back through the gardens and out onto the road. It was dusty, and the hills around us were sun-bleached and yellow. In the far distance, I could see the sparkling blue of the Mediterranean. Maybe I'd take Georgia to the beach. If I worked hard this year and proved myself to Alfredo, maybe I could get a real job in town and apply to get my sister back. We could all live together in a little house overlooking the sea.

I was halfway back to town when the blue lights appeared.

Carabinieri cars, speeding down the road toward me. I stepped to the side and waited for them to pass. The leather duffel suddenly felt as heavy as a tombstone slung over my shoulder. I was being paranoid. I'd seen how the police bent over backward for the infamous Mafia family. No one would investigate Bellisario or De Sanctis here. They were gods.

The cars got closer. Sweat slicked the back of my neck, a sudden and terrible foreboding hitting me in the gut. *Are they angling toward me?*

The cars pulled to a stop right in front of me, gravel and dust flying through the air.

The cops opened the doors, and the black metal of their handguns glinted in the sun.

"Put your hands up!" The shouts came from all directions.

"I'm just doing a favor for the *procuratore*!" I called, a certainty landing in my heart that I'd just fucked up.

"Hands up! Or I'll shoot, kid, I swear I will."

The chief of police was staring at me, a wild light in his eyes, and I knew right then and there that he was telling the truth. He would shoot. I'd walked into this, and if I wanted to get out of it, I needed to do what they said.

I dropped the bag and the package and put my hands up. Officers swarmed me.

"Okay, okay! Here, I'm complying," I called, then a sharp pain to the back of my head sent a veil of darkness rushing in front of my eyes.

The world fell away.

I woke up an unknowable time later to a light swaying feeling. A van hurtling over rocks? I sat and groaned, my head screaming at me. *Where am I?*

It was dark inside whatever kind of vehicle I was in. Old blood sat on my tongue, and my head was splitting. I swung back and forth, dizzy.

Before I could do more than try to get my bearings, the van stopped, and the doors slid open. Men in uniforms grabbed my arms and hauled me out. The door shut behind me, and they dragged me through metal gates and past security doors. The buzzes of the armed doors opening ricocheted around my head.

Where the hell are they taking me?

It was dark, so it wasn't easy to see, but bit by bit, as they hauled me down a long, sterile-looking hallway, I got it.

Prison. This was a prison.

They shoved me into a room with a metal table and handcuffed me to one of its legs, so I had no choice but to kneel beside it.

I had no time to process what was going on. The guards left, and a man entered.

Alfredo Bellisario.

"Well, well, Santori, seems like you need a lawyer, or should I call a public defender for you?"

I stared at him. "What are you talking about?"

"You know exactly what I'm talking about."

"I only took your things . . . I moved them according to your instructions!" I shouted.

He chuckled. "Do you really think you're here because of some drugs and money in a bag? You're here because you didn't listen to me. I told you to stay away from my daughter. You didn't. Now you'll face the consequences."

I shook my head. "You can't do this. I haven't done anything wrong."

"Oh, but you have. You have trespassed on that which was mine . . . my daughter. You're lucky to be alive. Honestly, the only reason you are is because I want to see you rot in here . . . I want to watch it break you."

"You can't do this," I repeated numbly, even knowing that those words were a lie.

A man like Bellisario in a place like this could do whatever he wanted. The guards would be in his pocket, and the cops, too. The judges, the whole rotten system. They could make a man disappear without killing him.

"Of course I can."

"Georgia won't accept it. She'll try to find me."

"Don't you worry about Georgia. I'll look after my daughter. You, enjoy the life you chose." He stood and nodded at the one-way glass.

Guards crowded into the room.

Bellisario slipped his jacket on. "Beat him, just enough . . . pissing blood should do it, for today. Repeat tomorrow and the next day."

"Yes, Signore Procuratore," the head guard said quickly and moved into the room as Bellisario walked out.

"Enjoy the hell of your own making, Santori."

18

GEORGIA

NOW

I woke with a start in the morning, roughly shaken awake by a huge tattooed and unfeeling hand.

"Get dressed."

I rubbed my scratchy eyes and sat up. My mercenary was already dressed in his usual uniform of unrelenting black. With his dark, dangerous good looks, he made his practical, utilitarian clothes appear straight off the runway. He had packed his things up and was now standing and staring out the window. The memory of last night slammed into me. Oh God. When he'd touched me . . . Damn me to hell. It had been hot. It had been the hottest thing I'd felt in well over a decade. *Pathetic, Georgia.*

I avoided eye contact with my mercenary, sure that he'd be able to see the shame on my face. I glanced around for my clothes . . . and froze.

There, at the end of the bed, was my bag from my apartment. The one I'd packed my meager meaningful belongings into.

I eyed my captor, studying his sharp profile in the morning light. He'd carried my things with him, on the run from the cops, even when I'd just escaped him. I didn't know how I felt about that. I didn't want to feel much of anything about it, but I couldn't lie to myself. I did have feelings about it.

"I said, get dressed."

"Where are my clothes from yesterday?" I pushed my confusing feelings out of my head.

"They're too bloody. Wear something else."

I got up and unzipped my bag. Everything was there, and it seemed untouched.

"There is one tiny problem with that," I revealed.

He turned to me, folding his arms over his chest.

I pulled out my half-finished dresses from the bag. I had a pair of flat sandals at the bottom, thank God, and my mementos box, but other than that, the bag was full of my half-finished designs. The hopes and dreams I hadn't quite given up on.

"This is all I have to wear." I held up a sliver of emerald satin.

"Wear it, then," my mercenary stated flatly.

"It's not . . . finished," I mumbled, feeling more and more like an idiot with every word. "In my defense, you said to grab the things I really needed because I was never coming back to my apartment, and then you gave me this tiny bag. Was I supposed to leave important things just to fit clean underwear and jeans? I didn't expect to get my outfit so dirty . . ."

I trailed off because he'd reached into his bag and pulled out a pair of black utility pants and a black long-sleeved shirt. He tossed them to me.

"Get dressed. We're leaving in thirty minutes."

Well, okay then.

We were taking a plane.

Of course we were. I had to have known that in some repressed corner of my brain, but I'd blocked it out. My psyche couldn't handle one more stress.

I hated flying. I'd done it exactly one time in my life, from Naples to L.A. I'd had a panic attack at the thought of leaving Naples that I'd never forget. It felt like dying. We'd lifted into the air, and I'd forcibly ripped free from my ties to the world. I was untethered. Lost. Objectively, it was a terrifying experience.

I chewed my lip as I took the clothes my mercenary had given me and changed. My heart was beating too fast, and I felt hot all over. A panic attack lurked just on the edges of my mind.

He watched me struggle to breathe.

"What is it?" he snapped at me, always too aware of what I was feeling.

"Nothing," I snapped right back. I knew I shouldn't expect sympathy from him, or consideration. Most of all, I didn't want to show him another weakness. Georgia with her crappy apartment and inherited debt and, oh yeah, her shitty father who had put her in danger. Oh, and she got turned on by being ordered around and manhandled. I couldn't add one more weakness to that list. I couldn't stand it.

I balled my hands into fists and got on with it. This was my life now. It rested in this man's tattooed, callused, uncaring hands.

Predictably, the clothes were huge and swamped me completely. I tucked the overly long shirt into the huge pants to try and make the waist a little tighter, then slipped on my flip-flops and shouldered my precious backpack.

My mercenary waited impassively at the door, and we left without a word. Half an hour later, we were boarding the private plane. It was so much smaller than a regular plane. My heart pounded even harder, and sweat drenched my face. It was tough to pull air into my lungs.

"Go." My mercenary tapped me from behind when I hesitated at the foot of the ladder. Feeling like I was going to the electric chair, I slowly ascended the steps.

I kind of was, in a way. My father had sacrificed my safety for his life and comfort. I was being taken to one of the most ruthless kingpins on the East Coast. It didn't matter that I'd known Renato when we were young. This was just business to him. A loose end. That was what my life had amounted to. Someone else's inconvenient loose end.

The plane was luxurious, from the soft leather seats to the shiny walnut paneling and even the spa-like scents in the air, but I barely registered it. Heat was building in my chest like a volcano in a bottle.

"Sit," my mercenary ordered, again tapping my shoulder. He forced me into a solitary seat at the front of the plane.

"Aren't I sitting with you?" I asked desperately. It was an effort to get the words out. Why I even wanted to sit with him, I had no idea, except I'd be more distracted with hating the man next to me than the plane taking off.

He didn't reply.

"I can't sit on my own!" I called to his departing back.

He didn't even hesitate to leave me. He just walked away. This frightening motherfucker who didn't even seem to sleep or eat. This monster who'd stolen my life and saved it at the same time, the one who'd threatened me at gunpoint and had hauled my box of mementos all over the city while evading the cops instead of dumping it.

The engine of the plane gunned beneath us, the drone of it cutting through my reason and breaking my patience.

The tissue box was in my hand before I could stop myself. I hurled it at my mercenary's departing back. In that second, I was so tired of it all. Tired of being dragged around, threatened, nearly killed. I couldn't stand it one more second.

The metal tissue box bounced off my mercenary's back. For once in my life, I had good aim.

He stopped. The flight attendant hovering near us covered her mouth with a dramatic intake of breath.

"I said, I can't sit on my own," I stated, my voice wavering madly. That hot feeling in my chest was pushing to come out. It wouldn't be contained.

"Take off as soon as you can," my mercenary instructed the flight attendant.

She hurried out of sight. Slowly, oh so slowly, my mercenary turned.

From behind us, the sound of the heavy door shutting thudded through the air. I swallowed down a feeling of rising nausea. *Oh God, this is it. We are locked in this metal box.* I couldn't breathe.

My mercenary approached, filled with lethal grace and menace. I couldn't keep a lid on my fears anymore. My breath was growing tighter and tighter. I was standing on a chair, a noose tied around my neck, and that, too, was getting tighter.

"What is wrong with you?" He stood in front of me. The back of his hand touched my forehead. "You're sweating."

A reluctant dagger of a chuckle left my tortured lungs. "Yeah, losing your mind isn't pretty, who'd have thought?"

"Losing what?" he repeated as the plane jolted into motion.

A small scream left me that I wasn't proud of, but I had no time to be embarrassed in front of this man. Holding the tatters of my mind together felt too difficult.

"Georgia! I'm talking to you," my mercenary demanded.

"I don't care!" I blurted out, caving in on myself. Fear was making it hard to speak. "I can't do this! I can't do any of this! Just kill me," I panted.

The idea suddenly made so much sense. I put my trembling hands on his chest, gripping his T-shirt and holding him close. I looked up into his dark eyes.

"Just kill me. Make it quick. It'll make both our lives easier.

Please, stop dragging it out like this. Just do it. I want you to do it," I pleaded. I wet my dry lips. It felt like my skin was going to crawl off.

The plane had started taxiing now, picking up speed. We swayed together.

"Get a grip," my mercenary ordered as I started to wheeze.

I really couldn't breathe. Maybe I didn't need him to kill me; I could do that all on my own.

One moment I was dizzy, reaching for air that wasn't there, and the next I was in his arms.

He carried me through the plane. My vision was going dark at the edges. I could see the tattooed skin of his neck where the design disappeared beneath the beard that perfectly lined the lower half of his face . . . it wasn't the worst sight to see before you died.

Distantly, a door clicked open, and then I was falling . . . landing on something soft . . . the movement jolted the remaining breath from my body. The bedroom was full of light from the doorway, but my mercenary kicked the door shut behind us, shrouding us in darkness apart from a small bedside lamp. I lay on the bed, crippled with panic. My lungs were cramped; they weren't getting enough air in.

My mercenary straddled me on the bed, his knees bracketing my hips. His rough hands cupped my face.

"Breathe, Georgia! Calm the fuck down."

I shook my head from side to side, white spots dancing in front of my eyes. I was going under. Drowning. I clawed at his arms, trying to hold on to something, but I couldn't. I just couldn't.

"*Merda*. I warned you not to test me one more time or I'd put you across my knee and turn your ass so red you wouldn't be able to sit for a week. Maybe that's exactly what you need right now." His growl seemed to come from far away.

Then he was turning me over, my face pressing into the bed and his heavy weight holding my thighs in place.

His hand smacked down hard on my ass cheek.

Ouch.

He matched the blow on the other side.

Fuck. That really hurt. I sucked in a breath.

"Did that get your attention?" he murmured and smacked me again.

The feeling of it radiated through me. It hurt like hell, and it was embarrassing. Being immobile and smacked. It was humiliating . . . Anger flowed across my panic.

"You asshole!" I wheezed, outraged.

He chuckled darkly. "Oh, look who can speak again. I guess that means my treatment is working."

I must have been the biggest idiot in the world, because I could've sworn that I'd heard a note of relief in his tone. Then his fingers closed around the waistband of my too-large pants and tugged them down.

"Hey!" I hissed at him, warmth beating in my already overheated face.

He was quiet for a second. "No panties is a choice."

"No, it's not. You didn't exactly give me any to borrow, did you, dickhead?" I shot out, my lungs loosening with every word.

Another sharp spank hit my ass cheek, sending stinging pain through me. The smack on the bare ass was something else.

"If you think it'll save your ass from me, you're wrong."

"God, I want to kill you," I ground out.

His smack moved to the other cheek, and everything inside me clenched. I felt so powerless. My hands were trapped beneath me, I was facedown, he was holding me utterly prone. I couldn't do anything to stop him. I couldn't fight him. I couldn't even try. The feeling of complete powerlessness built and built, while my mercenary spanked me again on the other side, his fingers dangerously close to my cleft.

"The feeling is entirely mutual, Mrs. Conti," he murmured. "Now, breathe."

I drew a ragged breath into my cramped lungs, the rush of oxygen making my head spin. *Whoa.* I'd gone too far into that panic attack. Passing out had only been seconds away.

My eyes felt wet. The tears stung my raw-feeling cheeks and sank into the bedspread.

His hand rained a smack down on my ass, and the feeling sent ripples of embarrassment through me. Shame, humiliation . . . you name it, I was feeling it.

"There you go, breathe again, nice and deeply. Let me feel it," my mercenary instructed. He put a hand high on my back. "Push my hand up with air. Fill your lungs right up," he commanded.

I found myself obeying, even though my whole being longed to defy this man. Tension started to seep out of me.

"Good girl. That's my good girl . . . breathe and calm the fuck down. You're safe here with me. You're not going anywhere. Not even God himself can take you from this plane or me. You can't change anything . . . all you have to do is accept it."

There was a loud sound beneath us. The wheels folding in? I shuddered again, my chest threatening to close once more.

His hand smacked me again, but it felt different. Softer, somehow. His fingers lingered after, his caress feeling indecently hot on my skin, like he could singe me with his very touch. My mind rebelled against the heat working through my blood. His hand was too damn close to my pussy, and God help me, I was getting turned on. I couldn't help it. It was the position, the powerlessness, the way his hands were so confident and masterful, like he knew exactly how to touch me. Like he knew my body better than I did.

"I accept that you're an asshole," I muttered into the pillow, my tears still falling. I wasn't crying, it was simply a tension release, but fuck, it felt good. It felt good to fight with all my strength and cry and push as hard as I could and then let it all go.

His hand moved over my ass, not smacking now, just feeling the skin.

"I think you need to accept a lot more than that if you want to save this precious ass of yours. It's already so perfectly pink . . . My handprint on your ass really suits you, Signora Conti."

"Stop calling me that!" I protested.

His finger made a long line down one cheek, then he slapped my ass, the weight of the cheek jiggling.

"Why? You don't like being reminded of your dearly departed husband when you're facedown, ass-up on another man's knee? Does it confuse your sweet memories of his touch?"

I snorted before I could stop myself. "My husband never touched my ass."

My mercenary's hand paused its sweet torture.

"Is that right?" he mused.

I gasped at a sharp pinch.

"Don't lie to me."

"I'm not!" I ground out.

His hand smoothed a circle over the place he'd pinched, sending pleasure spiraling through the pain. Somehow, it felt even better, like the pinch had woken up my nerve endings and heightened their sensitivity.

"I don't believe your loving husband would neglect to give his wife something she so clearly enjoyed."

"Enjoyed?" I squeaked, feeling called-out as hell. How did he know how good it felt? I attempted to sit up, unable to bear the thought of him knowing how his touch, delivered as a punishment, was turning me on.

"Yes, *cara*. Enjoyed . . ." he growled at me, then sent shock through my system as his fingers pulled apart my ass cheeks, exposing my most private places to him.

"What the hell?" I started but forgot my words.

His finger swiped down my ass and over my front entrance.

"You think I don't know how wet you are?" he asked in a quietly dangerous voice.

Before I could stop him, he gathered my hair in his other hand, forced my head back, and put that wet finger to my lips.

It sank inside, and I tasted myself on his skin. Musky and desperate.

"I can *smell* you, Georgia."

His words sent utter humiliation over me, and something else, so hot and wrong that I didn't know what to do with that feeling.

His hands traveled back down my body, and he parted my cheeks again.

"So, forgive me if I don't believe your husband neglected to give you what you so clearly like . . ."

He again stroked a finger down my cleft, and I shuddered. It felt too good. I was warm and empty, my panic gone, my muscles slack, and there was no escape. No escape from this man or the fate he was delivering me to.

"I warned you not to lie to me," my mercenary was saying. "I threatened to turn your ass red, but I had no idea how poor a punishment it would be, since you've enjoyed it so much. I'll have to think of something else . . . if you continue to lie to me."

I flushed, heat rolling through me. I felt like a beacon on a hill, burning hard, nowhere to hide, signaling that danger was closing in . . . *Run* . . . but it was too late.

I had no power here. I had no control. There was no escape.

There was only surrender.

"I'm not lying," I ground out, unsure why, exactly, I cared if he believed me or not. Maybe it was the principle of it, or I just didn't want this fucker to win again.

"Very well, in that case, you leave me no choice but to punish you for lying. Don't forget, you brought this on yourself," he murmured.

Heat dripped through me, lined with a sparking edge of fear.

"Try to not enjoy it too much . . . it is a punishment, after all."

His softly mocking tone sent that now-familiar heat of shame through me. There was no pretending. He knew this was turning me on. He knew how my body reached for his rough touch, even as my mind rebelled.

His wet fingertip traced up from my pussy to my asshole and circled it. I clenched down hard, trying to delay the inevitable, but there was no escape when he pressed his finger inside.

I cried out, jerking against him.

"Shhh, Signora Conti. Take your punishment well, and I'll give you a treat after."

"Fuck you," I spat.

My nerves lit up with pleasure and pain, a mesmerizing combination, as he eased his finger deeper into my ass. My cheeks were still stinging, my pussy was wet as hell and desperate for his touch, and my ass was gripping his finger tightly.

"No. Fuck you, Georgia. Fuck you and your perfect little asshole, and your fucking gorgeous pink ass."

His deep voice sent my eyes drifting closed, raking over my nerves, and firing a shudder through me.

"You have no control here. You have no say . . . I'm in charge. So, you might as well let go."

His finger fucked gently into my ass, and the pain fell away, that tight ring of muscle stretching just enough to take him. It felt unbelievably good. Wrong and taboo and fucking weird . . . and so fucking good.

I felt the second my mind decided to follow his confident orders. I felt the moment when the stresses and worries of the past week—and fourteen years—fell from my shoulders and I let go.

Surrender was sweeter than I'd ever imagined. I melted into a boneless mass underneath him. There was nothing in the world but the weight of him and the feeling of his finger probing my ass, sending pleasure spiraling through me.

He pulled his finger back, only leaving the tip inside, and I found myself pushing back into him, sending his finger deeper again.

That sealed it. I had fallen into ruin, and he knew it.

His other hand gripped my ass, spreading my cheeks apart again, while his finger pumped deep inside me.

He was watching his finger fuck my ass. I moaned, the thought somehow as hot as the act.

"Tell me the truth . . . did you let that man you married touch you like this?" he asked.

I shook my head, lost in the sensations.

"No. Never. Only you," I panted out. Could I come like this? I could. I knew it in a second. I hadn't been touched by anyone but myself in so long, I was going to come harder than I'd ever come before. And my mercenary was going to see it. Shame threatened to surface but dissipated. There was no shame in surrender.

"I almost believe you," he murmured, sliding his thumb over my pussy, pushing inside.

I gasped, my back arching as he started to fuck my ass and my pussy at the same time.

His rhythm was intoxicating; wherever I needed him, his touch was there. I couldn't control where he went, how fast, or how hard, and that undid me. I rose so fast, it would have been embarrassing if there'd been any space for that emotion in that perfect place.

I felt the peak rushing in. Was it obvious how long it had been since I'd last been touched? Could he see? I was humping his hand now, grinding my clit against his legs.

"Come for me, Georgia. Come with my fingers in your cunt and your ass." He sounded pained, like a man being tortured, stretched tight on the rack. His voice dropped to nearly a whisper. "Come for me and know that this ass is mine now, and only mine."

I couldn't be sure if those were really his words. They were too soft, and I was too lost in the pleasure streaking through me, racing on and on, reaching up and up until I couldn't bear it any longer.

The world exploded around me, and I came.

19

ELIO

I tore my hands from Georgia just as her cunt stopped gripping my fingers like a vise. I turned away, ripping open the door and leaving her there, red-cheeked, the bedsheets wet beneath her.

I couldn't take another fucking second of touching her. I was going to lose it, and I couldn't let her see. I slammed into the bathroom and locked the door. I leaned against it. The fingers that had been in her cunt screamed at me. I could still feel her wetness on me.

My other hand worked my pants down and pulled my cock out. I slid those slick fingers into my mouth and tasted her cunt for the first time in fourteen years.

Precum welled from my tip. I gripped my cock hard and pumped it furiously. I didn't need any slow warm-up. I was going to come, and it had taken every inch of discipline I had in me to stop myself from pulling my fingers from her plump, ripe cunt and forcing my cock in instead. She wouldn't even have had to move. She'd been perfect there, ass in the air, rosy from my spanks, her delicious hole calling to me.

She wanted me.

My *topolina* still wanted me.

I stepped to the sink. My balls drew up, the taste of Georgia in my mouth and the vision of her fucking my hand too much.

I came hard, jet after jet of cum striping the sink, the mirror, my soul.

Slowly, my senses rushed back. I caught sight of myself. My eyes were wild, contacts luckily still in place. My face was flushed and my clothes rumpled. My cock was red-tipped and wet. I looked unmade.

I was a fucking wreck. What the hell had I just done? Distracted her from her flying phobia by spanking her . . . it was already a stretch. Then I'd fingered her ass, made her come, and followed it up with this embarrassing display of weakness, blowing my load alone in the bathroom.

Hiding.

Fucking hell. I was losing it. I'd already lost it. Everything I'd worked hard to build inside myself. High fortress walls and a facade that wouldn't crack. The comforting numbness of winter in my chest, the chill keeping feelings at bay . . . it was crumbling.

Anger filled me, a hot and violent sensation. Fury at her, and at myself, and at all the years that had passed between us. Anger at her father, and the De Sanctis family, and everyone who'd been involved in the sorry excuse of a life I'd led.

Before I knew it, the anger pulsed outward, and my fist was flying at the mirror. It cracked hard, the glass splintering into pieces and splitting open my knuckles. The warm, comforting pain was a welcome distraction from the situation I was in. I didn't want to see my reflection. I couldn't meet the man in the mirror's eyes.

I stepped back and flexed my hand. Blood ran down my fingers and dripped onto the floor.

Blood and cum, failure, anger and violence so thick it suffocated me.

That was the ugly mess of being a person who felt too much. Of being the man she'd left behind.

I couldn't be him again. I wouldn't survive it. Soon, she'd be gone. Married to Jimmy De Luca. Just the thought of Jimmy touching her like I'd just done had me reaching for a shard of glass. I gripped it hard, and the pain sliced through that emotion. Georgia equaled pain. If I had to train my body like a fucking hound, I'd manage it. I was stronger than the frail object in my chest that used to beat. I didn't need it. I wouldn't be its bitch.

Gathering my composure, I slowly and methodically cleaned the bathroom, and then taped my cuts up with some bandages from the medical kit stowed in a cupboard.

Then I stepped out. She'd pulled herself together as well and was sitting in the isolated chair I'd attempted to put her in at the beginning of the flight. Looked like she'd changed her mind about wanting to sit with me. I ignored the sting of that simple gesture. *Good.* She should stay away. It was for the best, for both of us.

The rest of the flight passed in a blur. I fell asleep, an uncommon occurrence for me outside my room, or pretty much anywhere these days.

Feeling so much was fucking exhausting.

Remember the mission, Santori.

By the time we got to New Jersey, I was calm, collected, and I'd dusted off the mask I'd taken years to develop. *No. Never. Only you.*

Her words were sugar-laced poison. I wasn't biting. She was a liar. A performer. I wouldn't fall under her spell again.

We made our way from the private airstrip to Casa Nera in an armored car. It was a relief to be surrounded by my men, trained to my exacting standards, heading to a secure compound I had designed. Casa Nera was the seat of De Sanctis power in New Jersey. There was no safer place to be for the girl who had suddenly become important to dangerous people.

She matched my silence all the way into the compound. We didn't talk about the fact that I'd just made her come so hard she'd soaked through the mattress beneath her. I didn't let myself think about it. I didn't let myself think about it the whole drive home.

We drew up outside the main house, a Gothic-style rambling mansion, and the car door opened.

"Well, you've finally arrived," a familiar voice said from just outside the car.

Holy fuck, today had been a long day—and it was about to get longer.

I nodded to our driver, one of my best and brightest trainees, and got out of the car, waiting for Georgia to follow.

Jimmy De Luca stood on the gravel, wreathed in smiles. So, someone had already heard that they were getting married, it seemed. Jimmy appeared to have no objections. He stepped back and watched Georgia get out of the car and gave a loud, vulgar whistle. I shot him a deadly glare, and he snapped his mouth shut.

"Take Signora Conti to the blue bedroom," I told Ettore, the younger of the two men waiting patiently to see what I needed done.

He nodded and reached to take Georgia's backpack from her. She drew back, clutching it to her body. She looked at me questioningly.

"Go with him." My command forbade argument, and for once, Georgia obliged without talking back.

She stared distrustfully at Jimmy, who was currently leering openly at her, his greedy gaze running up and down her body. I took satisfaction in the fact that he couldn't make out much of her curves under her baggy clothes.

My clothes.

"Shouldn't she stay with me?" he asked as soon as Georgia and Ettore disappeared into the mansion.

"Why would that be? She's not yours yet, De Luca. Keep it in your pants."

"But she will be. What's the point in waiting to make it official? She might as well get used to me now." He grinned and thrust his hips forward in a lewd display of exactly which part of him he wanted her to get used to.

"Let's not disappoint her before the wedding. She's flighty as it is," I told him flatly.

Someone laughed softly behind me, and Jimmy's face went red.

"Hey, Santori, watch your jokes, buddy, not everyone has the same sense of humor. I'm a made man, in charge of the Vetiver, Renato's most profitable casino. Remember that."

I reached into the car for my own bag. His words used up the very last of my patience. Men like Jimmy never learned.

"Or what?" I turned on him, dropping my bag to haul him close, forgetting my own cool for a split second.

Shock radiated over Jimmy when I grabbed him. I never reacted in anger. It wasn't my style, and yet I couldn't stop.

"What are you going to do? You, the made man, the casino floor manager . . . compared to *me*? Who the fuck are you?" I didn't need to point out our differences. I was Renato's *sottocapo*. In the event of his death or injury, the men would answer to me. I was inner circle, family.

I pressed a hard finger into his chest. "You're nothing. Nobody. Don't forget that. Don't piss me off. Follow my rules until you're married. And yes, you're in charge of one of the smallest De Sanctis casinos. As long as you've not been breaking the rules . . . it'll stay that way. If not . . . we'll talk again."

Jimmy nodded numbly.

I let go of him and patted his rumpled clothes back into place, harder than was necessary.

"Our lives are all about respect, De Luca. If you don't respect me, I won't respect you . . . and you know what I do to men I don't respect."

I turned from him, ignoring my men's shocked expressions.

A slow clap sounded, and I glanced up at the stone steps that led into the main house.

Charlotte De Sanctis stood at the top of the stairs, still in her scrubs. She must have just left work. Despite being the new bride of the De Sanctis family, she continued her education and her work at a local hospital. The woman was determined to be the best damn nurse in the country, and Renato was determined to give his wife anything she desired. Salvatore hadn't been wrong. Charlie had tamed the mighty and revered Mafia boss, whether he'd admit to that or not. Though the taming only related to Charlie herself, and her sister at a push.

"I'm glad you're home in one piece." She reached out and hugged me.

Charlie was one of the only women I could tolerate in my space. Renato had chosen her, and that made her my family, too.

"That remains to be seen." I glanced inside, my eyes following the direction Georgia had gone.

Charlie raised a curious eyebrow at me. "Well, that's not like you . . . Also, I've never seen you wear those contacts at home."

I still had the brown contact lenses in. "Get used to them. I'll be wearing them for a few more days."

We turned and went into the house together. I had an apartment in Atlantic City, but I stayed often in the main house of

Casa Nera. I had my own rooms upstairs. Right next to the blue bedroom.

"Why's that? Don't tell me . . ." Charlie trailed off and looked upward, quickly working out more than I wanted her to. "Are you hiding who you are? From that woman? The one from Italy?"

I fought not to react, but Charlie still slapped a hand comically over her mouth.

"What?" I grunted at her.

"It's happening. The untouchable Elio Santori is breaking . . . She's someone important to you, right? Oh my God, I can't believe it. Does Ren know?"

I stared her down, doing my best to quell her curiosity, but Charlie just laughed.

"So, that's why he sent you to get her."

"He sent me because I'm the best," I muttered, knowing it wasn't the only reason.

Renato seemed intent on making me face my past head-on. *Asshole.*

She slapped my shoulder. "Sure he did. I can't wait to get to know her."

I shrugged her hand off irritably. "She won't be here for long," I warned her.

Charlie just chuckled. "Sure she won't. God, men . . . you're so funny." She was still laughing to herself as she drifted away down the hall toward the kitchen, leaving me standing in the foyer, fighting the urge to go and visit the blue bedroom.

"Here. You look like you can use it," Renato murmured hours later, handing me a glass of whiskey.

I rarely drank, but after the week I'd had, and now, being at home, safe in Casa Nera, I was prepared to indulge.

"The Ravellis are out for blood. I don't know what their plan is for her—kill her or just hold her and use her to threaten her father—but they're serious."

Renato nodded. "I heard that the prosecutor has more on Giuseppe Ravelli than he has over Zio Sal. But she's here now. And tomorrow, she'll be married to a De Sanctis man, and Alfredo Bellisario will understand that ratting out Zio Sal will be the end of his daughter."

"You told Jimmy already." I fell short of achieving a casual tone with my complaint.

Renato waved his glass at me. "Should I not have? I needed to make sure he'd cut other entanglements before the big day."

"He doesn't seem displeased."

"He wants to make his don happy. Climb the ranks. Also, she's Italian. I'm sure Jimmy is looking forward to home-cooked food just like his *nonna* used to make."

I coughed, the whiskey nearly going down the wrong way. "If he's expecting a domestic goddess out of Georgia, he'll be sorely disappointed. She had staff growing up, if you recall, and I've just seen how she was living . . . I don't think she cooks much." *Or eats for that matter.* Poverty was a cruel taskmaster, I knew that as well as anyone.

Renato shrugged. "I guess that's for Jimmy to find out." He was quiet, rubbing a finger over his lower lip absently, considering me. "I thought about holding off and waiting to see what happened when you brought her here . . ."

"Why would you do that?" I asked.

"To see if you had changed your mind about her being your business."

I wet my lips, the whiskey drying my mouth. I swirled the cut ice at the bottom of the fine crystal. "She can marry Jimmy. It's the safest thing for all of us. He might be a thieving, fucking idiot, but he's . . ." *whole*. I couldn't bring myself to finish that sentence.

Luckily, I didn't have to, because a knock at the door interrupted our conversation.

"*Bene*. Well, it's time to tell the happy bride about her future. *Entra!*" he called toward the door.

It swung open, and then, there she was. It had only been a few hours since I'd last seen her, but it felt like a lifetime all over again. Her eyes jumped to me, dark and expressive. I couldn't quite read the expression that passed over her features. She looked at Renato and frowned.

"Georgia, it's been a long time." Renato stood to greet her. He pressed a kiss to either side of her cheeks. "How have you been?" No one could ever accuse Renato De Sanctis of not knowing how to act like a gentleman.

Georgia scoffed. "I was doing better, before you sent your trained little killer robot to drag me across the country."

"I heard you encountered problems on your trip," Renato said smoothly, rounding his desk to sit, leaving Georgia to sit beside me.

I pulled her chair out for her, which she pointedly ignored.

She locked Renato in her gaze. "What's going on? Last I saw you, it was the feast of Saint Anthony in Castel Amaro, and now . . . you're sending armed men after me. Killers." She threw me an accusatory glare. "My father and I have never been involved in your profession."

Renato shook his head. "That's where you're wrong, I'm afraid. Your father was always involved. Neck-deep in the filthy pig shit of Mafia life. He just hid it from you well. I'm surprised how well. I suppose since you moved away when you got older, it was easier."

Georgia opened her mouth to argue, but Renato had had enough of listening.

"Your father's guilt is not in question. Neither are your future plans, I'm afraid. It's been decided. Your father wants you protected."

"You mean Salvatore wants me as leverage, right?"

Renato just shrugged. "It doesn't make much of a difference either way. The outcome is still the same."

"Which is?" Georgia asked. She was still standing, ignoring the chair. Her hands were curled into tight fists.

"You will marry a De Sanctis man and become part of the family." Renato waited a beat. "Congratulations."

Georgia paled. Her head started to shake back and forth, her whole body denying what he had said.

"I can't do that. I won't do that."

"You can, and you will," Ren said calmly.

"No! You know me, you wouldn't hurt me," she muttered, her eyes beseeching his.

"It's because I know you that I'm not hurting you. The Ravellis—the other family your father is threatening—would probably just send pieces of you in the mail until he got the message."

Georgia stared at me. That look was like a punch.

"You knew about this? Of course you did."

She appeared so betrayed at that moment, I knew I'd never forget her expression. It seared itself into my soul.

"Who?" she finally asked. Her hands were still little balls of fury, and she was vibrating with tension but forcing herself to find out as much as she could.

Her eyes flew to me again.

"Is it him?" She took a step toward me. "Is it you?" Her eyes held something precious and rare.

"No, I'm afraid not. My second-in-command isn't inclined to marry. The man you will marry is in the hall." Renato inclined his head to one of his guards.

Jimmy sauntered in.

Georgia continued to hold my hot gaze for a long time. Even after Jimmy arrived at her side, she stared at me. I couldn't break that gaze. I didn't want to.

"Georgia, allow me to introduce myself." Jimmy stuck his hand out. "I'm the man you're going to marry."

The man you're going to marry.

The words were wrong on a soul-deep level.

Georgia held my gaze with burning eyes so long, I started to think she was going to ignore Jimmy completely, but then she blinked, her eyes like shining jewels. Unshed tears shone within. She turned to Jimmy and recoiled from his hand.

"Oh, it's you," she muttered.

Renato chuckled. "Well, a lackluster greeting is better than nothing. Why don't you two go and get to know each other? Later my wife, Charlie, will help you pick out something to wear for the wedding."

"I don't have to wear anything special. I'm fine in this." Georgia curled her hands into the too-long sleeves of my black T-shirt. She hugged it to her like my clothes could protect her from her fate. She was wrong; nothing could.

"The hell it is! I'm marrying a piece like you, I want to show you off," Jimmy announced, glancing around for some male encouragement. His eyes paused on mine, taking in my lethal expression, and bounced away.

He grabbed Georgia roughly by the arm.

"We'll go and have a little date, get to know each other and all that." He yanked her back, nearly pulling her off her feet.

I was standing before I could stop myself.

"*Basta,* Elio. *Lasciali in pace.* Leave them in peace." Renato waved a hand at the closing door.

"He's hurting her," I ground out.

"Isn't that just what she deserves? You haven't forgotten what she did, I assume . . . Isn't this what you've always wanted? To see her fallen . . . humbled . . ."

No. Not like this.

I turned back to him and ignored his curious study of me. Renato wasn't cruel toward women; in fact, he went out of his way to ensure that the fairer sex was protected. The fact that he was letting Jimmy haul Georgia around told me that he was playing a different game here.

He surveyed me from head to toe and then leaned forward and put his elbows on the desk, studying me with interest. "You know, if I didn't know you better, I'd think you still loved this woman. The one who married someone else."

"I don't need to be reminded of our past. I live it every day."

Renato nodded. "Exactly. Maybe it's time to let some things go. A man can't carry the past with him forever. It's time to bury it. So, either leave Georgia to her fate . . . or do something about it."

"It's not as easy as that," I muttered.

Renato just shrugged. "Isn't it? I think that's for you to decide. This time . . . you choose."

20

GEORGIA

The brute called Jimmy dragged me out to the gardens at the back of the house then released me.

"There, get some fresh air," he said, taking a cigarette out of a pack in his pocket and lighting up.

I rolled my eyes and hid my face from him.

I wasn't marrying this man. I'd marry him over my dead body.

"So, you knew Renato when he was young, eh?" Jimmy grunted.

I was still blinking back tears, trying to hide my reaction from my so-called fiancé.

The moment when Renato had told me I was getting married, my eyes had immediately found my mercenary. For the smallest of seconds, I'd thought it would be to him, and I'd . . . been relieved. That was the horrifying truth that hurt to admit. I supposed the old adage was true. Better the devil you know.

"Hey, I'm talking to you." Jimmy poked my shoulder.

I faced him and folded my arms over my chest. "What?"

"You knew Renato when he was young?"

I just shrugged. "Yeah, I guess. A lot of good that's doing me."

Jimmy puffed up his chest. "I'd say it's done you a favor. I mean,

I don't want to brag, but I'm kind of a big deal in the family . . . I even run one of the De Sanctis casinos in A.C. You like gambling?"

"No." I turned away to fight a shudder.

Jimmy touched me on the shoulder, and I jerked back around.

"Don't touch me," I snapped at him.

His gloating expression morphed quickly into something ugly. "Watch how you speak to me. Tomorrow I'll be your husband, and I won't be disrespected at home. Get with the fucking program, or I'll have to show you who's boss here."

"And who is that? Renato?" I mocked him quietly, my survival instincts fried at this point. "You're certainly jumping to do his bidding."

"You stupid bitch, you should be getting down on your knees and opening that smart little mouth to show me how much you appreciate getting a merciful husband like me." He grabbed my shoulder and shook me, like he could shake some sense into me.

"That's never going to happen," I hissed at him, trying to stop my teeth from clacking together.

"Oh, yes it fucking is. Maybe we should go somewhere and have a demonstration right now."

"De Luca."

The quiet, commanding voice called to us from the doorway to the gardens, and Jimmy immediately stilled. We both spun to see my mercenary lounging in an archway.

He had his hip propped against the stone and his arms crossed, but there was no mistaking his pose for ease. He looked like a coil about to spring open.

"Is there a problem out here?" he continued in that quiet, deadly tone.

"Just a couple's spat," Jimmy said, his fingers still digging into my flesh.

My mercenary pushed off the wall and sauntered toward us.

He stared pointedly down at my shoulder, the place where Jimmy's hand still sat.

Jimmy dropped it to his side and shifted slightly away from me. "There's no problem," he repeated. He was afraid. It came off him in waves.

So, Renato hadn't simply sent some random made man after me. He'd sent his *sottocapo*, his second. My mercenary was an important man in his own right.

I met his dark brown eyes and felt like they saw down to my soul.

"If there's no problem, then I'll be taking Georgia inside. Mrs. De Sanctis needs her."

Jimmy raised his hands as if surrendering. "That's cool, man. I can wait one more day to have uninterrupted time with my new wife," he said, a smarmy smile spreading across his face.

A wave of sickness threatened to engulf me, but I pushed it away. I couldn't fall apart now. I had to figure a way out of this.

I walked stiffly inside. As soon as I was in, I lost my orientation. I swiveled around to find my mercenary right behind me.

"Charlie has had a dress brought to your room; go and try it on."

"Or what? You'll make me marry a fucking asshole?" I snapped at him. "Wow, I better be careful or my life will be ruined."

"Wasn't it ruined anyway? What were you even living when I found you?"

"A life. Sure, maybe it was shitty by your standards . . . but it was mine. Now—I'm just leverage for my father. I'm more than just a pawn to be traded back and forth when it suits people."

A muscle worked in my mercenary's jaw. "These are concerns you should have brought up with Renato. I can't help you."

"Can't? Or won't?" I shot out.

"Let me ask you this . . . Why should I help you?"

I stared at him, my chest deflating. He was right. He didn't owe me anything. He wasn't on my side just because he'd saved my life a few times. He'd just been doing his job, which he would continue to do, even if it involved marching an unwilling woman down a wedding aisle.

"Whatever. Take me to my room." I sighed and turned away.

I couldn't look at that man's face anymore. It was the similarity to Elio that was doing it. Muddling my mind and making me confused. Why should this stranger show me mercy? A jagged laugh left me when I realized that Elio Santori hadn't shown me any either, when he'd had the chance.

"Save going insane until after the ceremony," my mercenary said dryly as we walked toward my room.

I ignored him as much as I could ignore a man like him. He unlocked the door and let me in. On the bed, a beautiful white dress lay spread out. It was so pretty that I gasped, I couldn't help it.

"Whose dress is this?"

"I believe it's one of the ones that didn't make the cut. Renato bought every single garment his wife tried on."

I approached the simple and beautiful satin gown. It was lovely. Even with my picky eye for design, it was utterly exquisite. I touched the material gently.

"You need to try it on," my mercenary stated.

I shook my head straightaway. "It'll fit."

"I can't leave until you do. It's the boss's wife's orders, and what Charlie wants, she gets."

"Lucky girl," I muttered.

"If you knew what she went through before she married Renato, you wouldn't think so." He presented his back to me. "Change," he tossed over his shoulder.

Just wanting to be alone, and knowing that he would stick to his damn orders like glue, I took off the T-shirt I'd been borrowing and then the overly large cargo pants.

The dress was heavy, a many-layered concoction of frothy petticoats and beading. I stepped into it and pulled it up. It needed a strapless bra, that was for sure. I unclipped mine and tossed it on the bed, then raised the dress to cover my bare breasts. It had a strapless neckline and a corset back.

"It fits."

"You haven't done it up." My mercenary's voice felt like a touch on my back.

I twisted around. He was watching me. Heat flushed over my skin. It was like standing too close to a fire. Like his eyes could burn me.

"Well, I don't have arms on my back, so . . ." I forgot what I was saying when he approached me.

"Allow me, in that case," he said in a low murmur. "Don't be shy. I've seen more than your bare back."

I faced away, clutching the front of the gown to my bare chest as if my life depended on it. I'd never felt so exposed in my life. No, not exposed . . . seen.

In more than ten years of being married to my best friend, I'd forgotten what it felt like to be half naked around a man who liked women. It was a different feeling altogether. Heat trailed down my back as his fingers brushed my bare skin.

It was like I'd friend-zoned my own body, and now it was waking up. Very inconvenient timing.

"Thanks for the uncouth reminder of the mistake we made on the plane," I bit out, embarrassment rushing in.

"Uncouth? No, Signora Conti, uncouth would be reminding you of how you came so hard when I finger-fucked your asshole and your pussy that the flight attendants probably think you wet the bed."

I gasped, shocked by his filthy words.

"Uncouth would be reminding you how you rocked your tight ass on my fingers and took what you wanted . . ."

"Okay, I get it. Stop, please." My voice felt strained, like something was sitting in my throat.

He pulled in the lowest ribbon of the corset, cinching my waist. I gasped a little.

"Hold on to something," he advised. "I'm not known for my gentle touch."

I swallowed a knot in my throat the size of my fist. Was I nervous at his touch? I sure was, but worryingly, it wasn't the kind of nervous I should be. It was something else.

"Believe me, I know."

His fingers worked the ribbons, tightening the dress bit by bit.

"You're good at this," I remarked, feeling like the silence needed to be broken, in case he could hear my heart beating as loud as a drum.

"Mm-hmm, restraining people is a talent of mine," he murmured.

His hot breath warmed the very top of my spine.

"But not usually for fun, right?" I blurted and then flushed hotly. "I mean, of course, you can tie people up for fun all you want . . . it's just you have experience in a professional capacity," I rambled on.

He continued, unfazed, while I agonized over my words. *What the hell?*

I twisted my fingers together this way and that. An old habit.

"Are you nervous?"

"Me?" I forced a laugh. "Why would I be nervous?"

His hands left me. He was done. I turned around slowly.

"I'm just a captive in a heavily guarded Mafia compound, my

father is going to prison, and tomorrow I'm being forced to marry the most loathsome man I've ever met, probably at gunpoint. What's there to be nervous about?" I finished, my voice rising higher and higher until the last word.

"You seemed calmer ten minutes ago." My mercenary raised an eyebrow in question.

"That was before you started touching me," I snapped back, then realized what, exactly, I'd just said. What I'd revealed.

He tilted his head down farther, bending forward to look in my eyes. "Are you saying I make you nervous?"

"Have you seen you? Of course you make me nervous. I'm a perfectly rational person with a working endocrine system . . . a man like you will always make me nervous. You're dangerous," I added, in case it sounded like I was admitting how insanely hot he was.

His gaze drifted from my eyes to my lips and back. The heat that had been flushing through me, building with his every touch, was creeping up to my face.

"You're no picnic to be around either, *cara*."

Cara. Dear one. Another word lifted from the past. Sure, it was a common enough endearment in Italian, and this man's tone made it clear he was being sardonic, yet it reminded me again of him. My *cittaiolo*.

"Damn it, and I was trying my best to be a good little hostage. I wouldn't want to make your mission to ruin my life difficult," I ground out.

The shadow of a smirk pulled at his face. It made a startling transformation; a split second later, it was gone.

"Well, you might want to try harder." Then he did something that shocked me. He reached out and brushed a lock of hair from my forehead, guiding it back behind my ear.

It was a gentle movement. Gentler than I'd ever expect a man as hard as him to be capable of.

My breath caught when his fingers brushed my ear. It felt shockingly good. I was so touch-starved, my whole body thrummed with life at the meager contact. The pleasure he'd given me only hours ago rushed back, sitting in the air between us. We'd crossed a line there, in that luxurious little bedroom, high above the world, and we couldn't go back.

His gaze dropped to my eyes and fell, down and down. He looked me over with a darkness in his eyes that stole my breath. It was like we were caught in a spell for a long moment, and I didn't want it to end. Right here, it felt like time had stopped and tomorrow might never come. I wanted that more than anything. His gaze ran down my body, and he seemed to sway imperceptibly closer for a second, before catching himself.

He took a step back and then another.

"It fits." His voice was a low growl.

It took a second to remember what he was talking about.

I glanced down at myself. Ah, yes. The dress.

I smoothed my hands down the beaded corset. It was lovely.

"Yes. It does. It's very pretty for a prison uniform," I said.

My mercenary just stood there, silent. I wanted to know what was going on behind his taciturn facade more than ever. I wanted to open his head and pick out his secret thoughts.

Like always, he gave nothing away.

"Be good until the ceremony. Don't do anything to the dress . . . I'm warning you, or you'll be getting married in front of a roomful of people in your underwear." He headed for the door.

"I wouldn't . . . not something so lovely. I could never hurt it," I said, looking up and catching my mercenary's eyes.

He watched me for a second and then spun on his heel and left. The lock twisted with a sharp click behind him.

* * *

I found a full-length mirror inside the closet. It was the sight of myself standing there in the sweetheart-neckline gown, the white satin giving my skin a glow, that convinced me.

I had to get away from there. Earlier on the plane had been a moment of delusion, and it had given me the strength for one last stand. I couldn't stay there, with my mercenary, marrying some stranger. This was my last chance to grab for freedom. *What about the other guys . . . the ones following you?* The Ravellis. The other men my father was threatening to squeal on.

I was in New Jersey now. What were the chances that they'd already caught up? I could disappear here, somehow . . . I had to try.

It didn't matter what it cost me; I wasn't marrying Jimmy Sleazeball De Luca.

I'd die first.

After half an hour of wriggling to loosen the corset ties, I changed back into my borrowed outfit and got into bed. I waited until the house went to sleep. I lay fully dressed, not that I had an option for changing, until the grandfather clock in the hall chimed three A.M.

I got up. I'd already gotten a good look around the room. The only possibility was the window. I was surprised to find that the lock opened easily. The room had been very nice for a prison cell, so I was starting to think it was a place for guests and not prisoners. I strapped my bag onto my back. It was time to get the hell out of there.

I opened the window and stepped out onto the wide stone ledge that hugged the building and ran around the side. There was a tree not too far out from the ledge. Some of the wider branches were within touching distance. All I had to do was make it along the ledge to the tree.

And then across the guarded grounds and over the fortified walls.

One step at a time, I told myself. The ledge was firm. The night was cold, a big difference from the balmy evenings of L.A. I edged along the ledge, my heart pounding so hard it hurt. I shuffled past a window next to me, and then the end of the building came into sight. Thank God.

I continued my graceless shuffle toward the place where the ledge passed close to the tree. I finally reached it and had to stop, taking deep breaths and trying to calm myself down. My hands were shaking terribly, and I felt sick. But just the thought of Jimmy De Luca waiting at the end of the aisle for me was enough to steel my spine.

I had no choice.

I reached out for the tree and grabbed it easily enough. When I brought one foot to rest on it, the whole branch swayed. Okay, so maybe I was a bit heavier than I'd allowed for, but I could make it work.

I pushed my weight toward the tree and used the momentum to grasp a branch closer to the trunk. Slowly, I worked my way down the tree, putting my feet only on the biggest branches I could find. When I got near the bottom, I slowed, as the branches were sparser. I really had to reach carefully, feeling for a foothold.

I was only about ten feet from the ground at this point. I could just jump. I was facing in toward the trunk, my hands digging into the rough bark, while I tried to feel for one last foothold.

Suddenly, my foot gripped on to a firm but pliable hold. I let out a small sob of relief and transferred my foot to the branch and lowered myself slowly. I moved my hand and searched wildly for another place to hold on to.

"Just a little to your left," a voice helped from below.

I reached for the foothold, realizing what had just happened.

I'd been so intent on finding my way down the tree, I'd forgotten that being caught would render the entire exercise pointless.

I glanced down and swayed, nearly falling.

"Careful, Signora Conti, you wouldn't want to trip and fall and ruin your big day tomorrow," my mercenary's mocking tone drifted up to me.

Fuck, fuck, fuck. I was caught.

I froze there until the branch under my foot moved. So it wasn't a branch; it was his hand.

"Okay, I'm coming," I muttered and lowered myself.

His hand disappeared under my foot, and I slipped a few inches, then his arms closed around my middle.

My body pressed against his, his face level with my breasts, my feet swinging in the air.

"Put me down, then," I demanded hotly. I felt like crying. My only chance to get away was gone. Had there ever really been one? Probably not. Ever since this man had appeared in my life, I'd been trapped. There was never any escape.

A tear dripped down my cheek. I was no stranger to crying since Tommaso had died, but lately I'd been setting myself a new record.

His gaze searched my face. He wasn't as guarded as usual. Maybe it was the late hour, but it felt like his face was softer than normal. Maybe I was just imagining it. It was pretty dark out, with only the light of the moon to reveal him to me. A hint of something sweet and peaty floated to me. Had he been drinking?

"Don't cry, Georgia."

His deep voice, so familiar and yet so different, broke my heart all over again. Elio Santori had been my safe harbor. The boy who'd blazed into my life and changed it forever. I'd never felt safer than I had around him, and when he'd left, he'd taken that feeling of safety and never given it back. But this man was not him. Sure, he looked like him and sounded like him, but he didn't have his eyes, and more than anything, he didn't have his soul. The Elio I'd known would never be a mercenary for Renato De Sanctis. His *sottocapo,* no less. He might have taken the easy payday and run out on me, but there were still lines he wouldn't have crossed.

Still, despite knowing that this man had less mercy than a pile of rocks, I had to try.

"Let me go, please . . . just let me go," I whispered.

He was still holding me suspended against him. Slowly, his arms loosened just enough to send me sliding down his front. I felt every single ridge of his body.

"You could just look the other way, pretend that I'd escaped . . . Renato wouldn't blame you."

"I'd blame myself when the Ravellis caught you, which they would. The only things keeping you safe right now are me and this place. Without De Sanctis protection, you're lost. Would you choose that over me?"

"But I'm not marrying *you,* am I?"

"And if you were? Would you still be out here, trying to run away?" he pressed.

I changed tack. "I can take care of myself, better than you think. I would be okay out there."

His thumb rubbed across my lip, startling me and stealing my frantic words.

"It's done, Georgia. There is no escape, not from here, and not from me. There never was."

Anger surged in my chest. The fucking unfairness of it all. I parted my lips as his finger brushed past, and it fell just inside. He jerked against me. I swiped my tongue over the end of his thumb and then closed my teeth around it.

I bit down hard, and blood filled my mouth.

He just stood there and took it. He didn't fight back. I bit down again, daring him to push me away, but he only watched, impassive. Untouchable. I attempted to bite harder, but I couldn't. I just couldn't.

I pulled my head away, releasing his finger, and spit a mouthful of his blood onto the grass.

"Time for bed." His voice was quiet. He took my arm and firmly steered me toward the house.

"Please . . . just let me go," I cried, devolving into full-blown tears at this point. I stopped walking and tried to sit on the grass.

He hoisted me up into his arms and continued, without missing a step.

"I couldn't even if I wanted to," he told me mercilessly.

"And I guess you don't want to?" I didn't know why I said it. There was no point. No point at all. I guess I was just addicted to pain and disappointment by now.

He carried me silently through the house and up the stairs.

Instead of the room I'd been in before, he took me into the room next to it and set me down, shutting and locking the door behind him, then leaning against it.

"No," he said.

I forgot what question he was answering, so long had passed.

"No, you couldn't let me go?"

He pushed off the door toward me. "No. I don't want to."

I glared at him. "Why?"

He just shrugged, his impassive face giving nothing away.

"You're sick, you know that? You and Renato, and all the men you live with here, playing life and death with innocent people—"

His hand moved faster than I could duck away from it. His fingers pressed against my lips.

"Don't pretend you're an innocent person. You will tempt me to prove you wrong," he said, sounding grave.

I blinked at him. *What the hell?*

"No more talking for tonight. You've proven yourself unworthy of being trusted to sleep alone, so now . . . you sleep with me."

My eyes widened in alarm. He backed up a step and lowered his hands to the hem of his T-shirt. The next thing I knew, he'd pulled it up and over his head, tossing it precisely onto a chair in the corner.

"Sleep with you." I looked around the room. "This is your room, right? You put me in the room next to yours."

"I suspected you were a flight risk. I was correct." His lips tipped up in an unexpected smirk.

I was right, he'd been drinking.

"Tell me a woman who wouldn't try and run away when faced with Jimmy De Luca for a fiancé," I protested hotly.

The slightest ghost of a smile seemed to pass over my mercenary's face, then it disappeared so suddenly, I figured I'd imagined it.

"Well, now that you've represented the females of the world, it's time to sleep. There is no escape from tomorrow, Georgia. Not for any of us."

I frowned at him, watching him step back and move around his room. He was fishing in a drawer for something.

He turned around and revealed what looked to be scraps of material and a rope.

"Those better not be for me," I warned, panic jumping up my throat.

I backed away, and he followed. "I can't have you trying to kill me in the night."

"I won't try. I pinkie promise." *I'll succeed,* I vowed.

He just shook his head and advanced.

What came next was undignified to say the least. We tussled, me with abandon and him with great restraint. I'd never stood a chance of stopping him from tying me up, and the way he managed to do so within two minutes was really a blow to my ego. My hands were bound in front of me, and he'd tied some scrap of soft material around my neck.

He went to pull it up and silence me, and I backpedaled, shaking my head.

"Wait! Wait . . . please . . . Before tomorrow, I need some kind of reassurance." I looked him right in the eye. "I'm scared."

He met my panic steadily. "It's okay to be scared. It's smart. It doesn't change anything."

I shook my head again, and a tear dripped down my face. "I swear, I don't know what happened to my life. None of this was supposed to happen."

Another tear followed.

He watched them. His hand flexed at his side, as though he was fighting his own self-control. In the end his discipline won, and he watched me cry without touching me.

"I know the feeling." Then he pulled the gag up over my chin and silenced me.

I glared daggers at him. He tugged on the loop of rope between my hands. Of course he'd been good at tying up my wedding dress. He was a bondage expert, clearly.

That line of thinking sent me hot all over, and I was even more angry at myself. I was clearly focusing on trivial shit, like misplaced attraction to my literal captor, as a psychological trick to make me less scared of the future. It was my brain protecting itself. I had to believe that or I'd lose my mind.

"Lie down," he instructed me tightly, pushing me in the direction of his king-sized bed.

I shook my head and pointed at the floor.

"Lie. The. Fuck. Down." He gave me a look that would make saner women cry. "I've had enough tonight. Stop testing me."

What would this man be capable of if that steely control snapped? I dug my heels in and pushed back when he tried to tug me.

"Georgia," he growled in my ear.

He lifted me and hauled me to the bed, throwing me onto the mattress so hard I bounced. Before I could sit up, he was straddling me, lithe with that predatory grace of his.

He leaned over me and grabbed my bound hands, tying the loop of the binding rope around the metal bars of the headboard. I wriggled and writhed, bucking my hips and trying to unseat him. He fiddled with the rope, leaning forward so he could reach, his entire body stretched out along mine, and my mind went blank. His body weight was pressing me into the bed, his hips flush with mine, and his scent was everywhere. If I closed my eyes, I could pretend I was nineteen, hiding a boy in my room, waiting until my father went to sleep before pulling him into bed with me. Those stolen nights with Elio were my happy place, and my deepest pain, all at once. He'd taught me what it was to love and hate in sync. I wished I could be back there, in bed with my *cittaiolo*. The only man I'd ever loved.

My mercenary stilled once my hands were bound, but didn't move. I was still trying to shift him. Pushing up into him, trying to turn on my side, raising my hips up and down.

Then I felt it. Nestled right between my thighs and up on my pubic bone. Long, hard, and thick.

My mercenary was hard. He had me pinned to the bed, bound and gagged, and he was hard, rocking on me. And the plane wasn't that long ago, damn it, not nearly long enough for the fire he'd lit inside me to die completely. Desire roared back to life, igniting inside my veins. I didn't know what it was about this man that just made me want to hurt him and fuck him.

"That's enough, Signora Conti," he said thickly.

My heart was pounding. I was nervous. I was excited. I wanted to get lost in a different sensation tonight, something other than fear and panic. I wanted to be consumed by feeling, so intense that no other thoughts could exist in my head at the same time.

"I said, it's enough," he growled at me.

His restraint was being tested. He was dangerously close to losing control, and I wanted to see it. The smell of expensive whiskey fanned across my face. He tugged my gag down, and I sucked in a breath.

"Are you drunk?" I murmured.

"Why? You thinking of taking advantage of me?" he mocked.

I raised my hips once more, pressing on his hard cock. Daring him.

"Why have you been drinking? Drowning your sorrows?" I didn't know where the words were coming from, maybe some instinctive part of me that understood this dangerous man on a primitive level. He was upset, out of tightly held control. I bet he hated it. *Good.*

"Maybe I'm just celebrating early . . . a new addition to the De Sanctis family. A bride for De Luca. Maybe it's his bachelor party downstairs and I just got a lap dance," he murmured, goading me.

I scoffed. "Right. I've seen cardboard cutouts more likely to enjoy a naked woman gyrating on top of them. I'm starting to think you don't feel anything from the waist down."

"Try the neck," he countered.

I swallowed a hard knot in my throat. "Makes sense . . . how else could someone be so heartless? Were you born without one, or did you lose it along the way?"

A muscle ticked in his strong jaw. He lowered his face toward me, and one of his hands sank into my hair and tipped my head back. His lips brushed over mine.

"Neither. Someone took it," he murmured. "Someone stole it, and she's never given it back."

His face filled my entire line of sight. Everything I saw was him. A flicker of something dark and twisted burned in my blood. Was that jealousy? Over my kidnapper's lover . . . I'd lost my mind. It had finally happened.

A tear spilled down my cheek, born of frustration and fear. My tears had never been far from falling since all this had started. Had it only been a little over a week ago? It felt like a lifetime.

A shadow passed through his eyes at the sight of that tear. Then he ducked his head and ran his lips up my cheek, wiping the evidence of my devastation away with his mouth. He pressed a soft kiss to one eyelid, then the other.

"Don't cry, Georgia. I really can't fucking stand it."

Then he kissed me.

And kissed me.

His tongue swept along my lips, sliding between as soon as I parted them and stroking along my tongue. Heat enveloped me, so hot I felt like the places where he touched would be scorch-marked.

I arched into him, trying to bring my body closer to his. This was it. My last night of freedom before I was married off to a creep who made my skin crawl. I wanted this man. The one I felt drawn to, despite everything.

"You taste like lies . . . and fucking heaven," he murmured on my lips, moving lower.

"What are you doing?" I panicked. My hands were tied, and I wasn't going anywhere. Just like on the plane, I was in this man's hands. Excitement electrified my blood.

"This time I need more . . . directly from the source."

His hands fastened on my pants, and he tugged them down. I'd washed my panties earlier in the bathroom sink and dried them with the blow-dryer in my room. They went the same way of the borrowed pants. I should have been embarrassed, but I wasn't. I was getting married for the second time in my life to a man who I didn't love like a lover. A man I had no choice in marrying. I'd married Tommaso out of sheer desperation to save myself from a broken heart, and Jimmy De Luca—out of force.

My mercenary's hot breath fogged my thighs as he pushed my legs apart.

"Fuck. Does every single part of you have to be so fucking pretty?" he complained, leaning in and licking a hot, wet stripe up my slit.

I cried out. The touch was too intimate and sudden, overwhelming my senses. I wanted to crawl away and pin myself down at the same time. This man, this merciless mercenary, was pulling me inside out. My heart, still stuck in the past, couldn't reconcile my feelings for this man who looked like the only man I'd ever loved. My ghost, made flesh, but different. Cold and brutal, and at times kind and thoughtful. I couldn't figure him out.

But I wanted him. His mouth worked over my pussy, his tongue insistently slicking my clit. God, I wanted him like this. Dark and dirty, blurring the lines between right and wrong.

It was the only way I could give myself permission to do this . . . anything else felt like a betrayal of the past.

His finger worked inside me, curling up so it pushed on the front wall, my legs shaking.

"Why do you have to taste so good and smell so fucking good? Ambrosia has nothing on you, and it's fucking annoying," he said, his fingers pumping into my cunt.

I was going to come all over his face, and there was nothing I could do about it. All I could do was take it, and that fact was making me burn.

No control. No responsibility. No decisions to be made or morals to grapple over.

Just freedom and enough pleasure to set my soul on fire.

I was going to come; it was close. I was rising at a rapid pace. Maybe it was because it had been so incredibly long since I'd been touched like this, but I sensed it was more . . . it was him. This man who could touch me like no one else.

I was thrashing in his grip now, tightening my thighs around his head, and he laughed. It was a good sound.

"That's right, *cara*, fucking come and let me see it."

"Ahh!" A strangled scream left me as I came. My entire body tensed, and a wave of pleasure washed over me, my nerves tingling right down to my fingertips.

His hand pumped into me until I begged him to stop, the sensitivity just too much.

He shifted to his knees, ripping his pants open and taking his cock out. I stared at it. It was so thick and long, riddled with throbbing veins. He fisted it roughly and pumped himself, his body still angled over mine.

His gaze moved to mine, and his face twisted with pleasure. He came hard, his whole body shaking, his cock spurting long, white jets across my pussy. He panted, still working his cock, until the last of his spend dripped onto me.

With a sigh, he sank back and closed his eyes.

How much does someone as big as him have to drink to feel drunk?

After a second, he moved to the panties still caught on one of my ankles. He dragged them up my leg and helped me put the other leg in, then he guided them all the way up.

"Lift," he instructed.

"But—I need to clean up," I pointed out.

He tutted and shook his head. "No. You don't. You should smell like me. It's the least you can do for driving me fucking insane."

I lifted wordlessly, and he drew the panties up, over the mess of cum on my cunt, and snapped them into place.

He stroked a hand over the front of the material, wetting it through.

"There, that's how you should always walk around, Signora Conti."

Heat blazed through my cheeks. It was wrong and fucked up . . . but I liked it. There was something dark and possessive in his tone that made me feel wanted in a way that no man had ever wanted me, except for my ghost.

"Now, sleep. Big day tomorrow."

He pushed off the bed and stood. Going to the corner, he unrolled a thin blanket and tossed it on the floor, then added a pillow.

Without another word, he lay down, closed his eyes, and fell asleep.

21

GEORGIA

THEN

"I don't believe you," I said as I watched my father's sympathetic face. He was sitting behind his desk and had just delivered the unbelievable news that Elio had skipped town.

My father shrugged. "*Amore,* I wouldn't lie about this."

"He wouldn't. He wants to marry me . . ." I trailed off. *He's going to save me.*

"Where is he, then?"

"You've done something to him," I accused, standing so quickly my head spun.

"No, *amore,* I would never. You chose him, I would have respected that, gotten him a suitable job, made sure he took care of you and your future children, God willing. I would never hurt you."

My father's face was grave. I couldn't stand that expression.

I picked up my phone and scrolled for the number of the local police station. It rang a few times before someone answered.

"Hello, I'm calling to see if a young man has been brought in. Elio Santori?"

"Let me check . . . No, no one by that name. It's been quiet here today, actually."

I hung up without saying goodbye. "Just because he's not in the local jail doesn't mean you didn't do something to him."

"Georgia, please, stay calm. I have an idea of what happened . . . and even some evidence . . . if you'll trust me to show you?"

I flinched away when he tried to touch me, folding my arms over my chest. "Show me. I don't trust you, but I want to see."

My father nodded and pulled his laptop toward him. "I asked Elio to get the delivery that you were missing earlier. Somehow, it ended up at the De Sanctis house. Salvatore's right-hand man sent me this."

A CCTV video played. In it, Elio was walking into the kitchen of the De Sanctis house and over to a package and bag on the floor. He grabbed both and left.

"What did the bag have in it?" I asked, lightheaded.

"Nearly one hundred thousand euros," my father said quietly. "The last he was seen was leaving the property with the bag. The delivery box was abandoned just down the road from the De Sanctis property."

I stared at my father so long, tears burned my eyes. "What are you saying?"

"He took the money, *amore,* and ran. He was nothing but a hustler, after a quick buck. Getting saddled with a wife at twenty wasn't in his plans. He's gone."

I shook my head. "He wouldn't go. He wouldn't leave me. He wouldn't just leave me," I said again, pressing a hand to my chest. My heart was beating too hard.

My father's face was the picture of pity. I couldn't stand to look at him.

"Then where is he? What could keep him from you?"

I don't know.

But I was going to find out.

A month later, I was exhausted, but I hadn't given up, even though the scant information I'd uncovered had pointed to my father's theory being true.

Today, I was meeting with a taxi driver who the P.I. I'd hired had tracked down.

I sat in the meeting, numbness creeping over me.

"I gave the young man a ride to the train station. He said he was going to find someone . . . a girl. Said he had gotten what he needed here. Seemed eager to get gone."

A girl? His sister, or someone else? A cold feeling flooded my chest.

"He had a bag with him, a leather one. He was gripping it like it had the crown jewels inside. Gave a good tip, though . . . He hustled into the station, and I went on about my day."

The driver gave me the once-over, up and down.

"You okay, Signorina Bellisario?"

"Are you sure he came from the De Sanctis estate? He never said his name, right?"

I was clutching at straws, but I couldn't quit. Not yet.

"No, no names, but he had an accent. He was from Naples."

It was still circumstantial. It still didn't mean anything. It wasn't definitively Elio.

"The only other thing was his eyes," the driver continued.

The cold dug its claws into my heart.

"They were green, memorable . . . light and weird."

Just like that, my heart froze over.

Every night for a month, I'd sat at the window and shined the flashlight toward the barn. *Come to me. Come to me. Please. Come to me.*

No one had come. Elio was gone. He'd taken the money and left. He'd really left. And if he ever came back, for all I knew, Salvatore De Sanctis would have him killed for stealing from him. *Elio, what have you done?*

"Stop crying," Tommaso murmured, running his hands through my hair strewn across my pillow. Lately, I was either looking for Elio or crying, sometimes both at the same time. I'd never been so tired.

Today, I'd made it home before the tears had come, and now they wouldn't stop.

"Georgie. Stop," Tommaso murmured, his voice sounding wretched. "You need to shower. Come on, get up."

"Pass."

"No, I'm not taking no for an answer. You stink," he said and whipped the covers back dramatically.

"I can't," I sobbed.

Tommaso dragged me out of bed, losing patience.

I crawled to the window and grabbed the flashlight. I flashed it at the barn while tears dripped down my face.

"Georgia, stop. He's not there. He's long gone, and he's not coming back. He left you, sweetheart. He left."

I shook my head frantically. That earlier feeling that my heart was going to burst out of my chest returned tenfold.

Suddenly, I couldn't breathe. Spots danced in front of my eyes, and the air in my lungs burned.

I saw Tommaso reaching for me, then the world went black.

I sat in an exam bed hours later, empty. I had no tears left. I'd cried them all. I stared at the sun sinking below the horizon. My father had been to see me and left when I failed to speak to him. The doctor had already been in.

You had a panic attack. It was a severe one. Passing out allowed you to breathe again . . . it was a lucky break. The body's fail-safe.

The door opened, and Tommaso came in, shutting it behind him.

"Here, I brought you this." He lifted a bottle of red wine from a bag and shook it temptingly. "Times like these, you just need to get wasted."

I swallowed, my throat dry and raw, then reached for my water glass.

Tommaso sat beside me. "How are you feeling?"

"Like I just lost everything that matters," I muttered. "Like I don't want to be here anymore."

"The hospital?"

"Earth," I admitted with a sigh.

Tommaso gripped my hand. "Don't fucking say that to me. You're my best friend. Yes, this is shitty, and awful, but you've got a whole life to live. This cannot be the thing that destroys you."

"I can't get over it. I know I can't. I'm sorry."

"Fuck being sorry! Just snap out of it. Sure, take time to grieve, but then move on."

"I don't know where Elio is—" I started.

Tommaso snorted, his patience running out. "I don't care! He's not here . . . he's not here when you need him. Do you think he's dead? Did your father have him whacked?" he demanded.

I shook my head. "I don't think he would. He might not be the best person in the world, but he's still a prosecutor . . ."

"Okay, then, where is he? You called all the prisons and jails, every single hospital in the country near enough. Where is he?"

I didn't have an answer for that.

Tommaso looked furious and wretched as he twisted the cap of the cheap wine and took a swig. "He should be here. Even if it cost him everything, he should find a way. He ran away, Georgia. Took the money and ran. Fuck him."

I glared at Tommaso. "Stop it."

"No, I won't stop it. Fuck that guy. Something happened, or not . . . but he should be here. It's been a month."

"Stop. Just stop. Don't try and make me hate him."

"You should hate him. He fucked up your life and broke your heart. Hate him, Georgia, and move the fuck on. You have to live . . . you have to live." He pulled me close. "My dearest, sweet friend . . . you have to live. If you have to hate him to live, then hate him."

"How can I live? Here, in that house where we were together?" A sob caught in my throat. So, I could still cry after all?

"No, not here. Fuck here. Fuck your father, and Castel Amaro."

Tommaso fixed me with a determined look. "I know it's not New York, or Parsons, but California has a great design school, too."

"And?"

"And—my internship begins in a few weeks. Come with me. Live in your mother's homeland . . . forget everything here. Come with me to America. My parents want to set me up with some girl, a family friend over there, and see me married. I can't, Georgia, I just can't. Come with me instead."

"What? I can't come with you. My father would never let me and—"

"He would if we got married. Marry me, Georgia. Agree to be my lawfully wedded bestie, my fake wife, make my parents happy, and let's get the fuck out of here, together."

22

ELIO

NOW

Staff came early to get Georgia ready for the wedding. I hadn't gone back to sleep. I couldn't lie near her for hours, waiting for the moment. The temptation was too strong.

My identity had been built on a battlefield, forged from the pain and loss of the end of my youth, and the reason for it all was lying sleeping, her beautiful face tearstained and red, her hands bound to the bed. My bed. If I wasn't careful, I'd want to keep her right there, fuck the wedding. If I wasn't careful . . .

I went for a run as soon as dawn broke and then waded into the small lake to the west of the property. The cold water shocked my breath away but soothed the hot, burning sensation in my belly. My gut was churning. My heart was pounding. Last month, I'd have been able to swear that I hadn't felt the presence of that particularly weak organ in my chest for years—fourteen, to be exact.

Now, a mere week after being around Georgia again, I was crumbling. All my steely composure and hard-won mental fortitude, swept away like so many grains of worthless sand.

I returned to the house and headed for the kitchen. I wasn't going to hang around and watch Georgia get dressed to marry another man.

I drank coffee and watched Carmella get lunch ready, directing her staff like a drill sergeant. Carmella was a fixture of Casa Nera.

"*Ebbene,*" she said, sitting heavily across from me. "You seem glum this morning."

"This is just my face," I reminded her.

She scoffed and frowned at me. "Are you wet? You better not be getting that seat wet."

"I can't go back to my room. Someone is in there," I said.

"Ah, yes. Our blushing bride. I swear, you, Giada, and Renato—at one point I'd thought the three of you would all die alone, and yet . . . you're the last man standing. Don't you want to settle down, too?"

I sighed. "I'm not the marrying type. I don't hate anyone enough to marry them." I gave her a rare, crooked smirk.

She laughed and shook her head.

"I have to go and get the lamb dressed. I'll see you at the ceremony. I've got a new hat to wear," she said with a small smile, standing and rushing off.

I watched the bustle in the kitchen, a million miles away.

I hadn't been lying. I didn't hate anyone enough to stick them with me. I wasn't a whole person. There was no hope for me. I was beyond saving.

I didn't hate anyone enough to marry them . . .

Did I?

Inside the chapel on Casa Nera grounds, the incense was so thick, it was hard to breathe. I felt like I was suffocating as I watched Jimmy joke with his best man, making lewd gestures, right in front of the altar.

My suit was stifling, and my shirt and tie were trying to strangle me. I pulled at my collar and checked the time.

She was late.

Good. Maybe she got away.

Fuck. I was really losing it. If she had somehow gotten away, I'd just need to hunt her down again. I shouldn't feel excited at the prospect. I was unraveling, and I didn't have a fucking clue what to do about it. The memory of her lips on mine last night slammed into my head, taking over my vision, surrounding all my senses and filling them up. I'd lived in the dark for so long that one glimpse of her, my light, was going to drive me insane. I'd sat alone in the library for hours last night, glaring at the fire, drinking myself into a state, before going looking for her. Getting just drunk enough to stop make excuses for what I really wanted. I'd caught her just as she was climbing down the tree. Fucking fate stepping in. And I'd continued to take what I really wanted. I could still *taste* her this morning.

I'd thought I'd protected myself from ever feeling like this again, and yet here I was now, fucking sweating in my best suit and trying to work out how to stop a wedding.

Renato was sitting with Charlie in the front row of the chapel. Charlie leaned in and said something quietly to him, and he stood and crossed over to me. I was standing on the other side of Jimmy, resisting the urge to kill the fucker before Georgia ever made it to church.

"All good?"

I nodded tightly.

"You know, I got some interesting intel from Giada this morning."

I waited for him to go on. I wasn't in a chatty mood.

He nodded, turning to the entrance of the chapel. "Looks like

Jimmy's been a naughtier boy than we'd expected. Very naughty, in fact. We'll need to do something about him. Ah, here she is."

My eyes followed Renato's gaze, just as he gave me a smirk and returned to his wife. Music sprang to life, filling the air. Georgia was walking down the aisle.

All thoughts flew out of my head. It was a vision I'd tortured myself with a hundred times. If everything had gone down differently, would this have been my future instead of Jimmy's?

I couldn't tear my eyes from her, and to make it even more painful, she was staring right at me.

She walked toward me, her eyes never straying to Jimmy, the man about to be her husband.

She watched me up until the last moment, when the priest started to talk.

She turned away and focused on the priest as the guests sat. It was a little chapel and could only fit those closest to the family. In this case, it was Renato and Charlie, me, Carmella, and a few guys Jimmy worked with at the casino. He had no blood family.

The priest was saying something and Georgia was responding, then Jimmy. It was happening. It was really happening.

The witnesses stepped forward to sign the register, and then the priest was telling them to kiss. Mafia weddings, as a rule, were short and sweet. Better to get it over with before someone tried to escape—or got shot.

"Now you may kiss the bride," the priest intoned solemnly.

No. This was wrong. It couldn't happen. I'd been lying to myself that I could let it . . .

"Fucking A, Father," Jimmy goaded and grabbed Georgia, pulling her closer.

She put her hands to his chest and pushed hard. The tussle was immediate and ugly.

Charlie covered her mouth with her hand and made to stand as Renato held her back from getting involved. His eyes turned to mine. My oldest friend, he could read my mind better than I'd ever been able to.

I tore my eyes from my capo and watched the couple.

"Come on. I want to kiss my wife," Jimmy grunted and managed to fit his mouth over Georgia's, and something inside me snapped.

She's not yours. How dare you.

My self-control went out the window. The patience that had been growing smaller and smaller every single day dissolved . . . and my gun was in my hand before I could question it. I'd had a lingering suspicion that Jimmy was dirty, and it turned out I was right. Stealing from a De Sanctis casino proved just how stupid the motherfucker was. But really, it was just an excuse, right when I needed one.

I stalked toward the couple. My approach sent Jimmy's casino friends fleeing. The priest collapsed back, his face etched in fear.

Georgia managed to tear her face from Jimmy's kiss. She twisted toward me, and I stepped past her, putting her behind me.

Then I brought my gun to Jimmy De Luca's temple.

He staggered back against the altar and froze.

"For the crime of stealing from the De Sanctis family and breaking your oath of fidelity, I find you guilty," I said without emotion, then stepped closer and spoke in a low tone, just for him. "For daring to put your worthless hands on what is mine, I find you guilty." I stepped back and pulled the trigger.

The bang echoed around the room, and silence fell over the remaining people in the chapel. Renato and Charlie. Carmella and the priest. The good father scrambled to the side and attempted to run, but I was there, hauling him back.

"We're not done here, Father," I told him, my tone rough.

With a hard kick, I sent Jimmy's body tumbling from the dais.

"What do you want?" the priest asked, looking at me like I was the Devil himself.

"What else? You have a wedding to perform." I turned and grabbed Georgia's hand.

She was standing stock-still, her face a picture of frozen shock. Her side was spattered with blood, making her a gruesome work of modern art in her white gown.

"Marry us," I commanded the priest.

The father gaped at me. "I couldn't possibly—this is a great sin in the house of God."

"I don't think you heard me," I ground out, my voice low. I lifted the pistol again and pressed it to his forehead. "Marry. Us. Now."

The priest wet his lips, wiping the spray of blood from his eyes and straightening his cassock.

"Dearly beloved . . ." he began, his voice shaking.

I didn't look at Georgia. I couldn't. My emotions were too close to the surface. I was a volcano that had only just started to rumble. Nothing would be left in its wake.

"Do we have a witness?" the priest glanced around, fearful.

"I'm here, Father," Renato said smoothly. "Charlotte and I will be witnesses."

The priest nodded weakly and picked up the bloodstained register.

"I—the bride's name is the same, but what name should I write for the . . . groom?"

Something loosened in my chest at the inevitability of it all. Since the moment I'd heard that Georgia would marry a De Sanctis man, hadn't I known it would be me? Hadn't Renato known?

Like I could have ever let another man marry her. It was always going to be me.

"Elio. Elio Santori," I announced.

"Do you, Elio Santori, take this woman . . ." he droned on.

I finally turned and met the eyes of the only woman I'd ever loved. The only woman I could ever love.

Georgia's gaze was a punch to the gut.

"I do," I murmured, never taking my eyes from hers.

"And do you, Georgia Conti, take this man, Elio Santori—"

"She does," I interrupted and waved the gun. "Hurry this along, Father."

"Very well, I now pronounce you man and wife," he hurriedly spit out.

He stepped back, and I reached for Georgia. Her eyes were red from crying. I brought her close and stroked away a line of tears dotting her cheek like jewels.

"Elio?" she whispered as I leaned in.

"You may kiss the bride."

The priest's words were the last I heard before I kissed her, hard and unforgiving; my loss of control couldn't do gentle right now. I didn't know if I was capable of gentle at all, and yet, when I kissed her, I remembered for a moment—the boy I'd been. The man I'd dreamed of being one day . . . the family I'd longed to have.

Beneath the frozen river, currents still run.

Then sharp teeth sank into my lip, biting hard. Pain lanced through my mouth, and I released Georgia.

She stumbled back. Her hand came for my face, a hard arc. I let her hit me. The slap echoed across the church.

"You—you liar! I can't believe you!" she cried.

I swallowed my response. I'd just kicked a hornets' nest, and it was time to battle through the inevitable attack. But I didn't have to do it here, with an audience.

"Come outside, we'll talk," I told her.

She shook her head, her incredulous eyes narrowing.

"I'm not going anywhere with you. You're—you're an unfeeling, soulless . . . monster," she spit at me.

"Maybe so, but now I'm your God-given owner, and when I say we talk, we talk." I bent at the waist and threw her over my shoulder. Ignoring her protests, I turned and carried her up the aisle.

"*Auguri*!" Renato called after me. Congratulations.

23

GEORGIA

We got around the side of the chapel before the maniac set me down.

My mercenary.

My husband.

The boy who broke my heart.

Elio Santori.

I knew it. I'd known it was him all along. Despite his denials, despite his damn eyes, I'd fucking known it, and I'd allowed him to lie to me to keep my sanity. Hell, wasn't that why I'd lied to myself? Now there was nowhere to hide.

I pushed his hands away as soon as he lowered me to the ground.

"Don't touch me. You don't have permission to touch me ever again!" I hissed at him, trying to inject cool, hard vitriol into my tone to mask the hurt and shock I was feeling.

He stared at me, a muscle clenching in his tight jaw.

"And here I thought you'd be grateful not to have to marry Jimmy De Luca." His voice was cold. "My mistake. Shall I see if someone can scoop his brains back into his worthless skull and right the wrong?"

"You could never right the wrongs you've done to me," I accused. "And you think I'd want to be your wife?"

Elio stepped forward then, his chest colliding with mine. "Don't be confused, Georgia. You're not my wife."

I could only stare at him as he leaned forward, getting in my face.

"You're simply my hostage. It's just business. De Luca needed to be taken out. I did my job. Renato ordered you to be married into the family, I performed my duty. All of this is just work to me. It's nothing personal."

My slap took him off guard, turning his head with the ferocity of it.

"I hate you," I fumed at him. If I didn't get furious, I'd cry, and I wasn't giving this motherfucker the satisfaction.

I raised my hand to hit him again, and this time, quick as a whip, he grabbed my wrist.

"The feeling, Mrs. Santori, is entirely mutual. Now, we're going inside to discuss the rules of your new reality, and I'll get on with my fucking day. You—my hostage—will do what you're told. Jimmy wanted a beautiful trophy wife to fuck and show off. I have no such temptation." His gaze raked me from head to toe. "You have nothing I want, so behave, or your life will get a lot more difficult than it already has."

His eyes met mine, and I flinched away from his dispassionate expression. Sure, he had to have contacts in, I knew that now, but it wasn't just the color that was throwing me off.

"What happened to you?" I asked in a near whisper.

He became utterly still at my question.

"What happened to the boy with the easy laugh, who wrote poetry under the stars?"

He studied me, and I studied him back. I saw the tension in his jaw, and the haunted look in his eyes. His thick, tattooed throat bobbed with a swallow.

"You." His voice was heavy. "You happened to me—and I'll never forgive you for it. This conversation is over. I have no interest in dissecting our youth. Bring up our past one more time, I'll put you across my knee and make you scream. Though maybe that's exactly what you're angling for."

Heat rushed to my cheeks, and my mouth dropped open in shock.

"You're a pig," I mumbled.

"Maybe, but I'm also your husband. Being married to you and keeping you in line is part of my job, and I am truly talented at my line of work."

"What's that? Following orders? Killing people? Torture?" I spit out.

Elio just nodded. "Yes, and so much more. Consider this your only warning not to push me. None of this is personal, and I will employ my experience and skills to make you comply. You are my hostage and you'll be a picture-perfect one—or suffer the consequences."

"You're not just a cold, unfeeling machine . . . you're a tyrant."

He nodded slowly. "Yes—to you, yes, I am. Just think of me as your judge, jury, and executioner. The decider of your fate."

"You're drunk on your own power! Does it give you a thrill to make women kowtow to your demands?"

"Not all women. Just you. Now, get your ass inside. I've had enough of providing free entertainment for the men today."

I opened my mouth to protest, because of course I couldn't just go down without swinging. But he never gave me the chance. With a heavy sigh, he hoisted me over his shoulder again and started toward the house.

His hand landed hard on my backside when I wriggled in his grip. "There's something we need to do to make this marriage official."

He carried me through the house, and I stopped kicking and screaming, because honestly, it was embarrassing as hell. Everyone was staring at us. I squeezed my eyes shut and longed for the privacy of Elio's room. I had always hated everybody knowing my business, and this took it to a new level. Shouts rang out in Italian. Congratulations and then many bawdy comments, all aimed at consummation. The men watching assumed Elio was carrying me to his room to consummate the marriage. They were all animals. I hated every single one.

He set me down just outside his room and unlocked it with a key from his pocket.

I kept stealing glances at the man I now knew for sure had been the one and only man I'd ever loved.

Before, when I'd been trying to find similarities, they had been all I'd seen. Now, all I could see were the differences. His violence and coldness. His hardness.

"No one goes in or comes out, until I say so." He was speaking to his underling and holding my hand in a grip that would surely leave bruises.

The young guy's eyes strayed to me.

"Including her . . . and there's no need to look at her. Avert your eyes in her presence," Elio told him curtly, with all the warmth of a frozen river.

What had happened to Elio Santori to make him this ruthless, remorseless killer? *You could just ask him.* Right, because stopping to ask deep, searching, personal questions when you're literally under attack is a normal thing to do.

He opened his bedroom door and waited. I paused on the threshold.

"Shall I carry you over it? I didn't take you for superstitious."

I stepped forward into the room and glared at him. He entered more slowly and locked the door behind him. The world fell very quiet. My anger and shock from the chapel had petered out, but I was still reeling.

Elio took me in from head to toe.

"Turn around," he instructed me harshly.

"I will not consummate this marriage," I stated, firm. "I refuse. I protest. I do not consent to your touch, got it?"

I raised my chin at him and folded my arms across my chest, because honestly, I didn't know any other way to deal with this man. The one who'd broken my heart and now, all these years later, tracked me down and forced me to marry him.

"Yet I've already tasted your cum, *cara* . . . and you've already screamed my name while my finger was in your ass. I think that ship has sailed."

"Yeah, well, that was before I knew who you were."

He chuckled, a dark, familiar sound. A sound ripped from the past.

"So, you wanted to fuck a brutal stranger but not the boy you pretended to care about all those years ago? That tracks. You're still arrogant enough to think I want to stick my dick anywhere near you?"

I flinched at the icy mockery in his tone and shrugged.

"As long as we understand each other."

He reached into his pocket and withdrew a folding knife. He opened it languidly, and the wicked point caught the sunlight falling through the window.

"Now, back to the business at hand. I said turn around. You'd better get used to following instructions, Georgia, or this new life of yours is really going to hurt."

I scoffed. "Hurt? Like anything you could do to me could hurt me more than you already have. What are you going to do? Beat me? Stab me? Force me?" I shrugged again. "Do your worst. It's all I expect of you anyway."

A muscle ticked in Elio's stone-cut jaw as he watched me. Remaining silent, he pushed off the door and advanced on me. I turned and tried to sidestep him, but his arm quickly snaked around my waist and pulled me close.

"One day, my dear wife, you're going to realize that these little acts of defiance and tests are dangerous. You're going to understand how much I'm holding back only when I lose it. So be careful," he said.

I didn't understand why, but his words made heat break out across my skin. Something about how his voice dipped over the threat of losing his self-control. The way he'd sounded like the old him, the brave, charming boy I'd lost my heart to so effortlessly. He was warning me not to break that mechanical, robot-like cool that he had developed in the years we'd been apart.

I wanted to break it, though. I wanted to destroy him like he was destroying me. Why should he get to be the one with the clear, unruffled composure, while I was melting down into a hot mess?

There was a slicing sound, and then the damn corset of the dress was loosening. The bodice sagged as he cut through the ribbons up the back. His hot breath hit my bare shoulder, sending prickles all through me. His thumb brushed my skin, and I fought not to arch into his touch like a cat.

"Your control isn't mine to command." I twisted around. "You can't blame me for any of this."

His gaze hit mine and then dropped.

Colored contacts. Such a simple way to hide those noteworthy green eyes. Suddenly, I wanted to see his real eyes so much, I couldn't breathe.

I was pretty sure the sagging bodice and sheer strapless bra I'd been given this morning weren't leaving much to the imagination. I didn't care. I wasn't going to be the only one to suffer. I wasn't going to be the only one to go fucking insane.

His gaze moved across me, bringing heat to the surface of my skin.

"Take it off and shower," he instructed. His words were only a murmur now, but a command nonetheless.

"Why? Don't you like the horror show you made?" I waved my hand down the bloodstained side of the white gown.

He tilted his head to the side, his eyes holding a challenge. "I'm not the one who introduced darkness into our story," he said.

What? He took the back of the dress and tugged it down, leaving me in just my panties and the bra that barely fit. Thankfully, the ladies who'd helped me put the dress on had provided me with clean underwear.

He tossed the dress away and stepped back.

"But I am the one who will end it," he said cryptically and stripped off his jacket.

I watched his once white, now red shirt join it on the floor. Next, he reached for his belt, whipping it through the loops of his pants in a way that had my core clenching, hard.

"What are you doing?" I asked.

He pulled the zipper of his pants down and stepped out of them. He was wearing black briefs, and his cock was clearly outlined, pressed up against his belly. I stared. I couldn't help myself.

"I told you to shower. I was letting you go first. That courtesy has ended, *wife*."

Then he dropped the briefs, and my attention jumped to his bare cock, red and drooling at the tip, thick and hard and oh-so-dangerous-looking. He was hard. All this had turned him on. So, I did affect him on some level, even if it was just the base one.

Aware I was staring at his dick, I spun around and let out a laugh that caught in my throat. So much for appearing unruffled. "Right, like I'm going to let you—"

I didn't get to finish. His arms crossed around my back, and he was lifting me. His skin was hot. Burning me everywhere it touched. My back was to his front, and his cock poked at the top of my ass.

"You don't have to let me do anything. I'm not asking for permission." He carried my wriggling body toward the bathroom.

He dropped me unceremoniously onto the floor and locked the door behind him.

He nodded toward the shower stall. "Get in."

"No! You can't just order me around," I ground out, knowing I was lying. Of course he could.

He took the key out of the door and set it between his teeth, then brushed past me and entered the huge shower cubicle. He reached up to the rainfall showerhead, so much higher than I could, and placed the key on top of it.

Then he went for the faucet handles. The water turned on, and I tried very hard not to stare at his naked back. The man was a work of art.

Thick bulging ropes of muscle, tight in all the right places, and swelling out in others in a testament to pure physical perfection. His skin was sun-dusted brown, just as I remembered it to be. The tattoos were different, new, and the scars. So many scars. Elio's back was a map of the life he'd lived without me. My eyes snagged on a cluster of dots that looked like old bullet wounds, and another that was jagged and scarred, like a serrated blade had raked his flesh remorselessly.

He reached out and snagged my arm, dragging me under the water and breaking my stare.

"Stop it! I don't want to—" I started, just as he pushed my face under the fall of water coming from the huge showerhead.

"*I* don't want to see any part of another man touching you, never mind smeared across your face," he bit out, his rough fingers smoothing over my cheek, rubbing away the spattered blood.

Water was falling into my eyes, so I couldn't open them. I parted my lips to protest and got a mouthful of water, so I snapped them shut.

Elio's hand was on the nape of my neck, holding me just where he wanted me.

Hot water sluiced down my body, wetting through my underwear.

Finally deeming my face clean enough for him, he let me step back, and the water formed a curtain between us.

"Trying to waterboard your wife on the first day of marriage?" I spit at him.

He ignored my words and stepped forward, the water coasting over his head and down his beautiful, strong chest in rivulets. Jimmy De Luca's blood washed down the drain, erasing the evidence of the insanity of the last hour.

He squirted a long jet of shower gel into his large palm, and rubbed his hands together until long tendrils of bubbles ran down his arms, then he started to wash his chest. I was just stuck there, watching. I couldn't get past him. I was wet, wearing underwear, and getting cold. He cleaned himself methodically, and lastly, let his hands fall to his hard cock. I briefly watched him slide his hand up and down the taut, veined shaft before forcing my eyes away.

"So, I guess that answers my earlier question. It does turn you on to have a woman at your absolute mercy, to do with what you please."

"Again—just you."

I shivered, and Elio noticed. He stepped back and pulled me into the hot spray. This time, I was able to bend my head forward so the water hit the back of my neck and eased the tension there a little. Not all the way. I wasn't insane enough to relax when I was next to naked in the shower with the tattooed menace standing in front of me. He reached out again for the soap and squirted another jet into his palm. He held it out to me.

"Wash."

His grunted instruction only pissed me off. I was so angry. I was so sad. I was feeling everything at once, and it had to go somewhere, or I'd explode. I simply couldn't hold all those emotions inside at once.

I knocked his hand away. "Don't tell me what to do. I told you, I'm not going to follow your orders, so you can just lay off it already."

Elio's impassive face could have been hewn from stone. How did he manage that cool facade? It was impressive, and annoying as hell. I wanted him to burn with rage and frustration like I did.

"I said wash the blood off, Georgia," he said in a low tone that would have made someone smarter than me take notice.

"No," I stated calmly instead.

He sighed and lifted one shoulder in a gesture of defeat. *That was easier than I expected.* I'd barely formed the thought when he advanced.

"Hey!" I grunted.

He backed me into the wall. The cold tiles were a shock against my overheated skin.

"I said, wash. If you can't do that, I'll have to do it for you."

"Don't you dare," I hissed, twisting around to face away from him so I didn't have to feel his hot skin on my chilled body. My nipples felt like they could cut glass, and the thought of Elio feeling them pushing into his chest, of knowing how he affected me . . . I couldn't stand it. I tensed just as his hands landed on my hips.

They were soapy and slick. He ran them up my sides and over my stomach, and I put my hands on the tile to brace myself.

With a perfect slow and methodical grace, he began to wash me. His soapy hands ran across my stomach, roaming up my back and along my shoulders and neck, rubbing away any place Jimmy De Luca's blood had touched me.

And, damn me, I couldn't stop him.

I didn't want to.

I was so fucking touch-starved, his strong, insistent hands running along my arms and over my collarbones turned me inside out. So, this was what it felt like to be alive. I'd nearly forgotten.

His hand circled my neck, scrubbing away the blood that had congealed there until the water swirled pink beneath our feet. I was panting, my breath coming hot and short. His hand rested on my throat, his fingers digging in just a touch, enough to make my breath catch. I could feel his naked body brushing my back.

"What am I going to do with you, *topolina?*" he asked me, his voice a growl.

He was still hard, his cock poking insistently into the small of my back. His other hand had paused on my breastbone, just shy of touching my bra. I wanted the damn thing off. It felt offensively unwanted, that harsh, wet lace, when all I craved was to feel his skin on mine. As if he were reading my thoughts, his hand dipped lower, brushing the cups of my bra, circling my hard nipples that were pointing through determinedly.

He pinched one, and I gasped, water getting into my mouth.

"This isn't going to do," he murmured, and with a sharp, strong tug, he pulled the strapless bra down, forcing my breasts to pop free. His hand returned to the shower gel and then touched me again. He started on my left breast, the place where a fine patina of red had dried just above where the dress had sat.

"Let's get you cleaned up," he said quietly.

My heart clenched hard.

I closed my eyes and let myself sway back against his superior strength. It had been a long, long time since I'd had someone to lean on. And I had to be weak as hell, because I couldn't stop myself. His hand, still slick with soap, advanced across my breast, finding my nipple and tugging on it. My legs nearly gave out at that sensation. It was all too much for me. The steam rising around us, making the air thick, and the smell of jasmine and neroli, and Elio. He fogged my senses. His skin burned my back. He was so hot and hard. His other hand was still on my throat, gently holding me in place, his thumb playing over my pulse. As his hand shifted to my other breast, my head fell back onto his chest. God, I was a sucker. I knew it as clear as day and yet, I didn't want him to stop. It felt too good, and I was tired of feeling like shit all the time. My head was pressing into his collarbone, and he bent his face forward and nosed through my wet hair.

What was this sickness in my blood? How could I want him like this, after all that had happened between us?

Beneath this skin, a world waits to be discovered.

The poem he wrote, all those years ago, still as true now as it had been then. There had never been anything ordinary about the electricity between us when we'd touched. It had been magic, and it was still there. Stronger, even.

The hand on my breasts moved downward, and I mourned it for a moment, then it hit my lower abdomen and kept going. His fingers slid into the top of my panties, and I arched back, my hindbrain screaming for more. *Yes, touch me. Yes, remind me what it feels like.*

Relief flowed through me, thick and sweet. I couldn't deny it. I was relieved that he was Elio. I felt safer. I could breathe again. That was the shameful truth, deep down in the dark, where no one could see.

His hand around my neck slipped to my necklace, the chain pulling taut.

My locket. My testament to the past.

Fuck, I was such a pushover. A traitor to myself.

The reminder was like a bucket of ice water over the head.

I twisted away and rested my front against the wall, the cold of the tile slashing through my heated skin.

"Are you done? Am I clean?" I asked in a muted tone. I didn't turn and see Elio's expression. I couldn't take it. I couldn't risk forgetting who this man was. Once upon a time, he'd brought my entire world crashing down. He'd left me. I could never trust him again.

He was quiet, and then the heat of his body disappeared. I kept my eyes closed for a long while, until the soft snick of the door shutting hit my ears. I peered through the steam.

I was alone. He'd gone.

I grabbed my necklace, sliding my finger over the closed locket hiding my weaknesses inside, and holding it over my heart.

24

ELIO

THEN

I lay on my bunk, trying hard not to move and set off my injuries. Last night's assault had been extra vicious. It hadn't helped that I'd made it a game not to show any emotion when they hit me. Sure, the first few weeks it had been tough, but I was becoming hardened to it now.

Last night had happened because I'd been caught in the west wing when the kitchen deliveries were made. I knew the schedule of all external contacts with the prison . . . and one day, I would escape. Nothing could keep me here when she was waiting for me.

The week before, I'd been pummeled for bribing another inmate to make a call for me. The call had never happened.

The last four weeks, I'd truly learned what being powerless meant. I'd been beaten and starved and mocked. I'd thought I might die a few times . . . but I couldn't.

Not while she was waiting for me.

"Man, you must like pain. I've never seen another motherfucker go after it like you do. What, you really think you can escape, De Sanctis?" my cellmate asked, chewing the damn toothpick he was never without.

Sergio Ravelli was a low-level thug who was in for aggravated assault. He was older than me and had taken me under his wing, in a way, when I'd first gone inside. They called me "De Sanctis" because that was the name on my paperwork. No one knew I was here, and Bellisario had made sure I was admitted with a fake name. It boiled my blood.

"I told you that wasn't my name. Escape has to be possible."

"Santori, whatever. The way you're going about it, it's not. What you need is a sponsor. Someone important who will get you out. If you find one, ask for me, too. I can't stand the thought of being in here another ten years."

"I don't know anyone who'd help me," I told him confidently, just as a guard rapped on the bars.

"Santori. Visitor."

My heart leapt. Was it Georgia? Had she found me?

"Holy shit—look at that! Maybe your luck is about to change!" Sergio sat up and grabbed my arm when I passed. "But don't forget . . . you owe me, Santori. If you get out of here, you'd better find a way to take me with you."

I stared down at Sergio's hand, and something in my expression made him pull back.

"Just remember. If you figure a way out of here, it's for both of us," he repeated and stepped back.

I walked away without giving him a second thought. I had a visitor, and there was only one person in the world I could think of who would come and see me here.

When Renato De Sanctis walked into the busy visitors' room, I couldn't have been more surprised. Sure, I'd been getting closer to the elusive Mafia heir when I'd lived in Castel Amaro, but him visiting me was still a surprise. I thought he'd been in the United States. *Wait, is he here about the bag that Alfredo set me up to take?*

He pulled out the chair across from mine, waving me off when I went to rise.

"Don't get up, Christ. You look like you could drop dead if you moved too quickly."

I shrugged. "I'm tougher than I seem."

He studied me. "So I see. How is it in here?"

"How do you think?" I asked. "How long have you been back?"

Renato sat back. Half the inmates in the place were glancing at him fearfully. The young, calculating Mafia heir who would inherit a dynasty.

"Honestly, I came as soon as Zio Sal told me some of what happened. I'm not really clear on it, except that you got on the wrong side of the prosecutor, and he'll make sure you pay for that."

"Georgia. Have you seen her?" I asked quickly, desperate for any shred of news.

Renato shook his head slowly. There was something in his eyes that was hard to look at. Something terrible.

"I've not seen her personally," he said. "But she's partly why I'm here."

"What's going on?" I asked.

Renato took his time. He had a manila envelope on the desk beside him, and a newspaper, folded neatly.

"Alfredo Bellisario has it out for you, and considering your relationship with his daughter, I can imagine why. I don't know the details, I only know what Zio Sal knows . . . You took a bag containing drugs and money from the De Sanctis house and the cops found it on you. Alfredo means to keep you here . . . until you die."

I stared at Renato. *Die?* It shouldn't have been a surprise, but it was.

"I'm here because I don't like Bellisario or men like him.

Hypocrites. My uncle has a relationship with him, but I have none. I don't like to see men like him get what they want."

"Can you get me out?"

Renato shook his head. "It's not that easy. I'm not the boss . . . yet. Still, there is something I can do."

I held my tongue and waited to see where Renato was going with this.

"I'm here to offer you a deal."

"A deal?"

Renato nodded. "I know talent when I see it, and I'll be damned if I want to see someone I consider a friend die in a place like this." He glanced around. "The police have real evidence on you, so I can't get too involved with all of this . . . but I can swap you one sentence for another. You leave here and enlist in the Esercito Italiano. My contact will make sure you end up in the right place. You serve your country for however long you can stomach it . . . and when you're done, then you come to America and become a De Sanctis. I need men I can trust around me."

Esercito Italiano. The Italian Army.

"What about Georgia? I can't make any deals that affect her. I have to see her as soon as I get out of here," I told him, hope quickening my pulse.

There was that look again. Dark and terrifying. Renato dropped my gaze and picked up the newspaper.

"I brought you something. Don't give me your answer until you see it." His voice was carefully cool.

I opened the paper, and the headline slapped me across the face.

It was a regional rag, the kind of publication that thought local weddings were a big deal.

This time, they were right. It was a big deal.

There was a black-and-white photo of a couple standing in

front of a courthouse, Alfredo Bellisario clapping in the background. Doves were captured in flight over the heads of the happy couple.

Local Millionaire Claims His Bride

> Prosecutor Bellisario waves his daughter, Georgia, and her new husband off as they embark on their life in America. Tommaso Conti and his bride will settle in California, where he will intern at a financial services firm and Georgia will pursue her love of dressmaking.

Renato watched me as I waded through a turbulent storm of emotions. Georgia had married Tommaso Conti. She had married someone . . . she was married, and she was leaving Italy. I shot to my feet, panic making me careless.

The guard shouted at me to sit down immediately, and my wrist ached where I was handcuffed to the table.

I sank down. I couldn't leave. I couldn't see her. I was powerless. Powerless.

She was gone, and I was here . . . and I'd die here. She had left me. It seemed pretty clear. She'd found someone else to save her from Castel Amaro. I was surplus to requirements. Yesterday's trash.

Renato leaned forward and slid the paper away. It felt like the future I'd thought I'd have was slipping through my fingers. Gone.

"If you take my deal, you owe me . . . When you get out, you come to me first—"

"I'll go," I told him simply.

Renato raised an eyebrow at me. "You're sure? I don't want to sell anyone's soul for them or make them live a life they abhor."

"It doesn't matter." Ice formed in my chest. "Nothing matters anymore."

25

ELIO

NOW

After another eternity in the shower, Georgia finally emerged. That was fine by me. I'd needed the time to get my head in order.

I'd had a moment of temporary insanity, and my body had betrayed me. I wouldn't forget that act of rebellion. I needed to get myself, and my new wife, under control. What was done was done, and no one would forget what had happened to De Luca. Maybe they'd think twice about skimming from a De Sanctis casino. Now it was time to let my hostage know how things were going to be. Sure, maybe I'd been lying to myself that I could watch her marry another man, but there was no need to let the loss of my self-control run unchecked.

I was dressed and ready for her when she came out of the shower; I had trapped my swollen cock under my belt to try and get it to behave.

"Here, wear this," I told her flatly, tossing a ring box across the bed. I hadn't let her keep on the ring that De Luca had chosen.

She stared at the little box like it was a venomous snake.

"What is it?" she asked, distrustful.

"A collar—so everyone can understand that you have an owner."

She reached for the box and opened it. A soft gasp left her. I had no idea why I'd bought the rings. It had been years ago. They had reminded me of my mother's engagement ring and wedding band, I supposed, the ones my father had hawked for money only a week after she'd died. It had been a passing moment of weakness, especially considering that I'd never intended to give them to anyone. Maybe, if my sister ever had a daughter, I'd pass them down.

Now, Georgia stared at the two complementary bands sitting on the plush velvet.

"You want me to wear your ring? I thought I wasn't your wife . . . I was just a hostage."

"To me, yes, that's exactly what you are. To everyone else, you're my wife, and God have mercy on the soul of the idiot who dares to forget it."

She released a soft snort. "Be careful, Elio, I might think you're protective of me."

"You'd think right," I told her. "I am protective of my possessions. My car, my weapons, my apartments . . . my wife."

"Wow, fourth after apartments. What an honor," she muttered.

I watched her slide the rings on and stare at her hand. They looked right there, like they were just made to fit.

I tore my eyes away and shrugged my coat on.

"Where are you going?" she asked and eyed me. She was standing in my robe, and it was ridiculously oversized on her. Her dark curls were piled on top of her head, and she appeared innocent in a way she had no right to.

"Out. The door will be locked, so don't do anything dumb." I spun for the door.

"Wait! You're just going to lock me in? What will I do all day?" She seemed panicked at the thought.

"Sleep, stare out the window, I don't care. I have work to do. I'm not your babysitter. From this moment on, you will earn freedom from this room with good behavior."

She glowered at me. "I'm not your dog, I already told you."

"No, you're not. I would never own a pet. They're too emotionally demanding."

Her eyes flashed at me dangerously.

"I could kill you when you sleep, Elio Santori," she bit out through clenched teeth.

A dark chuckle left me. "You could try." I turned away.

"Wait! So, this is my life now? Locked in a room? I'll go mad."

"The human mind takes much longer to break than you imagine. With time, we can see—"

I cut off as she went for me, flying across the room like a possessed woman. I shifted to the side easily to avoid her attack and used the momentum to spin her around, tossing her onto the bed. I followed, caging her in with a hand on each of her wrists, holding her down.

"I told you to stop testing me, *topolina*."

"Don't call me that," she spit at me.

In my monotone life, her anger was a vivid slash. She was in color, and everyone else in black and white.

"Why not?" I heard myself ask.

"Because it hurts too fucking much," she responded.

It hurts?

She shoved me with her hips, trying to move me, but her robe had come undone, and her nut-brown skin was glowing against the white terry cloth, and fuck, I wanted to touch her.

My body was waking up, and it knew what it wanted. The only woman it had ever wanted.

I pushed thoughts of licking that soft skin and rolling her over and sinking inside her out of my head. Touching her only spread the poison. It was dangerous.

"Let's get something straight, here and now. I told you I was good at my job. I'm not just good at it. I'm the best at it. I've broken men so hard and well trained, they could watch their families die without shedding a tear. I've lived in hell, Georgia. I was remade there. I brought it with me when I came back to the world. You cannot win against me."

She stared at me, her eyes glittering. I knew that look. Tears were gathering, and I didn't want to be around to see them.

"You don't understand the privileges I've already given you. Clothes to wear. A bed to sleep in. Food to eat and served at a table."

Her brow furrowed, my meaning dawning on her.

I nodded. "That's right. I could keep you naked, chained to the bed, eating scraps from the floor and pissing in a bucket by the door. That is what the Ravellis no doubt had in store for you." *And they're still searching for you.* I didn't bother with the last bit; we both knew it, and it was my problem. She was mine to protect.

"Who are you?" Georgia murmured, her gaze running over my face.

I'd taken the contacts out after the shower.

"I know you look just like him, but I can't believe that you are. Elio Santori might have been a thief and a hustler, and he might have shattered me into tiny pieces, but he was ten times the man you are. You're not my *cittaiolo*."

Each word drilled into my composure, and splinters webbed the surface of my cool.

I had to get out of there.

My jaw clicked when I opened my mouth to speak, I'd been clenching it so hard.

"Like I said. Be good. Don't make trouble. I'll see you later."

I pushed away from her, easily springing up from the bed and heading for the door. I needed to punch something. Anger lashed through me, heady and potent.

I got to the door just as she spoke.

"Can the hostage ask for something?"

I paused for a second.

"What?" I asked without turning.

"A needle and thread. I can stay sane a long, long time if I have a needle and thread."

Without acknowledging her request, I strode out and nodded to Ettore, standing guard just beyond the door.

It shut behind me firmly, and I twisted the lock.

"Guard that door with your life."

I left him to watch the locked door. She wouldn't find the windows as easy to open in my room as in the others. Thanks to my safety paranoia, they were harder to open than any other in the building, except Renato's. I'd tried experimenting to see if sealing the room up better, making it impossible to enter while I was sleeping, would help with my insomnia.

It hadn't.

I needed to get Georgia out of there. It wasn't right to be living here in Casa Nera with a wife. We'd move into my penthouse in Atlantic City, where my personal guard could keep watch over her and there were far fewer men wandering around. My penthouse was where I employed the safety measures that Renato deemed too extreme for Casa Nera.

I headed down the stairs just in time to hear a low whistle.

"Well, well, if it isn't the trigger-happy groom. Congratulations, brother." There were few annoyances in my life quite as great as Bran O'Connor, my sister's new husband.

"Don't call me that," I muttered at him, stiffening.

He leaned in and gave me an entirely unwanted one-armed hug.

"Aww, come on man, cheer up. This is your big day. Cracking a smile wouldn't be the worst thing that's ever happened." Bran smirked at me, all confidence and Irish charm.

I'd hate the fucker if my sister wasn't so utterly enamored, and he didn't treat her like the queen she was.

"So, what happened? Who's the lucky lassie to have captured the ice man's heart and inspired such a takedown at the wedding, no less? I wish I'd been there, I bet it was a hoot."

"I shot someone in the head, over the altar," I said.

He just nodded. "And I bet that fucker was asking for it . . . touching your woman, right?" He elbowed me. "Giada thinks it's all because Jimmy or whatever his name was needed to be made an example of, but I think I know better."

I glanced at Bran. His knowing smile made my gun hand twitch.

"A man like you doesn't lose his cool. He doesn't make an example without thinking through when and where . . . This woman is important to you."

Bran studied me, and I met his probing look as blankly as I could. Clearly, the holes in my facade were only getting bigger, because the burly Irishman nodded confidently.

"I knew it. So, my brother has fallen for some poor soul. I need to meet her and give her my condolences in person."

"You don't need to meet her or talk to her, or anything," I snapped at him, feeling the situation careering out of my control. I wasn't ready to explain Georgia and my obsession to anyone. I couldn't even explain it to myself.

"Now, now, don't be grouchy. We came all the way here to see her for ourselves. Your sister isn't leaving without meeting the happy bride, you should know that by now."

Fuck.

My sister, Giada, was most at home behind a computer screen. Right now she was doing her thing, making sure that Prosecutor Bellisario got the message that his daughter had married a De Sanctis. Her fate lay in the hands of the De Sanctis family.

I was pacing the wall of windows in her office as Giada worked away. Bran was in the garden with Carmella and Charlie, charming the socks off both women, as was his gift.

I needed to go for a run, or to the range, or to just kill someone with my bare hands. My aggression was building up, and it needed out. The box I kept the past in was threatening to burst open, and I didn't know what the fallout would be. It was unpredictable, and therefore dangerous.

"So, it's done."

"What is?"

She held up one finger. "One, changing the names on the marriage license." Then another finger went up. "Two, Bellisario will get the message and rat on the Ravellis."

"Well done."

Giada raised a hand. "Question. What if they don't back down once they start getting into hot water in Naples?"

"They barely have a presence here in the U.S. Once their capo in Naples goes down, they will crawl out of their hiding places and go back to Italy to fight over the scraps of the business or to squeal on each other." I sat in a leather armchair and tried to calm the fuck down.

"Hmm, like Papa did," Giada murmured.

Ah, yes, the great, illustrious Santori Senior, who'd barely made enough money being a low-level thug to support his two children, had watched his wife die of poverty, and then turned around and tried to cut a deal in prison, without caring that he'd made me and Giada the kids of a snitch. Once the family he was snitching on got wind of him, he'd been killed. He'd left us a brutal legacy, and we'd just had to get on with it.

Strangely, I hated Prosecutor Bellisario and Georgia more. My father's betrayal I'd expected. He'd never hidden the kind of man he was.

But the Bellisarios? *Her?*

"Sorry, what did you say?" I focused on my sister, suddenly aware she'd asked me something.

"I asked how your little bride is getting on? I was pretty surprised to hear what happened . . . You did tell me you'd rather die than marry that specific woman. If I'd known it was going to be my own brother's wedding, I'd have bothered to show up and even would've worn a hat."

She was nearly pouting, and it drew a chuckle from me.

"It wasn't planned."

"But why do it? De Luca wasn't a big deal. Sure, he'd been naughty and got caught with his fingers in the cookie jar, but going by your usual punishments, it was more of a maiming situation. He'd lose a few fingers, or a hand, and learn his lesson. Executed in front of the don was a little much, when he'd just gotten married, no less."

"And now anyone who was thinking of following in his footsteps is discouraged."

Giada nodded thoughtfully and then smirked. "And you just happened to get the girl . . . the one you hate."

"Just business. There's nothing personal there." I stared my sister dead in the eye.

She just laughed.

"Sure there isn't. You're very convincing, but you forget that I know you. So, tell me about the new Mrs. Santori. You knew her, right? In Castel Amaro? Don't tell me she was your childhood sweetheart or something." Giada laughed again.

I saw the exact moment she realized she'd hit close to home.

Her face morphed from amused to stunned. "You're shitting me. She is? You've never spoken about her apart from asking for that report years ago. I thought it was business-related . . . but it looks like it wasn't."

"Until ten days ago, she was dead to me. I wish she still was."

Giada raised an eyebrow. "She hurt you?"

"She destroyed me. She hurt you, too, you just didn't realize it. She's the reason it took so long to bring you to the De Sanctis estate to live. She's the reason I ended up serving my fucking country for the better part of my life."

"Whoa, wait a second. Are you serious? How can there be a woman who is this important to you, and I knew nothing about her?" Giada exclaimed.

"I told you. She was dead to me."

"But she's clearly not dead! You just turned your back on her?"

"She turned her back on me. I don't mourn the dead, Giada, you know that. When you're gone, you're fucking gone, and she was gone." My voice rose toward the end of my words, my frustration with myself and the circumstances bleeding through my control.

Giada was incredulous. I rarely lost my cool.

She nodded, then reached out a hand and patted my arm. One of the few whose touches I didn't mind.

"Okay, I get it. She was dead to you . . . You never wanted to see her again. But Elio, you just married her."

And there was the fucking irony of the century right there.

"That reminds me, don't you think that the good prosecutor sent her the backup he was holding over Zio Salvatore? Has she mentioned it?"

I blew out a long breath. The fucking package from her father. I'd forgotten about it completely. That's how fucked up being near Georgia had made me.

"No, and she won't. She won't volunteer anything. I'll get it from her if she's got it. Let's see what he has on us, get rid of it, and leave the rest. Enough to sink the Ravellis forever. They'll get off our backs as they scramble to stay ahead of the law."

Giada nodded. "You want me to search her room?" She wriggled her fingers. "I've got the expert touch."

"No. I'll get it. She can't lie to me. Leave it with me."

"Where are you going?" Giada asked when I got up to leave.

I couldn't bear the thought of going back to my room at this point. I needed to be far away.

"I have to go out. I need to—just be far away from here, at least for a while."

I stood, and my sister followed, concern filling her face.

"If you want to help me . . . get the woman upstairs a needle and thread, or something to keep her from trying to climb out the window."

"Okay, got it. Get *your wife* a needle and thread," Giada said, following me.

I went toward the door.

"Giada," I warned her.

"What? Isn't that what she is?" Giada protested.

Yes. That was what she was. *My wife.* Something dark and possessive snaked through my blood at that thought. One of those demons I'd carried back from hell, alive and well inside me.

I turned on my heel and strode away.

26

GEORGIA

A knock at the door a short time after Elio left had me spinning around guiltily. I'd been carefully going through the contents of his room, looking for any kind of clue as to the kind of man Elio Santori had become, because I certainly didn't recognize him. Sure, his face was that of the devastatingly handsome man who had charmed me all those years ago, but his soul . . . that was very different.

The door opened, and a beautiful dark-haired woman lounged against it. Her eyes weren't the same, but the family resemblance was undeniable.

She had to be Elio's little sister. The one he'd always been planning to get back.

"I'm not interrupting your snooping, am I?" she asked lazily, immediately clocking my bent-over position at the bedside table.

I straightened up and shook my head. "No. I was finished."

I really was finished. Elio had nothing of any kind of personal nature in the room. Maybe he'd scrubbed it before locking me up in here. That was the only way to explain the fact that there wasn't a single scrap of personality in the whole place. It really was a prison cell.

"Good to know. I'm Giada." Elio's sister sauntered into the room and closed the door behind her.

The lock turned outside. So, there was still a guard there.

"Don't worry, you'd never make it past me to the door." Giada smirked, reading my thoughts easily.

"Yeah, you're probably right. I'm not a fighter." I surveyed her fit form. "I'm totally unprepared for life as a thug's wife."

Giada's eyebrows shot up, and she let out a cackle of laughter. "Thug's wife? If you think that about my brother, wait until you meet my husband. Thug life. Nice. Reckless and brave without anything to back it up, but brave nonetheless." She stopped in front of me. "I heard you know my brother from way back."

I nodded stiffly. She was making me nervous. She had an unpredictable aura about her, like she might hug me, or stab me. She sank down on the edge of the bed, leaving me awkwardly standing over her. As if my thoughts had summoned it, she reached into her back pocket and pulled out a wicked-looking knife. She twirled it easily between her fingers.

"You know, I'm not a big believer in women being forced to do things they don't want to. I don't like it on the street, or in my family. The De Sanctis family isn't big on it. It's against Renato's code; well, except when it came to his own wife. So, that begs the question . . . What made you another exception?"

I shrugged.

"He knows you, of course, so I guess that changes everything. It means that he chose this for you. Which means he thinks you deserve it."

"I deserve being forced to marry a murderer and being locked up in a room for the rest of my life?" I bit out scornfully.

Giada shrugged. "I don't know. Do you?"

I took a deep breath and smoothed my hands down the old T-shirt of Elio's I again had on. I still didn't have proper clothes.

"Look, as nice as this show of female camaraderie is, I had time penciled in to stare at the wall and cry, followed by screaming into the pillow. I really need to get on with it."

Giada stared at me and then burst into laughter, her red lips stretched wide. Maybe everyone in this house was a psychopath.

"That was a good one. I like that. You know, for a bride, Elio could have done a lot worse." She chortled, standing and flipping her knife around.

She moved it so fast, I barely registered the motion before it was pressing into my throat.

"But I need to let you know that if you hurt my brother, I'll cut your throat, bitch, anytime, anyplace."

"Your brother is the one imprisoning me," I ground out, alarm beating through me.

"Yeah, he is, which isn't like him at all. Something about you has him all turned around, and I don't like that. He's been through enough."

"What's he been through?" I heard myself ask. Suddenly, I wanted to fill in those blank years between us more than anything, so I could start to understand the man Elio Santori had become.

"What hasn't he? He lost his soul overseas. He came back different. . . . Get used to it. As for why you upset him so much, I guess you fucked him over when you were both young."

"It was the other way around, actually. He broke my heart."

Giada scoffed, pressing the knife harder into my throat. "Either you're stupid or a liar. The only way all of this is happening now is if you really meant something to him, and my brother doesn't care about people easily. You could count the people he cares live or die on one hand, and for some reason, it looks like you're included. If that's the case . . . there's no way he hurt you. You hurt him, and you should spend your life fixing it."

"I swear. He was the one." I stared into her dark eyes. "I loved him. He's the only man I've ever loved."

Giada pulled back. She tossed her hair behind her shoulder and snapped her knife closed. I took the first easy breath in a good ten minutes.

"Weren't you married before this?" She raised an eyebrow at me.

I just nodded.

She let out a chuckle. "Well, in that case, I guess you two have a lot of talking to do. Good luck with that, my brother isn't an award-winning communicator. I brought you this." She took a bobbin of black thread and a needle from her jacket pocket.

This was Elio's doing. He'd asked her to bring it. I didn't know how to feel about that.

"No offense, but your clothes are a little . . ."

"Unfitted?" I suggested.

She shook her head. "Stinky. You haven't got anything else to wear?"

"I didn't really have a chance to pack much." I sighed and stepped away. That fact should've been embarrassing, but I couldn't bring myself to care.

"Okay, well, leave it to me. Good luck with my brother, you're going to need it."

And with that, she rapped on the door and left without a backward glance.

The lock turning shut after her departure echoed around the room.

Someone brought dinner to my door, and two armed men set it up at the table in the window. Neither of them looked directly at me the entire time. Once they'd left, the door was once again locked, and I fell on the food. I'd missed too many meals lately, and I barely paused for a breath as I inhaled the meal.

Pasta with basil and tomato. Simple. Perfect. It was so good, I nearly cried. It tasted like my *nonna*'s pasta. I ate so fast that I nearly felt sick when it hit my stomach.

I sank back against the chair and stared at the moon rising in the dark sky. Tall trees reached for it, and stars sparkled. I hadn't seen the stars in a decade. L.A. stars were the kind on Hollywood Boulevard, not in the sky.

I hadn't met many of the Hollywood stars in person, either. All my dreams of designing my own line of clothes . . . of having a brand and a store . . . they all felt so far away now. All I had left of those childish fantasies were a few half-sewn designs that I didn't even love. My clothes used to be bold. It was haute couture or go home. I'd been so audacious as a privileged little daddy's girl in Castel Amaro.

Meeting Elio had changed all that. Not just the tragic end of our love story, but meeting him in general had introduced me to another side of the world. It was one my father had protected me from. Funny how the roles had reversed now. I was penniless and had been living in a shitty apartment with a door that didn't even lock and a loan shark paying unexpected visits to work out payment plans. And Elio? He was rich. I could tell by his clothes, the quiet expense of a man who only buys the best. Since I couldn't picture Elio shopping, he probably had some underling go out and fill his closet periodically with black suits, black shirts, and black shoes.

Tommaso had trusted me with dressing him. When we'd first moved to L.A., I'd gone to school and he'd worked. We'd been comfortable then, I supposed, though I didn't remember much.

The grief had weighed me down. I didn't manage to stay in school. I was too depressed and despondent. A few months had passed that way, until Tommaso started to see someone. He was a therapist. His name was Drew. I began counseling with him and slowly came back to the world.

I yawned, my jaw cracking.

Wandering through the past was exhausting. I just wanted to sleep and sleep, preferably before Elio got home and I had to work out how to act around him.

A niggle at the back of my mind reminded me of something important that I'd forgotten. I emptied my bag out on the bed. It was the one I'd had with me at work, the night the Ravellis broke into the atelier and would have attacked me . . . if not for Elio showing up.

He'd taken my phone and wallet, of course, but I still had some of my things. Most important . . . I tugged open the broken lipstick tube, and there it was. The flash drive my father had sent me. I had no idea what was on it and no way to find out. Elio wasn't exactly supplying me with a laptop. I tucked it back inside the lipstick case and put it in the inside flap of my bag.

I was so tired. So tired of running and being scared, and tired of feeling like my life was out of my control. I'd been feeling that way for a long, long time. Much longer than the last week or so. It had been years and years. Maybe even since the last time I saw Elio, when I'd been full of naive hope and love.

Elio coming into my life again was showing the differences in us starkly. An unforgiving light was beaming down on the choices we'd made to become the people we were. What had Giada said? *He's been through enough.* What had Elio been through? I was more curious about that than whatever was on the flash drive.

I lay down and snuggled into the covers. The half-finished

dresses hung in the front of the closet. A testament to how I had never managed to reach my dreams, but had never forgotten them, either.

I'd contemplated going back to school just when Tommaso's family had found out that Drew was living with us. They'd cut him off. School was out of the question. I got a job making custom alterations, we downsized, and then Tommaso got sick.

He stopped work, I worked more hours, and my dreams were pinned away out of sight again as I slowly lost my best friend.

After, Drew had moved away to deal with his own grief, and I'd ended up just like I was when Elio had found me. My life had become a tragedy when Elio ran away, and it had never quite turned around.

Lately, I'd been drifting aimlessly; just surviving, not quite living. The days had been blurring into one another as I worked hard, ate cheap, and existed every single day.

Now I was living again. I was feeling again.

Like it or not, Elio Santori had once again turned my life upside down.

Could I survive him a second time?

It looked like I was about to find out.

27

GEORGIA

Lightning flashed, and a boom of thunder broke over the house. Hot, wet air swept in from the open balcony. I rolled over in bed, pulling my nightgown off and tossing it away. The humid air was making my skin sticky. I felt feverish. I thought about the stables and wondered if Elio was sleeping out there or in the house.

Since that night a month ago, we'd been inseparable, but only when we were sure we wouldn't get caught. Elio promised he'd take me away from here, that we'd leave together, but it wasn't time yet. We barely had any money, no plan . . . We were right in the fresh bloom of love, and it felt impossible to think about anything else. There was a deep and abiding sense of safety and security. I'd met Elio. Everything else would work out.

I stood and crossed to the window, enjoying the damp air brushing my skin.

I took the flashlight I used for signaling the stables and directed it out into the rainy night. If he was watching, he'd see.

I flashed the light in our usual code and waited. Nothing answered me. Disappointment hit me hard. I wanted to see Elio. I wanted to kiss him. I just wanted to be around him, all the time.

Tommaso called it infatuation and told me I'd get over it soon enough, but I didn't believe him. This was different. A soul meeting its other half. I felt complete when Elio was near.

I lay back down and turned on my front, trying to cool myself down as much as possible.

I drifted in and out of sleep. My mind wandered over images of what our lives would be like once we left Castel Amaro. Maybe Elio could come to America with me . . . I had citizenship from my American mother, after all. She was the reason I had an English spelling of my name instead of Italian. Georgia, not Giorgia. I'd been named after the state where my father had met my mother. It was hard to imagine my workaholic father ever being romantic, but I guessed he must have been once.

A shift of cold swept over me, and a few drops of rain. Rain? I only had time to vaguely register it before he touched me.

I didn't move. I was half asleep and not really sure if it was a dream, but there was a wet hand trailing down my back. I shivered, the sudden chilliness a pleasure all its own.

Elio was here.

My head was turned toward him already, and I peeked through half-shut eyes. He stood beside the bed, outlined by a flash of lightning from the open balcony behind him. He'd clearly climbed up the outside of the building, seeing as he was soaked.

He stripped his wet T-shirt off and dropped his pants. Seconds later he was naked, his cock jutting out hard and ready before him. He shifted to the bed and lay beside me, his cool hands wandering over my back and across my waist. I shifted, rolling onto my side, and his palms closed around my breasts. I gasped, the icy feeling echoing through me, quickly followed by the pleasure of his touch. He circled my nipples and then leaned in and captured one in his mouth, sucking and nibbling. I wrapped my arms around his head, cradling it against me as he feasted on my chest.

"Weren't you sleeping, *topolina*? I was trying not to disturb you," he murmured, a wicked gleam in his eye. He leaned up and stared down at me.

"I am sleeping. Don't you see?" I turned back to my front and got comfy, playing along with his idea.

"Hmm, yes, you look asleep, perfectly innocently unguarded . . . mine to do what I want with."

He shifted across my back. He ran his tongue down my spine, and I gasped. He slapped my ass at the sound. The slight sting was intriguing.

"Oh, like that, do you?" He gripped my ass tightly, sliding his fingers down my cleft and feeling how wet I was.

I parted my legs in a very obvious sign of what I wanted.

"My, we are bossy in our sleep." He chuckled and settled between my legs. Then his body draped over mine and his cock prodded at my ass. He guided it lower, putting the tip to my entrance, his arms braced on either side of my head, keeping his weight off my back.

I stayed still. I played my part, enjoying the game.

He slid inside. I was so wet, I was more than ready for him.

He muttered a curse and glided right in, my muscles slick and desperate for his invasion. I felt incredibly filled by him. He pressed in as deep as he could and then stopped.

I fought the urge to move. I wanted to fuck myself on his cock, but I was supposed to be asleep.

He chuckled, like he knew exactly what I wanted, before he began. Slow and deep, he fucked me from behind, while I lay "sleeping." It was hot as hell. I had no control over our position, or his pace, or anything. It was freeing, and Elio knew it. He was always telling me to let go more, not to try and control everything. It was a hard habit to break. Right now, though, I had to admit, he was right. Giving control to him was hot.

His hand snaked around the front of me, and he strummed my clit. I had to bite the pillow to smother my moans. My father slept just across the hall. That would be an interesting way to reveal our relationship . . .

I was going to come. This angle was perfect, deeper than ever, and his hand on my clit was making me embarrassingly wet. A wet sound squelched while he fucked me. With a muffled cry, I came, the orgasm hurtling out of nowhere and slamming into me. Elio swore, my pussy clamping down on him. He stayed right where I needed him as long as possible, then pulled out. His cum splattered across my ass and lower back. I hadn't managed to get the pill prescribed anywhere yet—well, anywhere my father wouldn't find out about—so we were trying to be careful. There were a whole lot of flaws in that method, and we were both aware of it, but not enough to stop. His breathing was harsh, and he swayed over me, on his knees, his glistening cock leaking out the last few drops of cum onto my skin.

With a satisfied sigh, he lowered his hand to my wet back, and then he was rubbing the milky fluid into my skin. He massaged my ass and lower back, spreading his cum into my skin like oil.

"I like it when you smell like me, *topolina* . . . so you never forget whose you are."

I woke with a start as I came, just when dream Elio slammed into me for another round. Pleasure flooded through me, undulating waves that seemed to have no end.

I was on my front, sweat gluing my face to the sheet. My pillow was trapped between my legs, and I was humping it. In that dreamlike state, reliving that memory, my needy body had taken over.

I collapsed my pulsing body against the mattress, feeling boneless, relaxed for the first time in over a week . . . and then I saw him.

Elio was sleeping on a thin floor pad, right beside the bed. He had a pillow and a blanket, but that had been kicked off. He was drenched in sweat; his bare chest glistened with it. He shook his head, a soft murmur leaving him. He was panting.

He was dreaming about something, and it wasn't something good.

I wriggled to the edge of the bed and took the opportunity to watch him.

What kind of dreams could push a man as merciless and dangerous as Elio to have what appeared to be night terrors?

His head shook back and forth, and his hands clenched into fists. *Should I wake him?*

His eyes suddenly slammed open, and he stared at the ceiling. His eyes. Green, finally, and just as mesmerizing as ever.

I shot back in the bed and lay still, pretending to be asleep. Had he seen me?

Then there was a rustle. Elio getting up. He cracked his knuckles and drank water in long, desperate swallows. I wanted to peek, but I didn't dare to.

Elio moved around the room. I could feel when he passed me, even without opening my eyes. He went back and forth and then stopped. I had the feeling that if I opened my eyes, he'd be standing right in front of me. Watching.

I tried to breathe normally, slow and steady, but my heart was beating so fast. It had to be obvious that I was awake, right? He had to know. Seconds passed. Was he just standing there? I felt the heat of his skin on my cheek before he touched me. It was the only reason I could stop myself from flinching with surprise. His finger rubbed gently along my cheekbone. He brushed the hair off my forehead, where it had stuck to my skin. The memory of just coming, fresh off a dirty dream about this man, flooded through me. No, not just a dream. A memory.

Just as abruptly as he'd touched me, he was gone, going toward the table by the window, or least it sounded like that.

A metal scraping sound filled the air, then it fell quiet. After a moment, I got brave enough to crack my eyelids open a sliver.

Elio was sitting at the table with an array of guns set out in front of him. His attention was fixed on them, and he methodically disassembled the weapons and cleaned them. His tan skin glinted under the spotlight over the table. His tattoos were works of art. I could spend days studying the designs.

Giada's words from earlier replayed in my mind.

He lost his soul overseas.

A terrible foreboding hit my gut. The memory of that night, in my bed while the storm raged outside, was still close, lingering on the edges of my mind. Could he be the same man who only a few weeks later had run away from me? Abandoned me so thoroughly?

It had never made sense. Never. It had never felt right, but I'd had no choice but to accept it, slowly.

The real burning question was why did he hate me so much, if he'd been the one to abandon me? I felt a yawning pit of darkness stretching before both of us. The past rising to meet us. It looked like we'd have to confront those demons once and for all. There was no escape. No places left to hide.

Elio started to put his guns back together. When he was done, he set everything down and sat back. His eyes rose toward me, and I closed mine quickly.

It was quiet for a long while, and then the chair creaked like he'd moved. I opened my eyes again to see he'd picked up a revolver with an old-fashioned barrel. He stared at it for ages, then spun the chamber.

Is it loaded? Before my mind could go to that dark place, I watched him put the end of the gun to his temple and pull the trigger.

I jumped, clapping a hand over my mouth so I didn't scream. The click was loud. My heart was in my mouth, and I couldn't breathe. He sat with the gun still pressed to his temple and then lowered it. The tension seemed to melt from his shoulders. I'd rarely seen him relaxed since he'd stormed back into my life. He was always tense, coiled like a spring, yet tightly controlled. There was no relaxation or spontaneity. There was no room for ease.

The reality of what I'd just witnessed sank through me. Elio stood and switched the light off. He carried newfound calmness through the room as he walked back to the bed on the floor. Words to confront him, to reveal what I'd seen and ask him what the hell he was doing, filled my mind. I had to fight to keep them inside. He lay down, disappearing into the darkness. My words died. I didn't know what to say to Elio anymore to reach him. He was a fortress unto himself.

Tears came, and for the first time since Tommaso died, they were for someone other than myself. What had the world done to those kids who'd been young and starry-eyed in Castel Amaro?

My pillow wet through while I silently cried myself to sleep.

28

ELIO

I went for my run as soon as I woke up. Dawn was just creeping over the grounds of Casa Nera, the sky tinted purple. I pushed myself harder than usual. At the thirty-minute mark, my brain finally switched off and glorious quiet surged in. I ran for another hour.

The calm started to fade when I got back inside and unlocked the door to my room. The reason for the noise in my head was asleep. I found myself sitting on the bed. She was still wearing my clothes. Giada had messaged me yesterday to inform me that I needed to clothe my new wife before she decided to walk around naked.

Just the thought of Georgia making a point by strolling naked down the hallway of Casa Nera—packed with De Sanctis men—shattered my temporary calm. Giada had a point. My little hostage was going to need clothes. She was going to need her own room, and she was going to need something to keep her busy.

Yes, she was my hostage, but the undeniable truth I couldn't bring myself to say out loud was that she was also my wife.

My wife.

Finally, after so long . . . the universe had corrected its wrong. It had brought her back to me.

Tiredness pressed into me, like a heavy weight was pushing me down. I was an insomniac, but I was used to being tired. I lived with it. I ignored it, just like I'd ignored the fact that Georgia was out there, living her life, in the same country as me. Just like I ignored the memories of a life I couldn't forget and would always carry.

I shifted onto the bed beside Georgia. She had always been a sound sleeper. It looked like some things never changed.

God, the bed was comfortable. I hadn't slept in one in years. Usually, the softness rankled on my nerves, but now, it felt just right.

Just like that, I let go and drifted away.

I woke to the feel of something on my chest. Panic gripped me. Was it a person, a body? Was it debris? My mind scrambled to catch up with the present, and I nearly shot upright, and only just caught myself when the object on my chest gave a small snuffling snore.

A snore?

I glanced down. Georgia's head was on my chest. She'd migrated over to where I lay, and she was sound asleep on me. Her leg was slung over mine. My heart pounded. After years of being in peak physical condition, I was developing high blood pressure after only a few days of sharing my room with this woman.

She sighed and moved against me, burrowing her face deeper into my chest.

The smell of her hair and my shampoo drifted to me. I couldn't stop myself from running my fingers through it. My fingers caught on a tug at the end of the long length, and Georgia let out a small moan. Just like that, I knew I'd be hard all day.

So, she still liked having her hair pulled.

I had to wake her. This couldn't continue. This was dipping my hand right into the poison and expecting not to get infected.

"Georgia, wake up," I murmured gruffly.

My arm had crept around her back, and now, I squeezed.

She shifted against me, fighting my urge to wake her.

"Come on, *topolina*." There better not have been a note of begging to my tone.

I shook her lightly, and her eyes drifted open. They were hazy and unfocused, her gaze roaming upward until it hit my face. Her eyes latched onto mine, and I could tell she was still more asleep than awake.

A smile broke out over her face.

It was the most beautiful thing I'd ever seen.

An expression of pure relief and happiness.

"Elio," she whispered, her voice deep and husky with sleep. She was still there, drifting in the ether. "*Dove sei stato?*" Where have you been?

That look in her eyes . . . no one had ever looked at me like this woman had, a lifetime ago. No one could ever look at me that way again, because I wasn't the sort of man who could inspire such a look anymore . . .

Except from her.

I smoothed her hair back, locked in this stolen moment just a little longer.

"*Sono qui.*" I'm here. "*Sono sempre stato qui.*" I've always been here.

Her smile deepened. Sunlight hit her from behind, casting a golden halo around her dark waves.

Outside, far below the house, a loud bang sounded, probably deliveries stopping by the kitchen. The noise shattered the precious glass that had encased us in a memory.

Georgia's hazy expression snapped into focus and she jerked back, sitting up and pushing me away.

"What's going on?" She glanced wildly around.

"What's going on is that you still snore." I pushed off the bed and stood. "Get ready, we're going out."

"We are?" She jumped up. Her sleepiness had dissolved into excitement.

"You act like you've been locked up for years. It's been a day."

"Whatever. I need fresh air every day," she said.

"You lived in L.A.," I reminded her.

She rolled her eyes, but her excitement remained palpable. "Right, that's true. Anyway, I would love to leave this room, if my lord and master allows it."

I didn't trust myself to respond to that particular title, so ignored her.

After a shower, I found her waiting at the door for me.

"You're dressed?" I eyed the outfit I'd given her days before.

"Yes, I don't have anything else, and I have it on good authority that it stinks, literally." Her cheeks tinted pink at the admission. Was she really embarrassed to smell a little like old sweat around me? She had no idea how sweet she smelled. There was nothing about her body that wasn't a turn-on.

"I'll make sure to stay downwind." I reached for her wrist.

"What the hell?" she exploded as I slapped a metal cuff on her and then clicked the other end onto my wrist.

"I can't have you running off when we're outside Casa Nera."

"So, you've handcuffed us together?"

I just nodded and took her arm, steering her out into the hallway.

"That's right. Where you go, I go."

"Lucky me," she said.

* * *

Atlantic City might not be L.A., but there were enough high-end boutiques to keep even the pickiest of shoppers happy.

I walked into the first one we came to, my arm tucked around Georgia's, hiding our bound hands.

Assistants dressed in black with sleek headpieces fluttered toward us.

"We need women's clothes. A full wardrobe," I told them when Georgia failed to step in. "Pick things out," I instructed her.

She drifted toward a clothing rack, taking me with her. She moved some coat hangers, and her eyes widened.

"This stuff is expensive."

"Is it?" I checked my phone for any work-related messages.

Georgia wandered here and there, and I followed, her arm tightly gripped in my hand.

"Surely there's something in here you like?" I asked, my patience for shopping rapidly dwindling.

"Yeah, of course there is, but I'm not about to spend five hundred dollars on a shirt," she said, gripping the collar of the shirt in question. "It's not even sewn that well."

"Stop looking at prices and choose things. I don't have all day," I snapped at her.

"Sorry for caring if you waste your money," she snapped back at me.

She took a step away, and I tugged her back, just hard enough that she fell into my chest. I wrapped my other arm around her back and guided her against the railing just behind her.

"I've told you often enough that I'm not the Elio you used to know. I'm not some penniless hustler anymore . . . My time is more valuable than anything in this store."

She huffed.

"Roll your eyes at me right now, and I'll take you into a changing room and fuck your smart little mouth."

Her shocked eyes flew to mine. *Where the fuck did that come from?* Shit. The ability to hold back from all the things I wanted to do to her was crumbling.

Her cheeks warmed, turning a pretty pink. Her eyes slid from mine.

"Right. Like you'd dare do that here . . . and besides, I'd bite it right off."

"I'm sure. Let's not test that theory. Get a move on, or I'll choose whatever I want you to wear." Just the thought of picking out the sexiest clothes from the store and forcing Georgia to wear them around me was a fucking turn-on. It was ruined only by the fact that if anyone else saw her in them, I'd have to carve their eyes out.

"Big talk, Santori," she blustered, pushing me back.

I let her go. She was fully blushing now. My *topolina* was unsettled. That wasn't like her at all. I enjoyed every moment of her loss of composure. Considering how she was driving me slowly insane, it was only fair.

She started to hang things on the rack the assistants had left for her. When she was done, we headed toward the changing rooms.

The assistant hung the clothes inside and then held the heavy velvet curtain back for Georgia.

She hesitated, looking to me. I took hold of the curtain and stepped into the changing space, pulling Georgia with me.

"I'll take it from here," I told the shocked assistant.

"We—actually, we have a one-person-per-room policy," the assistant stammered.

"But you're making an exception for us," I told her firmly and shut the curtain in her face.

Georgia stepped back, and our bound wrists pulled taut.

"What now? She's going to think we're hooking up in here," she hissed.

"You're handcuffed to the man who forced you to marry him, and that's what you're worried about?"

"Well, I can't try things on with one hand," she said.

I conceded that, undoing the handcuffs around our wrists and tucking them into my pocket.

"I'll be right outside. There are no other exits, and I am armed."

"Of course you are, Mr. Mercenary." She turned around to yank a black jumper from a hanger.

I eyed the clothes on the rack.

"Everything is black . . . trying to tell me something?"

"Just dressing for my mood." She shot me a faux sweet smile and started to unbutton the shirt she'd borrowed from me. "We can match." She looked me up and down. She had a good point.

"Well, are you going to give me some privacy?"

I stepped out of the curtained changing room and settled onto the settee right outside. An assistant hovered near my side. Georgia in black didn't seem right. When she'd made her own dresses, they were all bright colors and patterns. My memories of her were all lemons and cherries in the dappled sun.

I waved a hand at the rest of the shop. "Can you guess her size from the things she took to try on?"

The assistant nodded eagerly. "Yes, of course. Is there something else you'd like her to try on?"

"No, she doesn't need to try it." I reached for the folded business paper sitting beside the couch. The store clearly knew their clientele. "Just ring it up and give it to my driver outside."

The assistant paused. "Er, which items?"

I waved a dismissive hand around. "All of it."

"All of it? All of what, sir?"

"The shop, what else?" I asked, growing annoyed with the continued questions.

The assistant backed away excitedly, just as the curtain twitched.

"Well, aren't you coming out to let me see?" I drawled.

Georgia peeked around the side. "Do I have to?"

I hadn't had any such intentions, but the clear reluctance on her face convinced me.

"Yes, of course. Get your ass out here now for inspection," I snapped.

She sighed. "This isn't the military, you know." Despite her acidic tone, she stepped out.

My brain short-circuited for a second. Sure, it was black, but by God, she was stunning. I'd had her swathed in my huge clothes this past few days. Now, there was no denying her hourglass shape. She was in a black clingy dress, some off-the-shoulder, tight-at-the-knee thing. Sophia Loren would have been envious.

"Well?" she demanded.

I stared. And stared.

"Hello?" She waved a hand in front of my face.

"You're lucky this isn't the military. You wouldn't last an hour without your CO coming down hard on your ass for attitude." I had to get a fucking grip.

"Yeah, well, just keep your fantasies of coming on my ass to yourself," she quipped and then jerked her eyes to mine in the mirror. She looked horrified at her own phrasing.

A laugh left me, unbidden and surprising. Like a rusted lock turning, warmth filled my chest. What was happening to me?

I found myself teasing her back. "Why would I do that and deny you so?"

She tore her eyes away from mine and took in her reflection. I could make out her ruby-red cheeks from here.

"Well, do I pass inspection?" she demanded hotly after a long moment of bearing my scrutiny.

I couldn't tear my eyes from the way the dress hugged her long legs.

I nodded and picked up the paper.

"Hmm, your ass is safe . . . for now."

I focused my attention back on the page. She huffed and went back into the changing room.

I'd like to say I ended the little game right there, but I didn't.

I made her show me every single outfit. All unrelentingly black, all hot as the fires of the inferno.

While Georgia stood staring critically at a pair of leather pants that personally I considered award-winning on her, the assistant from before sidled up to me.

"That's everything charged, wrapped, and sent to the car," she said with a warm smile.

Her eyes flew to my hand, and it didn't take a genius to see how she searched for a ring. I still didn't have one. A fact that would have to be remedied.

"Thank you." I nodded dismissively at her.

She didn't go, however. She lingered. I cast an irritated glance in her direction.

"Your girlfriend is a lucky woman to have a shopping spree with a man like you," the assistant continued.

A man like you? I wondered if she meant the killer part, or the mafioso, or the PTSD war veteran.

"You mean rich?" I proposed instead.

She tittered, covering her mouth in a way that she seemed to find demure.

"No, I mean, well, honestly, look at you. Money and good looks . . . your girlfriend has all the luck."

"She's not my girlfriend," I announced, casual, and turned the page of the newspaper.

Georgia swiveled from the mirror, my words catching her attention.

"She's not?" the assistant asked, her voice breathy and smile hopeful.

"No," I answered coolly. My eyes flickered to Georgia's. "She's my wife."

Silence met that statement, and there was a flicker of something that passed over Georgia's lips. Like the ghost of a smile. I couldn't turn away.

"Oh, well, she's even luckier then," the assistant rushed out.

"Hmm, tell her that," I drawled and set the paper down. "*Cara*, if you're finished, I think we should go."

Georgia's eyes widened at the nickname, but she nodded and cast a curious glance at the assistant as she ducked into the changing room again.

"I apologize, that was inappropriate. I don't know what came over me."

She was standing too fucking close. I stood and set down the paper. Then I took a few steps back from the unwelcome interruption.

"No need to apologize," I told her, firm.

Her face softened, and she drifted closer.

"No need to apologize because I don't care. I don't care about anyone except her." The words left me unexpectedly, and immediately I knew them to be true. Two days into this unwanted arranged marriage, and I was losing my head.

Two days in, and I didn't care.

29

GEORGIA

When we came out of the shop into the afternoon light, I couldn't bear the thought of being locked back up in that creepy old mansion again.

I whirled to Elio and clutched his hand with my free one. The wrist closest to him was already handcuffed to his. The psycho.

"Can we take a walk?"

He shook his head. "I've got work to do."

"Please, just a little . . . We could eat something." I hated the plea in my voice, but I couldn't stop it. I was close to getting on my knees and begging.

He shook his head again, and something inside me snapped.

I stopped on the street, only jerking forward when he tried to keep walking and found my weight pulling against the cuff.

He frowned at me.

"Even prisoners get more yard time than this," I snapped at him, barely holding it together.

He tilted his head to the side. "What the fuck do you know

about prisoners and their yard time? The closest you've ever been to being inside is watching a drama on TV."

I snorted. "Okay, fine, and you're an expert?"

It had just been a comeback, some kind of response to the shots he fired at me nonstop, but this one struck.

I could see in his eyes as soon as the words left me that they were true. I felt it in my gut.

Elio had served time. The man who'd never wanted to end up like his father had ended up in prison at some point after all.

He stared at me, and I stared right back.

"When?" was all I could manage. My questions had formed an impossible pile of dry kindling, and any second, a struck match could light the thing on fire and burn down the life that I'd known.

"Ask your father," Elio said.

Scratch. Hiss. Whoosh.

What the fuck?

"What do you mean?" I asked, wanting to know but also scared to find out.

Elio broke eye contact first. He peered down the street. His free hand pushed through his hair. It was shorn short these days, precise and no-nonsense. But the movement was the same as the past, when he had chocolate-brown waves tumbling across his forehead.

"There's a pizza place down the block." His voice was quiet.

Then he tugged me forward, and we were walking.

"What were you talking—"

"If you want to walk, drop it," he told me in a tone that brooked no argument.

I did want to walk. I didn't want to drop it, but it seemed I had little choice in the matter.

We walked in silence, my cuffed hand tucked in the small of

his elbow, like we were any other couple out for a stroll down a pretty tree-lined street packed with boutiques. I tried to ignore the screaming questions in my head. There was a display window on the way that caught my attention.

I hesitated at the glass, and Elio stopped too, following my gaze.

"All that time married to a millionaire like Conti, and you never made your designs available for sale."

"I never finished any of them."

He raised an eyebrow. "You had more than ten years."

I sighed. "Things didn't really go according to plan. I take it yours didn't either."

"What makes you say that? I'm rich, as you pointed out, powerful, second in line to New Jersey and a good chunk of New York."

"And yet you're so happy you play Russian roulette with yourself at night," I blurted out before I could think twice.

Elio continued to stare at the window display. The only sign he was bothered that I'd seen his little hobby was that twitching muscle in his solid jaw.

"Yeah, well, take comfort, *topolina*. One night, maybe you'll get lucky. Being a widow suits you. Maybe one day soon, you'll be mine."

"Don't say that," I snapped at him, my temper flaring even as my heart dropped.

He gave me a sidelong glance. "Why not? It's the truth. You already mourned the husband you really wanted, the one you chose, so I don't think you'll shed many tears for me."

"Elio," I started.

But he was turning away.

"There's the pizza place. I'm not taking the cuffs off, so eat one-handed or don't eat at all . . . Be the talk of the town, it doesn't bother me."

We crossed the street, the moment in front of the shop lost.

My heart felt like it was being tossed in turbulent seas, and my chest was an ocean of regret and confusion, and terrible, cutting longing. Longing so deep I felt it down to my very bedrock.

The pizza place was authentic and smelled delicious. It was standing room only. Elio battled to the front, letting his arm trail back so I could stay out of the fray, and managed to order, pay, and carry two bendy paper plates with slices. We sat outside on the curb, surrounded by others doing the same. There were teenagers messing around with friends, and some couples kissing. The pizza place sat in a small square, and there was even a fountain in the middle. On that sunny evening, we could have been in Naples.

A family of three passed by us, and the little girl in the stroller dropped her toy giraffe. The mom stopped pushing the stroller, and the dad jogged back for the toy. He handed it to his daughter and threaded his hand through his wife's. They beamed at each other.

Such simple, honest happiness. A display of richness that money couldn't buy.

I watched them until they disappeared around the street corner, and then I turned to find Elio watching my handcuffed wrist. The skin had turned pink and irritated underneath.

He sighed. "Promise me you won't run off and I'll remove it."

I considered his words. Running away wasn't even on my horizon right now. I was too intrigued by figuring out what had happened in his past to go anywhere.

I held out my pinkie to him. "Okay, but you have to make me a promise, too. You have to swear it."

He narrowed his eyes. "What promise?"

"You won't play that game again."

He jerked like I'd slapped him. His pale-green eyes fastened on me, demanding somehow. "Why do you care? I told you, it's the best-case scenario for you."

I shook my head. "I need protection, so I need you. I can't risk you leaving me alone in a den of wolves. You brought me here. You're responsible for me."

He stared at me so long, my hand wavered in the air between us.

"Are you asking me to save you, Georgia?" His deep voice made me shiver. No one did pure, unbridled power like him.

"Hmm, maybe the second time is the charm," I quipped and wriggled my pinkie. "Swear, and I promise not to run away."

Slowly, he brought his pinkie to fasten around mine.

"Deal."

After freeing my hand, he turned back to his pizza.

I devoured mine, even faster than he ate his. Now I wiped at the grease around my mouth, suddenly self-conscious. My cheeks felt hot. I was suffering through a second adolescence around this man, and it wasn't any easier than the first one. Only he could ruffle me like this.

He reached out and rubbed the corner of my mouth with a tissue. I found myself holding my breath.

He dropped his hand.

"We better get home." He helped me to stand, which turned out to be a good thing because my legs had fallen asleep at the curb.

I groaned at the leg pain and the thought of going back to Casa Nera.

"Is it too much to hope that that place burned to the ground while we were out?" I complained.

Elio just smirked faintly. "Let's go and see, shall we?"

Ten minutes later, we pulled up at a tall, swanky apartment building overlooking the harbor.

"Where is this?" I wondered when the car stopped outside and the driver got out.

"I told you we were going home . . . not to Casa Nera."

"Wait, Casa Nera isn't home?" I asked, eagerly following Elio out of the car.

He stood on the pavement and waited for me.

"It is to Renato . . . but not to me, and not for us. This will be our home, for now." He inclined his head toward the huge glass apartment building.

I couldn't fight my relief when we got into the elevator. Elio pressed his finger against a sensor, and a chime sounded.

"You didn't even press the floor button," I pointed out.

"It's programmed to my fingerprint. No one unauthorized can access the floor."

"Which floor?" I asked. The glass elevator shot upward, carrying us higher and higher. "The penthouse?"

"Only the best for the new Mrs. Santori," Elio stated flatly.

"Very funny," I said, but I couldn't deny I was happy not to be going back to Casa Nera.

The elevator opened into a sleek, dark hallway. Guards stood on either side of an impressively fortified door.

"Sir." Both men saluted Elio with tight precision.

Elio saluted them back.

"Does Renato know you have your own private army?" I asked as the locks disengaged on the vault-like door.

"Well, I am the mercenary, after all," Elio murmured and ushered me in.

Once we were inside, the men locked the door behind us.

"You don't have any security actually inside?"

"I don't need security inside," he said, leading me down the hallway to the huge open-plan living room.

Night had fallen. Floor-to-ceiling windows looked out over the Atlantic City marina, neon skyscrapers reflecting endlessly on the black water.

"So confident."

"No. Just experienced." Elio turned down another hall. "Let me show you to your room."

My room.

"Wow, this hostage is moving up in the world. I've got my own room and everything."

I followed behind him until we came to a door. He pushed it open and waited for me to enter.

It didn't look like the rest of the penthouse, from what I'd seen so far. This room was warm and inviting. Pale sage walls and dark wood surrounded a wrought-iron bed. The covers were terra-cotta and cream linen, and a thick wool blanket was tossed across the end. *Wait. Sage?* I glanced around the walls. The silence felt too thick as I met Elio's eyes. *One day I want to paint our bedroom sage green . . . it makes me feel safe.* My childish optimism and confidence felt like mocking as the memory hit me. My favorite color . . . the same color as Elio's eyes. Why'd he paint the room this color?

How long had he been planning on finding me and keeping me there, in the room next to his . . . his prisoner . . . his hostage . . . his wife?

What really happened to you? I wanted to ask, but I was scared to. *Tell me about the years I've missed . . . because something terrible enough happened that the boy with laughing eyes and a silver tongue became hard and cold . . . and yet still remembered the color I wanted to paint our bedroom one day.*

My heart softened. I watched him. His face gave nothing away about the simple gesture, but the way he avoided my eyes, it was clear. We both knew it meant something. That something was making my chest feel fuzzy.

The past sat like a boulder, holding my hope pinned down. I needed to know what had happened to this man. But I knew in my gut that once I did, nothing would ever be the same, and I wasn't sure I could cope with that.

"Make yourself at home. I have to go out."

"A *sottocapo*'s work is never done," I muttered, and then a terrible thought occurred to me. "Unless you've got somewhere else to go? I never thought about it before . . . since I'm your hostage and not your wife . . . if you had a girlfriend already." The thought made me sick with jealousy, though I'd never admit that out loud.

The silence was deafening.

Elio was impassive. I couldn't get anything from that guarded facade. I wanted to crack his head open and peer inside.

He stepped back into the hallway.

"I'll see you in the morning," he said quietly. "Don't try to run. You wouldn't get far."

"I believe you," I sighed, sinking down on the king bed. It was massive and cold.

I don't think I ever did, I admitted to myself. Not then, and not now. I hadn't got far.

I was still right here.

Waiting for him.

30

GEORGIA

I let myself wallow in my pity party for an hour after he left and then got up and dusted myself off. It was time to make myself at home, like he said. Best of all was the fact that the doors to his bedroom and office weren't even locked. That made me think he didn't share his space very often with others. Seeing how private he was gave me a kind of satisfaction I didn't want to examine too closely.

I started in his office. There was a laptop, password-protected, of course, and a painfully neat desk. That was about all. Not much to see there.

Next, I moved to his bedroom. In another life, I might have felt bad about invading his privacy. But considering how he'd left me with nothing but questions and no answers, locked up, penniless, phoneless, and desperate, I wasn't feeling too bad about it.

As soon as I opened the bedside table, it was clear this was where he kept his private things, not at Casa Nera. There wasn't much in his bedside drawers, but there was enough to give me a glimpse of the man he had become.

There were a couple of well-thumbed paperbacks and a set of

dog tags. I picked them up, staring at his initials etched into the metal. Where and when had he worn these?

I already knew he'd been in the military—that much was obvious from his bearing and training—but I longed to know the story behind it.

Where had Elio gone? What had he seen? I had a feeling that the *what he had seen* part was what drove him to sit at the table at night, clean his weapons, and roll the dice on tomorrow.

Beneath the dog tags there was a notebook I recognized like it was my own.

The one Elio used to write his poetry in.

I opened it, sliding my finger across the spidery black lines.

Beneath the frozen river, currents still run.
Beneath stone and concrete, seeds push through—
And those seeds can lift whole buildings.

The past sat on my shoulder and dug its claws in. He still had the notebook that he'd filled with words that summer. I gripped it tightly. I wanted to read it. I was that much of a masochist.

With a sigh, I sat on the bed with the notebook on my lap and gazed out the window. The city was dark, and the lights of the hotels and casinos glittered. Elio was out there right now. *What is he doing? Who is he with? Is he really working? Should I even care?*

He really could have a girlfriend. He'd been clear enough that I wasn't his wife, only his hostage. Surely his display in the clothing shop had been for appearances only. I could try to tell myself I didn't care if he was with someone else, but that would be a lie. And I didn't have the strength to lie to myself in my own head.

I *would* care. I would really care.

With a sigh I sank back, staring at the ceiling, my mind drifting back over the days we'd shared together. That whole sun-dappled summer that had passed too quickly—before my life had plunged into winter.

Unrelenting. Never-ending.

I still hadn't found spring.

The sound of a slamming door echoing through the penthouse sent me shooting to my feet.

A person?

I stood, panicking. Every time I snooped, I ended up nearly getting caught. I probably should just quit it. I clearly wasn't cut out for a life of crime. But common sense warred with my desire to find out more about Elio.

I shoved the notebook into my pocket, hoping my loose pants and baggy shirt would hide it.

I sauntered out of Elio's room, trying to seem like I hadn't been doing anything wrong.

A woman stood in the foyer, a discreet black headset in her ear. When she saw me, she stood straighter, clasped her hands behind her back, and studied some point over my head.

"Captain Toni Deponio, Mrs. Santori, performing a security sweep."

I felt like an absolute mess compared to this professional, disciplined-looking woman.

"Um, Elio said that there wouldn't be security inside the apartment," I pointed out.

"With respect, Mrs. Santori, that is only when he is in residence. Otherwise, I will be looking after you."

I sighed. "I don't need looking after."

"With respect, your husband disagrees."

Your husband. My face felt hot and itchy.

"Well, it's nice to meet you, Toni. Please call me Georgia."

"No can do, Mrs. Santori. Please go about your evening, and I will check the residence."

She gave me a salute, turned on her efficient heel, and strode off.

I stared after her. These people who Elio had watching his house weren't De Sanctis men (or women, for that matter). There was no way. These were all ex-military. More clues to Elio's mysterious past that I couldn't fit together.

Seeing as Captain Toni seemed as likely as a rock to let slip private information about her boss, I was just going to have to find out for myself.

You could just ask Elio.

Yeah, right, because he was really open to being asked about what had happened in our time apart.

The truth was, however, that Elio still had the poems that he'd written that summer. Love poems . . . to me. It made my heart feel like it could smash into a million tiny pieces.

That could mean anything . . . but it didn't mean nothing.

I couldn't go and read the notebook while Captain Toni was wandering around. The last thing I wanted was Elio finding out that I was snooping in his most private, personal memories. I'd justified it because he'd destroyed my life and forced me to leave everything I'd cared about behind. And yet . . . I couldn't deny that it was weighing on my conscience.

I really was done snooping.

I needed something else to do. Something other than sitting and thinking about the disaster that was my life.

I had just the thing.

For an upright, ex-military Mafia man, Elio sure had an impressive wine collection. To be fair, they were pretty dusty. He might collect, but it didn't seem like he enjoyed them often. I uncorked a bottle of red and swigged straight from it, settling down on the floor with my back against the kitchen counter, staring out the floor-to-ceiling window at the Atlantic City marina.

My mind lingered here and there, a bird hopping from the past to the present. I almost never let myself think too much about those days together. They had been so short but so precious. Thinking about them was like tracing an old scar that had never quite healed right and would always ache.

Now it felt like that wound had been opened right back up. And blood was running freely.

Before I knew it, the bottle of wine was empty, and my head was swimming. I had to hold on to the floor.

I had to be drunk. Because I never even heard him approach.

One minute, it was just me, gazing out the window, whispering to myself like a madwoman.

The next, a dark figure was crouched beside me, prying the empty wine bottle from my hand.

"What's going on?" Elio asked, his deep voice sending a rush of sparks across my skin.

"I've just been taking a walk down memory lane," I slurred, sloppy-drunk. "I don't recommend it. It's a fucking tragedy."

He studied me in silence, then stood. "You need to lie down."

I nodded, my head feeling like a puppet on a broken string. "Yes, boss," I sniped, putting my hands to the floor and trying to push up—only to immediately tip over. "Whoa." The world spun violently.

An Italian swear word left Elio's mouth, then he muttered something and reached for me. His arms were strong as he scooped me up and held me against his chest.

I inhaled the smell of him.

No perfume. No cigarettes. No gross club smell or evidence of another woman. He hadn't been with someone else. Why did that make me relieved? It shouldn't. I should be happy if he was making himself and his taciturn moods and cruel disinterest someone else's problem.

"You smell like you," I murmured into his shirt.

He turned and took me from the kitchen.

"Who else would I smell like?" he mused as he carried me down the hallway.

"Your girlfriend," I mumbled. "You've got one, right? Why wouldn't you have one?"

"I'm not really the dating type," he said cryptically. "And I don't know if you've heard, but I'm a married man."

A smile spread across my lips at his matter-of-fact tone. He glanced down, and one side of his lips lifted in a smirk.

"You like that?"

"Yes," I nodded. "Yeah. I like that."

We reached my bedroom. He pushed the door open with his foot and carried me in, heading toward the bed.

"Can I ask why you decided to get drunk as a fish tonight?" he asked and lay me down.

"I couldn't work out how to turn the TV on." I sighed and relaxed into the mattress.

"I'll show you tomorrow," Elio said. "Get some rest."

He turned to go, and—faster than I thought I was capable of—I snagged his hand and held him there.

"No, wait."

He stilled.

"I met Captain Toni," I added and tugged on his hand.

He let me pull him to the edge of the bed. He sat.

"Good. She's going to be your bodyguard when I'm not around."

"She's scary and awesome . . . Why a woman? Didn't trust me around a man?" I dissolved into giggles. It suddenly seemed so funny that Elio might think I was some kind of sexpot man-eater, when in reality, I'd only ever been with one man. Him.

"More like I don't trust them. I know better than to test a man with a temptation like you."

I wished it was brighter in there and I could see his face. But it was shrouded in shadow.

I gripped his hand like it was a lifeline in a turbulent sea—the only thing that could keep me alive.

"Be careful, dear husband. I might start to think that you don't hate me as much as you say you do."

"You can hate someone and want them at the same time." His voice was dangerously deep. "You taught me that."

Acting on sheer drunken impulse, I pushed myself up, bringing my face close to his. He stiffened, but there was no stopping me when I was this drunk. Suddenly, tempting Elio's iron-like control was all I wanted. I wanted him to see me. I wanted him to break his rules for me.

"So, you hate me, but you want me, and you have me here . . . all yours," I said.

In the dark, with only the neon glow of the city seeping through the windows, I could just make out his eyes. He was looking down at my lips. Heat surged through me.

I swayed toward him, leaned in, and landed a kiss on his lips.

His hands immediately closed around my shoulders and moved me back.

"What are you doing?" he asked.

A tear escaped my eye and dripped down my cheek.

"Why?" I asked. "You said you wanted me. You were lying, right? Just like then. You never really wanted me. You just wanted what you could take from me . . ." My voice broke near the last word. The damn wine had made me vulnerable and unfiltered.

He took his time to answer.

"I don't kiss drunk women," he said simply.

"That's nice to know, you're great at avoiding answering things," I said, dizziness taking over.

Oh, I'd really had too much to drink.

I lay back down, blinking at him a few times, my eyes growing heavier with each one.

"You're a professional. Did you train in how to survive torture?" I was so hot. I couldn't stand it. I pulled at my shirt, trying to unbutton it and take it off.

Elio's blunt-tipped fingers brushed mine out of the way and finished the job. I tossed the shirt across the room and flopped back in just my bra.

"But then, this isn't torture, is it?" I chuckled.

Elio stared at me. "Isn't it?"

I rolled onto my side and reached up to tap his nose.

"It's good," I said, "not to kiss drunk girls. You're still a good guy, though you kill people now. But if you only kill bad guys, does that made you a good guy?"

My voice was slurred, my thoughts slipping away.

"Me," I continued sleepily, my words barely making sense anymore, "I don't kiss drunk girls. Or drunk guys, either."

A pause.

"Do you want to know a secret?" I whispered.

Elio paused, then leaned in.

I pressed my lips to his ear. "I've never kissed anyone but you."

The confession was the last thing I said before the world drifted away.

31

GEORGIA

When I woke up, the world lurched so violently, I don't know how I managed to make it to the bathroom to throw up. Several disgusting and wrenching minutes later, I collapsed onto the floor and groaned.

What the hell?

I hadn't ever been this hungover. I wasn't a big drinker, and for a long time I'd been on so many antidepressants, I'd never bothered with more than a glass of wine here and there.

Now I was paying for the fact that I had basically zero tolerance. I'd been damn lucky to survive a whole bottle of wine.

"Mrs. Santori, allow me," a female voice spoke from the doorway.

I rolled over to see Captain Toni, fresh-faced and full of health. She had a medical bag in her hand.

She helped me up off the floor and back to the bed.

"You don't need to take care of me. I'm fine. It's my own fault."

"Feeling like shit is still feeling like shit, regardless of whose fault it is, if you'll pardon my language."

I laughed. I couldn't help it. The phrasing was so unexpected from Captain Toni.

I lay down and watched her unzip her bag.

"You got some aspirin in there?"

"Not quite," she said and pulled on some latex gloves, snapping them for good measure. Then she took out an IV with a long tube and needle.

"What the hell?" I reared back.

She reached for my arm regardless, her touch firm and nonnegotiable.

"Fluids, painkillers, and saline. You'll feel better in no time."

I watched as she swabbed my arm and then slid the needle in. She had a surprisingly gentle touch.

"I've been administering emergency medical aid for decades. Don't worry."

"Oh, I'm not, I just feel really bougie to be getting a drip for a hangover. Is this a rich people thing?"

"Pretty much," Toni admitted. "Colonel Santori ordered it."

"Colonel?" I repeated. "You served with Elio. I thought you didn't use titles in civilian life."

"It's hard to remember when it comes to the boss," she admitted. "If you could keep my slip-up to yourself."

"Of course. Anyway, it's not like I talk to my husband much."

Toni shrugged. "He doesn't talk to anyone much. But you are the first and only woman to visit this residence."

"You're here."

"Because of you. The boss doesn't share his space with people. He doesn't trust anyone." She caught my eye, and I could see her curiosity. "Except you, apparently."

I shook my head. "I wouldn't read too much into it. He just knows how powerless I am."

Toni let out a little chuckle. "You might be inexperienced and untrained, but in this house, I wouldn't call you powerless. Far from it."

I sighed as Toni draped the IV over the back of the headboard.

"You're going to be disappointed when you find out . . . your beloved colonel married a woman he hates."

Toni bustled around, tidying up. "The boss doesn't do anything he doesn't want to do, that much I know for sure. On that note, some things came for you."

"Really?" I sat up. "Clothes?"

"Clothes, I think, but something more than that. We can go and see, if you want."

Toni rigged me up a portable stand for the IV bag, and I wheeled it after her down the hall, past the huge living room to a room on the other side. She opened the door, and I stepped inside.

At first sight, I flinched, seeing several tall figures standing against the windows.

No, not figures. Dressmaker's dummies.

There were four in total, and on the opposite wall there were about ten rolls of fabric. On the large desk in the middle of the room were bags. In disbelief, I peered inside.

There were shimmering spools of thread in every shade imaginable, and a sleek pair of tailor's shears with polished silver blades. A pincushion bristled with needles, and a tape measure sat on top of rolls of tightly packed ribbons, lace edging, and tailor's chalk.

Everything I needed for my own dressmaking studio, right here, in these bags, and my own room to do it in.

I sat at the desk, incredulous.

"What is all of this? Why would he do this?" I looked at Toni, who just shrugged.

"I don't know, but like I said, the boss doesn't do anything he doesn't want to do. Which reminds me." She reached into her pocket and pulled out a sleek black cell phone. "This is for you."

I took it and turned it over in my hand. Honestly, I hadn't missed mine much in the last few days. The only person I might have missed checking on me was Erica. God only knew where she thought I'd gone. Was the LAPD looking for me because of the massacre in the dress shop? Elio didn't seem concerned. If anyone was experienced here with getting away with murder, it was him, it seemed.

"He's letting me have a phone?" I pressed my finger to the screen, and it unlocked. I just wasn't going to think about how he programmed my fingerprint to unlock it. Probably last night when I'd been out of it.

"To an extent. It can only call one number."

I opened the contacts and there it was, the only number in the phone. Added under:

My Mercenary.

I jabbed it, more out of curiosity than anything else. It rang three times, then someone picked up.

"You're still alive." Elio's deep voice came over the line and shocked me like a live wire.

I threw the phone across the room in fright.

Toni bent and picked the phone up from the chair it had landed on.

She put it to her ear. "Yes, sir. She is. She does. Very well."

She hung up.

"Here," she said and handed me back the phone.

I stared at it. "How come it can only call one number? Can it call 911?"

Toni shook her head. "Nope. It's specially made. Giada, the boss's sister, cooked it up. You can call your husband, and he can call you, and that's it."

"Great. What if I'm in a burning building and I need to call the fire department?" *Or the police to report my own kidnapping?*

"I'd still recommend calling your husband."

Well, it was clear where her loyalty lay. I shoved the phone into my pocket.

"Okay." I sighed. "What now?" I looked around the room. It was flooded with natural light. There was space and all the stuff I could possibly need.

"I guess you've got a lot to organize. Better get started."

A flicker of excitement lit in my belly.

"Let's do it."

By the time night fell, I'd organized my new studio seven different ways. I had my half-finished designs all pinned onto dummies. I'd been shocked to find the walk-in closet in my bedroom packed with not only the clothes I'd picked out, but the rest of the store. He was right, money wasn't an object to him anymore. It was hard to get my head around.

I couldn't lie; when I'd found the wardrobe, I spent nearly an hour trying things on. I was still neck-deep in the new things when a soft knock on the closet's archway that connected the walk-in to my bedroom sent me spinning around.

Elio lounged in the doorway, dark and dangerous and utterly lethal. His sharply cut suit did nothing to hide the power in his shoulders, and his piercing green eyes were fixed on me. Not on my face, though—on *all* of me, up and down, taking in the dress I was wearing. I'd been trying on a pale yellow one that fell to the knee and had a sweetheart neckline. The bodice was tight, and I couldn't reach the zipper myself. He walked toward me and wordlessly twirled a finger, telling me to turn around. I complied, and he pulled the zipper up. The feeling of his hot breath on my back weakened my knees.

"The clothes fit" was all he remarked.

I nodded. "They do. You didn't need to go to such expense, though. I'm just grateful to have fresh underwear."

"If you're implying that I'm trying to butter you up, or buy you with them . . . you're mistaken." Elio's gaze held my eyes in the mirror in front of us.

His hand slipped from my shoulder and ringed my neck, and I forgot how to breathe.

It sat like a tattooed necklace against the base of my throat.

"I already own you, *topolina*."

His fingers pressed lightly into the sides of my throat, constricting my breath just enough to send my heart racing. His front pressed into my back. I felt trapped. Suffocated. Liable to be consumed by this man.

I didn't hate it like I should.

My eyes drifted closed. I couldn't take him so near, the scent of him, and the look in those green eyes. It was all too much. I was already losing my head, there was no need to speed up the process.

"We're going out for dinner," Elio declared, releasing me and stepping back. "Wear the dress."

Then he turned and left me there, blood thumping in my veins, hands clenched into fists, genuinely unsure if I wanted to kiss him or kill him.

32

GEORGIA

We went to a private dining room in an upscale casino for dinner.

"Wow, the prisoner's getting parole tonight?" I mused as I grabbed a menu excitedly. Okay, a few days in, and I was already grateful for just getting to be outside.

Perfect. My mental health is looking really good.

"Just for a few hours, so don't get too worked up," Elio said to me calmly, watching me peruse the menu.

The food sounded amazing. I worked my way through the list, my mouth watering.

A knock at the door sent the security in the room on high alert.

"Wait, we aren't eating alone?"

Elio's eyes were trained on the door. "You'll be happy to hear that no, we're not. Be on your best behavior."

I blinked at him. "You're letting me be around someone else? What if I tell them you kidnapped me and forced me to marry you?"

Elio shrugged. "Feel free. If you think you'll find help or sympathy from the man we're having dinner with, you're sorely mistaken."

The doorway filled with a tall, broad man. This man was someone important and dangerous. Just the size of his security entourage told me as much.

The man approached, and a shock of recognition flowed through me.

His angular face and chiseled features were immediately familiar. It took me a second to place him, and then it clicked.

"Good evening, Mr. Santori. I'm glad that we finally found the time to sit down and talk business," the man said, looming over us.

His Russian accent was just as I remembered it.

I shot to my feet, feeling awkward just sitting while he waited to be greeted.

"And is this your lovely new wife—my, what a small world," the man continued.

"You've met before?" Elio asked, still sitting. But despite being the only one sitting, he wasn't weakened by the pose. If anything, the gesture rang with power.

It was an effortless display of dominance, and we all knew it.

The Russian smirked and shifted his eyes to me. "I had the pleasure of an introduction in L.A." He reached out then and took my hand. "Remind me, beautiful, of your name."

He brought my hand toward his lips but never made it. Suddenly, Elio was standing right beside me, his hand moving like a whip to leash the Russian's wrist, stilling the movement before it could be completed.

"It's 'Mrs. Santori' to you, Sokolov." Elio's voice was hewn from stone.

"Ah, yes, of course," Sokolov chuckled. He released my hand and shifted back. He eyed Elio with interest. "When I heard that you had married, I admit, I was surprised. I hadn't heard any rumors of an important new addition to the De Sanctis family. Unless this is a new relationship . . . the exciting first flushes of infatuation?"

"On the contrary," Elio said coolly, his expressionless facade back in place. "My wife and I have known each other since we were young."

The Russian nodded. "Ah, a first love then? Beautiful. Enjoy it, Santori. It is a rare find." He turned to me. "Your name was Georgia, wasn't it? I'm Roman. Roman Sokolov. It's a pleasure to see you again, Georgia."

I nodded, not particularly wanting to wade into the bristling tension between the two men.

"Let's sit. We didn't come here to chitchat."

Elio sat, and so I followed his example.

I had no idea what they were meeting about, except it appeared to be business and made me wonder why the hell Elio had brought me here.

"Sokolov runs Philadelphia. He and Renato might have shared interests, if they decide to work together," Elio told me. He shifted toward me, laying an arm along the back of my chair. "First, we need to see if we could work together."

"What your husband means is that if he approves of me enough, he might make the introduction to your capo, so I'll be on my best behavior tonight."

"You'll be on more than your best behavior around my wife," Elio said starkly.

"Elio!" I gasped. The insinuation that Roman might hit on me was embarrassing, to say the least.

Roman simply nodded. "Of course, another man's happy wife is never to be touched."

"A happy wife? So, if I wasn't happy, that rule wouldn't apply?" I asked.

Roman nodded. "Of course not. A woman should be happy with her situation . . . or it should be remedied."

I slanted a look at Elio. "Did you hear that?"

Roman laughed, a deep, rich chuckle. "Am I taking your line of questioning as a cry for help?"

"Sokolov," Elio said in a low warning tone.

"What would you do if I said yes?" I asked, enjoying the chance to get to Elio and make him feel awkward for once, instead of the other way around. "Would you take me away? Call the cops for me?"

Roman let out a boom of laughter and shook his head. "You've married quite the woman, Santori, congratulations. Women should be full of fire and never afraid to speak their minds . . . it keeps life interesting." He turned to me. "No cops, of course, and no, I wouldn't be taking you anywhere. A wife is a husband's property, like it's always been . . . I'd simply give your husband advice on how to better please you."

His gaze drifted over me. "It wouldn't be hard."

My mouth dropped open with shock at his words, but before I had time to respond, Elio tossed his napkin onto the table, picked up one of the many forks at his place setting, twirled it expertly between his fingers, and drove it through Roman's hand, pinning it to the tabletop.

I screamed, jarred by the sudden sight of blood splashing across the white linen. The security around the room tensed. De Sanctis men drew their weapons and held them on the Russians before the other side could even reach for their guns.

Roman grunted and swore. His security spoke to him in a rush of Russian, and he waved his free hand at them, sending them back to their posts.

"Elio! We need to get help or—" I babbled and tried to stand.

Elio tugged my arm so I fell back into my seat.

"Do you know what you want to order?" he asked me, nodding toward the menu.

I stared at him, dumbfounded. A man was bleeding right next to us, a fork impaling his hand and pinning it to the table, and my husband just asked me what I felt like eating.

"You'll enjoy the scallops here, and the *porcini tagliatelle*," Elio continued as if everything was perfectly normal.

Just then a waiter appeared, his eyes averted from the scene at the table.

"Georgia, what would you like to eat? Tell me or I'll order for you," Elio instructed, completely unruffled by the situation.

My mouth opened and closed, but I couldn't find any words.

Elio sighed and looked at the waiter. "Bring us one of everything on the menu. My wife is feeling indecisive."

He picked up his wineglass and settled back in his chair, his arm still lying across the back of mine, and regarded Roman.

He raised an eyebrow at the Russian.

"Well, Sokolov . . . apologize to my wife. Your bad manners have put her off her dinner."

Roman chuckled and nodded toward me. "I apologize, Mrs. Santori. Don't let me ruin your appetite."

There was a tense moment as I stared between the two men, and then I realized that Elio was waiting for me to speak.

"It's fine, really. Are you okay?" My voice was a muted murmur.

Roman shrugged. "I'm fine. It's just a scratch. In our line of work, you get used to a certain amount of liability. And Mr. Santori here, and his boss, are very dangerous men . . . as I'm sure you know. It was my mistake to flirt with his wife. I'm sure men have died for less."

I thought of Jimmy De Luca, shot in the head when he'd kissed me in the church, and shivered involuntarily. Elio Santori was a very, very dangerous man. He was watching me with those jade eyes, so familiar yet so unrecognizable from the boy I'd known. My heart thumped. My ghost, made flesh. Living and breathing, right there beside me.

And yet . . . it didn't matter what he did, or who else he hurt . . . I knew he'd never hurt me. There was nowhere in the world I was safer than by his side.

A very dangerous man . . . and my husband.

"Yes, he is dangerous. You shouldn't forget it, Mr. Sokolov, if you value your appendages."

Roman let out a cackle as he pulled the fork from his hand and wrapped a napkin around the wound.

"Consider me warned. Now, let's eat."

33

ELIO

I couldn't keep my fucking eyes off Georgia at dinner. Jealousy and possessiveness had stewed in my gut as I'd watched her talk to Sokolov. Why the hell had I brought her? Ah, yes, to send the message to my world and its important players that this woman was mine now. *Mine*. And there would be no mercy for anyone who forgot that.

I'd clearly never forgotten. Lie to myself as I might, the fucking walls of her bedroom of the penthouse were undeniable. How long had I been preparing the perfect prison for my little country mouse? How long had I planned to take her, and keep her? How long would I have been able to leave her alone to live her life, had Renato not sent me after her? Another month? A year? Had I always just been waiting for my patience to run out? Or Tommaso Conti to shuffle off the mortal coil and leave her alone and unprotected . . .

Now we were walking by the marina for no other reason than I wanted to delay leaving there and going back to the penthouse. I wanted to delay the moment when she'd disappear into her own bedroom and shut me out.

The last few days had made one thing extremely clear.

I was going to lose this battle she was unknowingly waging against my self-control. Her fucking whispered confession had haunted me, as had her drunken kiss.

I was going to snap.

And I wanted to.

Georgia had high heels on, and her entire body swayed with every step. It was hypnotic.

We were nearly at the yacht. I'd had it a few years, imagining that maybe once I did, I'd become the kind of man who worked less and went out and enjoyed his free time more. I'd pictured being on the boat, with the calm waters all around, and hoped that maybe, just maybe, they could calm me, too.

It hadn't worked.

The damn thing sat in the marina and mocked me whenever I saw it. A reminder of my failed attempts to be anything in this life other than the De Sanctis *sottocapo*. A natural-born killer.

Only one thing had calmed me in fourteen years . . . and it was this woman's touch. I was completely fucked. I could be calm and controlled and emotionless as hell, and Georgia might as well laugh at my efforts. Around her, I felt like a desperately-in-love twenty-year-old whose sun rose and fell by her smile.

"I would say this is romantic, but isn't this the kind of place where bodies get dumped?" Georgia said, waving her hand around the marina.

"No, the best places are up by Long Branch," I replied.

She stopped before realizing I was joking. To be fair, jokes felt like a foreign language in my mouth. I had very little experience with them of late.

"What? Are you shocked? Did you think as Renato's *sottocapo* I just push papers in an office? We both know what I am . . . what I've become." My voice was tightly controlled.

She frowned at me. "Yes, like your father," she said softly.

Ouch, that one stung. This was the problem with being so close to someone who'd known you when you were young. They had too much insight, making stunningly accurate ammunition to wage war with.

"My father didn't have an inch of the power I command now. Don't be confused. I am nothing like my father. He was weak, and he couldn't protect his family . . . In fact, your father has more in common with him than me," I pointed out.

She flinched and raised her chin, defensiveness taking over. "At least he tried to be good once."

"Did he? So did I . . ." I raised a hand and stroked her cheek. I couldn't stay away. "Those days in Castel Amaro . . . I tried to be good. I tried to be what you deserved, and look where it got me," I added, forcing myself to walk on.

"It got you here," she called out.

I stopped but didn't turn.

"It got us both right here, together," she continued.

It was true. Somehow, fate had brought us back together again.

We had just reached the gangway of the yacht when a dark shadow caught my attention. Farther along, in the boat just past mine, dark shapes were moving.

Trouble. I'd been waiting for the Ravellis to show up, and here they were, but in a greater number than I'd expected. *Damn it.*

I reached for my phone just as a shot rang out. I whirled Georgia around and covered her with my body, dropping us both to the ground, just behind a hulking boat lift. The shot flew over our heads, and a hail of fire exploded from behind us.

"What the hell?" Georgia gasped, scared. She gripped my arm. "Who is that?"

"My people are following us. I need you to get onto this yacht, go down to the bottom level, and lock yourself in the bathroom. I'll take care of everything else."

"Are these Ravellis?" she gasped.

"Yes they are, and they're here for you," I told her, peering over the top of the boat lift. My gun was in my hand, and I was ready to take out the threat.

Georgia's hand shook in mine, and I glanced at her.

"Don't be scared. You're not going anywhere. No power on this fucking planet could take you from me. I won't let them."

She blinked at me, the conviction in my voice ringing true. I'd never said anything truer than that.

"Now, when I say go, you go, and you don't look back." I was taking her high-heeled shoes off for her as I spoke. I pressed one into her hand, spiked heel facing outward. It never hurt to have a weapon.

She nodded, letting me guide her to the very side of the boat lift.

"Now, go!" I urged and started to shoot.

I covered her, and she ran as fast as she could, her bare feet slapping the sidewalk. She didn't draw their fire. So, that meant they were probably instructed to bring her back alive. I didn't know if Prosecutor Bellisario had done his duty and ratted on the Ravellis yet or not, but it seemed their plan hadn't changed yet. Get the girl and use her to twist her father's arm.

Well, it was too fucking late for that.

I was her husband, and no one would get through me.

Four men spread out in front of me, their movements precise and controlled. Trained fighters. No wasted steps. Four more took off behind me, aiming for my team, already running toward me. I tossed my gun. Covering Georgia had left me out of bullets. I'd have to do this the old-fashioned way.

The first guy struck fast, a sharp jab aimed at my face. I slipped left, feeling the punch rush past my cheek, and drove my elbow into his ribs. He let out a grunt and staggered back, but I had no time to follow up. The second attacker was already closing in, his foot snapping toward my stomach.

I caught his leg midair and twisted hard. His body spun sideways, his balance gone. Before he could recover, I slammed my knee into his chest and shoved him backward. He toppled over the edge of the dock, and a splash echoed in the night.

The third man, a thickset bruiser, came at me with a heavy swing. I barely ducked in time, his fist cutting through the air above my head. I countered with a sharp strike to his throat. He choked, stumbling back and gasping for air.

Then I saw the glint of steel.

The fourth fighter, faster than the rest, lunged at me with a knife. I twisted my body just as the blade slashed past, barely missing my side. I flashed my hand out, grabbing his wrist, and with a sharp wrench, I turned his own weapon against him. The blade buried itself in his thigh. His scream tore through the silence.

Behind me, movement. I turned. The first attacker had recovered and launched a spinning kick. I stepped in, cutting off his momentum, and caught him mid-turn. A quick sweep took his legs out, sending him crashing onto the dock.

That left only the bruiser. He stood there, panting, fists still raised but unsteady. I wiped my lip, feeling the sting in my knuckles.

"Still want to do this?" I asked, my voice calm.

His eyes flicked to the bodies around us. He hesitated. Then, slowly, he stepped back. Once. Twice. Then he disappeared into the darkness.

I tore my eyes from the sight of Ravellis fleeing me and my team, and nodded to Ettore to give chase.

"Ehi, bastardo! Guardate qui!"

I spun toward the shout just in time to see Georgia, her yellow dress bloodied, her body held against her attacker. Some motherfucker had caught her on the yacht.

"Santori! Stop right now, or she won't make it to tomorrow. Put your hands up!"

The rest of my security had moved away, chasing down the remaining Ravellis, who had made the worst mistake of their lives tonight by showing up at the marina.

I'd known they were coming. They hadn't scattered back to Naples as fast as I'd have liked. The justice system in Italy was taking as long as it could to put Prosecutor Bellisario out of commission. The man had to have gotten our message and known that his daughter was now part of the family. He should be ratting on the boss of these motherfuckers right now, but it all took time.

Time for them to keep thinking that they could threaten him with his daughter.

I was sick of it. It was time to end these fucks on American soil.

My team was pursuing the others. They wouldn't let any of them live.

This fucker, though, he was mine.

I put my hands up slowly, my eyes meeting Georgia's.

"I'm going to give you the best advice anyone has ever given you . . ." I called to him.

Georgia was terrified; I could see it in every line of her face. And yet, there was steel beneath that fear. There always had been.

My eyes flickered to the high heel in her hand, reminding her that she was still clutching it.

Her eyebrows jumped. She remembered. Of course she did. My clever girl. My wife.

"Right, like I need advice from you, Santori. You should just do us all a favor and fucking die!" the man shouted, his face red and voice strangled.

I chuckled. "Don't tell me the stress of coming here and trying to take out one of Renato De Sanctis's men is giving you trouble?"

"Not just any man." The underling grunted.

He pointed the gun at me, and I took an easier breath now that the dark muzzle wasn't pointed at Georgia anymore.

"You," he said. "Why can't you just die, man?"

I shrugged. "Would you believe me if I told you I was working on it?"

My gaze hit Georgia's eyes again, and the look I saw in them twisted something that used to be my heart.

"Now, that advice that I was offering you, for free, no less, is this." I shot Georgia a meaningful glance and got ready to move. "You're really not going to want to touch my wife. Ever."

The man sneered. "Right, and what are you going to do about it?" he began, but didn't get to finish, because Georgia exploded into motion.

She brought her hand holding the shoe flying up toward the attacker's face, the heel sinking into his cheek.

He roared and let her go, and the gun, aimed in my direction, went off.

I barely felt the bullet hit my arm. I was sprinting toward the two of them as they fought. He pulled back to hit Georgia, and she bent under his arm, so his blow went wide. They hit the railing of the yacht, and the guy tried to point his gun at her again, but she went after that arm, grappling for the gun.

I was almost there.

I was so damn close.

And then their weight shifted somehow. One second, they were grappling with the gun, pressed against the railing, and the next moment, they were going over.

"No!" I shouted, closing the distance between us.

Georgia's light dress was the only thing I could make out in the dark water. I dived off the railing and into the cold water without hesitation. My arm throbbed distantly, and I swam toward the two of them, but I couldn't see a fucking thing underwater. My heart was pounding, and something that tasted like fear sat on my tongue. I hadn't been afraid in a very long time. Not true fear.

Now I was fucking terrified.

I surfaced, my lungs burning and screaming for air. Gulping down a breath, I spied a body dragging something onto a nearby platform.

I sliced through the water toward them and grabbed the railing, hauling myself up.

The man was bent over Georgia, and I pitched myself at him. We rolled over the rough boards. He'd lost the gun, and now only had his hands to defend himself, which were a very poor defense for what I was going to do to him.

I wrestled him into submission, slinging my body over his and easily subduing his lesser weight, then gripped his head with both hands. He thrashed and heaved beneath me. I banged his head against the wooden boards hard. Once, twice, three times. The smell of copper hit the air along with the salt of the water around us.

He stopped fighting back. Rage filled me. Pure and unfiltered. Uncontrollable.

I roared at him and banged his head again and again, and then twisted it sharply and cracked his neck for good measure.

On my knees, I crawled to Georgia. She was lying still.

No. No. No.

I reached for her and pulled her into my arms.

"*Topolina,* wake up. You've just swallowed some water. Wake up," I urged, slapping her cool cheeks.

She was still. I gently laid her on the platform and lowered my mouth to hers, blowing air into her lungs and then starting chest compressions.

A move I'd done countless times, in jungles and deserts. I was still that merciless man, the one who'd lived nightmares, and yet, here, pumping Georgia's chest, I was also someone else.

I was a poor kid from Naples who'd found a reason to live again. A kid full of hopes and useless dreams and contradictions. A tough boy who wrote poetry. A drifter who wanted to buy the girl of his dreams a house of her own. An unloved boy who'd found a place to belong.

I breathed into her mouth again, her fragile chest expanding beneath my hands.

"Breathe, Georgia, breathe. I told you—you can't escape me again . . . I won't let you go." I pumped her chest. "Not when I've just gotten you back."

I pumped, and nothing else mattered.

"You asked me to save you once, *cara* . . . and I'm here now. I'm finally here," I muttered. Fuck, my heart pounding actually hurt. A real and terrible ache.

I leaned down to breathe in her mouth again when she coughed.

It was the best sound I'd ever heard.

She coughed, and coughed, and turned, hacking up seawater. I was on my feet and taking her into my arms.

"Elio?" she said.

I was moving across the platform toward my boat. The short makeshift pier joined with the floating dock. Seconds later, I was carrying her through the yacht. The staff were cowering behind the kitchen island. I barely spared them a glance as I swept past.

I reached my bedroom and kicked the door shut behind us.

The sudden bloom of light revealed the dark-red patches across her wet yellow dress. Blood.

"Are you hurt? What hurts?" I urged, my hands searching her body for the place where the blood was coming from. I had to stop it. I had to stop it right now.

"Where does it hurt, damn it?" I demanded. I couldn't find where the bleeding was coming from.

Georgia's hands held on to my arms, and I was pretty sure she was speaking. She was saying something, but I couldn't hear it. I couldn't hear anything but the pounding of my blood in my ears. It was like a scream.

I couldn't tell a fucking thing through the clinging wet material of Georgia's dress. I bent, grabbed the hem, and pulled it apart hard. It ripped up the middle easily.

I tore the dress right off, and finally, the sight of her smooth, golden skin came into view. I ran my hands over her. Her underwear was wet but unbloodied.

"Turn," I commanded and spun her around, holding her by the back of the neck to make her comply. I pulled the tattered remains of her dress from her and checked down her shoulders, her back, and over her thighs.

"Elio!" Georgia's sharp cry cut through my panic.

I focused on her face as she turned around.

"I'm okay, it's not my blood!" she said. "It's yours. I'm okay."

I shook my head. "No, you're not . . . you were nearly hurt, and I couldn't stop it."

"But I'm not," she insisted, and a raw laugh left me.

"No thanks to me." I moved my inspection on to her head. I ran my hands through her dark wet hair, feeling her skull for cuts or lumps.

"It's not really your job to protect me, you know that, right? Everyone is responsible for themselves at the end of the day."

No. That's not true at all.

"You're my wife. You're mine to protect until the day I die. *Mine.*" The last word left me in a possessive growl.

My lungs felt tight, and my body ached, but it was all far away somehow, behind the veil of panic that I couldn't see past. Soldiers didn't lose their heads. Losing control meant making mistakes, and hadn't I done nothing but that lately?

I couldn't keep my sanity around this woman. I was fucking up and making mistakes, and she was going to get hurt . . .

Georgia slid her hands up my cheeks, cupping my face. The sudden, voluntary touch stilled me.

"*Cittaiolo,*" she murmured. "I'm okay. I'm fine."

I tried to shake my head. I should explain to her how compromised my control was. How I couldn't look after her when my heart was beating so hard around her all the time; how my concentration was affected and my discipline torn.

Because I still loved her . . . after all this time . . . and I'd never stopped. Not even for a second. I had loved her then, and I loved her now, and I'd loved her all the time in between. I'd hated her, and I'd missed her, and I'd envied her, and I'd coveted her . . .

And through it all . . . I'd loved her.

Loving her was my one constant. My love for her was true north on my compass.

I didn't tell her any of that, however. I didn't have those words anymore. I wasn't the brave boy with a broken pencil and notebook who could spell his heart out on a blank page.

But—she made me want to be, for a shining, perfect moment.

I wanted to be that boy she'd loved. The one who could have deserved her one day. Not this broken man I'd become. An assassin, a ghoul, a stain on the world.

No, I didn't say any of that.

I showed her, the only way I knew how.

I kissed her.

She melted into my touch, her arms wrapping around my back and pulling me closer. I needed to feel her body close to mine. I moved back, ripping my wet clothes off. Fabric tore and buttons scattered, but soon enough, I was naked. I pressed her into the wall, enjoying every single inch where her skin touched mine.

"You're so cold." I nestled my warm body on her chilled skin. I'd nearly lost her. I'd nearly lost her again. I couldn't contain the horror of that thought.

I ran my hands over her, warming the coldest parts. I cupped her hands and blew on them and moved my hands to her breasts. Her nipples were freezing points, begging to be heated. I lowered my lips to the chilled buds and sucked them into the hot cavern of my mouth, rubbing my tongue over them until she cried out.

I returned to her mouth, kissing her fiercely.

"I told you that you couldn't escape me." I lowered a hand between her legs, ripping her panties down her thighs.

Her breath hitched, and she held on to my shoulders. I ran my fingers through her wetness.

"That command extends to death, you should know that."

I lifted her, and she gasped. I hoisted her effortlessly into my arms. She threw her arms around my neck as I leaned her shoulders against the wall and lined up my cock to her entrance, her legs wrapping around my hips.

"You're mine, in this life, and the next . . . I will never let you go."

And then I slid inside, pushing against her tight muscles. She was wet but so fucking tight. I supposed it had been a long time since her husband had died, and Georgia didn't seem like she'd been dating. I forced thoughts of other men from my mind. It didn't matter. Nothing that came before mattered anymore. I'd replace those memories of anyone else. I'd replace the touch of anyone else and make it mine, even if I had to come on every single part of her fucking body. She'd smell like me, be marked by me . . . be mine.

I went deeper, and she cried out. I was barely holding back. My relief at saving her was too strong. My fear of losing her had stretched my control too far.

I sealed my mouth to hers and forged into her as far as I could, her lithe body finally accepting my invasion. Then I pulled out and slammed back in. She moaned, the sound sending all the hair on my body standing on end. It was a sound I'd never dared to dream I might hear again.

The only blessing I'd ever need.

I fucked her steadily against the wall, forcing myself as deep inside as I could go. I wanted my skin to merge with hers, my heart to thud with hers, and most of all, I wanted to come buried deep inside this woman, so deep she'd never be able to get me out. Then I could taint her, just as truly as she'd tainted me. My sweet, beloved poison.

I was going to come. For the first time in fourteen years, I was coming inside a woman, and it was the same one as all those years before. The only woman I'd ever fucked. The only woman I'd ever wanted to. Georgia was right when she'd called me a robot. I wasn't a man like other men. I'd never wanted anyone other than her, and when she was lost, I simply hadn't wanted anyone. My blood rushed only for her. My heart beat only at her command. She thought she was my hostage, my leverage, a prisoner in this marriage. She had no idea that it was already too late for me. I'd always been her most devoted worshipper, even when I thought I hated her.

Now I was her slave.

"Elio," she said in my ear, holding on tightly despite my brutal pace. "Elio, I want to come."

"Then come, *cara*. Come with me deep inside you . . . right where I was always supposed to be."

She cried out, her body tensing and closing around me so tightly, I could barely pull out. Instead, as my balls drew up and my own orgasm surged through me, I pushed deeper in, pinning her to the wall with my cock, and came.

With a shout that was wrenched from my bones, I came endlessly inside her taut channel, feeling her turn even wetter and more slippery inside with my cum. Her thighs held me, keeping me inside. Her breasts were flattened to my chest, and her face turned toward mine as soon as I reared my head back. I kissed her, plunged deep, connected once and for all. I kissed her for all that she'd cost me, and for all that I'd suffered without her. I kissed her for all the lonely days and nights without her. I kissed her for how I'd scared her when I'd found her in L.A., and how I'd stolen her future from her.

I kissed her for how I had no intention of letting her go. Ever.

34

GEORGIA

When I woke, the world was swaying. It made sense, really, considering what had happened last night. The world today wasn't the same one as yesterday. It was forever changed.

I sat up. Sunlight flooded onto the bed from the high windows along the top of the walls.

Right, suddenly the bobbing made sense. I was on Elio's yacht.

A knock at the door sent me yanking the sheet up to my chin. The door opened, and Toni stood in the entrance.

"Good morning, Mrs. Santori. I've got some clothes here for you. If you get dressed, I'll drive you home."

"Where's Elio?" I wondered.

Toni's face didn't give anything away. "Working. It's past lunchtime."

"What?" There wasn't a clock in the room, and I had no way to tell the damn time. "You could have woken me earlier! I hope you weren't waiting for me to wake up."

"There're worse places to be on the clock than sitting on the deck of a yacht," Toni said primly.

I was starting to think she had quite the wicked sense of humor beneath her deadpan delivery.

"Anyway, it was the boss's orders not to wake you. He told me you were hurt last night."

"I'm okay. Everyone needs to stop worrying about me. It wasn't my blood." I wrapped the sheet around me and hung my legs over the end of the bed. "What about Elio's other security? Were you working last night?"

"No, I was off, since the boss was with you. Everyone is accounted for. You don't take down the Santori squad easily." Toni gave me a rare smile.

I nodded, relieved. The thought that Elio's closest people could have been hurt protecting me didn't sit well at all.

"I'll get dressed and come out," I told Toni, getting up and heading to the bag she'd brought me. When I caught sight of myself in the mirror, I nearly screamed. My hair was dried in damp snakes over my shoulders, my face was wild and black-rimmed with old makeup, and my lips were swollen like I'd been stung by bees. Worst of all was the stubble rash across my cheeks, and the bites down my neck. Elio hadn't been gentle last night . . . not by a long shot . . . and I had loved it.

I'd burned in his brutal hands.

I shoved my hair up in a bun, got dressed, and headed out to Toni.

Later, after being escorted home with more security than a president, I took a long shower and spent way too much time remembering every single touch of Elio's hands on my body. I dressed in some of my new clothes and went to my studio. Just opening the door still gave me a thrill, every single time.

I was deep into pinning a tricky area of a design when Toni appeared with a phone in her hand.

She passed it to me.

"Hello?" I asked cautiously.

Elio's deep, clipped voice spread across me like honey.

"Your father's lawyer is on the line. He insists on speaking to you personally. We need to know what your father's plan is."

Nice to talk to you, too.

"Okay."

"Get as much information as you can, Georgia," Elio prompted.

I sighed. "Yes, boss, anything else you want to tell me to do?"

"Yes," he replied, his voice deepening somehow, spreading fire through my body. "Rest up, you're going to need your energy later."

Before I could respond to that implication, the call switched, and my father's attorney was on the line.

"Mrs. Conti?"

"It's Mrs. Santori now," Elio interrupted, still on the call. There was an arrogant possessiveness in his tone that couldn't be denied.

"Of course, Mrs. Santori. Can you speak? I really need to speak to her alone."

"It's fine. My husband can listen . . . I give permission."

"It's not about what you want, Mrs. Santori; I represent your father's wishes."

"I'll go. I'm sure my wife will catch me up on the conversation shortly," Elio said smoothly and then seemed to disappear.

I pressed the phone to my ear. "What is it?"

"I am calling to tell you that your father has received the message sent by Renato De Sanctis. I delivered it personally. As a result, he will begin his deal with the prosecution, but the De Sanctis family will not feature in any of the bargaining."

I nodded mutely. So, Renato and Elio's plan had worked after all. At least I was an effective bargaining chip in this hostage situation; that was something.

"He is concerned about your welfare. He would like to be reassured that you are well."

"I'm fine."

"If you're not, just say the word and I can have charges brought against your new husband—"

"I said, I'm fine where I am. I'm safe. I'm so much safer here than I would be alone. My father still has delusions of grandeur, I see, to think he could do anything about the De Sanctis family or my husband. He can't. I have to live with the consequences of his actions . . . and the fallout of whatever dirty, illegal shit he was involved in my whole life. I will be making my own decisions from now on. I don't need or want his help."

The lawyer was quiet for a beat. "Understood," he said heavily. "If it means anything, I don't believe he anticipated any of this as a reaction to his arrest. He didn't think you—"

"He didn't think of me at all. I know. But he should know this . . . If anyone else had been head of the De Sanctis family, and if my husband had been anyone else at all, I'd probably be six feet under already. They are keeping me alive. Not my father."

I broke off, surprised by my own venom. No—when I really thought of it, I was furious. Livid. My father had lived a disreputable life, and in the end, to spare himself, he'd put me in danger. He was selfish, and he'd always been selfish. Ever since that day when he'd told me Elio had left, something had fractured between us. I'd never quite believed him. Not fully. It was a tear, one that had ripped the fabric of our relationship more and more every day since.

"I will communicate that to my client," the lawyer told me. "I will be in touch once there are further developments."

"Great. Looking forward to it," I snapped and hung up.

I handed the phone to Toni.

"Everything okay?"

"Not even remotely." I sighed and sank into the chair at my desk. I was sick of all of it. My father, trying to manipulate me even from prison, and now, trying to pretend he cared about me when I'd already been through hell because of him. I'd be dead because of him right now, if not for Elio.

I was done trying to pick sides.

I knew where I belonged.

35

ELIO

I listened to Prosecutor Bellisario's lawyer stumble through expressing her father's regrets and I heard the way Georgia shut it down. Something kindled in my chest at her venomous assertions. Georgia cutting ties with her unworthy father was satisfying as hell. Every day, her alliances shifted, bringing her closer and closer to being what she should have always remained. Mine.

After she hung up, I set my own phone down and turned on my laptop. Every single room in my penthouse, excluding only the bathrooms, had surveillance cameras installed.

"Everything okay?" Toni asked her.

She shook her head. "Not even remotely."

I watched a black-and-white Georgia sink into a chair at her desk and grip her head like it hurt her.

She looked so lost at that moment, small and vulnerable in that huge room, dwarfed by her large desk. It made me want to slay her dragons for her and build her a tower where no one but me could reach her.

Then she stood decisively and headed out of the room. I

switched between feeds. Watching Georgia was my new hobby, and I'd gotten pretty damn good at it. She entered her room and went to the tattered old bag that she'd hauled here from L.A. She'd need new bags and shoes to go with her new clothes.

She opened it and rooted around until she emerged with a tube of lipstick. With a twist of the lid, she opened it. It was a damn fake. I was impressed. She removed a flash drive and considered it. This had to be it. The proof of the De Sanctis misdeeds that her father had claimed would sink us. His insurance. It was right there, under my roof. How unfortunate for him.

Georgia considered the flash drive. Had she looked on it? Did she have any idea what she held? She tucked it into her pocket and left the room, making for her new studio.

Where was she going with it?

Her body swayed as she walked, an effortless femme fatale. I remembered the touch of her body last night. Sinking inside had been like coming home after a lifetime in the cold. I'd have her again. I'd have her every single night.

I was done holding back. Yes, my self-control had cracked, but I'd formed it anew. Staying away didn't work. I was done resisting Georgia's power over me. From now on, I'd have my wife whenever and wherever I wanted.

She was finally mine, and no power on this earth could take her from me.

I slammed the lid of my laptop closed and made for the door of my office. I worked in La Leonora, the jewel in the De Sanctis crown of Atlantic City, and Renato's favorite casino.

Ettore was stationed at the door, and he scrambled after me when I strode past.

"Boss?"

He wasn't expecting me to leave the office right now. I had a hundred meetings today, things to do for Renato. More important, I had the remaining Ravelli rats to hunt down and make pay for last night. I wanted to eradicate the lingering family presence from my city. From the entire continent. They deserved nothing less for daring to attack my family.

For daring to touch *her*.

"Have the strategy meeting pushed back. Get Giada to pinpoint Ravelli locations down to the hotel room. She dropped the ball last night and let us walk into a fucking setup. She owes me."

"Yes, sir." Ettore jogged along behind me. "Where are we heading?"

"Home," I told him shortly. "I'm going to have my wife for lunch."

Ettore frowned at me. "You're going to have lunch with your wife?"

I couldn't fight the smirk that passed across my lips, and I shook my head.

Ettore's eyes bulged at the sight of my half smile, as if he'd just seen the Devil himself.

"Let's go."

I found Georgia in her studio. The idea to give her a room to make her dresses had been a natural one. She needed something to occupy her and keep her out of my hair. If she was busy, she wouldn't be trying to escape or poking her nose where it didn't belong . . . she wouldn't be a distraction.

Right. How is that working out?

It was an exercise in futility. Her smile at discovering the room and her new equipment had warmed the hollow in my chest.

She was wearing another of the dresses I'd bought her. It shouldn't be possible, but the thick white linen dress, with a skirt that fell to the knee and nearly covered her completely, was as titillating as lingerie on this woman. She stood and went to a tall stack of shelves, going up on her tiptoes to reach for something, and I quickly stepped forward and closed the door. The breeze from the movement brought the hem of her dress indecently high. Ettore was outside, after all, not to mention Toni. Was I really jealous of other people's eyes on my wife? Yes. It was why I'd assigned her a female bodyguard, after all; well, that and the fact that Antonia Deponio was one of the best soldiers I'd ever known, and she'd saved my ass more times than I could count.

"Allow me," I said and reached past her.

She jerked against me, falling into my chest. She twisted around and leaned on the shelves, looking up at me.

"You're home."

"Hmm." I pulled the box she'd been aiming for down from the top shelf and held it at my side. "Did you miss me?"

She scoffed, but her cheeks turned pink. "Hardly. I manage on my own just fine . . ."

"Was that what you were doing when I found you? Managing just fine?"

She swallowed hard and shrugged. "I was okay."

"No, you weren't." I couldn't resist tucking a stray curl behind her ear. "But it's okay. I wasn't either."

Her dark eyes held mine, and a lot passed between us in that moment. Last night had been the first night of uninterrupted sleep I'd had in more than a decade. It was the first night I hadn't even thought of playing the damn roulette game. Though I hadn't played it with a loaded weapon since the night I'd found out that Tommaso Conti had died. I'd never play it again that way. How odd that after all this time, I'd found something to live for again, and it was the person who'd threatened that desire in the first place. She'd broken me, and now it seemed like only she could fix me.

Life had some sense of fucking irony.

"I think we need to talk, *topolina*."

She nodded, a jerky, uneven movement. "Yes, I think we do."

"Let's do so over lunch."

36

ELIO

We ate in the dining room in front of the stunning views of the water. We talked about nothing, simple and easy, something I hadn't experienced in a long time.

When the dishes were cleared, Georgia's smile dropped, and she sighed.

"So, I found out about my father. Were you listening?"

"Do you think I was listening?" I was genuinely curious if Georgia had any idea how much surveillance I had on her. From CCTV to the GPS chip, to bodyguards who would follow her when she eventually started to leave the house without me, she'd never be far from my eyes.

She lifted a shoulder, uncaring. "He promises that the De Sanctis family won't be used in his deal with the state. He's going to snitch on the Ravellis instead, just like you wanted."

Her expression was grim.

"And that upsets you?" I asked.

She shook her head. "Not really. I guess the alternative was never going to happen."

"The alternative being . . ."

"He doesn't snitch on anyone. He pays for his wrongdoings with honor. He doesn't put me in danger just to shave a little time off his sentence. He did things wrong; he should pay. He's a cheater and a coward. He loves himself more than me," she finished.

Ding-ding.

I took no pleasure in seeing Georgia finally realize what a reprehensible piece of shit her father was. Before she'd come back into my life, I hadn't taken pleasure in anything at all.

Now, my pleasure lived in her smile.

"It doesn't matter what he does now. Salvatore wanted it taken care of so he could die gracefully. That mission has been accomplished."

She nodded and bit her lip, holding her words inside until she couldn't anymore.

"So, does that mean . . . you don't need me anymore? Is the hostage situation over?"

I pinned her with a look. "Do you feel like a hostage?"

She shrugged. "I promised not to run away, but I can hardly call who I want or go for a walk if I want to. Sounds like being a hostage to me."

"Forgive me for being cautious. The Ravellis did try to kill you last night. And may I remind you that you yourself threatened to kill me in my sleep only a few nights ago?" I quipped.

She rolled her eyes. "And you told me that I was nothing to you and nothing could tempt you to touch me . . . Seems like we're both liars."

"You think because of last night . . . you have some irresistible hold over me?" I asked, arching an eyebrow at her.

Sparring with her was more enjoyable than I remembered, but I had to be rusty at it, as my words sent heat flooding to her cheeks. She pushed her chair back and stood.

"Whatever. I'd say there's no need to be an asshole, but we both know that just comes naturally to you," she snapped and made to stride away.

She didn't get far. I stood and, in a fluid motion, pulled her to me, turning her so her back was to the table. Her eyes were bright and embarrassed. Her cheeks were red, the shame trailing down her neck. I'd left marks. It thrilled me to see that I'd left love bites on her skin. *Good.*

"You do." I sank a hand into the hair at the nape of her neck and gripped the back of her head. "You win . . . *topolina*. You do tempt me. You do torment me . . . you always have. I'm tired of holding back. You're not my hostage. You're my wife, and I'll treat you as such."

I tipped her head back, forcing her lips to be presented to me, a feast for me and only me. Then I kissed her, hard and ruthlessly, softly and carefully. I kissed her all the ways I'd missed kissing her for so long.

I pulled my lips from hers as I lifted her onto the table, pushing her knees wide so I could press my body in between.

I kissed her again and guided her back so she was supine on the polished wooden surface, her legs open, her hair a dark cloud around her head. Her eyes were fixed on me. Excited or scared, I couldn't tell. I no longer cared.

"Everything comes to he who waits . . . and I have waited a lifetime for you, and I'm done. From now on . . . I will not hold back."

Her breath hitched in her chest, her dark eyes full of excitement. "I'm not asking you to," she told me.

I tugged her panties off, then balled them up and tucked them into my pocket.

"What are those for?" She raised an eyebrow at me.

"No one touches your panties but me," I told her thickly, stroking a finger down her pussy. God, she was beautiful."Not even the cleaning staff," I added.

"You're crazy," she breathed as I leaned in and smelled her musky, sweet scent.

"Hmm, you seem to have that effect on me," I agreed and then licked her.

My tongue worked her from her hole up to her clit, where I stayed. Licking and nibbling on it, I had to hold her hips down on the table to get her to stay still. Her hips danced.

Her hands sank into my hair, tugging at the short strands.

She was rising. If I weren't such a jaded cynic, I'd almost believe that she hadn't been with anyone in a long time, she was so responsive.

I laved her clit hard, eliciting a scream, and she rose toward her orgasm. I pulled back.

"No!" she protested hotly.

I straightened up, dropped my pants, and took my cock out. Now that I'd crossed that line and been inside her, there was no going back. I needed to be there as much as possible. The world made more sense when I was inside her. My demons weren't as loud, and the past no longer breathed down my neck when I was home, deep in Georgia.

I pushed, parting her tight muscles. She leaned up on her elbows and watched me enter her. Her gaze was riveted to the place where my cock disappeared into her perfect cunt, and my eyes were riveted to her.

My wife.

Finally.

I slid right in, deep as I could, and fought off the lethal grip of her muscles trying to expel me. I wasn't going anywhere. Lowering a hand to her wet, swollen clit, I rubbed my thumb across it, and she groaned, falling back to the tabletop and surrendering completely.

Her muscles loosened, and I thrust, thumbing her clit the entire time. She raised her hips to meet my every movement. I should have put a pillow beneath her hips. She'd lost some of her lush curves in the years we'd been apart. Her lifestyle in L.A. had left her poor and hungry. I was well familiar with that feeling. I'd never forget it. I wouldn't let Georgia feel it again. She'd never be poor again, in debt, or hungry. Never. As long as I lived, and beyond. She'd never want for anything.

She was rising once more, her beautiful face twisting with pleasure. Red and sweaty, she was more beautiful in her honest reactions than anything I'd ever seen.

"I'm going to come," she panted, her eyes flying to mine. She looked almost scared.

I simply nodded. "Yes, you are, and I'm right behind you."

"It feels so full," she said, biting her lip.

"It is full . . . full of me, your husband," I added, my balls drawing up. God, I was close.

She gave a strangled cry, her hands scratching at the wood of the table.

"Elio!" My name on her lips when she came was a benediction.

No matter what horrors had passed between us, or trespasses that had occurred, I knew at that moment that we could live again. Despite all odds . . . suddenly, there was a sunrise on the dark horizon after more than a decade of night.

Beneath the frozen river, currents still run.

Her pussy closed around me, holding me in place so tight, undulating inside, drawing my cum from me ruthlessly.

Liquid burst from her, soaking the table and showering my cock. I rubbed her clit and drew it out, the spray a glorious fucking sight to see.

"Oh my God, oh my God," Georgia sobbed through it.

I pulsed inside her, coming hard. Her tight cunt milked me, pulling every last drop from my balls. I was breathing hard, the pleasure a rush I'd long forgotten. My heart was pounding. Undeniable.

"What the hell? Oh my God," Georgia muttered.

I pulled free on a rush of her juices and my cum. She looked embarrassed and stared at the pool on the table below her.

"No, not your god . . . your husband made you squirt, *topolina*," I said.

She flushed scarlet.

I stroked her wet, sweaty hair back. "But you can call me your god if you want."

I bent down, positioning my face near the table, just beyond her cunt. I licked a long stroke against the wood, tasting her cum.

Her breath hitched. I licked the liquid again, and again, leaning forward to place a kiss on her twitching pussy.

"Every single bit of you . . . every single drop, inch, strand of hair, freckle, and nail . . . is perfect . . . and mine. Got it?"

She stared at me, mesmerized.

"I said, got it?" I repeated, straightening up.

She followed in a daze. I lifted her off the wet table and placed her on the floor.

"I got it," she said.

Her dark eyes were luminous, her cheeks rosy, and her hair a mess. I wanted to pull her close and consume her, take her to bed and spend the rest of the day there, but there was work to be done.

"Now, you have something else of mine, and it's time to hand it over," I told her. I stepped back and pulled my pants up, tucking my shirt in and returning myself to normal as best I could.

She leaned against the table. "What is it?"

"The flash drive. Your father's insurance. It's time to hand it over." I held my hand out.

She stared at me, surprised I knew about it, but somehow not upset. She felt around in her pocket and took it out.

"Here. I was going to give it to you. I don't care what's on it. I wish he hadn't sent it to me."

I took the flash drive. "Forget he did. You don't have to worry about it anymore."

"What are you going to do with it?" she asked.

I slipped it into my pocket. "Nothing too nefarious. As long as Alfredo does what he's promised and keeps the De Sanctis name out of his mouth, there won't be any problems."

"And if he doesn't? What if he decides to tell on Salvatore anyway? This whole marriage thing will have been pointless . . . What if he doesn't care about me as much as you think he does?"

"Impossible," I said shortly and grabbed my jacket.

"Why's it impossible?" she asked and followed me.

"Because loving you isn't something a man can recover from—or forget. It's a lifelong condition."

Her eyes widened at my words, my confession sitting starkly between us.

"I'll see you later," I bit out before leaving.

I met Giada at La Leonora and handed over the flash drive. She sat at her desk and plugged it into her computer.

"Now that we know that Bellisario is singing to the prosecution about the Ravellis, the question is, why are they still coming after us? Last night they nearly hurt her, Giada. It can't happen again."

Giada slanted her eyes toward me. "And this is the woman you hate, right?"

"Giada," I growled at her.

She just laughed, then sobered. "About that. We need to talk. My little electronic birdies have found something regarding the Ravellis. I'm not sure this is about Bellisario anymore . . . it seems more personal than that."

"Personal? What could be personal? I've never met a Ravelli before."

Giada wagged her finger. "That you remember . . . Take a trip down memory lane with me. You were twenty years old and incarcerated in Poggioreale Prison. You had a cellmate . . ."

The memory hit me like a ton of bricks. Sergio Ravelli. My cellmate when I was inside before Renato got me out.

"Fuck." I sank onto the sofa across from her.

"And there it is. Apparently, Sergio rose through the ranks in the family after he served his time . . . and he holds a grudge against you. What happened? Did you spurn his advances?" She smirked.

"I didn't get him out when Renato offered me an escape . . . I left him to serve his sentence."

I knew in my gut now, that was what had started this. That was why they hadn't stopped. Sergio wanted payback for that slight, and for however many years he'd had to serve after I'd left. I'd never had the possibility of getting him out, of course, but he wouldn't care about that.

"Hmm, so you betrayed him back then, and now you've gotten between him and the woman he needed to get ahold of to protect his capo. Looks like you're really on his shit list."

"I'll take him out. If he's here in the U.S., then he'll die here."

Giada nodded. "What if it's more complicated than that?"

"Complicated how?"

"I heard rumors of a Ravelli engaging the service of a certain mercenary . . . L'Ombra."

L'Ombra. The Shadow.

An assassin of the highest order. He had quite the reputation in Naples. Very few knew his real name, though he made no effort to keep it a secret. Massimo Lucciano. He held no alliance to any family. He worked for the highest bidder, or when he felt like it. The guy was like smoke. One of the best.

If Sergio Ravelli had sent L'Ombra after me, then Georgia would be caught in the crosshairs. It would be impossible to keep her separate.

"I'm sure Sergio would love L'Ombra to take both you and your new wife out . . . After all, Prosecutor Bellisario could still recant his testimony. No one has been charged in the Ravelli family yet," Giada voiced my thoughts.

"Which means this isn't over," I stated flatly.

"If L'Ombra is involved now . . . then it might just be beginning."

I thought of Georgia safe in the penthouse but longing to go outside. Her unfinished clothing line, and all the things her decisions had ended up costing her.

"It doesn't matter. L'Ombra or not, I'm going to finish it. If Sergio wants me enough to hire L'Ombra, then I'm more than happy to make their job easier."

Giada studied me. "You're going to them."

I nodded decisively. "I'm not waiting around for Sergio's henchmen and hired killers to come after me. I'll take the head off the snake and deliver that flash drive to the prosecution while I'm at it, once you scrub our name from it, of course."

"And Georgia?"

"She'll be safe at Casa Nera. The might of the De Sanctis family will protect her against those inept Ravellis."

Giada sighed. "If you want me and Bran to stay over there while you're gone . . . just ask." She smirked at me, but her smirk dropped when I nodded.

"I'd appreciate that."

"You're serious!" She gaped at me. "You never ask for help from the O'Connors!"

"That's because they are a bunch of wisecracking, bare-knuckle thugs with no finesse," I told her. "That being said . . . Brandon isn't without his strengths, and he puts family first. I'd appreciate extra eyes on my wife."

Giada beamed at me.

"What?"

"You just said it," she teased.

I blew out a breath and headed out of the room, my little sister right on my heels.

"You said it! I can't wait to tell Georgia. Damn, I wish I'd recorded it!"

"Giada!"

My driver pulled to a stop in the underground parking garage beneath the building where my wife was sitting in her studio. I knew that for sure because I'd indulged my little hobby of watching her on the CCTV to placate my anxiety.

Anxiety was distracting. It allowed mistakes to slip through. Unfortunately, a threat to Georgia filled me with the kind of gut-twisting anxiety that was impossible to ignore.

Just one more reason why she needed to be locked away at Casa Nera.

The full presence of De Sanctis men, who I'd personally trained, would be looking after her, as well as my most capable sister and her husband. As much as Bran O'Connor might irritate me, I couldn't deny his skills or his strength.

I got out of the car and slammed the door shut behind me. In the corner of my eye, a shadow moved. I froze for a second.

My driver was walking ahead of me, and two security men

flanked my sides. Since the threat of L'Ombra had entered the picture, it wasn't the time to be lax with security. I could take on Massimo one-on-one anytime, but not like this, surrounded by uncontrollable variables, civilians, and too fucking close to where Georgia was.

I continued, my awareness snapping and biting, searching every corner, my ears straining for any sound. I whistled a jaunty tune beneath my breath, and the conversation among my security team stopped.

It was a little signal that something was amiss.

Silence fell, punctuated only by the echo of our footfalls. I nodded to one side, and the two security guys flanking me peeled off. I discreetly drew my weapon. A few lanes over, a couple had just gotten out of their car and were talking loudly.

When I was assessing the chances that Massimo would fire on me here and now, the couple lowered those chances significantly. L'Ombra didn't do witnesses, and he didn't kill anyone outside his contract, either. As much as an assassin could have a code, he had one.

I walked steadily toward the double glass doors that housed the elevators. The couple was just behind me. I held the doors open and turned, looking out at the garage. All seemed still.

I could see my own security circling around the sides of the parked cars a few aisles over, checking from behind to see if they'd find anyone hiding.

I knew they wouldn't.

I could feel that the eyes which had been watching were gone. This was a warning. He was collecting information, making his plan. This was a reminder that he could get to us anywhere and anytime.

"Boss, we didn't find anyone, but this was sitting on the second reserved parking space for the penthouse."

It was small. Nothing more than a broken game trinket . . . to anyone else. To me, it was a warning, and its meaning was clear.

Not just a plastic little nothing . . . a sign that you'd been marked for death.

A broken hourglass . . . with no sand remaining. The calling card of L'Ombra.

Sitting in the second reserved parking space for the penthouse.

Georgia's spot.

37

GEORGIA

I was back in my studio when Elio strode through the door and his people scurried around to follow his sharp commands.

"Pack some things. You're going to Casa Nera," he commanded from across the room.

"Where are you going to be?"

"I've got some cleaning up to do."

He turned away, calling Toni over to speak in a rapid murmur. My heart clenched hard. I didn't want to go back to Casa Nera alone.

I'd just gotten Elio back. Now a terrible fear filled me.

"Cleaning up those men . . . the ones who are after me?"

"It seems I've managed to get myself in their line of fire as well. None of this is your fault, Georgia," Elio said before the guilt could spiral through me.

"No, it's my father's," I muttered mutinously.

Elio simply nodded. "I'm not going to argue with you on that count. Go and get your things, *cara*. You need to leave as soon as possible."

"Just I need to leave?" I watched his team move around, their expressions serious. "You just said that you're also a target. Why aren't we leaving together?"

Elio paused and dismissed Toni.

He jerked his head toward the door, and his people left, shutting the doors after them.

"We are not the same. You are mine to protect. It's the only thing that matters."

My lungs immediately threatened to close at the idea of being sent away alone. I swallowed hard, but my mouth was already dry. *Great.* A panic attack, just what I needed right now.

"I don't want to go there alone. I don't know anyone . . . I don't trust anyone." *But you.*

"The men there have been trained by me. You can trust them. Moreover, Toni and Ettore will be there, as well as my best men."

"And what about you! If Casa Nera is a safe place to go, why don't you come, too?" I reasoned.

He shook his head. "This has dragged on long enough. I can take care of whoever they send after me, as long as no one gets in my way."

"So, I'd just be in the way, is that it?" My worry morphed into irritation.

"Yes." He turned away.

I snatched at his sleeve. "So, I go there, and you disappear, and what . . . I wait fourteen years to find out what happened?"

My lungs were tightening. Fuck, I hadn't had a panic attack in years, and now I'd had two in as many weeks. Because of this man who had come back into my life, everything I'd learned about staying calm was slipping through my fingers.

You never learned how to stay calm, you just gave up caring about things.

I turned to grab on to the table and dragged air into my lungs.

He touched my back, and the simple gesture felt overwhelming as I tried to fight off dizziness. This was his fault. He'd dragged me here, married me, made me love him again, and now he was yanking it all out from under me. Again.

He was leaving me again.

I couldn't breathe.

I shrugged his hands away and struggled to stay calm. I had nowhere to go. Conflicting emotions collided in my chest, wild and untethered.

"My people can keep you safe."

"Not like you can," I pointed out.

Was he going to stay here and take on all those men who kept coming for us?

His mouth pulled up at one side. A smile. They came more often to him lately. Soon, it would nearly look natural.

"I appreciate the vote of confidence, *cara*. But you don't have to worry about me. I can take care of myself, and I always have."

Something snapped in me at that statement. It was all too much. The threat hanging over us, the past that had fucked us both so thoroughly.

"Oh, I know that! Believe me, I know! You certainly took care of yourself when you stole that bag of cash and skipped town and left me behind all those years ago!" A twisted chuckle left me, and I pushed at his chest when he tried to reach for me. "Don't gaslight me into thinking I'm overreacting about being left by you—*again*."

"What the fuck does that mean?" he growled at me.

"You left me once and it nearly destroyed me, and now you're doing it again!"

Silence fell between us, and Elio stared at me like I'd slapped him.

"We both know who left who. Don't try and rewrite our past."

"Our past—you have no idea what happened after you left," I

snapped at him, then whirled away and went to the display case at one side of my studio, picking up the damn memento box that I'd dragged across the country.

Elio just watched me storm over to the table and fumble it open.

"Did you look in here?" I asked and ripped the lid open.

He shook his head slowly.

"Why not? You don't care that much about me to know? I mean so little to you nowadays that you don't even care what I'd bother trying to preserve?"

"Georgia. We don't have time for you to lose your mind right now," Elio ground out.

I had the box open, and the contents spilled across the table. His eyes drifted to the photos and papers from the box and then slid away.

I collected the photos and shoved them at Elio.

"Look at my family pictures—look at them!"

"I don't have time to walk down memory lane with you right now."

I scoffed, but air had become too precious, and I could barely afford it.

"You just don't want to know the truth, because then all those years of hating me would have been for nothing," I wheezed out and slammed my eyes closed. "You want to blame me. It's all my fault, right?" The words left me before I could call them back.

I knew he blamed me, though I wasn't sure why. His sister had alluded to that much. The past was a yawning dark chasm that threatened to swallow us both. It had to come out. We had to put those demons to rest.

"Are you punishing me? Is this the game?" My voice was high and desperate, untamable.

"Punishing you? You have no idea about the ways I've been punished for loving you!" he roared at me.

I stilled, my lungs growing tighter. His sudden rage shocked me. I'd never seen Elio lose control like that. Even when killing or maiming, he wasn't emotional. His eyes were blazing, and his expression was livid.

"I was punished in prison, every single fucking day, for loving you. For daring to touch you—I was beaten every single night."

"What?" I wheezed out.

"Then I was shipped off, far from home, alone, in the blistering sun, fighting other men's wars, representing other interests, while I lost my fucking soul! And I didn't care—I didn't even try to fight it, because if I couldn't have you, I didn't need it anyway."

His words echoed around the room and arrested my panic attack completely.

My lungs released and filled, and the fight left me. I closed my eyes, allowing my mind to drift.

"I saw you—footage of you stealing some bag with money in it and running away . . . And then a P.I. I hired found some taxi driver who claimed he'd driven you to the train station . . . a young man with a Naples accent and light green eyes."

I opened my eyes to meet his.

"You."

He stared at me, shocked into silence.

"I sat at my window every night for weeks flickering that damn light toward the barn. Every night I was sure that the light would flash back. You'd have come back for me . . . but you never did."

Elio wet his lips and cleared his throat. "You married Conti," he reminded me.

I nodded and looked down at the photos I was still clutching in my hand. I pulled out one in particular and handed it to Elio.

"I married Tommaso because I couldn't stay in that house without you. After knowing you . . . I couldn't stay. I'd break completely. So, I married Tommaso, and I ran away like you."

I pressed the photograph into his hand.

"That was my family."

He swallowed hard but didn't glance at it.

I sighed. "If you believe a word I'm saying, you'll look."

Slowly, he lowered his gaze to the photograph. I knew what he was seeing. It was a picture of Tommaso near the end. He'd been bald and bedridden but still smiling. He was sharing his bed with the one person he'd loved . . . the partner of his dreams. They were holding hands.

"That's Drew. Tommaso's partner. They were together nearly thirteen years. Can you believe it . . . the first gay bar we went to in L.A. when we arrived, and they met. Nothing can keep soulmates apart."

I followed his gaze to the picture.

"He lived with us for a decade. The happy couple and their friend—me. Tommaso was always scared what his parents would think if they found out, and he was right to be. They cut us off when they found out that Drew was living with us, and it wasn't him but me in the spare room."

The photograph fell to the table as Elio stared at me.

"Are you telling me you married your gay best friend and lived the life of a fucking nun for the last fourteen years?"

"Yes. If you don't believe me, here—" I yanked off my locket and threw it at his chest. He caught it, his reflexes unbeatable. He held it in his fist.

This was it. Honesty. In the past couple of weeks since this man had stormed through my life and changed every single thing, facing the past had been out of the question. It wasn't the right time. We were fighting to survive. There was no hurry . . .

But the look in his stormy gaze now told me this was the time. He'd been waiting for this conversation for fourteen years, just like I had. He'd been waiting . . . just like me.

I took a deep breath and spoke through my fears and insecurities.

"I think you were waiting for me, too, somehow, against all logic and reason. Weren't you?"

I held my breath while I anticipated his answer. I hadn't even been aware I was going to say the words, but somehow, I knew with stone-cold certainty that I was right. Elio wasn't an approachable man. The person who had found me in L.A. wasn't some hot-blooded man who indulged his desires. He'd been my robotic, untouchable mercenary. I was willing to bet he'd been that way for a very long time.

Since me.

He swallowed, and the way his well-defined muscles bobbed in his tattooed neck was a thing of beauty.

He opened his mouth to answer, but a knock sounded.

Toni opened the door and looked at Elio.

"Boss, the plane is ready and waiting at Strawberry Field."

"Thank you, Toni," he said and tore his eyes from mine.

Disappointment filled me, just as the words sank in.

"I'm flying to Casa Nera?" Panic threatened to overtake me again before logic intervened. Why would I fly when the drive was only a couple of hours?

Elio shook his head. "That's for me, don't worry."

"For you? Where are you going?" I caught sight of his expression. Reality dawned on me. "Wait—you're not going to the Ravellis, are you?"

"I told you not to worry about me, Georgia. I can take care of myself." He caught my eye. "As long as I know you're safe. It's time to go. Toni has packed you some belongings."

His men entered, dressed in unrelenting black. His hand moved toward me like he was about to cup my cheek, and then it fell, and he turned away.

"Elio!" I shouted after him.

He wouldn't look at me. It was happening. He was leaving again, and there was nothing I could do. I could barely process everything we'd talked about in the last few minutes.

I backed away from his men, who were approaching, and pointed a shaking finger at Ettore, who was closest to me. "Don't touch me. I'm not leaving!"

Then Elio was there. "Don't worry. No one touches you but me."

My breath was coming hard.

His hands landed on either side of my face, and the acrid sweetness of the cloth he held suffused my head. The world went fuzzy around the edges.

Elio's voice was deep and hypnotic. "Still so stubborn. Just know this . . . Even before you let me know that you've loved me and only me your entire life . . . I was ready to do whatever I had to, to keep you safe. Even before I knew you'd never wanted to leave me . . . I would have protected your life until my dying breath." He tipped my chin up and placed a kiss, soft as a feather, on my forehead.

It felt like a goodbye.

"Just what do you think I'm willing to do now to keep you safe?" A last soft kiss and a murmur. "I'm going to take care of you, *topolina*, and not even you can stop me."

The world was falling away under my feet, and the touch of his hands was the last thing I remembered.

That bastard.

I woke with a start to find myself strapped securely into the backseat of a luxurious Jeep as we bounced and jolted along a small rural road.

Toni and Elio's younger guard, Ettore, were in the front. I twisted around to check out the back. Two sleek black cars followed behind us.

"Rise and shine," Toni called, twisting around to see me.

I squinted at her. "It's dark outside. What the hell happened?"

"You were about to have a panic attack."

"So Elio drugged me? Your boss is nuts."

"Not as nuts as your husband," Toni said and smiled at my expression. "I mean, I've never seen him act like this before, and I've known him for ten years."

That's right. She has. She knows all about Elio. More than me.

"Lucky me, I guess I just bring it out in him."

"It appears to be your unique talent." She stared down at her phone and frowned.

"Ettore, take Route 2 ahead," she said quickly.

Ettore nodded and turned left at the next junction. The two cars behind us branched off in different directions.

"Where are they going?" I asked.

"Confusing and redirecting any possible tails," Toni explained. "We're nearly there."

I slumped back against the seat and thought of Elio. Where was he now? Already in the air, thousands of miles above us? Where would he take the fight?

Italy . . . where he'd be greatly outnumbered.

If he died there, then our story really would be the greatest tragedy ever written.

We were driving on a twisty, dark road, the headlights illuminating trees on both sides. I had no idea where we were.

"Turn right," Toni said quietly.

Ettore glanced at her. "You mean left?"

"These are Giada's instructions," Toni said.

Ettore shrugged and did as he was told.

We entered a slightly more built-up area. Ettore glanced around. "I think this is wrong," he said.

We passed a sign for a military airstrip just up ahead.

"Okay, I'm sure this isn't right," Ettore said. He made to turn around and then stiffened.

"No, it's right. Keep going." Toni's voice was strange.

Ettore was silent. The car progressed down the street toward a metal gate in the distance.

"I think Ettore's right. This can't be the way." I peered out the window.

Silence surged inside the car. Something was off. I looked between Toni and Ettore, and that's when I saw it.

The black glint of a gun pressed against Ettore's side.

"Toni?" I asked cautiously.

"I don't have a choice, Mrs. Santori. I'm sorry."

"You're betraying Elio?"

"Yes, I'm betraying Elio, and if I thought he'd survive this, then I'd expect to answer for it . . . but I have no choice. Stop here."

Ettore pulled the car to a stop. Panic welled inside me. I had to do something. Save Ettore, get away . . . something to stop this plan from falling into place.

I can take care of myself . . . as long as I know you're safe.

Elio's words from before swirled in my head. Of course, how could they ensure that they had the advantage over a man like Elio? By throwing off his focus and giving him something else to worry about. Some*one*.

"Toni, please, don't do this. Let's go to Casa Nera and talk to Renato. He'll help you."

Toni spit out a bitter laugh. "Renato De Sanctis doesn't care about anyone but family, and Elio will kill me himself once he finds out what I've done. I expect that. I know that . . . but if I can save her, then none of it matters."

"Her?"

Before Toni could answer, a tap at the window nearly made me scream.

Toni jerked her head to Ettore. "Get out."

"Antonia," he started.

"Get out, Ettore, if you want to survive this."

"If I don't die protecting her . . . I'm dead anyway," the young man said with a sober, mature expression on his face that I'd never seen before. He was so much older than his years in that moment.

"Your choice, not mine," Toni said coolly, and then the gun went off.

"*No!* Ettore!" I screamed, losing all self-control.

The door opened, and Ettore fell out onto the ground outside, moaning. Moaning was good. Moaning wasn't dead.

Toni got out the front, and I slid across to the other side of the car and pushed open the door. I wanted to check on Ettore. I got two steps, then I hit a hard chest and bounced backward.

The man in front of me was wearing the same solid black that Elio did. He was just as tall and broad, too. He had a thick dark beard hiding the lower half of his face. Dark slashes of eyebrows framed eyes so black, they seemed to be carved-out holes in his skull.

He had a dark scarf of some kind wrapped around his neck and over his head, making him nearly impossible to identify.

As I stared up at him, he tilted his head to the side, studying me back.

"Mrs. Santori, it's a pleasure to finally meet you. I'm Massimo, and I'll be accompanying you on your flight."

I backed up a step, and Massimo smiled. There was something utterly terrifying about his calm amusement.

"She doesn't like to fly." Toni's voice came from just behind me.

I whirled around to take her in.

She appeared faded somehow. Defeated but resolved.

"Is that right?" Massimo asked, his voice suddenly closer than before.

I twisted around to see him, but it was too late. He was right there. A sharp pain pricked my neck. Coldness flooded me, turning the world blurry. I stumbled, but Massimo was there, holding me up.

"She'll have a tracker somewhere," Toni said from a million miles away.

"Of course she will. Santori is a thorough bastard, and this woman is his wife. Don't worry about it."

The world tilted. He'd picked me up. I couldn't move.

"He'll come for her," Toni called, somewhere behind us.

"Yes, he will. And I'll be waiting," Massimo said, dark certainty in his tone.

It was the last thing I heard before I went under.

38

ELIO

The plane ride had been tense. Now I was holed up in a De Sanctis safe house just outside of Naples, preparing for the next step.

I'd chosen to send the bulk of my trusted men with Georgia. Sure, she was only driving to Casa Nera, but with her went my only reason to live.

If they hurt her, or she died . . . I'd lie down and die, too. It would finally be time. But first, I'd take out Sergio Ravelli for all the trouble he'd caused me.

I pulled out the small snapshot I had of her from my wallet. It was just a picture from her apartment that I'd cut Conti out of. She was smiling at the spot where her former husband had been standing. I wanted more pictures of her. Albums' worth. I wanted to capture her smile again and again, and I wanted that smile to be reserved for me. I wanted to see it every fucking day. I wanted to see it every morning, and every night . . . Fuck, I wanted it so badly it felt hard to breathe.

For the first time in fourteen years, I wanted to live.

A rap sounded at the door, and one of my men appeared.

"Boss, Giada says she's been trying to get through to you."

"I'll call her back."

It was a few years after I'd left Col Moschin that I started to employ my former squad mates. Experiences in the Special Forces bonded people on a soul-deep level. When they got out, at loose ends and trying to fit themselves into civilian life, I understood their struggle. Renato didn't worry about my team. He understood the compulsion but also knew my first allegiance would always be to the De Sanctis family. He was the man who had gotten me out of prison, after all. He'd also delivered the news about Georgia.

The news that had sent me into hell . . . news that had turned out to be a lie. Renato hadn't known, of course. I supposed that no one outside of Conti and Georgia had known. I hadn't even suspected that Conti was gay. It hadn't crossed my mind, because in my mind he had to be infatuated with Georgia, because who wouldn't be?

I pinched the bridge of my nose.

She'd been living with her husband and his partner for thirteen years.

She'd never replaced me.

She'd thought I'd left her . . . taken a bag of cash and run away.

I guess I want you to save me, Santori. I want you . . . I just want you.

I closed my eyes, filled with pain and regret like I'd never known before. It was just such a fucking waste. Fourteen years I'd hated her, blamed her for all of it, and all the while, she'd been out there doing the same.

If I hadn't been a heartless bastard who was more intent on ensuring his own peace of mind, I'd have looked her up years ago when I'd gotten out of the military and demanded to know why she'd married Conti. I'd have seen the truth with my own eyes.

She wouldn't have been able to do the same . . . I was a ghost. She didn't have the resources to counter my sister's efforts to hide my existence from prying eyes.

No, the fault was mine, and I was going to fix it. I was going to take out every motherfucker who had dared to threaten Georgia, and then, when it was done, I was going to give my wife the life she deserved . . .

No one was going to get in my way.

I'd changed out of my suit and into clothes I could move easily in. Pockets for weapons, and black to blend in. I stood in front of the mirror in the safe house and slowly shed my pretense of being a civilian, becoming the mercenary that my wife called me. I slipped knives into sheaths on my arms and thighs. Extra clips went in there, too, as well as my guns. I pulled a long case from the safe in the corner of the room and carried it to the dining room table to set up. I put an earpiece on and fiddled with it.

"Comms check, over."

"I hear you. How was the flight? Catch any good movies?"

I ignored my sister's glib remarks. "Is she at Casa Nera?"

"Should be any second now."

I'd left for the private jet before my security team had left for Casa Nera. The security escort for Georgia had waited a good ten hours, until the dead of night and Giada was sure that no one was around.

"Keep an eye on it," I told Giada.

"Yes, boss. Now, would you like to know where Sergio Ravelli has been staying lately? You'll never guess . . ."

"The Bellisario villa, right?" I didn't even have to think about it.

"How did you guess? Were you and Sergio much closer than you pretended you were in prison? You can tell me. I won't judge, but if this is a scorned former lover, I can understand the situation better."

I blew out a sigh. "Very funny. What happened to that property? How come the Ravellis can just move in?"

"Looks like old Alfredo had a lot of gambling debt lately. He was deep in the shit with the Ravellis. Probably why they were so certain he was going to squeal on them and needed to try and get to Georgia so urgently. As you know, Zio Sal doesn't stay at the De Sanctis estate out there anymore, so the town has been up for grabs, and it seems like the Ravellis went for it. Did you bring the flash drive?"

"Yes." I patted my pocket that held the tampered-with evidence. Giada had removed everything related to the De Sanctis family. I'd hand it over as evidence . . . if any of the motherfuckers made it through the night.

"Okay, so we know where we're going . . . I'm getting my darlings in the air."

Before changing, I'd taken Giada's drones to the rooftop and set them up, so she could remotely control them by satellite.

Keys were clacking away in my ear as my sister did her thing.

"And they're up," she said with satisfaction. "I can see your safe house . . . Wait, what's that?" she muttered.

I checked my weapons once more. A glint of something metal shone from the table, beside my phone. I'd emptied my suit pockets earlier and found it.

Georgia's locket.

I picked it up and opened it, revealing a tiny dried flower pressed against a creamy background, preserved behind glass.

A heliotrope.

My heliotrope. She'd kept it.

I lifted the chain over my head. It was long; she used to keep the necklace hidden, and now it hit me at my collarbones. I pressed it against my skin for a second and then fastened my bulletproof vest on top of it.

I didn't need dog tags with my name on them anymore.

If they needed help identifying my body, this locket would suffice.

This body belonged to her . . . and it always had.

It was my last thought before the mission went to shit.

"Elio! Get down!" Giada shouted.

I was still pressing the place where the locket sat when the world exploded.

I woke with a start and nearly tumbled off the gurney bed I was lying on. I grabbed on to it just in time to stop myself from falling off. Everything was white. An alarm was beeping wildly beside me, and I realized that there were electrodes attached to me.

Hospital.

I was in the hospital.

Slowly, I sat up again and looked around. There was a window into the hallway, and a doctor talked to two men in blazers. Cops.

The beeping was driving me mad. I pulled the drip out of my arm, and the sensors went too. The machine made a long, flatlining beep until I yanked the power cable from the wall.

"Sir!" A nurse appeared, speaking in a rapid flood of Italian. "You can't take that off! You've been hurt. You were in an explosion."

"Where are the men I was with at the house?" I demanded.

"They are here, too. They are more hurt. One is in surgery," the nurse said, plugging the machine back in.

Fuck. None of this was going to plan.

I found my hand drifting to my neck and patting for the locket. It was gone.

"Where's my stuff? The clothes I was wearing . . ." I trailed off.

The nurse paled. Of course, I'd had half an armory strapped to me when I'd been brought in. I'm sure the police outside had questions about that.

"The clothes are in the locker there. The other items . . . they are being held by the police."

Shit. Still, they probably only took the weapons I had on me. My sniper rifle was in the house. Hopefully it was still there.

First, I needed to get out of here without trouble from the cops. I sat back as the nurse bustled around me.

"I have to tell the doctor that you're awake." She glanced toward the window.

The doctor was standing with the cops. Perfect.

"Can you wait? I'm really dizzy. I think I need to sleep some more," I asked her and summoned the best exhausted look I had. I didn't need to try that hard.

She hesitated and then nodded. "Okay, next time you wake up . . . we have to tell them."

I nodded. She meant the cops. Sure, she could tell them whatever she wanted . . .

When I was gone.

I watched her leave the room and then pushed myself out of bed. The locker beside the bed opened easily, and I got dressed. Tucked into a pocket that rested just above my heart, I found the locket. I had no guns or weapons, and my Kevlar vest was gone . . . but I had this.

Mia ragione.

My reason to live.

I pulled it over my neck and tucked it under my jacket.

I had what I needed. It was time to go.

The first rule of being prepared was always have extras. I went to the wreckage of the safe house first and sifted through the debris. A whole day had passed while I was in the hospital. I'd glanced at my chart as I went out the door. Suspected concussion. I'd gotten off lucky.

Still, I'd lost twenty-four hours.

I found my sniper rifle in the mess that was the bedroom I'd been in. Luckily, it had been the least hit, and the case could take a few hard knocks. I carried it outside to the car we'd driven from the airport. It was parked four blocks away. Never leave your assets all in one location. Thankfully, the keys had still been in my pocket. I got in and drove even farther, until I was backed into a space in a deserted parking lot, where I could see all around me.

I went into the trunk and took out the backup weapons cases. For the second time in twenty-four hours, I strapped myself up with guns and knives. I took a backup phone from a pocket in one of the cases and called Giada.

"Oh my God, are you okay? That was fucking crazy," my sister said, answering immediately. She had that wired note to her voice that told me she hadn't left her post in twenty-four hours, waiting for news. I'd seen her do it before, existing on energy drinks and anxiety. Hopefully Bran was making sure she was taking care of herself.

I reached for the satellite link I'd need and put it in my ear.

"How are the drones?"

"Dead. You've got one spare. Be gentle with her. What about your other men?"

"In the hospital, and hurt. I'm not bothering them with this. They've done enough."

"So, you're going in alone, after they tried to blow you up."

"I don't have a choice."

Giada was quiet.

"What is it?" Dread formed like ice in my veins, and I just knew something even worse had happened.

"She didn't make it here, Elio . . . We think Massimo caught her."

I stared at the dark night beyond the parking lot, emotions I hadn't felt in a decade brewing in my chest.

"She's not dead. Don't you dare tell me she is," I warned my sister.

"She's not! I don't think that she is. Her tracker is still working . . . transmitting a location. It went haywire for a bit, when I first realized that they were taking too long to show up here, but it's transmitting normally now."

"Where is she?"

Giada cleared her throat. "Actually, you'll be happy to hear that she's not too far from you."

"Where?" I demanded, but I knew. Of course it would come to this.

"Castel Amaro. The Bellisario villa. They've taken her . . . home."

39

GEORGIA

A hand was moving slowly through my hair when I woke. For a moment I thought it was Elio, and we had fallen asleep in the orchard that overlooked town. No one was missing us, and we could steal a few more minutes of peace before we headed back home.

Then my stomach lurched, and the dream shattered. I turned to the side just in time to vomit on the floor.

"Shit, are you okay?" Toni's voice came to me. She was sitting with my head on her lap. We were in the back of a car.

"What's wrong?" a deep voice asked from the front.

"She's sick. Too much sedative back-to-back."

"It's fine, it's not my car, and besides, we're here."

The car stopped, and I sat up with a groan. The door opened, and a smell flooded into the car, recognizable even over the stench of vomit.

The scent of warm earth and olive groves. Fig trees and night jasmine. It was a smell I hadn't thought I'd ever inhale again.

It flooded my head and sent me back in time.

"Out you get, Mrs. Santori," the deep voice continued.

Yes, that was right. I'd forgotten about the man. The dark shadow of a man who had injected me with something.

Massimo.

Toni helped me out of the car, and I yanked my arm from her grip.

"Don't help me. I don't need your help," I snapped at her.

Her face was pained as she followed behind us. I straightened my spine, wiped my mouth with the back of my hand, and spit on the ground just beside Massimo's booted feet.

His mouth pulled into a smirk. "I like fire, Mrs. Santori, but save it for the Ravellis. This is nothing personal. Your husband is just a name on a contract for me, and you are just the method of attracting his attention."

"Wow, your sense of honor is impressive. What a man," I murmured, my eyes challenging him. Why exactly I was pissing him off, I had no idea, but I just couldn't go easy.

He chuckled and turned away, unfazed.

"Let's go. They're waiting. Once you hand over Bellisario's daughter, you've made good on your agreement. They'll let Sara go."

Toni flinched. "Do you promise?"

Massimo nodded. "I am a man of my word, always. You know that, Specter."

Specter?

We walked across gravel. Toni was at my side.

"Who is Sara?" I asked her.

She hesitated, then sighed. "My wife . . . well, not officially. My—partner. I'd never hurt the boss . . . never . . . but then *he* kidnapped Sara." She shot a furious glare at Massimo walking behind us.

"Why'd he call you Specter?"

"It was my call sign."

"You served together?"

Toni sighed again and nodded. My mind worked furiously over what the hell the implications of that were, considering that Elio also knew Toni from the military.

"Sara—she's pregnant. We've tried IVF for years and it's not stuck, but now," she shot me an agonized glance, "it's twins."

Fuck.

"Don't worry. They don't want to hurt you. They just want to force your father into silence," Toni said.

I scoffed. "How do you think they're going to do that?"

Toni was quiet.

"Enough chitchat," Massimo grunted from behind us.

As we walked, a house came into view.

I stumbled. It was the house of my childhood.

We went past the front gates and across the gardens. Men with guns were dotted here and there, watching us.

Massimo pounded on the door and waited, just behind us.

The door swung inward, and a man I'd never met stood there.

He smiled deeply at me and stepped back.

"Welcome, Georgia. I've been waiting for you."

Inside was nearly unchanged from the place I'd grown up in. The same art lined the walls, and even the same pictures were hung. Me as a teenager riding a horse. Me graduating high school with my wreath of laurel leaves.

My father holding me as a baby.

"Come through here." The man led us deeper into the house to the sitting room, where there were drinks laid out on the coffee table.

"Help yourselves."

"This isn't a social call, Sergio. This is the end of a job." Massimo took up too much space in the room. A black hole of darkness and violence.

"It's not the end, since Elio Santori is still alive and kicking."

Massimo nodded. "Yes, that's true . . . but I'm sure he's on his way. It wasn't my idea to put him and his men in the hospital so that cops could be watching them around the clock."

Sickness lurched through me again, and I barely managed to fight it down. *Elio is in the hospital?*

The Ravelli man, Sergio, sneered. "You were taking too long."

Massimo just stared at him. "And now, thanks to you, it's taking longer."

Sergio tightened his fists and looked like he was about to argue.

"The job is practically done, so you can go ahead and give me the name now," Massimo said, staring a hole through the other man.

Sergio shook his head. "Practically done isn't done. After. I'll give you the name after . . . if you can even manage to kill Santori."

"Such confidence." Massimo glowered at Sergio. "It's like you really think you have nine lives, Ravelli, and you can afford to irritate me."

Massimo stepped closer and loomed over him. Silence fell.

"Now, before you piss me off, why don't you be a good fucking host, Sergio, or we might fall out." Massimo's tone was chilling, and clearly I wasn't the only one to think so.

Sergio turned to Toni.

"Since you came through, your little girlfriend will be released. You can leave."

Toni glanced at me. "I want a guarantee."

"A guarantee?" Sergio laughed and then jerked his head toward his man, who was on the phone.

A cell was put in her hand, and she listened to someone talking on the other side.

She closed her eyes, the relief visible on her face, and then handed back the phone.

"Happy? Now, get out of here."

Toni swallowed hard.

"Mrs. Santori," she murmured.

She looked wretched at that moment, and in an instant, I forgave her. I understood her.

"It's okay. I'll be fine. Elio's on his way," I told her quietly.

"I'm sorry."

I just shrugged. "You did what you had to, to save the person you love. I get that. But Toni . . ."

She gazed back at me.

"You'd better disappear before Elio gets me out of this. You'd better be far, far away," I warned her. If there was anything that I'd learned about the man Elio had become, it was that he wouldn't take the betrayal of one of his inner circle lightly.

Then Ravelli men were pushing Toni out of the room.

Sergio watched me with reptilian eyes.

"So, this is the woman who caused the downfall of Elio Santori. I have to say, he has taste . . . you are lovely."

I stiffened and raised my chin. He circled me, appraising me like I was a pound of meat at the butcher's.

"And you're pathetic," I couldn't stop myself from saying.

Sergio stopped and raised his eyebrows at me. "Excuse me?"

"I said it's pathetic how all your men in L.A., countless faceless losers, couldn't bring down Elio. It's funny that you think you can defeat him here and now."

Sergio glared at me. "Yes, well, that's why you're here. Besides, I didn't have help then." He jerked his head toward Massimo.

"This all started because your whore of a father wouldn't keep his mouth shut when he was arrested. After years of bending over and taking whatever the capo wanted to shove his way, he decided to grow a spine . . . but only to save himself. You know"—he reached out and grabbed my chin—"when I heard Elio had decided to marry you instead of cutting off body parts and sending them to your father, I was surprised, but meeting you . . . it makes sense. He owes me, you know . . . he left me to rot in prison and took the easy way out like a little bitch," he spit. "He owes me. In return, I'll take you . . . his lovely wife."

He leaned in, his fetid breath touching my skin. His lips landed on mine, and I bit down as hard as I could. Blood filled my mouth. I savaged his lip, and he punched me as hard as he could on the side of the head.

I fell to the floor and stayed down. Massimo pushed between us and pinned Sergio to a chair.

"This wasn't in our deal, Sergio. I'm not here to watch you slobber over an unwilling woman."

"No, you're not. You're here to kill Santori. What I do with this bitch to send a message to her father is none of your business," Sergio spit, holding his lip. He glared at me. "You're going to pay for that. I think I'll take a finger first . . . or maybe a fucking ear."

Fear flickered through me, and my lungs felt tight. A panic attack, after just throwing up and being sedated twice, wasn't going to be great. I didn't really know how I was going to manage it.

But I didn't have to worry about it, it turned out.

At that very second, the lights shut off, and the entire house plunged into darkness.

Massimo chuckled. "Mrs. Santori, your husband is here for you."

40

ELIO

"Okay, it's a go," Giada said in my ear.

I was waiting at the back wall of the property for her to remotely cut the power. All the streetlights on the block went dark.

"Very precise work," I muttered as I climbed the wall and dropped down the other side.

"Hey, I only blew the grid for this part of town. That's tough. I'm in another country, don't forget. If you want to isolate the house, go find a fuse box."

"Okay, okay, I take it back. Good job."

"Thank you. Now, there is a man up ahead, judging by heat signature."

"Got it." I slipped on the thermal imaging goggles. Thankfully, they'd been stowed away in the car when the safe house had exploded.

Sure enough, there was a man stumbling around. I got close enough to hear him swear and then snapped his neck. He fell to the ground.

"One down, about thirty to go," Giada said.

"On it."

I moved systematically, circling the house and picking off the external security.

The real threats would be closer to Sergio, and then there was Massimo himself. L'Ombra.

I was finishing off the last of the external security when Giada spoke.

"Okay, I can see Georgia . . . at least, I think I can. She's the only one the size of a female inside. They are taking her to the kitchen."

The kitchen overlooked the back garden and stables. It was directly below her old bedroom.

"There's someone moving toward you. Someone big."

Massimo.

"I need a place I can fight him without interruptions."

"The stables. There's nothing there except a few horses."

"Good idea."

I wasn't far from the stables now, since I'd been working my way around the perimeter of the grounds. Now, I snuck inside there, keeping low. The smell of hay and horses was immediately familiar.

I hid myself in a stall and pulled a gun, then waited.

"He's coming your way," Giada said.

I nodded, staring into the darkness beyond the stall.

Massimo was the real threat. Everyone else was bullshit. They wouldn't kill Georgia right off. They needed to scare her father. There was still time to get Ravelli Sr. out of jail and get the criminal charges dropped if the prosecutor recanted his testimony.

That alone would stay Sergio's hand. He wanted me dead, revenge for leaving him to rot in prison . . . but he knew he couldn't manage it himself, so he'd hired Massimo.

The real question was why L'Ombra had agreed to a mission like this.

It wasn't like him at all.

Silence fell that felt deeper than before. It had dimensions, this silence, and I knew he was here.

"Apollo, do you come in, over?" L'Ombra's mocking call came to me.

Apollo. God of the sun. My old call sign. The scent of hay and sweat thickened the air, the low snorts of horses the only sound between us. Moonlight filtered through the gaps in the wooden walls, casting broken shadows over Massimo's face. He drew level with me. His stance was wide, controlled—just like I'd taught him.

He pulled a gun from his waistband and held it up. "I'm unarmed . . ."

I fought a snort but didn't quite manage it.

His head turned toward me, and then he was charging over the stall's half-door.

He landed right in front of me as I stood and aimed a punch at the side of his head. I wouldn't shoot him. He used to be on my team. It was impossible to see him as the enemy, despite the reality of the situation.

The punch glanced off his temple when he spun around and faced me.

"Long time no see, boss." Massimo smirked at me.

He'd always been able to laugh in the face of death; murder and mayhem didn't faze him. In fact, it was quite the opposite.

He lunged first, his boot crunching in the straw. I twisted, barely dodging the jab meant for my throat. My back hit the back wall of the stall. Massimo came in again, faster this time, a brutal hook aimed for my ribs. I caught his wrist, twisted, and drove my elbow toward his jaw. He ducked and countered with a knee to my stomach. It wasn't the first time we'd fought. We used to make a game of it. For a second, it felt just like it had then, until the pain set in.

Pain exploded through my core, but I absorbed it, using the momentum to spin and drive my shoulder into his chest. We crashed to the floor, rolling in the dirt and straw, fists colliding with flesh. He got on top, his forearm crushing my windpipe. My vision blurred. I struck blindly—*one, two, three* shots to his ribs—before hooking my legs around his and reversing the position. I slipped a knife out of the sheath on my forearm and held it to Massimo's throat.

Now I was on top. Now I had the advantage. I pressed my blade to his throat, just enough to make the fight go out of him.

"Why are you here, Mass?"

"What can I say? I hate not being invited to a party, so I'm crashing. Good to see you, Colonel Santori. It's been a while."

Massimo chuckled. He'd always had that psychopathic edge. A man who thrived on chaos and darkness. I'd felt it even then, when he'd been an up-and-coming recruit and I'd been his first commander.

"Not long enough. Why did you take this contract?" I demanded, pushing the knife harder against Massimo's throat.

"It was a hell of a payday." Massimo laughed.

"Try again . . . and tell me the truth."

"Why shouldn't I take it? Should I have let someone else take it and come after you? Besides, Ravelli has something I want."

"What?"

"A name. An important one. I need it."

"And so you kill me, and he gives you the name? What name?"

"You wouldn't know it. The man wasn't someone you'd know."

"Try me."

Massimo sighed. "Unless you have very intimate knowledge of

local steel manufacturing around 1988 in these parts, I doubt you'd know."

"Wait, steel manufacturing around Castel Amaro?" Giada said in my ear. Her keyboard clacked. "That rings a bell."

"I might know more than you think," I told Massimo.

"Got it!" Giada said excitedly. "There's a ton of information on the drive that the prosecutor sent to Georgia, all about the first work they did and who they worked with. A steel business came up, as did the names of the people in charge."

I told Massimo as much.

He grinned. "Well, fuck me, Colonel Santori, you've still got it. Do you mind?" he asked and pushed the knife from his throat.

I let him.

I sat up, and he wiped blood from his broken nose.

"How did you get Georgia here?"

"I twisted Antonia's arm . . . stole her partner. Don't worry, both are fine."

"Why?" I demanded and got to my feet.

"Because I had to get you here . . . How was I supposed to know you'd decide to come on your own? I needed to play along with Ravelli to get the name." Massimo smirked up at me. "I thought we could torture him together . . . just like old times."

"Mass . . ." I sighed with annoyance. "You scared my wife, and Toni betrayed her. I should kill you both."

"But you won't." Massimo was full of confidence. "Give me the flash drive . . . and I'll consider my contract canceled."

"You never renege on a contract, or so your reputation would lead me to believe."

"It's true, but I don't keep contracts with dead men . . . and I believe Sergio Ravelli is living his last hour of life right now, isn't he?"

I tucked the knife away, tossed the flash drive to Massimo, and took my sniper rifle from my back. "An hour is generous."

Massimo nodded, tucking the flash drive away in a pocket. "I like her, by the way . . . your wife."

I considered him. "Be careful. I could still kill you, you know."

His booming laughter filled the stables. I offered my hand to him, and he took it. I pulled him to his feet.

"So, he's insane," Giada said, having listened to the whole exchange.

"Undoubtedly. Update on Georgia."

"In the kitchen."

"The doors are open," Massimo said conversationally behind me. "I tried them on the way out."

"What are you saying?"

"I'm saying, we divide and conquer . . . lure your wife out here and pick off the men around her on the way. That'll already make a dent in their manpower. I'll return to the house and take care of the rest."

"I want to snuff the life out of Sergio Ravelli myself. I want to watch the light drain from his eyes . . . for daring to mess with my wife."

Massimo's eyes widened, and he looked genuinely shocked, shaking his head.

"So, it finally happened . . . you care about someone. You're compromised."

"One day, you'll realize how empty a life of vengeance is . . . Living in the shadows, just existing . . . collecting contracts and money. None of that matters."

Massimo watched me, then shrugged. "Maybe so, but it's all some of us have. Until next time, Colonel." He saluted me sharply, stepping back and melting into the shadows.

"I don't mean to pry, but I got all of that on tape and I'm totally playing it for Georgia. '*I want to watch the light drain from his eyes . . . for daring to mess with my wife.*'" Giada cackled in my ear.

"Focus," I snapped at her.

She chortled away for a few more seconds.

"So, let's go with L'Ombra's plan. But do you think there's a way to lure Georgia out to the stables?"

My gut lurched as I felt the past and present collide.

"Yes," I said with perfect certainty. "I know a way."

41

GEORGIA

I sat at the kitchen table right by the window and stared out at the moonlit garden. Right now, outside somewhere, Elio could be fighting for his life against Massimo. I was terrified. I felt sick. I couldn't even think or worry about what would happen to me if Elio lost. If he did, I didn't care what happened. They could carve me up and ship me to my father inch by inch. I would be dead anyway.

There were about ten guards standing around the kitchen, watching me. It should have been comical. I didn't know what they thought I could do by myself. I didn't even have a weapon to defend myself with, but apparently Sergio Ravelli was taking Elio seriously. I wished he weren't. If only he'd underestimate him.

That didn't seem to be the case.

A slight breeze blew through the gap in the kitchen door. I stared at the yard and then looked up at the stables, remembering that night we'd first slept together. Life had seemed so shiny and full of hope then. I'd been excited to live, because I'd met him, the man who made every second exciting. We were going to leave

Castel Amaro and see the world. We'd had our whole lives ahead of us . . . and now, I might lose it all again.

Elio was right; I hadn't really been living alone, without him . . . I'd just been waiting.

I was staring at the dark stables when I saw it.

A light flashing in the darkness.

Flash-flash, pause . . .

I'd know that pattern anywhere. That code had lived in my brain for fourteen years.

Come to me.

Adrenaline surged through me. I considered my escape. Elio was telling me to run to the barn, and I'd follow his orders off the ends of the Earth, trusting him to catch me when I fell. I didn't stop to think. I didn't let my panic take over.

I trusted Elio's plans to work.

I trusted him, period. If I was going to die here, I'd do it trying to reach him.

This time, I'd trust him until the end.

I glanced around casually, checking the guards' positions. They were chatting among themselves, clearly feeling safe. I waited until the one closest to me turned around and started to argue about the latest football match—and then lunged for the door.

The handle moved beneath my palm, and then I was outside. The men closest to me grabbed at me, but I twisted away, putting my head down and running toward the stables with everything I had.

Someone beside me reached out for me, and a strange zipping sound echoed around before he fell. Someone got close on the other side, and he also fell. A fine spray of blood hit my cheek, but I kept running. The men beside me kept falling, picked off one by one. Some still had their hands outstretched toward me, just about to grab me.

Not one managed to touch me.

They fell as I ran, perfectly protected by my merciless mercenary. There was no hail of bullets. Each shot was exactly precise. Not one of the men got up.

I reached the stables and slammed inside.

One man was still behind me, doggedly on my heels. He'd been right behind me the entire time and had clearly used me as his shield.

I ran down the central aisle of the stable, aiming for the ladder at the end. I didn't make it. The guy behind me grabbed my hair and yanked me back, just as Elio's legs appeared from the space above the hayloft. He dropped and landed smoothly, pointing a gun at the man behind me. A sharp feeling pricked me under the chin.

"Move and I'll cut her throat," the man's voice wavered. He was terrified.

Elio didn't bother answering him. His gaze fixed on me.

"You trust me, *cara*?" he asked. "Nod if you trust me."

I didn't stop to think. I bent my head and nodded.

The bullet zipped over my head and hit my attacker between the eyes. His hold went slack. He fell to the floor, and I stood there, shaking all over.

Then Elio was in front of me, bundling me into his arms.

"It's okay now, *topolina*, you're safe." He smoothed my hair back and looked me over, his gaze running across me, searching for injuries. It snagged on my bloody lip. A remainder from when I'd bitten Sergio and he'd clocked me.

"Who?" Elio's voice was utterly lethal.

"Sergio . . . he kissed me . . . and I nearly bit his lip off," I admitted.

Elio took a shuddering breath and then pulled me close, pressing a kiss to the top of my head.

"That's my good girl. My wife." He breathed into my hair. "My love."

My heart clenched hard, and everything else that was going on suddenly felt far away. It was all happening behind thick glass. It couldn't touch us.

"My love?" I repeated.

"Yes, my love. I've thought of you as a lot of things over the years apart . . . my poison, my betrayer . . . my killer . . . but through it all, you were always my love. My one and only everything. Now, I need you to—"

"I'm not staying here without you! I'm going with you. This time, you're not leaving me behind. Where you go, I go," I said determinedly.

Elio stared at me and then smiled. The darkness shifted in the stables, the place where he'd asked me to marry him.

"Abso-fucking-lutely. I've learned my lesson. You're not leaving my side."

He took my hand in his and threaded our fingers together.

"Let's finish this."

Inside the house, it was silent as a tomb.

Bodies were strewn across the floor. I stared at the formation.

They were laid out head to toe in a line leading toward the stairs.

An arrow formed of bodies.

I glanced at Elio, horrified.

"This way," he murmured.

I stayed behind him, and we walked up the stairs. He had a gun at his side, and I could feel his focus. I felt safer than I'd ever felt before, protected by this man.

We reached the top floor and started down the hall. At the end of the passage, at the doorway to my father's office, two dead bodies were propped up on either wall, their arms stretched out to point at the open doorway. The black rectangle seemed to gape. I was scared to see what was inside.

"Who did this?" I whispered to Elio.

"Massimo. He's a creative soul."

A strangled cry sounded from the room before us. Elio squeezed my hand, and then we were stepping inside.

Massimo was sitting at the desk, his feet up, arms behind his head.

"The gang is all here, Sergio. Now the party can get started." He grinned at us. "I see you found us easily enough?"

"Your directions helped," Elio said dryly and checked in the corners of the room.

Everyone was dead, it seemed, except for Sergio. He whimpered somewhere in the room.

Massimo clicked on the desk lamp, and the whole bloody scene came into focus.

Sergio was trapped beneath the desk chair—no, not trapped.

Impaled.

Two legs of the chair seemed to be driven through Sergio's legs. Two long metal pokers from the fireside were driven through his spread-out arms. He was sprawled out in a cross shape, and Massimo's weight on the chair made it impossible for him to move.

He was crucified to the floor.

Blood formed a pool around the desk.

"I figured it made sense to end Sergio and his little vendetta here, where it all started, Alfredo Bellisario's study. The place where the prosecutor made his deals and did his dirty work."

"I'll tell you the information," Sergio groaned. "But you can't kill me."

Massimo laughed. "I don't need your information, Sergio. I have everything I need, and I didn't have to betray a brother-in-arms to get it." He stared at Elio. "But no matter, I know he understands me."

He stood suddenly and stepped back, gesturing down to Sergio like a waiter presenting a particularly delectable main course.

"All yours, Apollo," he said to Elio and winked at me. "A little insider nickname for our dearly beloved Colonel."

Elio nodded to Massimo and turned to me, pulling a long, wicked-looking knife from his belt.

"I didn't know what to get you as a wedding present, *cara* . . . but now I do. A life free from danger. That is what I promise you."

Then he turned and made his way across the room.

"Don't look. You don't have to," Massimo said, standing beside me. He shifted his body and hid the desk and Sergio. "You never have to look . . . that's your husband's job now."

Then Elio was there. "No, not my job."

I fell into his arms. He brought me close and kissed the top of my head.

"No?" I pressed myself as close to him as I could.

"No. My honor and privilege . . . my birthright. Protecting you . . . loving you, is my legacy, *topolina*, and I'm the luckiest bastard in the world."

42

GEORGIA

We went to the De Sanctis estate, only a few miles away, while Massimo Lucciano disappeared into the night. Giada had already redirected Elio's men from their failed mission to escort me to Casa Nera, and they headed directly to my childhood home to clean up the mess.

Elio fished out a key, hung by a string, from an old well in front of the De Sanctis estate, and let us in. The heavy metal gate creaked when we pushed it open. The garden was overgrown, and the path to the front door was nearly hidden under wildflowers. Dawn was just breaking on the horizon when we got inside.

I was tired and wired at the same time.

"Are you sure it's okay?" I wondered as we stepped inside.

The grand foyer was still awe-inspiring, even if it was a little dusty and faded.

"Zio Sal invited us himself. He has more than a few estates dotted around Napoli, don't worry. We won't be disturbed here."

With that, Elio turned to me. "I think it's time to finish that conversation from the other day."

The adrenaline that was still leaping through my system jumped to attention again. "It is? Aren't you tired?"

"Not of you. Never of you," he said quietly and lifted me into his arms.

"Hey, I can walk."

"You don't know where we're going," he pointed out and started up the marble stairs.

"What are you looking for?" I asked.

Elio took us in and out of the long procession of bedrooms upstairs.

"The least dusty one."

"So, you don't know where we're going either?" A laugh escaped me.

He chose a room and put me down, backing me into the wall and cupping my face. "Is this going to be a pattern? Sassing your husband?"

I nodded solemnly, and his face creased in a smile.

"Good."

Then he kissed me. Long and hard, soft and melting, he kissed me until my knees were weak, and the only thing holding me up was his strong, solid body against mine.

His hands fell to my jacket, and he slipped it off my shoulders.

"I've thought about what you told me . . . I had time, plenty of time on the flight. And it sounds like you've been waiting for me."

Always.

"You've loved me and waited for me all this time, haven't you?"

His deep voice sank through me, comfort like I hadn't felt in a lifetime.

I fought a roll of my eyes at his words. "No. I wasn't *waiting*. I didn't think you were coming. You left me, remember . . . you didn't love me like I loved you, and after that, I wasn't interested in loving anyone ever again. Once was enough." My breath grew short when he pulled my T-shirt up and over my head.

"*Loved*. Past tense," Elio said. "So, you stopped loving me, *cara?*"

I swallowed hard and raised my chin. "No. I could never manage it. I loved you then, just like I love you now. I don't think I can stop."

He inhaled deeply at my words. I felt more naked than I'd ever been in my life.

"What about you, though . . . you stopped, didn't you? You blamed me for all of it all this time . . . don't you hate me?" How could he forget the way he'd felt about me all these years? The stain of my father's meddling had marked us both so deeply.

My bra was next, and it fell to the floor, immediately replaced by Elio's hands. Thick, callused fingers tugged at my nipples and sent heat spiraling through me.

He let out a satisfied sigh and moved closer, pressing his forehead to mine, even though he had to bend to do it.

"*Beneath the frozen river, currents still run* . . . Those lines were prophetic, I just didn't know it."

He stroked my breasts until I was panting. I held on to his arms when he bent and sucked one nipple into his mouth, rubbing his tongue across it.

He moved to the next one, and when his mouth left me, the dueling sensations of cold and heat exploded inside me as the air touched my wet skin. I shivered. Fully alive and awake. Feeling everything all at once, after years of feeling nothing.

He kissed the corners of my mouth. "I didn't understand then that loving you would be the most enduring emotion I'd ever have. Stronger than hate, more undeniable than anger, more persistent than despair . . . You've been with me through it all."

I opened my mouth to speak but didn't trust my voice not to

break. He slid his hands downward, unbuttoning my jeans and pushing them off my hips.

"You were my ghost, Georgia . . . you've haunted me, and honestly, it was enough. You lived like a nun, and I—I stopped doing anything but surviving."

Now it was my turn to be shocked. "So, you really were waiting for me, too?"

"Not just because I was waiting for you, but because hating and loving your ghost was enough. Your memory was enough for me . . . even if we never met again."

His hand glided into my panties, and I died a little at his possessive, confident touch. He handled my body like it was his own . . . like he had every right to it, and he did. He always had. Heat burned inside me at his caress, even as my heart hurt for the things he'd endured alone, thinking I'd left him.

"My father did this, didn't he?" I murmured, sadness and resentment colliding inside me.

Elio nodded slowly and then tilted his head to the side. "You want me to kill him for you? Or I can just have him tortured in prison . . . Your call."

The derisive offer split the tension down the middle, and a laugh spilled from me, which trailed off into a gasp when he ghosted his fingers along my slit and found my clit.

"A mood killer, from the trained killer," I said.

He chuckled. I couldn't find balance. I was happy and sad, regretful and grateful.

He thumbed the tears from under my eyes with his free hand. "Why are you crying? Did I scare you?" he asked.

I shook my head. He had his demons. He had lived in hell.

But he could never scare me.

"Even when I didn't know who you really were . . . you didn't really scare me," I said. "You saved me. You've only ever saved me."

"Well, you saved me, too . . . more than you know. If there was any shred of humanity left in me, burning through the darkness . . . it was my love for you." Then he kissed me again, his finger pumping inside me. "Now, my little country mouse, now that the dragons are slain and the demons are vanquished, you're left with just one to deal with."

His lips curved in a grin as I gasped, just about to come.

"And I'm going to make you scream."

Salvatore De Sanctis called in some old favors with the local cops and had the whole night erased from record. Elio's men flew in and took care of the bodies. The DIA pushed forward with the charges against the capo of the Ravelli family, and five prominent players, including the capo and his sons, were arrested.

The De Sanctis estate had been closed up for the better part of five years. Women from the village came to open it up, airing out the stuffy rooms and dusting off the past. The swimming pool was cleaned and the gardens cut back. Within a week, it was thriving again.

Renato and Charlie came to stay, as did Giada and her husband, Bran.

"Are you ready to go shopping? I know all the best places. You'll be inspired to design a whole line of dresses just for me . . . with space for knives, that's important," Giada said, then snagged a croissant from the table and took a big bite.

I was sitting in the orangery, looking out at the pool where Elio was doing laps. I couldn't stop staring.

"What are you doing?" Giada asked when I failed to respond.

"Enjoying the view," I said and sipped my coffee.

She followed my eyes and then groaned. "That's my brother."

I just smirked at her. "And my husband . . . Looks like he's not alone."

Bran had wandered out onto the sun-drenched poolside and was watching Elio, no doubt making some kind of smart-ass commentary.

Giada sank down next to me and kicked her feet up on the window ledge. "Okay, I take it back, the view is great."

We watched in companionable silence for a few minutes.

Charlie appeared in the doorway. "Hey, are you ready? Change of plans . . . Georgia needs to stay here. Elio will bring her into the city in a little bit. He has a surprise."

She was taking a short break from her work and studies. We'd become friends effortlessly. In the month since Elio had come back into my life, suddenly, being lonely felt like a distant memory. I had girlfriends and family, I had a husband, and I had a purpose again. My life in L.A. had wrapped up neatly. Erica was on her way to visit me soon, and I'd heard that the killing spree at the dress shop was unsolved. It seemed that someone had wiped all the CCTV footage of the location and all the blocks around it that night. I had a pretty strong feeling that that someone was sitting next to me. The more I got to know about Giada, the more terrifying she was.

"A surprise? I wonder what that could be," I said.

"Maybe you're pregnant," Giada joked.

"I feel like she might know before Elio." Charlie sighed, sinking down into a chair and taking a slice of melon from the platter on the table.

"If the man were a mere human, maybe, but this is my brother. He knows all . . . he's always watching. He's probably taking your temperature at night and studying your discharge with military precision."

"Giada!" I protested and threw a pillow at her. "That isn't an image I need to have right now."

"You should know who you're married to. Anyway, in that case,

Charlie, let's get going. Our husbands' money isn't going to spend itself."

"I make plenty of money myself, thank you." Charlie laughed and stood. "And I happen to know that you more than pull your weight building the De Sanctis fortune."

"Like I'm going to spend De Sanctis money. I've got O'Connor money for that."

Their voices drifted away as I watched Elio boost himself out of the pool and dry off.

Ten minutes later, we were parking down the street from a house that sat just off the square.

The Bellisario villa.

"I wanted to see something with you," Elio said, taking my hand in his.

We went through the house and out into the back garden.

The house was painfully clean. A lot of the furniture had been removed, as well as rugs and soft furnishings. They'd been too stained, I supposed. I should feel worse about that than I did.

The garden was full of flowers, and life. Bees buzzed about the lavender, and the sunflowers had lifted their heads to the sky.

I paused and looked at the stables. "Is that where we're going?"

Elio grinned. "Come to me, *topolina*." He pressed a kiss to the back of my hand.

We headed toward the building.

Inside the stalls, there were three horses. Their heads poked over the stalls, and they watched us curiously.

"I can't believe the Ravellis were taking care of them," I muttered.

"They weren't. The vet has been out. They need a good diet, care, and attention . . . all the things I used to do for them. Best job I ever had. Taking care of the horses . . . sleeping with the boss's daughter. That was the life."

"Shall we run away and start a horse ranch somewhere?" I asked.

He laughed.

"Maybe not. I'm not thinking of changing jobs, but this town, this house . . . it needs a new story. A new legacy . . . Renato and I think the De Sanctis family should reinstate its presence in this town. He has charged me with that job . . . if we want it."

"If *we* want it?"

"I told him I had to ask the boss." He smirked at me. "My country mouse needs to decide if she's ready to come home. A terracotta house with sage green bedrooms and horses in the stables . . ."

I stared around the beautiful building. The sweet smells of the garden, and the earthy scent of hay and horses. The view of the house from behind was spectacular. It was a family home. One for a family to live in. A garden for children to run around in.

A new legacy. A new story.

"Plenty of designers have ateliers in two countries . . ." Elio continued.

"Designers?"

"Well, that's what you are. Time to make those dreams come true."

I spun around to look at him.

"That's my dream. What's yours?"

He tucked a strand of hair behind my ear.

"You. It's always been you."

Beneath stone and concrete, seeds push through—
And those seeds can lift whole buildings.

A Year Later

GEORGIA

CASTEL AMARO

After a morning working with my team on my first-ever upcoming show, I left Erica in charge of catching up with the PR team and went for a swim. My favorite place to swim wasn't the swimming pool just beyond the stables at home. It was the secluded lake that sat a few miles outside of town.

I rode my favorite horse, Vento, there. Yes, a year ago I was living off ramen, had a loan shark banging down my door, and had worked my hands to the point of early arthritis. Now I was working on my first collection, and I split my time between Atlantic City and Castel Amaro, going into Naples when I needed to talk to stores and make production decisions. I rode horses in the countryside and was wildly in love with my husband.

After years of misfortune and tragedy, Elio coming back into my life had turned it all around. He had saved me after all in the end, and I'd saved him right back.

I tied Vento up to a tree to let him graze, then stripped down to my bikini. The shore of the lake was dotted with pebbles. I passed over them, enjoying the way they pressed into the soles of my feet. The water was cool and refreshing.

I walked out until I could swim and then dived beneath the glassy surface. When I came back up, I lay on my back and floated, enjoying the feel of the sun on my exposed skin. It was funny; even though I'd lived in L.A. for so long, this was the first summer in years that I was sunbathing and swimming.

Vento snorted from the shore, and I turned to see that he was no longer alone. My blood immediately heated to see Elio standing in the shade beneath the tree, stroking the chestnut horse's neck.

He was back. He'd been away on business for the past few days.

He left Vento and walked toward me. His suit looked odd in the idyllic rural setting. Usually, he opted for worn-out jeans and T-shirts to work with the horses at the house or wander the countryside.

"Nice outfit . . . city mouse," I called to him, treading water.

He grinned at me as his hand went to his suit jacket. He shed it like it wasn't a bespoke designer piece and discarded it on the stones. His shirt followed next.

"I haven't been home yet. Ettore told me you were up here."

Ettore, the youngest man in Elio's private guard, who had chosen to be hurt over failing his boss. Toni had spared him, shooting him in the leg. He'd recovered well and was back at work.

Shirtless, Elio stole my breath away. His hands went to the waistband of his pants, and he pulled his belt out of the loops with a dramatic swish that had my mouth falling open.

"Now you're just showing off."

"I told you I was experienced with restraints, *topolina*." He smirked, cast the belt aside, and dropped his pants.

"Hey, no complaints from this end," I murmured, my heartbeat picking up. I took in Elio's body. I'd never get tired of looking at my husband.

"Where's the bodyguard I assigned you?" Elio walked into the water.

"I don't know . . . he can't ride fast enough to keep up with me. Better get Toni back," I said.

Elio's eyes narrowed. "Not happening."

"We'll see," I called back.

Toni and her partner were living up north near the Alps in a ski town. Giada had found her for me. I knew she wanted to be brought back into the Santori fold, but Elio was being stubborn about it. I'd wear him down.

"I warned you not to ditch the bodyguard again."

"Like anyone will find me up here!"

"Still, it's not a risk I'd like to take. You broke the rules, *topolina*."

A thrill went through me at his dark, intense expression.

"Oops." I shrugged and then let out a shriek when he dived under the water, darting quickly for me.

I swam away, kicking my legs and trying to move as fast as I could through the cool water, but it was no use. Elio was too damn fast.

His arms went around my waist and tugged me backward. He surfaced behind me with an explosion of expelled breath and hugged me to his chest.

"I'm starting to think you just like breaking rules."

"Only yours . . ."

He was right. I did like breaking his rules. I liked his delicious punishments and his wicked imagination.

"Hmm, let's see what we can do about that." He tugged me back and swam us toward an outcrop of rocks, his arm loosely locked around my neck like he was saving my life. His cock brushed my back now and then, hard and probing.

I reached under me and grabbed it, and he swore. I slid my hand around him, squeezing his impressive length.

"It's too late to be a good girl now, Georgia."

The warmth in his voice filled my soul up to the brim. Sure, I'd seen him in meetings and talks with dangerous men. He was soulless. A man without mercy. A man you shouldn't cross, in charge of the security of the De Sanctis family. Renato's *sottocapo*. But alone? He was my *cittaiolo*. Again. Just for me.

We got to the rocks, and Elio sat on a broad, smooth one that was hidden under the water. He pulled me onto his lap, my back against his front, and hooked his ankles around mine, forcing my legs apart.

His hand wandered down my front and slid between my thighs. His fingers traced down my slit and slipped inside me, his thumb rubbing my clit. The hand that was around my waist shifted up to my face, cupping my jaw. Some of his fingers fell inside my mouth, and I sucked on them as he pumped his hand into me.

Before I came, my trembling muscles giving away how close I was, he lifted his hand free of me and turned me around so I could face him. I slid one leg across him and nestled on his lap. He shifted his hips and pushed inside me, impaling me.

"Did you miss me?" He cupped my face and sank deep.

I wrapped my arms around his shoulders and nodded.

"I missed you. I can't sleep without you . . ." I admitted, rising and falling on him.

"Good," he growled. "That's only fair . . . since I'm a wreck without you. I haven't slept, I've barely eaten . . . It's hard to breathe when you're not next to me."

His hand wandered down my back and gripped my ass.

"That being said . . . don't forget your punishment . . ." His finger traced my asshole and surged inside.

I gasped, my pussy clenching tightly around him while he invaded my ass. I bit my lip and swallowed down another gasp.

"Oh, no. You don't get to hide how much you love it when I fuck you in both holes, *cara*. Let me hear how much you love being filled by me," he said then kissed me hard, his tongue snaking into my mouth.

His possession was complete.

I moaned deeply into his mouth, and he raised his hips just right to rub me in all the best places. I was climbing higher and higher with every second. His finger in my ass withdrew, and I made a noise of complaint that had him chuckling.

"Don't worry . . . I think you're ready for more," he said against my lips.

"More?" Nerves battled with anticipation. "How much more?"

Using the water to carry my weight, he lifted me and then tilted me back on his lap, his strong hands holding me easily.

"Everything." He pressed the tip of his cock to my ass.

My eyes widened, and my heart pounded hard.

"Do you trust me?" he asked softly, his cock breaching my ass.

"Yes," I said without thought. "Always."

He smiled against my lips and pressed deeper. It felt like I was being split in half and remade at the same time.

His hand lowered to my clit, and he circled me there, his cock shallowly thrusting into my ass.

"Tell me how good it feels, *cara* . . . because to me it feels like fucking heaven."

He brought his pale-green eyes to mine.

"You feel like heaven . . . you *are* heaven, to me . . . the only one I've ever sought to reach. The only paradise worth fighting for."

"I'm going to come, I—I'm going to come right now," I panted, my thoughts dissolving. I couldn't think. I couldn't speak. There was just the feeling of the water around us and his body under mine. His cock, pumping steadily into me, and his hand circling my clit, making me shake.

"Come, *cara*. Come with me, now," he growled in my ear.

And I did.

Maybe I was a good girl after all.

After, we got dressed and got onto Vento. Elio sat behind me, cradling me in his arms, his hands on the reins. He'd learned to ride like a pro. He was a natural. Seeing him taking care of the horses was the most peaceful sight.

We rode, and he took something from his pocket and tucked it under my bracelet. His wedding ring flashed in the afternoon sunlight as he picked up the reins again.

"I saw these when I was looking for you."

Heliotropes.

"They're beautiful."

The vivid purple shone against my tanned skin.

"They are an interesting little flower . . . if you remember?"

Vento walked on slowly, taking his time to travel the small paths back toward the villa.

I shook my head, even though I did remember, and rested it back against Elio's broad chest.

"Tell me."

"As you wish. Purple often symbolizes mysticism and dreams . . . which makes sense, because for fourteen years, I've dreamed of you. Heliotropes turn their heads to track the sun, showing devotion . . . In Victorian England, they were given as a sign," he continued and leaned down to speak in my ear. "*I adore you,* they said."

"And don't forget that they were named for Helios, the god of the sun . . . like you, Apollo."

"I am no god, *topolina,*" he chuckled. "In fact, I might be the very opposite. A mercenary, a devil . . . whatever I am, know one thing beyond all doubt." He tightened his arms around me.

"I'm yours."

"The feeling, my mercenary, is entirely mutual."

ACKNOWLEDGMENTS

I want to take a moment to thank all those who made this book possible. My amazing cover designer, Angela; my editors, Emmy and Lauren; and my ideal reader and friend, Katarina, who always gives me the early feedback that helps me work out my characters!

I also want to thank my master marketer, my husband; my family for their support; and my 20Books Madrid ladies. You know who you are.

xx

PHOTO: JOANNA SILVESTRI

MILA KANE is a previously independent bestselling author. She is obsessed with cats, coffee, and antiheroes just the right side of insane. She writes dark and dirty romance with the alpha-holes of your most filthy nightmares. She only writes SAFE stories, and no matter how dark and twisted the story might be, there will always be a happily-ever-after guarantee. She was born and still lives in Scotland.

Check out her books, deleted scenes, character profiles, and more at:

milakane.com
Instagram: @milakanebooks
Facebook: @MilaKanewrites
TikTok: @milakanebooks

ABOUT THE TYPE

This book was set in Jenson, one of the earliest print typefaces. After hearing of the invention of printing in 1458, Charles VII of France sent coin engraver Nicolas Jenson (c. 1420–80) to study this new art. Not long afterward, Jenson started a new career in Venice in letter-founding and printing. In 1471, Jenson was the first to present the form and proportion of this roman font that bears his name.

More than five centuries later, Robert Slimbach, developing fonts for the Adobe Originals program, created Adobe Jenson based on Nicolas Jenson's Venetian Renaissance typeface. It is a dignified font with graceful and balanced strokes.